LEXINARY

Dictionary of Invented Words

Javier Enríquez Serralde

LEXINARY

Dictionary of Invented Words

Selected Neologisms
from the Novels

of

Javier Enríquez Serralde

neolog Eds.

neolog Eds.
414 N. Court Avenue. Tucson, AZ 85701. USA.
Calz. del Hueso 160 Edif. G-103, Fuentes de Coyoacan, Mexico City 04850
Mexico

Linguistics, grammar, lexicography & style (Spanish): Carlos Herrera de la
Fuente, Ph.D.

Lexicography & copyediting: John Green

Cover Design: Rob Bahou

Logo design: Javier Enríquez Serralde

Typography & layout: Eugene Rjin Santori

Author's photograph: Rob Bahou

ISBN: 978-1-946761-45-3

Printed in the USA

www.comoseteocurrio.com

To Lisa, my muse,
who tolerated my verbal, written
and behavioral idiosyncrasies.

To Alesi,
my test case.

PREFACE

My intention in literature has been to compose symphonies of words which simulate pleasurable music and awaken new, *straphalaric* sensations in the readers' minds. To express such music and to convey something yet indescribable or sensations not-yet-defined, I created thousands of neologisms. Some of my concoctions sprang from old, ancient and — why not? — future languages, while some others appeared in front of me as vibrating, onomatopoetic sounds from contemporary tongues. The beauty of the old Spanish poems of El Cid, the English of Alfred the Great, the exquisite tempestuous salad of Norse, Angle, Saxon, Latin, Gaelic and French in Chaucer, the modern-sounding waves of Apuleius, and numerous more modern writers that would take too much space to mention, for example, are nothing but delicacies from which I steal to cook my own sounds, my poetry in prose. This is how I tell my stories.

Over the years, I've constantly declined to define my neologisms. I wished to induce in the reader aesthetic pleasure and an individual interpretation of my words. I wanted for my readers to define each word as they felt or not to define at all and go with the flow of the narrative. The reason behind that is that in my novels each word, phrase or sentence can have more than one meaning. Thus, I wanted to maintain an interpretative freedom for the reader. But my publisher, Fernando Valdés from Plaza y Valdés Editors, persisted and insisted for two decades that I write a dictionary to define my neologisms. I jokingly said no, since I knew the labor-intensive task that would be required to define thousands of words. However, after

Fernando's coaxing and cajoling, I began to compile and define some neologisms. When I defined about 200 terms, my eyes opened. I *opticated*. I observed the explanation of the neologisms and felt the wonder behind the minds of my characters.

Working on this *Lexinary* forced me to immerse myself in new-to-me subjects such as semasiology, onomasiology, lexicology and other *ologies*. I am not and do not pretend to be a lexicologist nor am I versed in linguistics. My work in the written arts, including this *Lexinary*, remains fiction, but visualizes new, far-off plausible horizons in literature.

I decided that 'dictionary' (from Latin *dictionarium*, manual or book of words, from *dictio*, derived from *dicere* 'to say' and *nary*, which evolved from *narium* to indicate manual) was not a suitable term to title this work. The thought of my readers 'translating' neologisms or following instructions on how to pronounce them was abhorrent to me. My purpose was not to create a manual of diction. My intent was to provide a limited number of definitions with my own characters' interpretations. Therefore, I decided to title this compilation "Lexinary," from the Greek word λεξις, *lexis*, meaning word.

In Spanish, narrative in the written sense consists of novels, short novels and short stories. In my opinion, each one of the neologisms defined herein is, in some form, the shortest form of a narrative. I believe that certain definitions are *microstories*.

To those familiar with my work, this *Lexinary* could be of assistance to clarify hidden, esoteric components of my novels and to explore the roots of my literary experiments. But, to anyone else, this *Lexinary* may be a curious source of laughter or reflection.

Here comes the brief, boring part. In the midst of this labor I realized I should keep an eye on the book's length. I decided not to include words that could be easily understood, such as *urinatory, suppositorized, hypermaculated, menstruatory or horizontalize*. I settled to choose words that could offer a supplementary representation of the spirit of my work. For these reasons I arbitrarily established several criteria to select and validate a reasonable number of terms which are, but not limited to:

- Defining sensations, feelings or emotions, known or not, that:
  - ➤ have not yet been defined,
  - ➤ have been partially defined,
  - ➤ differ from contemporary terms or definitions.
- Describing fictional things, concepts, objects and circumstances as well as facts that, although obvious or common knowledge, have not been described.
- Including preferentially neologisms composed from Greek and Latin roots.
- Introducing words from other languages that are not found in English dictionaries. For example *affriolant* in French, *flitzcaca* in German or *arrancar* in Spanish. For this English translation I excluded terms derived from English that I included in the Spanish *Lexinary* such as *conundrum, septum, keg, bawdy, pervasive, besmirch or serendipity*.
- Contributing knowledge.
- Defining paradoxes that could provoke reflection. And, more importantly,
- Being funny.

To circumvent what commonly happens in some dictionaries worldwide, I avoided:

a) Defining a word with simply another word.

b) Including words that have only a slight variation from existing and already defined words from other languages, such as variations in British and North American spelling like *aluminium* and *aluminum* or adding or subtracting a letter to an existing word.

c) Defining a word utilizing an existing verb or adjective and adding a prefix, such as "un," to them (eg. *un*appear, as there is already *unapparent*), unless I felt such an addition would contribute to any of the points in my aforementioned inclusion criteria (eg. **unprudish**. adjective. Having had, but losing any sense of modesty, especially with regards to matters of nudity or sexual nature).

d) Changing a prefix of Greek origin to one of Latin origin or vice versa with the same meaning. For example, *bichromate* instead of *dichromate,* by replacing the Greek *bi* for the Latin *di*, meaning "double."

e) Using a second neologism to define a neologism, with limited exceptions. These exceptions, defined elsewhere in the *Lexinary*, are identified by an asterisk (*).

f) Including proper names, with one exception, unlike the Oxford Dictionary of English.

To circumvent the tedious extension and repetitions of a *real* dictionary, I defined each neologism in only one form. That is, each word is defined solely as a substantive, adverb, adjective, noun or verb. Otherwise, this *Lexinary* would have been several times larger.

Penultimately, as Samuel Johnson wrote, "Language is the dress of thought," the words herein represent voices and mindsets of a wide range of characters. Their thoughts vary according to each individual worldview, educational level, cultural background, experiences, interests, prejudices, obsessions, etc. and thus, the definitions reflect the heterogeneity of those voices.

To conclude, in a few words, this concise *Lexinary* is the dictionary of the ineffable.

Javier Enríquez Serralde

A

abelligic. adjective. **1.** Not having personally witnessed or experienced war or conflict. **2.** Abelligerated.

abiobiogenesis. noun. *Biology.* Biological principle according to which all living beings are engendered from other living beings who, in turn, proceed from inorganic elements or inanimate constructs.

abiodict. noun. *Psychology.* A person who loves or exhibits loyalty to inanimate objects.

abiowarp. noun. **1.** The unique behavior of cables and wires in entangling themselves without human or animal intervention. **2.** Abioligation.

abjucracy. noun. **1.** An economic, political, and philosophical movement that endorses logic and common sense in every governmental process and criminalizes bureaucracy for being an instrument of psychological torture and social control. **2.** Abureaucracy.

ablefaria. noun. A female who is aggressive during daylight hours and inconsolable during night hours, leaving only small windows of time at sunrise and sunset for normal communication.

ablutter. noun. **1.** A person whose skin turns dark blue following strong punches. **2.** Acinoplexic. verb. *Informal.* **3.** To beat the shit out of someone.

abomitaph. noun. **1.** A message of hate engraved on the tombstone of a loved one. **2.** A loathsome headstone.

aburemia. noun. A strong aversion to passion.

acaresty. noun. *Economics* **1.** An economic theory that promotes gold as the sole monetary standard for all currencies, refuses fiat fraud of paper and electronic digits and promotes the abolition of strategized inflation. **2.** The economic theory behind aurolition.*

acargatism. noun. Tedious ritualistic and ceremonial

mannerisms used by alchemists when trying to transmute metals.

accentology. noun. *Phonetics.* **1.** The study and comparison of spoken accents within a single language. *Linguistics.* **2.** The study of written representation of accents.

accrit. adjective. **1.** Being exiled from time and space. **2.** Deleted from existence. **3.** Accritated.

achrony. noun. The total absence of time.

aclimize. verb. To make the best of whatever situation one encounters.

aclust. verb. To double-doubt someone's reasoning or logic flow.

acolmenated. adjective. **1.** Living in a tiny apartment or room amongst many tiny apartments or rooms. **2.** Living aplethorated* like a social insect.

acorrain. verb. To corral a person into a very small space.

acosmotic. noun. A person who staunchly refutes any theory related to cosmogony.

acostigate. verb. To pursue and cause someone a psychological torment with the sole objective of teaching that person a lesson.

acrastinate. verb. **1.** To preemptively do something today in a hurried, shoddy fashion, which had been planned for tomorrow in a methodical manner. **2.** To do something earlier than planned without increasing the quality of the product or the task performed.

acrinnity. noun. The caustic quality of a cry emitted by an animal or a person in imminent danger of death.

acrobe. noun. A being that always lives on the edges of life.

acuggulate. verb. To hit a prey with a powerful strike, followed by another punch of medium intensity and, when the prey is groggy, to asphyxiate it with constant pressure.

adamalyte. noun. *Geology.* An unbreakable material found during deep excavations in Antarctica.

addicpassive. adjective. *Psychology.* Being capable of causing a conditioning addiction without the awareness of the targeted person.

adego. noun. **1.** A person who is next to his or her own self. **2.** A person who is attached to the self one used to be.

adimensional. noun. Immeasurable, intangible and unimaginable by three-dimensional beings.

admignody. noun. Admission of ignorance.

adopostol. noun. A person who disseminates a doctrine that refutes any doctrine.

adrendous. noun. *Forestry.* A forest with no trees.

adynaphobia. noun. Fear of something or someone that does not move.

ageitude. noun. **1.** Variable period of time in which a person cares for and nurtures both growing offspring and elderly parents. **2.** Aggilescence.

agglinate. verb. To obtain information from various sources, generally with difficulty.

aggrenate. verb. To display with assertiveness and certainty a familiar activity, but with a degree of roughness.

aghenic. noun. **1.** The body of a person occupied by the mind of another. adjective. **2.** Not knowing one's biological parents. noun. **3.** An entity unable to reproduce.

agnaglot. verb. To chew conspicuously with the mouth wide open.

agnaglottic. adjective. **1.** Having the habit or custom, culturally or otherwise, of chewing conspicuously with the mouth wide open. noun. **2.** A person who agnataglots.*

agnocemy. noun. Vastly prevalent acquisition of ignorance in an active, voluntary fashion, generally a consequence of oversaturation of trivial, cloying information transmitted by global multimedia.

agogandrosy. noun. An attribute that repels any masculine characteristics.

agogannate. verb. To absorb internal strength from being the center of attention of an audience.

agonagyny. noun. A mental battle against intrinsic or acquired femininity.

agotorick. adjective. (from *age-otori* in Japanese). **1.** Looking worse after a haircut. **2.** Feeling disappointed or depressed after enduring an event intended to enhance one's beauty or attractiveness.

agricline. noun. **1.** Inability of a farmer to induce rain when vehemently desired. **2.** Agripluvistasia.

agymize. verb. **1.** To live a sedentary life without any form of physical activity. adjective. **2.** Practicing full-time domestic nudism. **3.** Agymnasited.

ajesullation. noun. *Philosophy.* A theory that contests the deity of Jesus Christ and validates his philosophical contributions written by his descendants following his suicide in the year 63 A.D.

alberration. noun. A grave, unconscious blunder against the customs of a society.

alcanite. adjective. Enduring physical distress or torment without any desire for vengeance.

alcurnickle. noun. A proletarian sybarite.

aletromic. adjective. The secure, vigorous and decisive, yet slow steps of an athlete performing a light activity.

alexinate. verb. To abruptly say something defensively.

alexissity. noun. *Psychology.* Anxiety combined with feelings of defenselessness anticipating challenges or critiques.

algophize. verb. **1.** To convert an object into a thing. **2.** To reduce something to the condition of a thing it previously was not.

allopsych. adjective. **1.** Feeling the perception of being outside one's own mind. noun. **2.** A person who has the distinct sensation of being outside his or her own mind.

almation. noun. *Religion.* The precise moment in which a soul adopts a body in the Christian mythology.

almell. noun. A twin soul.

alphanumerism. noun. *Statistics.* A mathematical movement aiming to rename and alphabetize the numbers from zero to one hundred to facilitate the work of computer programmers and statisticians.

alsenescence. noun. Decision to throw away a long cherished object once it is finally realized, after a long period of storage, it is no longer of use.

altack. verb. To interrupt someone in a manner that shocks.

amalgachronation. noun. **1.** Fusion of different timelines into one. **2.** The effect of mixing several future probabilities with those of the present and past. **3.** Temporal chaos. **4.** Chronofusion.

amanterism. noun. **1.** A friendship with interludes of a sexual nature. **2.** Decoitism.

amasiant. noun. A person in a couple who live together in matrimony, without marriage.

ambisahuciant. noun. A person who bears both desperation and confidence simultaneously.

ambitropism. noun. *Psychology.* Propensity of a monad to move toward both sides of its dualistic existentialism.

amblid. adjective. Feeling weak, without any physical or emotional strength.

amboptiate. verb. To look at both sides alternating back and forth.

ambulatia. noun. The familiar sound produced by a known person's footsteps.

ambutelency. noun. A condition in which an event or circumstance is subject to multiple interpretations, usually highly diverse or opposite to one another.

ambuthrall. adjective. Lacking ability in the art of walking normally.

amiloflexic. noun. **1.** Animal or person that cannot be manipulated or behaviorally molded. **2.** Something that cannot be molded anymore. adjective. **3.** Unable to be molded due to excessive malleation.*

amistation. noun. Subconscious magnetism that attracts two strangers to become friends.

amistatus. noun. **1.** The true degree of friendship or closeness one feels for another person. *Informal.* **2.** Gut ejiis.*

amoricide. noun. **1.** A mannerism that destroys a passion. **2.** (in a couple): An involuntary gesture, tic, facial expression or physical behavior of a person that, whether new or not, annoys the other to such a severe degree that it triggers the termination of their relationship.

amphally. adveb. **1.** Forceful, pushy behavior with no apparent motive. **2.** Assertiveness without having a clue about the specific topic, event or circumstance.

amphity. noun. **1.** Repetitive lateral movement of the head executed by religious tradition, by fixation or following a traumatic childhood. **2.** Amphicephaly.

anaceptualism. noun. *Philosophy.* A philosophical theory which sustains the reality of notions not yet exposed, admitting their abstract existences by the fact that thoughts cannot be negated simply because they have not yet been conceptualized.

anadesiry. noun. *Literary.* Bazaar of desires that have yet to be wished by anyone.

anaffluence. noun. A force that impedes a confluence between things or beings.

anampleic. noun. A person with an aversion to being hugged by another person of the same gender.

anandrosis. noun. The opposite extreme of masculinity.

anapudency. noun. **1.** Lack of modesty. **2.** Inability to feel embarrassment.

anaritene. noun. *Anthropology.* **1.** A humanoid lacking one of the two posterior laryngeal cartilages. adjective. *Psychology.* **2.** Incapable of pronouncing words correctly.

anaster. noun. **1.** A continuous disaster. **2.** A disaster that evolves into another disaster, which in turn generates an additional disaster and so on until a state of massive disaster is perpetual. **3.** Finansepsia.*

anastic. noun. A person without family, home or country.

anastrophy. noun. A sudden circumstance that favorably changes someone's fortune.

anasty. adjective. The absence of progenitors or descendants.

anceslitigio. noun. *Law.* Legal process against someone's forefathers who contributed a genetic pool that coded for diseases or unfavorable conditions which caused said person to live in constant pain.

anchomate. verb. To twist a hand and forearm behind the back to immobilize a person.

andexistence. noun. Absence of consciousness or feeling of inexistence for a period of time.

andragogna. noun. An ugly, graceless woman who in reality is a man.

andralgist. noun. A substance, person or event capable of inducing pain in a man's genitals.

andrauxine. noun. *Biology.* Recombinant phytohuman hormone, of vegetable and human origin that promotes growth by means of cellular elongation.

andrem. noun. **1.** A group of men who live together in a household and are totally dependent on their matriarch. **2.** A group of husbands of a polygamous woman.

androgest. noun. **1.** A man who successfully carries a fetus to term in some part of his body. **2.** A pregnant man.

androgynephobia. noun. Obsessive aversion to men and women.

androlexor. noun. A man who futilely attempts to defend his own masculinity, usually in unfavorable circumstances.

androlint. noun. A man who in a gathering of men does not establish verbal communication with any of them.

andromeseusness. noun. The feeling of extenuation in the masculinity of a man.

andromisanthrope. noun. **1.** A man who dislikes and shows hatred to people who hate men or anything masculine or related to the male gender. **2.** A man who hates misandropus.* adjective. **3.** Displaying hostility against andromisoics.*

andromisoic. noun. A man who disdains and displays hatred toward anything of masculine nature.

androparitis. noun. *Law.* Cause of divorce; generally the inability of a man to perform any task, to assume any responsibility, and to depend entirely on a woman.

androticnia. noun. A remnant of masculinity in the body of a person.

androvalence. noun. The number of men with whom a woman is capable of sharing her love simultaneously.

andruge. noun. A person who dresses in expensive rags.

anecstasy. noun. **1.** An overwhelming feeling of self-repugnance during extreme states of abhorrence or disdain. **2.** An overwhelming feeling of repugnance at one's own appearance.

anegopathy. noun. *Psychology.* **1.** Absence of self-empathy at the moment of imminent death. **2.** Adoption of a passive attitude and total inaction when sensing death.

anempathy. noun. *Psychology.* **1.** Insensitivity to or inability to react to graphic acts of violence and cruelty; generally the effect of pervasive use of exaggerated violence in movies and multimedia. **2.** Violesthesia.* **3.** Phenacultry.* **4.** Empathectomy.*

anestoloid. noun. A person with the absolute inability to reason.

anfile. verb. To give someone false hopes with dogged assertiveness.

anikhi. noun. A mobile entity capable of incorporating ephemerally and sequentially in several persons.

animalate. verb. To create animal figures with the meal of an infant to encourage eating.

animaspit. verb. To impale someone's self-assurance with loud and grotesque language.

animastia. noun. An intention to cleanse the soul by self-abrasion, self-flagellation or any other punitive acts on one's skin.

ankymesis. noun. A transient paralysis following a shock, powerful impression or a sudden, unexpected pain.

anonerist. noun. A person who sleeps without dreaming.

antannual. noun. *Literary.* **1.** Concerning a year prior to last year or years before, especially as nostalgically recalled. **2.** A long, long time ago.

antaphrodisy. noun. **1.** Protracted decrease of libido in long-term monogamy. *Medicine.* **2.** Chronic anestrosis characterized by bradygony, absence of mydriasis and lack of tachycardia during sexual arousal. **3.** Progressive erosphyxia* that could develop into sexidity.*

anteclosion. noun. **1.** Closure of an envelope or a membrane. *Botany.* **2.** Active closure of petals of a flower. *Biology.* **3.** Sealing off of a shell in a chrysalis, an egg or an embryo to block its exit, hatching or birth.

antethical. adjective. *Ethics.* **1.** Of, relating to, or dealing with anything that goes against a set of moral norms that guide human conduct in a specific place and time. *Sociology.* **2.** Relating to social norms that falsely guide humans with the objective of manipulating them.

antetime. noun. One of the times in the paraterit.*

anthal. noun. Collection of experiences and desires of yesteryear that a person remembers with serenity and pleasure during old age.

anthannal. adjective. Belonging to or relative to yesteryear.

anthocol. noun. *Ecology.* **1.** An organism that seriously modifies or destroys the environment in which it resides. *Derogatory.* **2.** A politician.

anthracide. noun. **1.** Excessive loss of human life as a consequence of simultaneous wars, genocides and epidemics. **2.** The deliberate killing of a large group of people by non-human beings.

anthrastinct. noun. **1.** An instinct present exclusively in human beings. **2.** A human reflex not yet discovered in other animals.

anthrasty. noun. **1.** Repugnance at humanity overall. **2.** Extreme dislike or aversion to human beings.

anthriscern. verb. To perceive the intrinsic nature of a person at first sight.

anthromaniate. verb. **1.** To play with a person who wishes to enter a social circle by demanding vexing behaviors and cumbersome activities from said person. **2.** Burguesate.

anthropalist. noun. A cloying man who nauseates a woman or a cloying woman who nauseates a man with continuous affected affection.

anthropocystemy. noun. **1.** The proportion of obesity in a population. *Medicine.* **2.** Endemic obesity principally caused by oxysthesia* and phenatechnia.*

anthropority. noun. *Philosophy.* An oligarchical philosophic doctrine that classifies people into instruments, farmed slaves, debt serfs, domesticated entities, taxpayers or enemies of the State in order to effectively control a society.

anthropsist. noun. A person who exhibits a metallic appearance in hair or skin.

anthrosty. noun. A logical system that quantifies the limits of human potential.

anthrotrophy. noun. *Commerce.* Manufacturing method to produce organic material derived from inorganic substances for transplantation of human organs.

anthrovolution. noun. *Philosophy.* Philosophical theory that validates technology and its consequences as inherent elements of human evolution and, therefore, as harmonious components of the natural evolution of the biosphere.

antibiony. noun. Habitual compulsion to talk to inanimate objects.

anticlosion. noun. *Sociology.* **1.** The sudden disappearance of a cultural movement in a society. noun. *Psychology.* **2.** The expected end of an accepted psychological principle.

antideparture. noun. Variable and protracted period of time between the announcement of someone's departure and the actual departure.

antiminal. adjective. A sense of being in the immediate past while balancing on the threshold of a present conscious moment.

antipheretion. noun. *Psychology.* **1.** A strong sense of being different from all other family members. *Literary.* **2.** The pervasive inner questioning: "How did I get here?"

antipheth. verb. To pretend to be different and act differently without being different.

antiphylactic. adjective. Attempting to prevent something retrospectively.

antispectron. noun. *Physics.***1.** Phenomenon of non-gravitational light absorption in which no light can escape. *Biology.* **2.** Phenomenon associated with certain organisms that absorb light and darken their surroundings.

antisperation. noun. *Politics.* A set of strategies used by a despotic government to evaporate the hope of its citizens. Example: *Faux*-flag events.

anxilation. noun. Anxiety without a cause.

anximitant. adjective. **1.** Imitating the mannerisms of an anxious person. noun. **2.** A person who easily becomes anxious when seeing someone anxious. **3.** Anxichopraxic.

anxitist. noun. A person with nothing to do who acts as if in a hurry.

aparveate. verb. To imitate an infant's mode of speech with adult mannerisms.

apavullate. verb. **1.** To silence someone forcibly. noun. **2.** A silence compelled in someone by an external cause.

apenied. noun. **1.** A man who lacks a penis. adjective. **2.** Absence of a reproductive organ in a male. **3.** Adparephallic.

apimanist. noun. A person with obsessive devotion to bees.

apincuous. adjective. **1.** Lacking any sense of proximity. **2.** Lacking any ties to anything.

apirogamy. noun. Extinction of the flame of love or passion in a marriage.

aplethorated. adjective. Feeling of being compressed and deformed by excessive quantities of things, people or emotions.

aplethoration. noun. Excess in the number of things or beings that realistically fit in a defined space so that they are compressed and about to overflow.

apodynamism. noun. *Physics.* Re-establishment of motion of something or someone that had stopped moving.

apondate. verb. **1.** To ponder without logic or to reach a conclusion contrary to the facts or the likelihood of truth. *Informal.* **2.** To think in a circular or backward fashion.

aporist. noun. *Informal.* **1.** Moniker of a physician with the reputation of making erroneous diagnoses or providing inadequate care to patients. **2.** A physician who does not inspire confidence in his or her patients. *Archaic.* **3.** Barber or surgeon without the dexterity to perform bleeds and who often caused swelling, hematomas and apostems.

aport. verb. To arrive or reach a place involuntarily or randomly.

aposcientate. verb. **1.** To become conscious of something beyond its *raison d'être.* **2.** To recognize one's essential self and deep attributes in relation to the surroundings.

apotellation. noun. *Medicine.* Unquestionable medical law supported by each phase of scientific methodology, including observation, experimentation, hypothesis, theory and law.

apparrion. noun. Painful long-term immobilization of people or scarecrows by forcing them to maintain both arms extended, mimicking a horizontal line.

appellition. noun. Immediate bond between two persons when realizing they share the same last name.

appetity. noun. *Psychology.* Pavlovian reflex to elicit appetite by imagining ingestion of delicacies.

appillingous. adjective. **1.** Being extremely honest but lacking discernment. *Informal.* **2.** Being open and sincere almost to a fault.

apprastide. noun. **1.** Automatic reflex in a woman about to apply makeup consisting in opening eyes and mouth. **2.** Apprastomation.

apromart. verb. To abusively exploit sea resources.

aprounsel. noun. A person who hears counsel with apparent interest and evaluates it with suspicion.

aranid. noun. (from *aranyhíd* in Hungarian). **1.** The blinding reflection of the sun on a body of water. **2.** The glistening reflection of the sun on the ocean.

arbit. noun. A tree that owns itself.

archecho. noun. An echo coming from a distant past perceived with various senses.

archefally. noun. Creation of pseudo-archaic art by a non-artist without knowledge of ancient art.

archiplist. noun. **1.** A person who explains and re-explains subjects that he or she does not understand. **2.** Someone who conveys inconsequential information over a long period of time.

architechnon. noun. *Archaic.* **1.** Architect. **2.** Etymologically correct title for a person who studied and practices architecture.

ardescence. noun. A state that resembles the condition or sensation of being in combustion.

aretascence. noun. A narrative so unbelievable that it seems to be the exploits of a mythological hero or a god.

argony. noun. **1.** Condition that resembles asphyxia. **2.** Intoxication following inhalation of pure argon.

argotostic. noun. **1.** A person who macerates a written or a spoken language. **2.** Osurist. **3.** Barramist.* **4.** Verbosurist.

arimatist. noun. An old man who acquires the mannerisms and scars of a mythological warrior with old injuries sustained in lifelong battles.

aristoverbia. noun. The peculiar speech patterns of a plebeian pretending to speak like an aristocrat.

arithmetize. verb. *Mathematics.* **1.** To execute simple arithmetic calculations while protruding the tongue outside the mouth. **2.** To protrude the tongue outside the mouth when trying to remember how to spell a word.

armerogeny. noun. Sexual arousal provoked by a person's non-pheromonal smell.

arragous. noun. Phenomenon by which the present emotional state of a sentient being is caused by a past experience.

arrank. verb. **1.** To rip something from the roots. **2.** To tear out something that is stuck, fastened or fixed with violent and vicious force. noun. **3.** The feeling of having the soul torn out with malice. **4.** Evaxanime.

arrebocy. noun. **1.** Sexual attraction to a person by means of surreptitious or disguised seduction. **2.** Subtercoquetry. **3.** Hermeflirtesy. **4.** Esoterborsia. **5.** Cryptertany. **6.** Corparrecy.

arronate. verb. To hit and insult someone simultaneously.

arteity. noun. **1.** Spontaneity and innovation in the creative process. **2.** Creative quality in art that matures with age while diminishing the nonchalant improvisation of youth.

arthrofolphide. noun. A woman with a specific type of arthritis attributed to promiscuity and a chronic venereal disease acquired in youth.

arthrolepticity. noun. Sensation of weakness when the joints feel ankylosed, stiffened and tightened by an overwhelming external force.

artiphilia. noun. *Psychology.* Egocentric affectation that eventually leads to social blindness.

aruspition. noun. Imitation of speech patterns, facial expressions and general mannerisms of those who pretend to foretell the future.

arxitla. noun. **1.** A woman who seduces a young girl. *Mythology.* **2.** In the Teotihuacan mythology: A lesbian aquatic nymph.

asamist. noun. A slave or subordinate who rebels passive-aggressively against his or her master or boss.

asbazdic. noun. Urban area of affluent residences surrounded by slums.

ascarynate. verb. *Biology.* To insert cells inside other cells.

ascetimize. verb. **1.** To convert a person to an ascetic life. **2.** To hermitize. **3.** To anachorize.

ascetology. noun. Lucrative study focused on understanding the ascetic behavior of greedy hedonists.

ascheplation. noun. Uncomfortable sensation of suddenly finding that time has jumped, surged forward or is in reverse from the usual present moment.

asculpy. noun. *Psychology.* Repugnance and disgust toward oneself provoked by an insurmountable feeling of guilt.

ascurist. noun. **1.** A person who when pronouncing certain words emits an annoying gagging noise that sounds like the prelude to a vomit. **2.** A non-Dutch native speaker who correctly pronounces the word *gracht* in Dutch.

asomism. noun. *Theology.* **1.** Fine-tuning the assembly of a body and a soul. **2.** Afinaminament.

aspaculaint. noun. Someone who habitually, but with no purpose, goes from here to there and from there to here.

aspamnemic. noun. A memory or thought that triggers frantic waving and flapping of the arms.

aspavule. noun. The expression of childish distraction in an adult.

aspaxilia. noun. The contorted face of an adult expressing bafflement that resembles that of a perplexed infant face.

aspeculator. noun. **1.** A person unable to speculate. **2.** A mirror that reflects images in the opposite sense of a reflection.

asperant. verb. **1.** To have hope that something unexpected will arrive or happen. noun. **2.** A period of one thousand seconds.

asperrandric. noun. **1.** A gruff man who is invariably brusque, insolent, and impertinent despite circumstances that require compassion. Example: A man asking his wife to time the delivery of their child before the commencement of a ball game. **2.** A grotesque man with bad taste.

aspersensist. noun. **1.** A deeply perceptive person. **2.** Someone who detects, associates, links and remembers details that generally are not perceived by others.

asphalgenic. adjective. *Engineering.* Generating or precipitating the formation or construction of new roads.

aspide. noun. **1.** A mangrove that grows in a swamp of acid waters. **2.** An acid mabalon.*

assomachia. noun. Psychological torture technique in which the body of the tortured person is never touched.

asteristist. noun. **1.** Someone with the habit of drawing asterisks in the air to emphasize what is being said. **2.** Parenthesist.

asterometer. noun. *Astronomy.* Instrument used to measure stars, planets, satellites and asteroids.

astheistic. adjective. Praising someone with truths and compliments using a reprehensible tone of voice.

astigmania. noun. **1.** Obsession of an artist or an art critic with certain points or dots in a painting. **2.** Pointalism. **3.** An anally retentive pointillist.

astralic. adjective. Perceiving the surroundings through swift, voluntary astral trips.

astralite. noun. An astral body that initiates an astral trip at the precise moment its physical body is engaged in an important conversation.

astrophobia. noun. *Psychology.* **1.** Capricious concern about being crushed by a meteorite. *Psychology.* **2.** Nocturnal anxiety caused by the possibility that celestial objects might fall on Earth. *Psychology.* **3.** Fear of astronomers.

asyntempy. noun. Without time barriers.

ataguhr. noun. *Commerce.* A bar for gay and bisexual people with specific preferences.

atinguist. noun. A non-naïve person who lacks malice toward anyone else.

atmostereo. noun. *Physics.* **1.** A thick vapor emanating from a solid body. *Astronomy.* **2.** Vapor emanating from a celestial body.

atominatory. adjective. Being capable of pulverizing a soul.

atorist. noun. **1.** A person who is not a sightseer or a vagabond, but likewise ambulates from place to place with no specific direction. **2.** A stroller with neither curiosity nor the desire to prowl.

atrabilisity. noun. (from Latin *atrabilis*, black bile). A melancholic and irritable condition.

atragolliate. verb. To forcibly squeeze someone's neck.

atrapy. noun. The sensation of being trapped between two or more predestined overlapping and intersecting lives.

atrichote noun. A person with soft, hairless skin.

attineity. noun. A peculiarity of destiny that provides what is searched for or needed at the least expected moment.

attinereity. noun. The discovery by accident of that which has been persistently and systematically looked for.

audiochrony. noun. Ability to hear the movement of time.

augurable. noun. A benefit or a pleasure that occurs predictably.

auguralist. noun. A person who, through the medium of theatrics, predicts and promotes better times during a calamitous period.

augurolysis. noun. **1.** Invalidation of a prediction. **2.** Invalidation of an augury with valid reasoning or facts.

auriculeum. noun. *Anatomy.* The portion of the ear that extends from the middle ear to the internal part of the earflap.

aurolition. noun. *Law.* Legislation that criminalizes both devaluation and inflation and establishes gold as the global monetary unit and the economic basis for all finances. It derives from acaresty.*

auscultanism. noun. *Religion.* **1.** Cult of the seemingly magical properties of auscultation. *Psychology.* **2.** The placebo effect that the presence or the touch of a physician has on a patient.

austronium. noun. *Chemistry.* The extremely rare super-heavy element of atomic number 119 discovered in Australia in the late 21st century.

autelist. noun. A person who blesses himself and truly believes in its benedictory effects.

auticonny. adjective. Venerating one's own image reflected in a mirror.

autobstetrician. noun. A woman who gives birth by herself and rejects any assistance.

autogynmast. noun. Capacity to develop breasts or to change their size and shape at will.

autojenity. noun. **1.** An uncomfortable sensation that one's body, or part of one's body, originated from outside oneself. **2.** Something intrinsic to oneself that is perceived as foreign.

autolyte. noun. A car-shaped toy made of stone for children in a post-apocalyptic society.

autophory. noun. Capability to put up with oneself as if one was a beloved friend.

autopluviation. noun. Increased probability of rain following the washing of a vehicle.

autosucogus. noun. Feeling that follows the realization

that a deep sorrow is only half sadness.

avaricity. noun. **1.** The highly pervasive greed of people and corporations in cahoots with a government that causes wars or exploits other countries. *History.* **2.** One of the main causes of war. **3.** A cause of poverty in the majority of a population.

avariture. noun. **1.** Insatiable drive to accumulate vast quantities of goods and wealth by any means, regardless of the damage caused to others or of the long-term consequences. **2.** Irrational fear of not having everything.

avastag. adjective. Having no offspring.

avernocracy. noun. **1.** An extremely repressive government regime. **2.** A punitive government. **3.** Hematocracy. **4.** *Informal.* A government from hell.

avolutness. noun. Incapacity to adapt, evolve or improve in life.

awary. noun. (from *mono no aware* in Japanese). **1.** The bittersweet feeling of a fleeting moment of transcendent beauty. **2.** An ambivalent emotion of pleasure and sadness after perceiving ephemeral beauty.

ayody. noun. **1.** An uncomfortable or painful feeling of both vacuum and pressure in different parts of the body. **2.** Vacuumness.* **3.** Painful vacitress.*

aztlanitis. noun. *Literary.* **1.** A place where the sierra is transformed into hills and the paths grip the ground. **2.** A place where the hills become wider toward the beaches and where the air is most fresh.

azupyre. noun. **1.** Sweet smell that may emanate from a bonfire. **2.** Syrupyre. *Informal.* **3.** Sugarsmoke.

B

babatell. noun. Slovenly hanging skin from chin or neck resembling a turkey neck in the obese or old who recently have had a sudden loss of weight.

babile. adjective. *Informal.* Lacking intelligence or common sense and being filled with hatred against people or events.

baddema. noun. **1.** Collection of prosaic ideas stated in a discourse or argument. **2.** All words in a text considered superfluous that can be extracted without modifying the nature or the message of said text.

bajosoprano. noun. *Music.* A hoarse castrato singer.

baladinate. verb. **1.** To remove from a work of art that which appears to be inconsequential without affecting the whole. **2.** To rid a garment of adornments.

baladite. verb. **1.** To eliminate futile or redundant words from a text. **2.** To give a text or a manuscript more substance.

ballapus. noun. A rag with healing properties that absorbs headaches when worn as a headband.

balleter. noun. *Informal.* **1.** Underwear that is too tight. **2.** Stricturepants. **3.** A man who displays one or two testicles that sneaked out the underpants. **4.** Sacabolas.

ballupy. noun. A monologue that is tedious due to the numerous words used, but not because of the nature of the message.

bancking. noun. *Law.* A crime committed by a financial organization with the goal of making exorbitant profits via sophisticated accounting deceit.

bapile. noun. A woman who, pretending to be a man, cross-dresses in women's clothes and gives the impression of being a real woman and not a male transvestite.

barahacont. verb. To bless a god in his or her own temple.

barity. noun. **1.** The overwhelming, uncontrollable

urge to enter bars, cantinas, pubs, cocktail lounges or taverns. **2.** Tavernity. **3.** Cantinasity. **4.** Pubicity.

barragania. noun. The anticipation of a pleasure that produces goose bumps.

barramist. adjective. A person of any educational level who cannot avoid speaking his or her mother tongue incorrectly.

barraphia. noun. **1.** The action of a woman who bares her bottom and dives in, rear end first, because she has not noticed that the toilet seat is up. **2.** Toilimmersion.

barristery. noun. Law office.

bascunet. noun. *History.* Loose garment used by women and men in Gomorrah, highly valued by Gomorrites.

basfugee. noun. An immigrant from the Basque country.

batarchomnesia. noun. The mumbling of faraway memories when everything is lost.

bathopathic. adjective. Imitating the words and tone of voice of someone else in a sarcastic and angry manner.

bathycate. verb. To sink into depression before any unfavorable circumstance occurs.

bathyfurn. noun. The ability to grasp a concept in depth or to intuit the real purpose of a process.

bathygnation. noun. Submersion into the depths of one's mind as a vehicle to find one's soul.

bathymatism. noun. *Philosophy.* Realist movement, opposed to cryopreservation, that proposes to add depth to existence instead of prolonging it.

bathythanastia. noun. Extremely profound meditation that resembles the sensation of dying.

bathyvencity. noun. Quality of living intensely without hedonistic practices.

bawsia. noun. Obsessive behavior of an adult who enjoys playing with infant's toys.

bazophian. adjective. Smelling like a combination of fecal material and food refuse.

bedappio. noun. *Prie-dieu* used specifically for sexual activities for holy procreation.

beggantropic. adjective. Having the tendency to improvise supplications.

beguerrer noun. **1.** A cowardly mercenary. **2.** A warrior that openly shows fear.

beguijerative. adjective. Susceptibility to being stung by insects.

beldite. noun. A young woman, notable only for her physical beauty.

bellastrop. noun. **1.** Sublime art created under penurious circumstances. **2.** Strotting* art.

bellatia. noun. A beautiful but clumsy woman, unable to move with grace.

bemaric. noun. **1.** A radio without control buttons, keys, tuning knobs, etc. **2.** A radio that randomly and automatically tunes stations, seemingly at will.

bemelic. adjective. Having naturally sticky skin.

bemolisia. noun. Property of certain stones that when crashed or fused together produce a sound in a lower semitone than their original, independent sounds.

bengot. noun. A vindictive person who gives the impression of performing a good deed during an act of vengeance.

benigntory. noun. A place where those who pretend to perform good deeds gather together to plan future actions.

beocus. adjective. Absorb someone else's sorrows.

beozoric. adjective. Affirmed to be a direct descendant of a beocus.*

bephite. noun. Debt of honor.

berlanda. noun. A woman's garment consisting of a combined vest and miniskirt made from different materials.

besothopia. noun. *Mythology.* Mythical civilization where nonverbal communication was transmitted by besothopol.*

besothopol. noun. *Linguistics.* **1.** Wordless language executed by smacking one's lips in various contorting ways that produce sounds resembling kissing. *Mythology.* **2.** The language of the mythical civilization of Besothopia.

bestilence. noun. Innocence of the naïve who thinks him or herself to be a messenger of God.

bethomio. adjective. **1.** Holding the second or third rung down on a low-grade hierarchical scale. noun. **2.** A person who is commanded to do something.

beyondegrave. noun. **1.** A mysterious world with only one entry called the portal of death. **2.** Inexistence. **3.** Masalla.

bibliocephalic. adjective. Accurately retaining the majority of the information read in many books.

biblioptician. noun. A person who compulsively glances at books and reads none.

bicapitality. noun. **1.** Common trait in homosexual couples who share authority, tasks and responsibilities in domestic settings. *Psychology*. **2.** The dramatic sentimental turbulence that affects some gay couples. *Politics*. **3.** The dualistic economic and power forces that influence a democracy.

bidigiclup. adjective. Comfortably fitting two fingers in an orifice.

bienfasch. adjective. **1.** Appearing aesthetically well dressed despite wearing rags. **2.** Eleganragged. **3.** Sophistandruge.

bienvenniate. verb. Generic welcome given in accordance with the social etiquette of a location or occasion.

bigendrick. noun. **1.** State of shock when a heterosexual being suddenly awakens in a body of the opposite sex. **2.** A being of one gonality* living in a host of a distinct gonality.*

bigofant. noun. **1.** Phantom mustache. **2.** Space between the upper lip and the nose of a clean-shaven man that inexplicably gives the impression of just having shaved a long, lush mustache. **3.** Impression that the frondinella* is larger than its actual size and that it would look less unattractive with a mustache in any gender.

bigorria. noun. adjective. Slovenly, unkempt woman by choice or conviction.

bihoost. adjective. Purposefully drowned twice by the same person.

biloquium. noun. **1.** Colloquium of two. **2.** Situation between two persons in which one believes they are conversing while the other only hears a monologue.

bimenstruist. noun. adjective. A woman who commonly endures two menstruations per month.

bimorbid. adjective. Suffering simultaneously two diseases that are not related to one another.

bimorbous. noun. **1.** Doubly gruesome spectacle or circumstance. **2.** A person with an uncontrollable, uninhibited ghoulish mania. **3.** Phenacultry. adjective. **4.** Causing multiple ghoulish states.

biobathic. adjective. Pretending to comprehend the origin, meaning and depth of life.

biobricate. verb. Self-lubrication of mucosal tissues with biological substances from someone else.

biocaducity. noun. *Biology*. **1.** Genetic coding that determines the average natural longevity of a species and that of individuals of each species. **2.** Bioexpiry. **3.** Prothanasia. **4.** Telobioptosis. *Biochemistry*. **5.** DNA-programmed obsolescence in living organisms. *Philosophy*. **6.** Ontolilepsis.*

biochronoscence. noun. *Biology*. **1.** The predefined period of multi-systemic degeneration regulated by specific biological clocks in each species and the individuals within a species that concludes with death. *Medicine*. **2.** Ontosis.* *Philosophy*. **3.** Ontolilepsis.*

biocosmia. noun. **1.** Collection of living beings in the observable universe. **2.** Panbiocosmia.

biocrypton. noun. *Biology*. Spore or microorganism encapsulated in amber during a past geologic era that when freed in the present continues its life and biological cycle.

biofallacy. noun. **1.** Profound feeling of being betrayed by destiny. **2.** Overwhelming sensation of physical and mental defeat due to ugliness, incapacity, disease or senility.

biofume. noun. Entity made of smoke.

bioidem. noun. Each one of two persons who, while not being fraternal twins, identical twins or clones of one another, look identical.

biosilepsy. noun. *Biology*. A trait or behavior of an individual or a group of individuals within a species that is dissimilar to the traits and behaviors of the genus and species of said species.

biosophism. noun. *Philosophy*. Philosophic theory that rules out monads and recognizes life as godless, evolving, random interactions between organic and inorganic substances.

biostofan. noun. *Zoology*. Family of primitive Triassic crustaceans from which extremophiles and thermophiles evolved.

biostrofid. noun. Organism or organisms of one species that drastically modifies the number, organization and ecological balance of numerous other species.

biotherga. noun. The last frontier between life and death.

biotocastism. noun. *Biology*. Evolution theory proposing that selective processes of environmental pressures favor the random evolution of species, dependent on the adapting behavior of some individuals and their descendants in response to said pressures.

biotron. noun. *Biology*. **1.** An apparatus that accelerates biological processes. **2.** An apparatus utilized to accelerate physical and mental activities and life as a whole without diminishing the relative longevity.

biovitral. noun. An eye which, when reflecting light, resembles a brilliant stained-glass window.

bipady. noun. A neurotic fixation with using double pads for the comfort of computer mice.

biparasitis. noun. *Biology.* Chronic irritation occurring in two individuals of distinct animal or vegetable species when mutually intending to parasitize each other.

biponomy. noun. The study of bipolarizations.

bipretition. noun. Propensity of trousers without a belt to tighten on a person's hip, seemingly at will.

biroluga. noun. A woman with long and abundant down above her upper lip.

bisetile. noun. A decorative table with two feet which maintains its balance by a precise weight distribution.

bisomnism. noun. Mental state in which two sleeping persons share the same dream.

bispeciologist. noun. A person with two specialties in two different, unrelated disciplines.

bispectrolic. adjective. *Optics.* Having two tones of the same color.

bisthenic. adjective. Becoming mute when in the company of two or more people.

bithanater. adjective. **1.** Having died on two separate occasions. noun. **2.** A person who has died twice.

bithrolist. noun. A physician with two specialties.

bitofrious. noun. A priest or monk wearing a soiled soutane or habit.

bituate. verb. To participate in the cause of death of someone, indirectly and unknowingly.

bixile. noun. A person exiled twice.

blacule. noun. *Biology.* Microscopic spark that generally occurs between two or more cells in active communication.

blanfette. noun. Coarse piece of antique cloth used to clean objects or animals.

blaspet. noun. **1.** Insult combined with a spell that is effective by virtue of a precise position of the tongue in relation to teeth and palate. **2.** Lingutelio. **3.** Glossaret. **4.** A truly harmful curse.

bledda. noun. **1.** A convoluted form of legal deceit that takes possessions away from their owners. **2.** Depoil.*

blefarasthenia. noun. Incapacity or lack of strength to open the eyes.

blefareate. verb. To blink repeatedly with both eyelids.

blefarostatic. adjective. Maintaining an immobile posture without blinking.

blefasculation. noun. **1.** Wide opening of the eyes to complement an expression of affected surprise when listening to the conversation of a person of authority or a celebrity. **2.** Maximum aperture of the eyelids that accompanies a massetetion.*

blefasgia. noun. Intense languor in opening the eyes on wakening.

blemagation. noun. Contagious feeling of relief among coworkers when they believe a problem is resolved at the moment of identifying someone who probably can resolve such a problem.

blenitis. noun. *Medicine.* Inflammation of mucosal tissues in several parts of the body.

blenodipsia. noun. Uncomfortable situation when having the nose aplethorated* of dry mucus that blocks breathing, without handkerchief in hand and unable to sniff forcefully or to wipe with a sleeve, by virtue of being in a silent ceremony.

blenosis. noun. *Medicine.* Systemic degeneration of mucosal tissues following chronic autoimmune blenitis.*

blesser. noun. A person who blesses someone else and believes his benediction to be effective.

blopira. noun. A woman with lips painted in an intense color and a thick dark line outlining the lips' contours.

blotta. noun. **1.** Collection of intangible refuse. *Psychology.* **2.** A set of deep-seated frustrations, traumas, phobias and resentments that occupy and shade a great portion of a person's mental processes. *Cybernetics.* **3.** Undeletable digital debris.

blove. noun. *Informal.* Cluster of hair, desquamated skin, human excretions and other varied rubbish mixed with soap residue that builds up in the bathtub drain.

bokett. verb. (from *boketto* in Japanese). To gaze vacantly into the distance without observing or thinking.

bollymastia. noun. Breasts that resemble volleyballs in form and shape.

bonatier. adjective. **1.** Pretending to be good-natured. **2.** Keeping a blotta* under tight wraps.

boncordia. noun. Something beautiful that cannot be seen, smelled, heard, tasted or felt, but that triggers a sense of well-being or pleasure.

bonggio. noun. A badly made bun.

bookous. adjective. Pretending to have read one or more books but remembering absolutely nothing about them.

boretech. noun. **1.** Lack of teaching techniques. **2.** A mediocre teacher.

borotte. noun. A father resigned to accept the abuses he receives from an offspring.

borrevian. noun. **1.** An acquaintance without family relations who lives close by. **2.** A known neighbor with no kin relationship.

botrophioid. noun. An unattractive man who persists in meeting a beautiful woman despite her numerous refusals.

bozonia. noun. **1.** A woman with a mustache. **2.** The sudden depression that engulfs a woman when her reflection shows a sizeable stray hair on her chin.

bradexplosive. adjective. An aroma derived from cooking or baking that scatters effectively and appears to become omnipresent.

bradoscule. noun. Tender and respectful kiss on the forehead of the recently deceased.

bradyambulate. verb. **1.** To walk slowly and steadily without hesitating or claudicating. noun. **2.** The idiosyncratic heavy walk of some adults that does not resemble either parsipody* or presbipodia.*

bradybulant. adjective. Exhibiting a slow, petulant tone of voice with marked insecurity.

bradybully. noun. A measured, excessively ceremonious speaking style that uses exaggerated enunciation and volume to emphasize each word.

bradychronia. noun. Perception of the sluggish pace of time in difficult moments.

bradydidactic. adjective. **1.** Instructing strategically. **2.** Teaching methodically while boring the students.

bradyfulminancy. noun. *Psychology.* **1.** Frustrating sensation that time passes rapidly while actions and events are perceived in slow motion. **2.** Simultaneous tachychronicity* and bradyophtalmia.

bradydigitation. noun. Affectation of a salesperson when briskly manipulating one's purchased items while pretending to do it carefully and meticulously.

bradyoxy. noun. *Medicine.* Slow distribution of oxygen throughout tissues due to arteriosclerosis, anemia, hypoglobulinemia or other conditions.

bradypendent. verb. *Aeronautics.* To descend with rapid speed and gradual altitude.

bradypodious. adjective. **1.** Uniquely slow manner of walking. noun. **2.** A healthy young adult who walks slowly. **3.** Premature parsipody.*

bradytachodony. noun. Direct, real-time images perceived as halting or faltering, accelerating and breaking in a vacillating fashion, like early cinematographic images.

braggalate. verb. **1.** To pull up someone's underwear from behind. noun. *Informal.* **2.** Wedgie.

braggate. verb. **1.** To make a superficial statement in an ostentatious manner and exhibit satisfaction with oneself. **2.** To wildly embellish a personal story or a fictitious anecdote to others.

brasmotic. adjective. Getting easily upset without apparent motive.

brita. noun. Array of emotional and physical characteristics that constitute the essence of a person.

brogaterant. noun. **1.** A person who irritates children by slandering their parents or siblings. **2.** Boggard. **3.** Pedolough. **4.** Bruminfant. **5.** Pediabrign.

bromaneer. noun. **1.** A person who firmly believes himself to be living in a minefield of free radicals. **2.** A nutritional warrior who tries to fight against microscopic antinutrient soldiers. **3.** An active paladin against cellular terrorism in the war of attrition against antinutrients and globalization. **4.** A combatant for bromatlism.*

bromatilism. noun. Movement that proposes to fight against the global, corrupt antinutrient bombardment that blocks noble nutrients.

bromatilist. noun. Neophyte missionary of seemingly sound nutrition.

bromatologist. noun. A person who practices gastronomy and nutrition without studies or qualifications in either field.

broohagg. noun. *Informal.* **1.** An unattractive woman who dominates her husband. **2.** An ugly kaddaka.*

brummery. noun. **1.** Collection of words emanating flatly and hesitantly from the mouth of a person with a hazy brain. **2.**

Disjointed speech pattern with slurred words in the inebriated. **3.** Morphosy.*

burbule. verb. **1.** Emit tangible words with the shape and consistency of bubbles. **2.** Pronounce fragile, empty words that are quickly broken and forgotten.

bureaucrallast. noun. **1.** The minister in a municipal ministry dealing with intangibles. **2.** An unimportant, local man with a government title.

bureaution. noun. The inevitable peculiar tendency of any organization to become bureaucratic once reaching a certain size.

bursasion. noun. **1.** Female action of pulling out everything from her purse with the exception of what she is looking for. **2.** Burseculation.

bushobamic. noun. *History.* Historical period that marks the severe decline of the Unitedstatian superpower in the 21st century.

butagge. noun. *Psychology.* **1.** Persistent psychological excoriation that flays the conscience when a loved one dies before one has had the opportunity to apologize. **2.** Grudd. **3.** Rosidiol.

C

cabiphoned. noun. **1.** Body position of a person consulting, reading or writing on a small telecommunications device. adjective. **2.** Being engrossed with or totally absorbed in the screen of a small electromagnetic contraption.

cabycephalic. adjective. *Zoology.* **1.** Having the head located in a distal part of the body. *Informal.* **2.** (of a person) Thinking with the rear end.

cachett. noun. The bulky cheeks of the just awakened.

cacoforia. noun. The ability to endure adversity with dignity, resignation and without question.

cafond. noun. (from *cafuné* in Portuguese). **1.** The act of running one's fingers, gently but deeply, through someone else's hair. verb. **2.** To caress someone else's hair.

cafrenoid. adjective. Driving a vehicle aggressively, without precaution and yelling frequent insults at other drivers.

caft. verb. **1.** To intend locomotion using four limbs with the insecurity and clumsiness of a newborn calf. **2.** To terneate. noun. **3.** A drunk man creeping into his home to avoid detection.

calatro. noun. Event, invention or discovery that, in addition to being in itself a remarkable achievement, also constitutes a significant milestone in the progress of humankind.

calcigeneous. adjective. *Physics.* **1.** Emanating warmth after accumulating heat from a non-heating source. **2.** Radiating heat from an internal reaction of two or more components.

calendogonous. adjective. **1.** Being frequently and inexplicably hot or sexually aroused. **2.** Having multiple and ever-changing sexual partners. **3.** Kaleidogonous.*

caligely. noun. Sudden, violent sensation of bitter cold with uncontrollable muscular contractions alternated with the feeling of being ablaze with smoldering heat burning the body from inside out.

caliginia. noun. **1.** A vagina in the shape of a challis or a funnel. **2.** A virginal posture in a portrait or statue representing a female saint.

calitrigeny. noun. **1.** Capacity of certain acidic or spicy foods to elevate a body temperature when ingested. **2.** Pyrocity. **3.** Capsicholia.

callipetmy. noun. Active and purposeful concealment of the truth.

calmetrism. noun. *Mathematics.* **1.** Theory proposing to change the measurement of time to the metric decimal system. **2.** Doctrine that insists on modifying measurement of minutes, hours, days, weeks and months into the metric system, maintaining the second as the main unit of time. **3.** Decichronometrism.

calmterk. noun. A person who is excessively slow, imperturbable, and stubborn.

calomain. noun. *Informal.* A coquettish homosexual man.

calout. noun. A man who obeys his wife's instructions and urinates sitting down.

camofia. adjective. **1.** Having a less than attractive facial profile. noun. **2.** Unsuitable and unattractive model to pose for a cameo.

camprell. verb. To see a person today as if in earlier times.

campth. noun. **1.** Inability, due to mediocrity or incredulity, to recognize the greatness of a well-known relative or a friend. **2.** Campeignity.

camputa. noun. *Informal.* Rural prostitute.

camuflacciate. verb. **1.** To simulate that something is not limp by giving it the impression of rigidity. **2.** To joke offensively.

canannette. noun. *Literary.* The heavy, ethereal iron chains a person drags through life trying to do what is believed to be an obligatory duty.

cancamick. adjective. Having the predisposition to prowl without cause or reason.

cancine. noun. A castrated lamb that happened to procreate.

candaphus. noun. *Literary.* Crust that envelops the fleshy capriciousness of a woman.

candelagyny. noun. The unique feminine cadence in the walk and mannerisms of a woman that awakens venereal desires in others.

candello. noun. *Astrophysics.* **1.** Astral photometric unit of luminous intensity equivalent to a trillion (a billion outside the

U.K. counting system) or 10^{12} candelas. **2.** Teracandela.

caneforiol. noun. *Archeology.* Ancient container of small size for holding flowers.

canforial. adjective. *History.* In ancient Greece, having performing dogs in a public spectacle.

canglibose. noun. **1.** A woman who becomes seductive despite wearing rags. **2.** Bonafash. **3.** Sexyrag. **4.** Our Lady of Harvest. *Literature.* **5.** A captivating woman wearing rags and feathers from Salvation Army counters. *Music.* **6.** The reverberant singing voice of a Canadian male poet.

canglious. noun. Hanging piece of skin under the earlobe.

cangond. noun. **1.** An uneducated, disheveled man with halitosis who tries to pursue an amorous relationship. **2.** Bodrius.

cangoot. adjective. Being absolutely resolute and without options.

cangulate. verb. To walk or run with intermittent jumps like a kangaroo.

canifer. noun. *Botany.* A tree of the Family Abietaceae with masculine and feminine flowers sequestered on separate branches, with scaly leaves and

conical fruits resembling the snout of a dog.

canimate. adjective. Being extremely energetic, nervous and jumpy with frequent involuntary muscular contractions like a Teacup Chihuahua dog.

canipodial. noun. A peculiar fast-paced walk in which the person is looking straight ahead with his sight fixed only on one point of the horizon.

canistery. noun. **1.** Establishment where dogs are kept in captivity for religious reasons. **2.** Canitery.

cannat. noun. Curly gray hair on someone who previously had colored straight hair.

cannibanoia. noun. *Medicine.* Psychiatric condition consisting of imagining eating the cooked flesh of a loved one.

capassent. verb. To concur positively by nodding the head.

capiflex. verb. **1.** To move the head downwards and laterally. **2.** To amphicefaliate.

capigyrate. verb. To turn the head ninety degrees in any direction.

capippate. To raise one's head with the neck extended to the limit.

capiton. noun. **1.** Biological plug. *Medicine.* **2.** A bioabsorbable lid to cover the hole after a trepanation or a brain surgery.

capnandro. noun. **1.** Human smoke. **2.** Smoke emanating from human cremation.

capneobathy. noun. Property of a type of smoke that descends instead of going upwards.

cappaman. noun. *Informal.* **1.** A person experienced in performing castrations. **2.** A dexterous castrator.

carconid. noun. **1.** Sawdust produced by wood-eating insects. **2.** Type of skin that resembles carcosoid* scales.

carcosoid. noun. The rough quality of a truncated and ragged cliff.

carcosoma. noun. *Medicine.* Fleshy skin growth that, when reaching a certain size, hangs loose and looks like a semisolid teardrop.

carcosomiasis. noun. *Medicine.* Prevalent condition in certain predisposed families characterized by multiple carcosomas* in young adulthood.

carenchemia. noun. Burning sensation occurring when someone despicable touches one's skin.

carendong. adjective. **1.** Having the non-lustful need to constantly touch or caress other people. **2.** Caressimia. **3.** Touchison. **4.** Eulust. **5.** Carimania.* **6.** Carssious.

carestism. noun. *Economics.* Economic theory that proposes and implements inflation to impoverish and control human beings.

caribalt. noun. *Informal.* A person with a concave, malodorous, hairy face, resembling an armpit.

carimania. noun. *Psychology.* **1.** Non-erotic need to feel direct and frequent contact with the skin of other people, particularly loved ones. **2.** Excessive touching or caressing other people without sexual desire and disregarding gonality.* **3.** Carendong.*

caripoth. noun. **1.** A person who constantly has a solemn or angry expression. **2.** Carigrump. **3.** Facrugh.

caripult. verb. To motivate someone to do something relevant at the most opportune moment.

cariroost. adjective. Acquiring the facial expressions of an angry cockerel.

carmophletoid. noun. **1.** A person with a wide, sagging face, droopy eyes and flattened nose. **2.** Carmopleth. **3.** A faulty Olympic sky-jumping structure.

carndamotha. noun. *Informal. Vulgar.* **1.** Damned be your mother. **2.** Damn your camel too.

carnived. noun. Vegetarian doctrine that warns of the deadly dangers of systemic dispersion of toxic substances following consumption of any meat.

carosserous. adjective. **1.** Being difficult to awaken. noun. **2.** Megamodor.

carracarra. noun. *Informal.* **1.** An aggressive and cranky old woman. noun. **2.** Grumpy and bitchy old man born with an erroneous gonality.*

carrecarre. noun. *Informal.* **1.** Uncontrollable explosive diarrhea. **2.** Doomrun. **3.** Futile attempt to run to a bathroom when suffering uncontrollable diarrhea.

carreter. noun. **1.** Wide unpaved road suitable for four-wheeled vehicle transit only. **2.** Anempetrolled.

carrouha. noun. *Informal.* **1.** Derogatory insult to an intrigant woman. **2.** A slanderous, gossipy woman.

cartaviat. noun. **1.** Very thin, light paper used for airmail correspondence. **2.** Papair.

cartocapnia. noun. **1.** Long distance communication using smoke signals. **2.** Carthoom. **3.** Smoke brief.

cartoonderly. noun. Exaggerated, comic-strip-like transformation of the personality and character of some elderly people.

carushlette. noun. **1.** Wealth of wrinkled skin under the chin and jawbone in the obese and old. **2.** Carnosed dewlap. **3.** Corrugated double chin.

cascabat. verb. **1.** To carry or manipulate something clumsily and gracelessly. noun. **2.** Torpeosis.

casconate. verb. To punish someone by divulging his or her devious acts.

casdacrie. adjective. Involuntarily shedding tears when yawning.

catagra. noun. Thin layer of soil that surrounds a dead body during putrefaction.

catalepsis. noun. Invalidating *a priori* possible debatable points.

catamerge. verb. To submerge someone in a brutal manner, with such strength and violence that sizeable quantities of fluid are displaced.

cataptosis. noun. Physical empathy for someone else's vertigo.

catarumb. verb. To flatten, demolish or destroy a

construction in an astonishing manner.

cataruna. noun. *Zoology.* **1.** Marine telosteal fish. **2.** Edible fish similar to herring, but smaller and less tasty, with a posterior dorsal of green color with silvery tones that lives in the temperate waters of North and South America.

catastrissis. noun. Morbid human thirst to find out about daily catastrophes that happened to others.

catastropic. adjective. **1.** Being predisposed to frequent catastrophes. noun. **2.** A person with a predisposition to experience frequent personal catastrophes due to not thinking one step ahead.

catharchy. noun. **1.** Expression of sluggish surprise combined with confusion identifiable by flaccid cheeks, open mouth and eyes contaminated with sleep. **2.** Miralenna.

cathepuly. noun. A sexual posture in which both partners are in a sitting position during coitus.

causicarnia. noun. Spontaneous combustion in humans.

caustiporn. noun. Burning pain a man suffers in his penis after coitus with the most entrancing and inflaming prostitute of a particular locale.

cautivirgin. noun. A woman who uncompromisingly protects her virginity with extreme prudishness until she sells it to the highest bidder.

cavagina. noun. *Medicine.* **1.** Speleologina. *Informal.* **2.** Vagina of the cautivirgin* resembling an unexplored cave.

cavanicle. noun. **1.** Eccentric wine enthusiast. **2.** Inhabitant of a wine cellar.

cavilescence. noun. A bizarre thought with strange shapes, textures, smells, and feelings that seem to be truly an alien thought and that in turn generates an alien sensation.

caviparlant. noun. **1.** A person who normally thinks out loud. **2.** Selfcluse. **3.** A person who talks to oneself, animals, plants, and inanimate objects.

cellastration. noun. The deep frustration of an ambulatory hematophagous insect trapped in a sealed room empty of vertebrates from which to suck blood.

celleng. noun. Feeling of having an orgasm moments after having an orgasm.

celofacial. noun. Perplexed expression when realizing that a memory is not a remembrance of a lived experience, but rather the remembrance of an elusive dream that one has been attempting to recollect for some time.

celogenator. noun. **1.** Real or imagined trigger of innate jealousy. **2.** A trigger that catapults a person suffering from zelostenoity* into an explosive tornado of jealousy, violently destroying everything around him or her.

celoggoogh. noun. **1.** Intense re-arousal soon after an orgasm. *Psychology.* **2.** Orgasmic tenesmus. *Medicine.* **3.** Coitus tenesmus. **4.** Antonym of cuasiplation.*

cementrige. noun. Cement dust scattered by the wind or by workers mixing concrete.

cennondic. noun. The noise heard during absolute silence.

cenolysal. adjective. **1.** Unfrowning. noun. **2.** Event, action or thought that unravels a frown.

centripheral. adjective. **1.** Maintaining the same distance from a center point. noun. **2.** Dynamic property of not getting closer or farther away from the center. **3.** Relating to or situated on the center or close to the center of something.

centripherism. noun. **1.** Artistic movement in painting and sculpture in which the essence of the work is in the periphery.

adjective. **2.** Riding a horse, a mule or a donkey sidesaddle.

cephalokleptia. noun. The ability of an intrigant to enter the minds of others.

cephalomin. noun. A man who nervously turns his head from side to side when urinating in a public restroom or outdoors.

cephamime. noun. A person with a facial expression that resembles that of a mime.

ception. noun. **1.** Action of incomplete perception. **2.** Frustrating sensation when perceiving something incompletely.

ceptrid. noun. A muscular man who fears being observed.

cerdiff. adjective. *Informal.* Extremely offensive insult toward the unkempt.

cerdillism. noun. Full surrender and complete obedience after experiencing cerdillition.*

cerdillition. noun. Minimal obedience borne of intense emotions of rage and despair along with a complete feeling of impotence on being the target of an injustice by an authority.

cerigge. noun. A person who would willingly tell the truth if he or she were able to do so.

cerollary. *Archaic.* noun. Ancient chandelier used in Minoan equinox ceremonies.

certident. adjective. **1.** Being absolutely certain or convinced of something irrational or illogical. **2.** Insisting on being absolutely certain or convinced about something despite the vast evidence to the contrary.

cerunite. noun. Substance excreted by ear cells that provides cerumen or earwax with its distinctly bitter flavor.

cetamea. noun. Turbid trail of urine left by a harpooned whale.

chactalism. noun. Fractal quality of an entity in the fourth dimension.

changor. noun. **1.** A feeling of being mildly sick with no signs or symptoms of disease. **2.** A sensation of no vitality, demotivation, with unidentifiable discomfort in the body that does not reach a threshold of pain, feeling heaviness in head and body or perceiving an uncomfortable external pressure. **3.** Slightly under the weather.

charpid. noun. Sound of human distress, very much like the chirping of a small bird.

chemflay. verb. **1.** To peel someone's skin with chemical substances during torture. **2.** To utilize an alternating combination of strong alkalis and acids to torture someone in the manner of chemical flaying. **3.** To chemodesull.

chemissant. noun. *Chemistry.* **1.** A chemical substance that converts healthy cells and tissues into fecal matter. **2.** Chemodefecant. *Informal.* **3.** Chemshit.

chilldom. noun. *Philosophy.* **1.** A temporary hollow state of mind. *Psychology.* **2.** An acute or chronic sensation of being hollow.

chineiriness. noun. **1.** Open demonstration of fake sincerity. **2.** Pretended chineiry.*

chineiry. noun. Open display of interest conveyed by voice or gesture to experience something, or to do something for someone else.

chirittage. noun. **1.** Incessant mixture of whining and wailing complaints in an extremely fastidious, acute tone, uttered by small children to express their discontent with something trivial. **2.** Loud, ear-piercing screech of small children or animals.

chiroviosk. noun. **1.** Vicious and damaging vaginal rape executed with the hands alone. **2.** Defiling someone's chastity with the hands. **3.** Quiroviolation. *Informal.* **4.** Handrape.

chirurtics. noun. **1.** Punitive therapeutic technique consisting of stabbing needles in random parts of the body. **2.** Puniacupuncture.

chispiron. noun. Microscopic vibration produced by electrical charges during intercommunication between two or more cells.

chistolik. noun. Loud, distressing, triumphal, comic or agonized noise some people make when sneezing.

chondilorrhage. noun. *History.* **1.** Multiple joint leakages of people tortured on a rack. *Medicine.* **2.** Generalized synovial fluid effluvia caused by massive traumatic cartilage dislocation.

chondrophobia. noun. **1.** Aversion to eating cartilage. **2.** Refusal to eat animal cartilage when sharing a meal with people from a culture who customarily consume animal cartilage. *Informal.* **3.** Kehladisgust.

christiacle. noun. **1.** A merchandize stand outside a church. **2.** An anxious salesperson waiting for churchgoers to get out of Mass.

chromophonia. noun. The ability to perceive sounds as colorful moving shapes.

chromosmetic. noun. **1.** A facial paint used by people who wish to give the impression of being in estrus. **2.** The natural facial tint of a woman in heat.

chronal. adjective. **1.** Relative to time. noun. **2.** A measure of time using the decimal system. **3.** Measurement of time in non-linear time. **3.** Computation of the radial direction and the relative velocities of time. **4.** Valuation of time and times in distinct radialisms.*

chronam. adjective. **1.** Wandering through time. **2.** Traveling through dream-time with no specific moment targeted. noun. **3.** A person who hallucinates a time period not lived in.

chronatelity. noun. Ability to circumvent the passage of time.

chronesthesia. noun. **1.** Unique capability to perceive both the real and the relative speed of time. **2.** Unique sensibility to perceive the real radialism* and the relative speed of time.

chronity. noun. Invisible hatch separating and dissolving the general illusion of individual realities.

chronodimensialism. noun. **1.** Unique variety of properties of the present in different dimensions. **2.** Transdimensional convolution of the present in distinct presents characterized by parexacticity* of instants to happen and the relative exactness of what is happening at the precise moment of which it is happening.

chronofusion. noun. **1.** Blend of differing times into one. **2.** Amalgachronation.

chronolevity. noun. **1.** Intrinsic quality of the weighty lightness of time. **2.** Ability to synarch,* transmegunate,* or protocept* instants.

chronoligic. adjective. **1.** Comprehending in, out and through time. **2.** Possessing chronospheric* ability, experience and dexterity. noun. **3.** Someone who possesses chronoristic knowledge.

chronolisp. noun. Awareness of having the time to repeat a task because one did not perform it properly the first time.

chrononihilism. noun. *Psychology.* **1.** Depression triggered by the passage of time. **2.** Bathycated* with time. **3.** Future error radialized* in the past or in the par7aterit.* *Philosophy.* **4.** Late 21st century subculture philosophy with the motto *we are all going to die anyway.*

chronopalent. adjective. *Literary.* Having the innate ability to tangibilize* time, mince it and swallow it raw.

chronopathy. noun. Incapacity to feel, sense or perceive the passage of time.

chronopetry. verb. **1.** To retain memories in layers. **2.** To place a remembrance above a recollection above a reminiscence above an impression. **3.** To lapidate old reminiscences with new memories.

chronophagia. noun. **1.** Incapacity to realize the duration of the time lapsed while being deep in concentration. **2.** Cheated by time when under coma or unconscious.

chronophone. noun. Instrument of great precision to measure the intensity of time frictions.

chronoprison. noun. *Literary.* **1.** Metaphor of time perceived by three-dimensional beings. **2.** Absolute restriction of time travel to those who do not comprehend totitemporality.* **3.** Chronosphere.*

chronorradial. noun. The radial directions of time along with the relative velocity of time.

chronorreactivity. noun. Submissive acceptance of uncontrollability when perceiving the relative haste of time.

chronorrhage. noun. **1.** Sensation that time passed rapidly without realizing it. **2.** Regretful feeling of having wasted time. **3.** Unproductive chronophagia.*

chronorrhea. noun. The condition of suffering frequently from chronorrhage.*

chronosphere. noun. **1.** Tridimensional metaphor of totitemporality.* **2.** Prison where three-dimensional beings are slaves to time. **3.** The only remedial concept of time for those who do not get it.

chronostetion. noun. Relating to or denoting a short-term grant of time as a loan that does not alter the course of life and that is not possible to pay back.

chronosthesic. adjective. **1.** Having the ability, dexterity, gift or experience to perceive the curvatures of time. **2.** Having the capability to sense chronotistically.

chronotropy. noun. A purposeful attraction, concurrence or interconnection with time by virtue of having no other option.

chrontichism. noun. **1.** Quality of insupportable lightness of time. **2.** Insospennable* chronolevity* in which humans gravitambulate.*

chumpollog. adjective. Chewing, licking, twisting or biting of the lips when someone is apologizing.

circancision. noun. Circumcision performed by a neophyte rabbi.

circoma. noun. *Medicine.* **1.** A circular tumor. *Sociology.* **2.** A cancerous circle within a society.

circumcerebration. noun. A memory that circulates and re-circulates in the mind with no apparent end.

circumclitorization. verb. To manipulate the clitoris with circular or elliptical movements.

circummane. verb. To constantly twist one's hair with one's fingers.

circumship. noun. **1.** A cyclical phenomenon in which citizens, perceiving that they are oppressed by their government, organize a revolution, defeat the old regime and set up a new ruling system nearly equal in despotism and re-oppress its citizens. **2.** The almost invariable cycle of retyrantion.*

circumtection. noun. **1.** Egocentric refection on one's own actions. **2.** Retrospective replay of regrettable actions felt in an intransigent manner. **3.** Egospection.

circumtine. adjective. Anxious mental circling around a problem and being unable to solve it.

circumverbiation. noun. **1.** Purposeful whirling of

words with long tiresome phraseologies on diverse topics with the intention of confusing the listeners. **2.** Wordplay for self-aggrandizement. **3.** Pompous word game for the speaker's self-enjoyment.

citizenate. verb. *Sociology.* **1.** To diminish the education of a population by limiting or restricting the quality and quantity of pre-university studies. *Politics.* **2.** To mediocritate.*

civispabilate. noun. *Sociology.* **1.** Mass awakening from the illusion of a free society and seeing the truth behind a government. verb. **2.** To cleanse the senses of a population and enable them to recognize the truth about a government.

civispavick. verb. *Politics.* **1.** To withdraw from the dream of a *faux*-free society. **2.** To wake up to the reality of this moment.

clach. verb. To evanesce slowly, or to pass out of sight, through long periods of time.

cladipully. noun. **1.** Affectation of disgust about something that is secretly desired. **2.** Tactic or trickery to obtain what is vehemently sought by feigning apathy or disapproval.

clammitone. adjective. Routinely speaking pretentiously as if reciting a gothic poem or an obscure philosophical thesis.

clarimesser. noun. **1.** A person who clarifies messages. **2.** Someone who interprets, translates, conveys or deciphers what was not clearly stated or written.

claucholia. noun. Mood or state of mind that goes up and down or comes and goes without any predictable pattern.

claudichord. noun. *Music.* Musical instrument, precursor of the clavichord, with the peculiarity of a sound delay following the striking of a key that confounds and amuses audiences.

claustrell. noun. Enema frequently administered by monks and nuns to one another in cloisters for bowel cleansing and for enhancing spiritual conductivity.

cleavacity. noun. The distinctive qualities of firmness, roundness and proximity of two female breasts to create a highly esthetic cleavage.

clepsidric. adjective. *History.* Pertaining to the old world, from the invention to the decline in usage of clepsydras or water clocks.

clinisensiate. verb. To perceive conditions, syndromes or diseases in others at first sight, generally by physicians with diagnostic talents and extensive practice.

cliospeher. verb. To force someone to adopt the shape of a ball either by coercion or violence.

cliphagy. noun. **1.** A custom of eating in a reclining or totally lying down position. **2.** Playful suction of the clitoris during cunnilingus.

clitosclotion. noun. **1.** Hardening of the clitoris following sexual arousal. *Medicine.* **2.** Non-exudative edematous clitoritis of idiopathic etiology.

cloffonge. adjective. Someone who, despite being well groomed and dressed for a gala event, behaves inappropriately.

clongony. noun. A highly abrasive copulation involving scratching, biting and episiocussions.*

coconfidant. noun. Individuals who mutually confide each other's secrets or intimacies.

cocottier. noun. *Informal.* The head of a sentient being.

cognispansion. noun. *Law.* Action of divulging all knowledge without restriction, including any state secret, commercial patent, restricted information, copyrighted material and miscellaneous esoterica as well as every datum designated as confidential.

cognometer. noun. An instrument for measuring and indicating the true knowledge of a person, generally an intracranial device equipped with neurotransmitters' attractants.

cogto. noun. Depressing feeling that surges with the realization of knowing someone too well.

cohette. verb. To ignite someone's wrath with subtle morbidity and premeditation.

coldation. noun. **1.** Act of insistently bothering a person to the limits of his or her patience. **2.** Harm someone by eliciting uncontrollable rage and thus triggering damaging physiopathological consequences. **3.** Angericide.

colicom. noun. *Medicine.* **1.** Medical condition characterized by an overgrown, dehydrated and deformed large intestine due to chronic constipation. **2.** A person affected by this condition.

collague. noun. The hose politicians use to water their lies over a population.

colobard. noun. Mutilated ghost who ambulates without limping.

colotrancher. noun. *Medicine.* Surgical instrument used to stitch an infected colon.

colpophagistic. adjective. **1.** A person who customarily aspirates and swallows the fluid during cunnilingus. **2.** Comecolp. **3.** Cunninker.

combule. noun. *Medicine.* Pearly dilation at the base of connective tissue tumors.

combusteer. adjective. Having the ability or predisposition to upset people.

comeggy. noun. The eye of a matrimonial turbulence where the desires of a man and a woman fuse together cohesively only to implode into a split.

comeshitter. noun. *Informal.* **1.** A person who evacuates sperm and seminal fluid with feces. **2.** A receptive sodomite. **3.** A man who shits sperm. **4.** The worst insult for a closet homosexual man.

communitarize. noun. Publicly share something that was previously private.

comprehendery. noun. **1.** Cluster of cerebral functions that together enable a person to find a justification for the essence of things, events or concepts. **2.** Collective mental machinations that allow a person to understand notions, principles or happenings.

comprimation. noun. Disconcerting feeling that originates when realizing that there are unidentifiable and unknown tangibles and intangibles.

comproverse. noun. Gathering of perverted persons with the objective of planning a massive act of perversion.

comprovert. adjective. **1.** Being a pervert in quality and quantity. **2.** Becoming a pervert by assisting and participating in a comproverse.*

comuppancy. noun. Punishment or random fate someone endures and justifies as being deserved.

concattugate. verb. To intend to acquire or to mimic the talents of others while underestimating one's own talents.

concomadre. noun. The comadre of someone else's comadre.

concomassia. noun. Lethargic sensation during an intense state of alertness.

concuniant. noun. **1.** A person who accompanies a person to visit another person or place. **2.** An object that is visible in the presence of another object despite their simultaneous appearance being extremely rare. **3.** A phenomenon that happens when another unrelated phenomenon occurs, their simultaneous occurrence being extremely rare.

condetest. verb. **1.** To admit that someone is correct about something all the while knowing that is not true at all. It is generally applied to a person who believes himself to be physically, mentally or morally superior to the other person. **2.** To acquiesce that something is true or valid when knowing that it is not.

condetestable. adjective. **1.** Deserving to be condetested.* noun. **2.** Someone who, characteristically blinded by pride, concedes to the will or volition of someone else.

conepesia. noun. Mild anguish on realizing one is having a bad or immoral thought.

conguge. verb. To rub a sorrow in the face of someone else.

conicephalic. noun. **1.** A baby with a cone-shaped head following a difficult birth or use of forceps. noun. *Informal.* **2.** Insult to a person who is dumb, has a cone-head or has cuneiform scars on the face. **3.** Conehead.

coniotah. adjective. *Informal.* **1.** Insult to a blatantly promiscuous woman. **2.** Vaginasta. noun. **3.** A man who hits or punches in an effeminate manner.

coniphallus. noun. **1.** A male with a cone-shaped penis. *Medicine.* **2.** Androfalloconoid.

conmagtism. noun. Visual attraction to a document labeled with the word "CONFIDENTIAL", especially when the document is sealed and the word is typed or stamped in large, bold letters.

conmicrity. noun. **1.** Cluster of undefinable trivialities that, over time, carry enough weight to dissolve a marriage. *Biology.* **2.** A parasite that copies the host's antigens to circumvent potential anti-parasite immune responses in said host.

connagination. noun. Ability of a person to sense the imagination of someone else.

connathene. noun. *Politics.* Political organization constituted of people without political power with the expectation of assuming true legislative, judicial and executive power in a future regime.

connenpocial. noun. **1.** Numerical scale that quantifies human traits or qualities ranging from cruelty to kindness. The results are expressed in a numerical logarithmic scale with distinctive separation of groups in ascending order which include: cruelty, nechicia, anempathy,* sympathy, empathy, mercy and kindness.

connimuse. verb. To recompose, re-harmonize, rearrange, or pretend to improve upon an existing musical composition.

connintresty. noun. **1.** An interest shared by two or more people. **2.** Mutual realization of two strangers sharing one or more interests.

conopillation. noun. Coitus through a *chuppah* placed on a bed.

conoscience. noun. Branch of conscienciology that studies the how and the why of recognition and sense in the sense of sense, cognition and recognition.

conotheque. noun. **1.** A place where strangers gather together to meet and get to know each other. **2.** An establishment that sells promises of love for a set price.

conteemput. verb. To treat or to consider someone with contempt.

contemperation. noun. **1.** Feeling that a person, animal or object does not merit consideration. **2.** The sense that a person, animal or thing lacks any value. **3.** The intent to ignore something or someone regarded as despicable.

contempocature. noun. *Politics.* Twenty-second century political and economic theories that aim to change governmental systems of the world on the basis that the contemporary world is a mediocre and cheap cartoonish portrait of a Greek tragedy or a B-movie.

contorsition. noun. Quantum contortion of chemical elements when entering and exiting different dimensions.

contraday. noun. **1.** A day of the week dedicated to no work and no holiday. **2.** A nameless day of the week. **3.** A day out of established time.

contradecant. verb. *Physics.* **1.** To separate solid objects in a container by centripetal shaking to bring to the surface the denser objects. *Informal.* **2.** To shake a container with pistachios in such a manner that the closed pistachios are left at the bottom for the next person intending to eat them.

contrafag. noun. **1.** A heterosexual man who claims not to be a homosexual despite evidence to the contrary. *Music.* **2.** A musical instrument that is larger and longer than a contrabassoon and sounds an octave lower in pitch.

contraffactive. noun. **1.** Facts or figures that are, systematically, not true. **2.** Not based on facts or true events. **3.** The opposite of real.

contragonal. adjective. Opposing the concept of gonality.*

contrair. noun. **1.** Air not suitable for breathing. **2.** Artificial white trails marking a blue sky in linear or grid pattern unsuitable for breathing.

contral. noun. Feeling of control a prostitute can exert over a man to give her money.

contraltern. noun. A colleague in a nonprofessional association with no mission or objectives.

contramal. noun. Evil combating evil.

contrangle. noun. *Geometry.* Angle on the other side of the referred angle.

contrapette. noun. *Archaic.* **1.** Small area of shaved hair above the forehead signifying virility. **2.** Contratonsure.

contraputtie. noun. **1.** A woman not linked or associated with the practice of prostitution despite evidence to the contrary. *Informal.* **2.** A woman who argues she is not a whore despite her risqué clothing and behavior.

contrasage. noun. The unalterable quality of a past event because it has already occurred.

contrasolt. adjective. **1.** Always clumsily dropping something. noun. **2.** Fumbliest.

contrel. noun. Feeling of control a man can exert over a prostitute to give him pleasure.

conundratal. adjective. **1.** Being completely baffled. noun. **2.** A maneuver for gaining time to think. **3.** A paradox in the process of being solved by a scientist or a fully thinking being. **4.** A puzzle with no solution for a common man.

conuntouos. noun. A passive-aggressive, clearly bureaucratic action or non-action with the objective of wasting someone else's time.

convexe. verb. To transform a shape from concave to convex.

convidumb. noun. Certainty that someone is irrational or something is illogical despite vast evidence to the contrary.

cooptiate. verb. **1.** To observe something or someone attentively along with other observers. noun. **2.** An event witnessed and observed together by two or more people.

coprodontia. noun. Presence of teeth in fecal matter.

coproeroticism. noun. Sexual arousal when smelling or touching fecal matter.

coproscope. noun. Microscope used exclusively for analysis of fecal material.

coraggicide. noun. **1.** Action of murdering someone by triggering their own anger repetitiously. **2.** Passive assassination of an ill-tempered person.

corbatist. noun. **1.** A woman who gets sexually aroused by pulling a man by the tie. **2.** A woman who frequently jerks a man by the tie. **3.** Tiebatist.

cornetologist. noun. A person who studies brass musical instruments but cannot play them.

corpophoric. adjective. Bearing the body of someone else after being incorporated in said body.

corrious. noun. **1.** A man who is both strong and lean. *Informal.* **2.** A man with leathery skin that seems glued to his bones.

cortamigg. noun. **1.** A woman who frequently ends friendships by having sexual relations with the husbands of her female friends. **2.** Frientiette. **3.** Instrument used to pulverize breadcrumbs and other food detritus and recycle them in home gardens.

coscometaneous. adjective. **1.** Originating from the same region of the cosmos as other intelligent beings.

2. Cosmometan.
3. Cosmometant.
4. Cosmometanish.
5. Cosmometanian.
6. Cosmometanoid.
7. Cosmometanoic.
8. Cosmometanean.
9. Cosmometaner.
10. Cosmometanench.
11. Cosmometanese.
12. Cosmometaning.
13. Cosmometanunian.
14. Cosmometanyan.
15. Cosmometanican.

cosmicle. noun. All which originates in the cosmos.

cosmodicity. noun. **1.** Collective natural laws that determine the average longevity of the cosmos. **2.** Thanastellation.

cosmogen. noun. Native inhabitant of the cosmos.

cosmolabier. adjective. *Literary.* **1.** Traveling through life at full speed with a cognitive windshield. **2.** Lacking the ability to process perceptions as well as lacking interest in how to do so.

cosmoling. noun. An inhabitant of a region of the cosmos.

cosmolizing. adjective. Socializing in the cosmos with other cosmolings.*

cosmoma. noun. **1.** The name given to intelligent inhabitants of Earth by a more evolved species from elsewhere in the universes. **2.** The term "humanity" in an extra-earthly language. **3.** Cosmos cancer.

cosmometer. noun. *Astronomy.* Instrument used to measure the variable size of the observable, perceptible or immediate universe.

cotraitant. noun. Each one of the persons who mutually confides each other's secrets or intimacies and then shares them with others.

counterbestiality. noun. *Military.* Strategy consisting of fighting extreme violence with even greater violence.

counterpretation. noun. **1.** Interpretation distinct from what a person says or said. It generally occurs in a couple. **2.** Contradictory interpretation between two or more people who lived through or witnessed the same event or circumstance. **3.** Near-opposite stories remembered by a husband and a wife regarding a trip taken together or an event both attended. **4.** Divergent cooptiation.*

countersadomasism. noun. **1.** A negative response by a sadist when a masochist asks to be hit. **2.** Passive-aggressive behavior of a sadist toward a supplicant masochist.

counterverity. noun. *Religion* and *Politics.* **1.** Diffusion of a belief or myth by comprehensive propaganda. *Philosophy.* **2.** The absolutist phase of the etimy.* *Commerce.* **3.** A contraffactive* marketing strategy.

cowarth. adjective. *Informal.* **1.** Provoking a fistfight in a group of people with the premeditated intention of not participating in said fight. **2.** Calientamadres.

cracient. adjective. Continuing to grow physically and mentally past the average period of growth or normal development.

cracyment. noun. A cruel punishment given to a member of a defeated regime.

cranealgia. noun. *Medicine.* Headache that stretches throughout the cranium.

craniupus. noun. Derogatory manner of referring to someone with a defect in their cranial anatomy.

cremiony. noun. Involuntary facial expression of a person who experiences sudden terror or a sharp pain.

crenoid. noun. **1.** A surface with toothed irregularities that gives the appearance of not having any curvatures. **2.** Dentated.

crestomatt. adjective. **1.** Having hanging skin off several parts of the body. noun. *Medicine.* **2.** A person suffering from severe carcosomiasis* who appears to have an inverse crest. **3.** A person with carucholettes.

cricka. noun. A gonad of a genotypic male with a feminine phenotype.

crimortization. noun. *Law.* A late 21st century movement that criminalized interest-first amortization and exposed its fraudulent nature. *Sociology.* **2.** Movement that made people aware of the fraudulent nature of banking practices. **3.** Movement that gave rise to mortization* and lexicamortization.*

crimortize. verb. *Law.* To reform practices of banks and financial institutions (after crimortization).*

crisotist. noun. Person who tolerates extreme heat customarily in charge of a maintaining hot furnaces and industrial ovens.

crispable. adjective. **1.** Having the predisposition to crumble or shatter into tiny pieces. **2.** Brittle.

crispallous. adjective. Someone with limited information about a subject who pontificates using prefabricated sentences in an assertive manner.

crispeant. adjective. **1.** New, clean, shiny, and crumbly.

Informal. **2.** Old and sparklingly clean.

crispogeneous. adjective. Causing sudden, temporary severe muscular contractions.

crossimption. noun. **1.** Sudden cessation of sexual arousal without cause. **2.** Prelude to erotion.* **3.** Erophluge. **4.** Consequence of erosphyxia.*

crucispheral. noun. Relating to or denoting a sphere in the shape of a cross.

cryobradylism. noun. *Commerce.* **1.** A profitable business that rents cold chambers for short-term hibernation with the purpose of reducing a person's metabolism and allegedly elongating their lives. **2.** Commercial enterprise of human hibernation. **3.** Ecobiologic hibernicism.

cryoducated. adjective. **1.** Having been raised or educated in a cold and sterile manner. noun. **2.** Someone educated by extreme discipline and with no enjoyment of learning.

cryomommized. noun. A cadaver transformed into a mummy by desiccation in constant, intense cold.

cryonit. noun. *Medicine.* The unbearable pain of instantaneous freezing of the body or part of the body.

cryop. noun. **1.** A common insect pest in domestic freezers. *Entomology.* **2.** A fruit fly of the species *Drosophila cryogaster* adapted in laboratories to survive in subfreezing temperatures that is now a common dweller of human habitats.

cryopanation. noun. **1.** Frozen mist on a glass, crystal or marble surface. **2.** Frozen fog on the exterior of a windshield.

cryptolith. noun. *Medicine.* Extremely small renal stone hidden in a glomerulus that causes intense pain in a very defined point with no relief until it grows larger and is removed.

cryptonegate. verb. *Psychology.* **1.** To hide a desire from oneself and others. **2.** To hide a wish or a desire fearing that it could be perceived as abnormal, dishonorable, or bad in some respect.

cryptopreterit. verb. **1.** To hide a secret or an artifact belonging to the past. **2.** To visit or to stow oneself away in the past for extended periods of time.

cryptoscope. noun. *Literary.* **1.** Optical instrument used for viewing the mysterious and esoteric fringes of life. verb. **2.** To panomarate* clandestinely

upon specific targets. **3.** To ulonsiate* people.

cryptounce. noun. Unit of weight for the immaterial.

crytohedrus. noun. A hypocrite who displays varying rehearsed facial expressions corresponding to his or her current pretensions.

cuasify. verb. To convert a pseudosomething into a pseudothing.

cuasiplation. noun. **1.** Satiation of a nymphomaniac. **2.** Cellangurry. **3.** Coital or orgasmic exhaustion.

cubicephalic. adjective. Having a head in the shape of a cube.

cubiony. noun. *Philosophy.* **1.** Human right to live life without imposed decrees or excise. *Law.* **2.** Enforcement of true freedom for the people and by the people.

cuchuric. adjective. **1.** Perceiving people only by their form, shape, color and texture and not by their essence. **2.** Quaphic.

cuclill. verb. **1.** To genuflect with no intention of manifesting humility, devotion, courtesy or respect. **2.** To bow or kneel with no purpose or intention.

culach. noun. (from *culaccino* in Italian). A mark left on the table by a moist glass.

culpachryma. noun. A solitary tear shed by a woman

accompanied by an almost inaudible whimper or sob because she is unable to find any additional argument, which thus triggers a profound state of consternation in a man that ignites a protective instinct towards her.

culpastule. noun. *Medicine.* A region in the brain that controls the feeling of guilt and varies in location dependent on the intensity of guilt.

cunungo. noun. A facial expression of confusion and sleepiness immediately following a sneeze.

curcurreteca. noun. *Botany.* A small, leathery-leaved evergreen tree from South America (family Cucurbitacea) with a bitter fruit well known for its childish hallucinogenic properties.

curniclash. noun. An intention to carry out an act of infidelity, without the participation of a third person, which is suspected by the spouse or sexual partner and precipitates a conflict in the relationship.

curvangularity. noun. Peculiarity of curved angles in another dimension.

curvigyneous. adjective. Reminiscent of female curvatures.

cusculation. noun. A completely novel sensation.

cutastrus. noun. *History.* Array of small diameter, red-hot cylindrical irons used in medieval torture to burn the entrails of the condemned through anal penetration.

cyberdiv. noun. *Commerce.* **1.** Instantaneous electronic and fair exchange between currencies. **2.** Electronic wire transfer through the pannet* that costs cents, regardless of the currencies exchanged.

cybernnation. noun. Disappointing or depressive emotional state a computer program user experiences when a new version of a program is launched and the previous program that was beginning to function properly is now incompatible with the newer operating systems and is considered obsolete.

cybolia. noun. A sensation of feeling outdated.

cyclognoma. noun. *Medicine.* **1.** Ulcer or blister excreting malodorous fluid from the crutch area or the gluteus of cyclists. *Sports.* **2.** Braggadytis. *Informal.* **3.** Brovagronia. **4.** Nickergroin.

D

dacronosis. noun. *Sociology.* Loss of social sensibility caused by persistent consumerism and indiscriminate use of plastic products and energy in an economically privileged population.

dacryonatriosis. noun. *Medicine.* Fistula surrounded by salty scabby deposits inside the eye of people suffering from chronic dacryonatritis.*

dacryonatritis. noun. *Medicine.* Inflammation of the lacrimal sac due to high concentration of salt in tears.

dactyloptera. noun. *Zoology.* A frog capable of sustained flight. A batrachia of the order Anura, large family Ranidae, familia Dactilopteridae equipped with membranous skin webbing the fingers and called metacarpian wings.

darjagon. noun. An insult held between the teeth without actually articulating any words.

darsic. adjective. Speaking in a scratchy guttural manner.

darthflo. noun. *Medicine.* A microscopic dart containing a precise drug dosage on the tip that is administered by injection.

datisson. noun. The action of an employee carrying documents in a visible manner to create the appearance of being a diligent worker, when in reality he or she has not accomplished much of anything.

deamanize. verb. **1.** To slander and tarnish the integrity and manhood of a family man who has been successful in his field. *Informal.* **2.** To spread suggestive, morbid, spicy or comic rumors that a heterosexual man is a closet homosexual.

decadentude. noun. A luxurious display of self-indulgence during a devastating period of decline in financial, moral, or physical health.

decalorize. verb. To remove calories from a meal or from a dietary regimen.

decaptivize. verb. **1.** To rescue or release a human or animal from captivity. **2.** To free a person from jail or prison.

deceiviator. noun. **1.** An expert in the art of deceit. **2.** Someone who repeatedly causes people to believe something that is blatantly untrue. *Politics.* **3.** Propaganda master. *Commerce.* **4.** A banker. *Informal.* **5.** Advertising executive.

decharon. verb. *Medicine.* To revive a person immediately following a cardio-respiratory failure.

dechation. noun. *Psychology.* Disconcerting sensation of feeling oneself turned off immediately after being turned on.

dechizophrenic. noun. A seemingly normal person who previously was schizophrenic.

deciviate. verb. **1.** To cheat by means of absence of action. **2.** To passively swindle by not doing or saying anything, simply allowing a particular circumstance to unfold without intervention so that the fraud can occur in an apparently natural manner.

deconilor. verb. **1. To** strip away a virgin's maidenhood in a nonsexual manner. **2.** Hymenate. noun. *Medicine.* **3.** Hymenectomy.

deconomize. verb. *Law.* **1.** To financially drain entire populations through deceptive legal and political maneuvers. **2.** To economically drain someone dry, generally by a corporation using legal means.

decound. verb. **1.** To publically declare and share a secret doctrine or esoteric knowledge. **2.** To dehyde.

decrystallize. verb. To remove the natural geometric regularity and the symmetrically arranged plane faces or the transparency from a crystal or from something crystalline.

deculture. verb. *Sociology.* **1.** To increase quantity and distribution of trivial, irrelevant information through multimedia, while facilitating access to useless leisure activities. *Politics.* **2.** To maintain dominion over a population by strategically diminishing their culture. **3.** To precipitate agnocemy.*

dedeify. verb. **1.** To remove the attribute of deity from someone or something. **2.** To deideny.

dedesirt. adjective. **1.** Taking away from something or someone the strong sense of being needed or wished for. **2.** Having lost the quality, attribute or trait of being wanted or needed.

dedination. noun. Sensation of having a heavy burden upon one's shoulders.

dedoquiblant. adjective. **1.** Having a peculiarity which shocks most people. **2.** Deckiblant.

defaciate. verb. **1.** To punch someone in the face repeatedly, inflicting severe damage. **2.** To insult someone with strongly emotional personal affronts in rapid succession.

defester. verb. *Medicine.* **1.** To heal an inflamed, purulent and fistulized ulcer or wound. **2.** To remove a festeration.*

deffemine. noun. A man who has or shows characteristics regarded as typical of a woman, but does not demonstrate effeminate affectations.

deflactant. noun. A non-sensual, non-attractive woman who dresses in sensuous attire, makeup and hair styling.

defrigeriant. noun. A person who, with a mannerism or a phrase, instantaneously turns off any sexual desire toward him or her.

degarm. verb. **1.** To tear undergarments from a person in a fierce or passionate manner. **2.** To remove someone's underpants forcefully without pulling them down from the legs. **3.** To debragg.

degood. verb. **1.** To steal goods or wealth from a person using legal maneuvers. **2.** Depoil.*

dehush. noun. **1.** A sudden burst of exuberant utterances by a person who is normally quiet and reserved. **2.** Dequieteer.

dehydrocarbonize. verb. *Nutrition.* **1.** To eliminate carbohydrates from a dietary regimen. **2.** To remove hydrocarbonicity from something or someone.

deidolithus. noun. An intellectual or a highly educated person who is temporarily affected with paralysis when the topic of religion is raised, but once recovered destroys a religious argument with a minimal number of logical questions that are not logically answered.

deidophoby. noun. **1.** Fear of deities. **2.** Contempt for deities.

deiniric. adjective. **1.** Dreaming of oneself among deities. **2.** Dreaming of interacting with gods, virgin-mother goddesses, angels, saints or prophets of a religion.

deintrine. verb. **1.** To actively erase the mental echoes of a voice. noun. **2.** Focus concentration to ignore someone's cloying verbosity or annoying tone of voice.

delabaration. noun. Drastic diminution of both the lumbar vertebrae curvature and the gluteus muscular mass that occurs in mid-life to old age.

delacle. noun. An out-of-sight place where servants observe their patrons eating.

deland. verb. *Aeronautics.* To separate from a surface when initiating a flight.

delinciat. noun. *Psychology.* **1.** A delinquent or criminal act that is savored as delicious when anticipated or actually being committed. **2.** An action that, despite inducing guilt over breaking a moral norm or law, is enjoyable when planned or executed.

deliragia. noun. **1.** Irrational fury in someone striving to convince someone else to believe in a doctrine. **2.** Obscene dream that triggers a guilty feeling.

delitherapy. noun. **1.** Subtle, obscure treatment employed by a therapist who assumes each patient to be a species of derelict, without letting the patient know what is being done. **2.** Esoteric treatment of a sick person by a condescending healer.

delitruous. noun. *Physics.* **1.** A solid that during decomposition or degeneration releases particles that form a liquid. *Medicine.* **2.** Psychiatric care that makes patients increasingly worse.

dembellish. verb. **1.** To make someone or something less attractive by removing or magnifying details or features. **2.** To deprettify.

democrisis. noun. **1.** Apparent effervescence of a democratic regime just before the breaking point, when the constituents realize that the regime is actually an oligarchic plutocracy. **2.** Effervedropsy* on the threshold of collapse. *Medicine.* **3.** Synchronized parasitic larvae hatching and being confronted by overwhelming host immune responses.

demollent. verb. *Politics.* **1.** To overwhelm a person with detailed tallying of numbers and confusing paperwork. *Sociology.* **2.** To confound and distract a population with entangled paperwork and cumbersome taxation structure to deflect their attention from the real source of control and deconomization.* *Psychology.* **3.** To shut someone down emotionally. *History.* **4.** To punish someone with the 3-cube torture.

demophonous. noun. *Politics.* A political maneuver consisting of conducting brief interviews with people from a small area to form and convey the overall opinion of a population.

demorgony. noun. *Sociology.* The awakening, union and synergy of a population.

demotionate. verb. *Psychology.* **1.** To diminish an emotion or the awakening of an emotion using a constant increase in an unrelated stimulus. noun. **2.** The loss of knowing who you were.

demulgrand. noun. **1.** A person who insults someone in a complimentary tone and flowery wording without the victim realizing the insult. verb. **2.** To overly compliment someone while surreptitiously despising and criticizing.

denaturist. adjective. **1.** Favoring all technology while abhorring everything natural. **2.** Aluddistic.

denchulment. noun. **1.** A psychological and hormonal treatment for pretty or effeminate men striving to become more masculine. **2.** Dembellishment.*

dendronicy. noun. *Psychology.* A habit or a psychological ailment of someone who, at work or at home, maintains an exasperatingly disengaged, passive attitude in voice and manner and carries out his

duties with the speed of a tree absorbing water.

dendronitic. noun. A sleeping position where arms and legs stretch awkwardly in all directions like tree branches.

denthos. noun. *Informal.* **1.** Swear word used to express anger or frustration. *History.* **2.** Exclamation to praise someone or something so enthusiastically as to imply condemnation. Expletive derived from the Middle English expression *God's teeth.*

depaysed. adjective. (from *dépaysement* in French). **1.** Feeling uncomfortable in another country. noun. **2.** Strong nostalgic feeling and sadness when in another country and missing everything related to one's own country. *Psychology.* **3.** Not finding oneself. **4.** Feeling disoriented. noun. *Informal.* **5.** *Jamaicón* Syndrome.

depenition. noun. *Medicine.* Surgical technique consisting of the extirpation of the interior part of the penis while maintaining the top epithelium or skin and the nerve structure during male-to-female transsexual surgeries.

deperd. noun. **1.** Acts and actions to minimize correlations of information and the synthesis of ideas. noun. **2.**

Waste of mental potential. verb.
3. To minimize thinking.
deplessure. verb. **1.** To annoy
a loved one repeatedly on an
emotionally sensitive topic.
2. To anger someone with
premeditation and malice.
deplicate. verb. To confuse
someone by speaking obtusely
about a subject the listener
ignores.
deplommet. noun. A valuable
object someone drops
accidentally on a sidewalk
that other people step on
unintentionally.
deplonge. noun. **1.**
Bittersweet feeling following
a reconciliation. **2.** Cautious
euphoria that follows a truce
with a loved one. **3.** Sensation
of joy and relief that follows
a resolution of an emotionally
charged disagreement.
depoil. verb. *Law.* **1.** To seize
someone's goods via highly
bureaucratic means. noun.
Economics. **2.** Pervasive robbery
or appropriation of goods
via turgid and misleading
bumbledoms. **3.** Degood.*
depoiler. noun. *Law.* An ad
hoc corporate lattice that
systematically appropriates
money and goods from a large
portion of a population in a
slow and progressive manner.

depoptition. noun. *Medicine.* **1.**
Physiological suicide at a cellular
level that is felt in some or
various organs or systems. noun.
2. Apoptosis wreaking havoc.
deporiast. noun. A person,
fired from his work, who hides
his shame by saying that he is
"between jobs."
depory. noun. Desperate
and depressive state of an
unemployed person after being
fired, when realizing that he or
she faces a long, incomeless and
undeserved period of rest.
depravullant. adjective.
Provoking mild shivers, like
the news of a terrible tragedy
affecting many in a faraway
place.
deration. noun. An agreement
between two people to
sever their personal, private
relationship but to continue
interacting with one another for
the sake of a third party.
derenmenia. noun. The lament
of a rich person who has rapidly
lost all of his/her wealth, said
wealth having been effortlessly
obtained.
dermopath. noun. A person
who continually suffers skin
diseases and is perpetually
healing from one outbreak when
another malady emerges.

dermoplasia. noun. *Medicine.* Intermittent, deciduous, tumor-like skin growth.

derrelation. noun. A circumstance when something relevant is deemed irrelevant by a person with a certain level of authority but not necessarily knowledge, understanding or common sense.

derrevolve. noun. **1.** Active quiescence. **2.** A new bureaucratic department. verb. **3.** To unmix. **4.** To unblend. **5.** To deagitate. **6.** To unbeat. **7.** To unwhip. **8.** To reorder something.

derrilicuose. noun. *Physics.* **1.** The increased fluidity of a liquid by means other than heat. **2.** Melted liquid.

derromp. verb. **1.** To create entropy from chaos. **2.** To involuntarily repair something that was broken on purpose.

deschizophry. noun. The joining of two disparate parts to create a whole.

desculpture. noun. A sculpture that has lost contour, form or proportion, as if melting.

deseoteca. noun. Establishment where all desires not attained are stockpiled.

deshivall. noun. A woman who appears beautiful from far away but when seen at close range, her imperfections render her hideously ugly and totally unattractive.

deshiver. verb. **1.** To dissipate shivering in someone by means of tickles, jokes or other distractions. **2.** To distract a person who is shivering with non-titirigeneous* stimuli.

desilopidy. noun. A quality or talent that someone vehemently desires and in fact has, but is incapable of using, developing, or putting into practice.

desimpine. adjective. Valuing a desimpinion* when it comes from the mouth of a celebrity or an authority figure.

desimpinion. noun. **1.** Opinion someone offers in matters that he deems uninteresting. **2.** An opinion that restates the obvious. **3.** An opinion lacking value by the person proffering it.

deslivy. noun. *Psychology.* **1.** Any relief, ease or comforting feeling that is perceived as pleasurable. *Informal.* **2.** Pleasure derived from a physiological relief such as: the relief of defecating following a long wait with multiple evacuating contractions, or the pleasurable consolation when urinating after a prolonged retention in which there has been a feeling of swelling eyes and that the body was about to exude urine from every pore of the skin.

desmall. verb. To hit someone hard and repeatedly until that person becomes moribund.

desmile. noun. **1.** Fake smile to mask a twisted expression of pain. **2.** Pain glaswen.*

despaciate. verb. To slow down something in an attempt to match the speed of everything else.

despharry. verb. To stay at home involuntarily while friends are out enjoying themselves painting the town red at a bar, club or party.

desphiront. verb. **1.** To hit with one's fist the face of someone with a stupid expression that seems to beg loudly to be punched in the face. **2.** To punch the face of a jeek.* **3.** To dechonur.

despirit. verb. *Psychology.* **1.** To purposefully snatch someone's enthusiasm knowing the depressive consequences that can be created by such an action. noun. *Sociology.* **2.** The intentional depressive effect of global mass media on its disparaged audience.

despiritation. noun. (from French *l'esprit de l'escalier* meaning formulation of the perfect reply too late) **1.** The combined feelings of remorse, regret and being upset with oneself for not having reacted, answered or done something in response to being insulted, humiliated or abused. **2.** The emotion that frequently affects the treverter.*

desquat. verb. *Informal.* To stretch one's legs or to get up from a squatting position.

destinator. noun. *Theology.* **1.** The name of a future god. **2.** *Deus posterus.*

detimize. verb. **1.** To bring to light or to openly expose a taboo that was considered for a long time an irrevocable truth. **2.** To decover. **3.** To mythunveil.

detram. verb. To scale dry the rheum of the mind.

deyaulee. noun. An ephemeral dizziness that occurs at the onset of a *déjà vu.*

dezoolated. adjective. *Ecology.* **1.** Having no animal life. noun. *Psychology.* **2.** A severe condition of divorcement from one's natural "animal" instincts in flight, fight, self-defense, hunger, procreation, etc.

diablepharic. adjective. Having the ability to see through one's eyelids.

diachronal. adjective. **1.** Happening through time. **2.** Using one or more of the chronal* systems.

diadelectic. noun. **1.** Ability to use ignorance and inexperience as advantageous questioning instruments during an interview, debate or project development. **2.** The use or exploitation of an intogobility.*

diaerct. noun. Malevolent spectral force that seeks domination.

diafficient. adjective. Something that through something else produces an effect on a third something.

diafideism. noun. *Philosophy.* **1.** Non-religious doctrine that defines and implements strategies to decrease the education of citizens and to spread concocted fear in order to diminish the reasoning capacity of the citizens to discern or discover facts. **2.** Citizenate.*

diagunne. verb. **1.** To implant mental blocks or memory lapses with artificial, non-lived memories. noun. *Psychology.* **2.** Personality disorder of amnesic or hipomnesic people characterized by inventing a life comprising feelings and events not lived. verb. *Medicine.* **3.** To fill mental lacunae with fictitious memories. *Medicine.* **4.** Amnesic paraplethonoia.*

diahert. verb. **1.** To reprimand someone through someone else. **2.** To change, prevent or pressure a person's behavior via a third party, messenger or representative. **3.** To put

pressure on a person through a third person to influence the opinion of a second person.

dialecture. noun. Terrible diction and articulation of words by someone with an advanced degree who is trying to teach a subject in which he or she is supposed to be an expert.

diamnemology. noun. **1.** The study of the nature, storage and transmission of memories. **2.** The study of the transomnesic* phenomenon.

diamnesy. noun. **1.** The use of diverse technologies to transfer memories between two or more persons. **2.** Transomnemia.*

dianimport. noun. A task, responsibility or assignment that suddenly becomes important which initially was not important.

diantelligence. noun. The study of the refraction of distinct types of intelligence.

diapilot. verb. To perform a task subconsciously that requires the attention of multiple senses, coordination and complex calculations and operations while the conscious mind is busy with other matters. Example: Driving a car for a while before realizing it.

diaputate. verb. To take an exceedingly long time to consider irrelevant minutia before evaluating valid advantages and disadvantages and making a decision.

diastoma. noun. *Medicine.* **1.** Contagious mouth disease transmitted through direct contact with mouth mucosae, generally through kissing. **2.** Pathologic oscuglossia. **3.** Glossasculopathy. *Botany.* **4.** A purple weed.

dickent. verb. To subconsciously squeeze something with one's fingers and damage it by not realizing the force applied.

dictiomb. verb. **1.** To untangle or rearrange hair by passing one's fingers through it, generally from front to back. **2.** To pretend to be calm by performing mannerisms to convey cleanliness or feign indifference.

dictionate. verb. **1.** To research the pronunciation of a word in a dictionary. **2.** To attempt to improve diction with the help of a dictionary.

difecant. adjective. *Medicine.***1.** Having the property to induce defecation. noun. **2.** Someone possessing the ability to trigger a bowel movement in someone else by saying something obnoxious, threatening or off the wall.

difficultation. noun. Realization that the performance of a task is more difficult than initially thought before performing said task.

dignigendry. noun. **1.** A warm feeling of pride or satisfaction in the attributes or accomplishments of one's progeny. **2.** Honorable behavior of a bigendrick* being in its host.

digniptosis. noun. **1.** Severe sensation of hopelessness and inadequacy when one's sense of pride is lost. **2.** Disillusion when dignity is destroyed.

dilaby. noun. **1.** The mutual touching of lips between two persons as an affectionate sign of greeting or love without sexual desire. **2.** Kiss on the lips without a glossioscle.*

dildomania. noun. *Psychology.* **1.** An obsessive desire and frequent use of plastic replicas of an erect male sexual organ. **2.** Priapomania.

dinandrous. adjective. *Psychology.* **1.** Perceiving oneself as abominable and despicable. noun. **2.** Utter self-distaste for the inability to join a club that would not allow one to be a member.

dioidocercus. adjective. Having the shape of a tail.

diontony. noun. *Philosophy.* Period of transition in the transmigration between one entity into a fully distinguishable *other.*

dipsonostia. noun. **1.** Vehement desire to learn and comprehend. **2.** A strong impulse to memorize facts, absorb and assimilate knowledge on all subjects.

distramnesia. noun. Notable decrease in memory during periods of stress.

ditiramble. adjective. **1.** Ambulating through life babbling embellished flatteries to admired people or figures of authority. *Informal.* **2.** Dribbling suck-up.

dockinstrik. noun. **1.** An overly strict teaching method based on applying negative feedback and punishment. **2.** Docestring.

docotract. noun. **1.** A sexually penetrated person who actively forces the depth of the penetration. **2.** Genucoxil.* **3.** Pullasion.*

dodeplegia. noun. *Medicine.* Diminution of feeling and movement in four limbs as well as the malfunctioning of two or more organs.

dolotic. noun. A stimulus that engenders pain in some people, but normally does not induce pain.

dolotist. noun. *Psychology.* A person who feels pain when feeling a physical stimulus which does not provoke pain in most people.

dolycosmism. noun. *Astrophysics.* **1.** Theory that rejects the Big Bang Theory as well as the size and the expansion rate of the observable universe. *Physics.* **2.** Neocosmic* theory that casts aside, as underestimated, the size of the perceived universe and mathematically demonstrates the size of the universes (T_U) as a Preternal Unit* (*PU*), concisely described as $T_U = PU$. This formula is derived from the equation: $T_U = \Omega - 1t$. A Preternal Unit is expressed as $UP = \Omega - 1^q t$ [where Ω is eternity (previously expressed as infinitum ∞) ^{q} is timespace continuum (previously referred to as space-time continuum) and t is a time unit]. **3.** Dolycosmology.

domoclast. noun. A person who premeditatedly destroys a marriage, a relationship or a family unit.

doncell. verb. **1.** To adopt a child from a proletarian family into a family belonging to a nobility. **2.** To adopt a natard* from known parents.

dontoccia. noun. *Medicine.* **1.** Stress bruxism. **2.** Tensional teeth grinding.

dontox. verb. **1.** To grind teeth, producing an irritating noise, during periods of stress. noun. *Informal.* **2.** Scared shitless teeth grinding.

dorcaldow. noun. *Meteorology.* **1.** A hot, thick fog. *Meteorology.* **2.** Fog passing through a valley or canyon on a clear day.

dormack. verb. To pretend to be asleep when alone and not being watched by anyone.

dormittle. verb. To pretend to be asleep when being watched by someone else.

dowr. noun. **1.** To give money, goods or property to a husband-to-be. *History.* **2.** Valerian dowry.

dozethak. **1.** A person incapable of teaching something effectively. **3.** Docenthach.

dragget. noun. **1.** The frustration a vehicle driver experiences when changing a lane of slow circulation to another lane appearing to circulate at a faster speed and finding that suddenly the new lane is slower than the first lane. **2.** Linemellitude. **3.** Drarth.

drainment. noun. **1.** The action of emptying all fluids from a body cavity. *Psychology.* **2.** The action of unloading all the emotional buildup within one's psyche. **3.** Blotta* cleansing.

dramaton. noun. *Music.* **1.** A musical note played with inflated drama. *Psychology.* **2.** A person who dresses and behaves himself or herself as though they are very important and wishes everyone to think so. *Informal.* **3.** An aging homosexual who dresses in tight and colorful clothes.

dramaviraggy. noun. A well-practiced affectation when slandering someone.

drance. noun. **1.** A decisive and critical period someone goes through. *Psychology.* **2.** Emotional state a person experiences in a paramystic* state. **3.** A prolonged trance whether positive or negative.

dranduelo. noun. **1.** A false and overtly affected demonstration of mourning and deep sadness following the death of someone not loved, not close, nor personally known to the mourner. **2.** A series of faked wails and cries for payment at a funeral parlor.

drexellious. adjective. *Psychology.* Disconcerting and depressive feeling of inferiority when in the company of others considered superior in a particular field.

drossant. noun. *Politics.* Prolonged propaganda of

fear and terror a government advertises, with alarming tone and frequency, about fictitious dangers with the covert objective of causing public consternation to deflect the citizens' attention from government corruption and incompetence.

dubilation. noun. **1.** Instantaneous state of doubt that immediately follows the perception of a shocking event. **2.** Brief moment of deep confusion before something extremely obvious and upsetting happens.

duga. noun. Unexpected inheritance received from someone unknown.

duplatic. adjective. Exhibiting a facial expression that conveys the stupidity of someone experiencing a double doubt.

duradurate. noun. Someone or something that surpasses the average lifespan or shelf life by virtue of being hard, refractory or stubborn.

durand. verb. To calculate the likelihood of two events occurring simultaneously.

durantility. noun. **1.** The likely quality of two or more different circumstances that happened at the same time. **2.** An undistinguished zalahazar*

or a zalahazar* minus one. **3.** Synchrondomness.

dusack. verb. **1.** To try not to think of something. **2.** To make forceful, yet unsuccessful efforts not to worry about something.

dusch. verb. **1.** To spray someone's torso and abdomen with high-pressured water. *Informal.* **2.** To hose down the dirty chassis of the unwashed masses of humanity. **3.** To duchennyze.

dynamania. noun. Frequent use of force or violence toward a mechanical object or an electronic apparatus that has stopped functioning properly.

dynastat. noun. *Physics.* Apparatus with components that rotate at high speed to detect and record rapid movements of something and display those movements later on in slow motion to detect movements at a femtosecond level or 10^{-15} seconds.

dynatur. noun. Avaricious, anempathetic* and sociopathic traits inherited by offspring of rulers, monarchs and inbred nobility through a set of dominant genes.

dysbarysm. noun. *Medicine.* **1.** Centrifugal pain accompanied by difficulty in feeling the natural barometric pressure. *Psychology.* **2.** Dysesthesia.

Informal. **3.** Making silly faces while scuba diving.

dysbeep. noun. **1.** Peculiar mode of walking in slippers, characterized by an erratic and dramatized clattering. **2.** An annoying click-and-drag rhythmic noise produced by a person wearing loose shoes. *Medicine.* **3.** Dysbipedy. **4.** Dysbipodia.

dysceptic. adjective. **1.** Openly and falsely expressing doubt about something secretly believed. noun. **2.** A person who affectedly announces disbelief in someone or something when in reality believing it deeply.

dyschission. noun. Methodically examining each part, component or possibility of a plan, but then postponing any interpretation or decision about it.

dyscracid. adjective. **1.** Having difficulty in distinguishing differences between different doctrines, ideas or opinions. *Literary.* **2.** Left on the shoals of indiscernibility.

dyscreency. noun. **1.** Incapacity to believe something. **2.** Logical questioning about something that seems unbelievable. *Psychology.* **3.** Cognitive dissonance.

dysculpery. noun. **1.** Insincere and vain attempt to apologize.

Commerce. **2.** A corporate department where apologies are assembled and offered according to their clients' finances. **3.** An establishment where manufactured apologies are sold.

dysdox. noun. Anomaly in the ability to comprehend opinions, mistakenly confusing them with facts or conclusions.

dyslunt. noun. *Psychology.* A person who has suffered separation from both past and present realities so that when new experiences are added, the person becomes ever more separated from his past reality.

dysmallic. noun. *Medicine.* **1.** The state of a person who is preoccupied and anguished by an event that happened unexpectedly. *Psychology.* **2.** A shock that follows a person for a long time.

dysmeneucy. noun. Field or study centered on examining and cataloging memories.

dysmneic. adjective. **1.** Exhibiting impediments to organizing or finding recollections. *Medicine.* **2.** Having difficulty navigating through one's own memories. *Psychology.* **3.** Sensing or feeling lost in time within one's own life.

dysnaudial. noun. **1.** Incapacity to discern subtle sounds.

Informal. **2.** The damaged hearing of a cannoneer.

dysnescent. adjective. **1.** Maintaining a stubborn attitude throughout life without realizing it. *Psychology.* **2.** Believing that one's own perspective is the only truth.

dysnism. noun. Difficulty in performing mental tasks during periods of stress or while being entertained.

dysnomer. noun. **1.** Inaccurate name for something or someone. **2.** Transnomia. **3.** Wonliner.*

dysodiator. noun. A person who hates discord.

dysonaudic. noun. **1.** A person who involuntarily or customarily has the ability to avoid listening when hearing. **2.** A complaint a man receives from his wife about his inability to listen. **3.** Paracynic. **4.** Dicynic. *Medicine.* **5.** Incapable of discerning sounds.

dysparly. noun. **1.** Discordance between a person's desire and the way he or she conveys it. **2.** Gynelalia.* *Phonetics.* **3.** Dysmenparlia.*

dyspose. verb. To get rid of something that belongs to someone else by clandestinely throwing away.

dyspulence. noun. *Medicine.* **1.** Brain dysfunction due to overabundance of memories. **2.** Dysmneopulence.

dysrag. verb. *Law.* To falsely label or prosecute a person as an anarchist, terrorist or Enemy of the State for mentioning a fact or a truth.

dysregant. adjective. **1.** Ignoring other people persistently. noun. **2.** A person who pays no attention to associates or colleagues within an organization.

dysregition. noun. Passive action of a person who realizes he or she is the center of attention and continues the task at hand, disregarding any opinion or critique.

dysrumpation. noun. **1.** Temporal interruption in the friendship of two good friends. **2.** Crackamy.

dysrupcady. noun. The end of solidarity between people or groups of people.

E

eab. noun. **1.** A student from a developing country studying abroad. **2.** Ethnofugee. *Medicine.* **3.** Exudative mellicerous cerumen. **4.** Oozing liquid earwax.

eade. noun. *Literature.* **1.** A literary work considered plagiarism by some but highly regarded by others for its widely inspired use of various styles that are clearly unabashedly copied from multiple sources. **2.** Eclectisity.*

eakle. noun. *Zoology.* **1.** The sudden development of a penis in females within specific mammalian species. **2.** Eclampsophaly.

ealm. noun. *Sociology.* **1.** Proactive prevention of future social aberrances, beginning with a full spectrum analysis of the root causes of problems plaguing a society. **2.** Etiosocilaxis.

eammity. noun. **1.** An erroneous self-serving belief held by the leaders of a system or organization that its leadership is effective and unanimously supported by the subordinates. **2.** Effervodropsy.

eanus. noun. *Law.* **1.** Contemptible and prosecutable state practice to openly hide or make data inaccessible, usually for fifty to ninety-nine years, regarding criminal, immoral and unethical acts of leadership. **2.** Escotondrism.

eawee. noun. **1.** A person who spontaneously and unconsciously imitates the expressions of someone enthusiastically recounting a story. **2.** Echomaniac.

ebble. adjective. **1.** Living or occurring outside time or on a distinct timeline. **2.** Ectotemporary.

eblon. noun. **1.** A rough imitation of the tone of voice and gestures of an authority figure by a small child or a mentally challenged person. **2.** Inatimulation.

eccleschoic. noun. **1.** The apparent altruism and justice feigned by a government and foisted upon its citizens. **2.** Etnocaristeo.

ecdyl. noun. *Medicine.* **1.** A painful skin disease of unknown origin consisting of massive desquamation that leaves the majority of the dermis exposed and hypersensitive to any contact. **2.** Escalvipela.

echidnous. noun. *Anthropology.* **1.** An individual within certain human races who lays eggs. **2.** Androviparous. **3.** A thick-skinned, unintelligent egg-laying human. *Informal.* **4.** A derogatory term for a foolish or lazy person who does nothing productive, as if nesting on artificial eggs without a thought.

echodor. noun. **1.** A smell that returns or echoes back into the nose of a person. *Informal.* **2.** Echosmish.

echollum. noun. The echo that follows an overwhelming silence.

eclaff. noun. **1.** An uncomfortable, lengthy pulsation that commonly blends into the preceding and the following pulsations. **2.** Esthagauck.

eclaption. noun. *Informal.* **1.** Forceful and repetitive collisions between two pubis. *Medicine.* **2.** Episioplexion. **3.** Plesipsia. **4.** Episiollide. **5.** Epitocussion **6.** Episiocussion.

eclectisity. noun. Harmonious, esthetically pleasing mix in the arts.

eclecturous. adjective. **1.** Despising everything eclectic. verb. **2.** To hate any work of art that is eclectic.

eclesity. noun. Uncertain quality of a conspicuous success.

eclitic. noun. The quality of being equally as arrogant as other arrogant people in a given group.

ecsphisy. noun. **1.** A grimace of disgust when imagining being forced to swish and swallow the semen of a giant quadruped. **2.** Estomaperphous.

ecsyde. verb. **1.** To warp reality with knowledge of the cause. **2.** To transcend a paradigm from a tridimensional paradox on purpose. noun. **3.** Existengnoll.

ectapt. verb. To perform, or appear to perform, adequately in deplorable conditions.

ectocrine. noun. *Physiology.* A gland or a component of a glandular system belonging to an organism that is located outside the body of said organism.

ectoflex. noun. **1.** A mirror that reflects what a person wishes rather than a true reflection. **2.** Minospecle. **3.** Dereflex. **4.** Ectoreflux.

ectofoggie. noun. Formation of fog on the exterior of a vehicle's windshield.

ectointroptiation. noun. Introspection from the outside, attempting to objectively visualize oneself as if through another person's eyes.

ectoplosmia. noun. Dramatic vomit of ectoplasm by a medium in communication with spirits having a hilarious sense of humor.

ectoptic. adjective. **1.** Having the ability to see outside while trapped within a non-transparent solid substance. **2.** Seeing through closed eyelids.

edictment. noun. A committee's decision to fire or eliminate a person from an organization once the person demonstrates having learned the way the organization actually works.

edurnitude. noun. *Education.* **1.** A system of education stressing strict discipline and total immersion. **2.** A system of education based on pressure and stern discipline.

eepie. noun. **1.** Mutually reciprocal and consenting sodomy. **2.** Equisodomy.

efemisculate. verb. **1.** To make a woman ineffective or weaker. **2.** To deprive a woman of her role or identity.

effagule. noun. **1.** The final facial expression of a person before dying. *Archaic.* **2.** Espermortis.

effaptous. noun. **1.** A man who displays his ponytail close to the crown of the head, imitating that of a woman. **2.** Equisetalic.

effedor. noun. **1.** A highly intelligent, sentient, non-carbon-based extraterrestrial being with a genome formed by six nucleotide pairs. **2.** Exdecarbiling.

efflugy. noun. **1.** Sudden and unexpected efflux of air from the vagina. **2.** Inaventorra. **3.** Soplagynon.

effulpurtion. noun. **1.** A trait of a company executive consisting of generating useless tasks to be performed by subordinates and colleagues. **2.** Realization that an executive career consists of assigning activities that are peripheral or wholly unrelated to productivity or the company's objectives. **3.** Executition.

effutrion. noun. *Ecology.* **1.** Rapid desiccation or drying of a large body of water or a sea by a natural or an artificial cause. **2.** Eschetalation.

egapist. noun. **1.** A likeable person who expresses truths about someone in varying tones of voice, from castigating to complimentary. **2.** Etymulguous.

egatude. noun. **1.** Ability to grasp concepts, synthesize them and relate them to one another. **2.** Eusynnitude.

egett. adjective. **1.** Provoking a sneeze. **2.** Sneezogenic. **3.** Sneezatory. **4.** Estornutatory. **5.** Estornugenous.

eggressive. noun. *Phonetics.* The blowing or puffing sound of a particular syllable in certain languages that requires expulsion of a significant quantity of air from the mouth to be pronounced correctly.

egolantric. noun. An egocentric person demanding to be idolatrized.

egolicit. verb. **1.** To demand, ask or supplicate with tireless insistence, to obtain something tangible or intangible for the pure pleasure of gain. **2.** To insist with obnoxious or cunning persistence in pursuing a sexual relationship. noun. **3.** Self-satisfaction through conquest.

egolidarity. noun. Circumstantial adhesion to the cause of others solely for selfish interests.

egonfort. noun. **1.** A person who pretends to be in disagreement or uncomfortable

simply to be the center of attention. **2.** Egodiscort.

egopathy. noun. **1.** A vehement desire to be greatly appreciated, admired or adored while neither expressing that desire to anyone nor doing anything to earn it. **2.** Tacipreinity.

egotomist. noun. A person or event that destroys the self-assurance and the self-image of an egocentric person.

egration. noun. **1.** General feeling of a population when realizing their governing leaders have betrayed them. **2.** Espaldism.

egregist. noun. A person who is drawn to other people not belonging to his or her own social status because he or she believes they have something new and entertaining to share.

egrettary. noun. A person who, on arriving at a place, announces that he or she has to depart immediately.

ejackler. noun. **1.** A person who does not respect the personal space limits of others, invading their reasonable, yet undefined, borders. **2.** A trespasser of comfortable proxemics. **3.** Elolimator. **4.** A person with a failing proximeter.*

ejiss. noun. **1.** The feeling of multiple electric currents surging through the entrails. **2.** Electromilgh.

ejol. noun. **1.** Domestic worker with the responsibility to sexually satisfy his or her master(s) under the guise of being a personal masseur. **2.** Embamasseur.

elephodon. noun. *Informal.* A person with overgrown and curved canine teeth resembling elephant tusks.

ellachinent. adjective. **1.** Discovering that one has the incorrect gender. **2.** Quality of having the wrong gonality.* noun. **3.** Equivogonality.

eluptia. noun. **1.** Worldwide, massive annihilation of targeted human beings. **2.** Rigorous selection of potential survivors during a global genocide. **3.** Etnoetmosis.

embeclism. noun. **1.** A set of inquisitorial and torture techniques, developed by Nicolau Eimerich (1320-1399), to exhaust a person physically and mentally, adopted by modern states against alleged terrorists. **2.** Eimerichism.

embestial. noun. An introverted, calm and decent person who suddenly turns loud, indecent, rough and aggressive without motive or provocation.

embettie. noun. *Psychology.* **1.** A feeling of both fear and excitement combined with a sense of doubt immediately before a fight, a battle or an annual employee review. **2.** Embattailed.

emblicous. noun. **1.** A person who boldly conceals his thoughts from everyone else. **2.** Enceferrous. adjective. **3.** Stubbornly and passively persevering in not revealing certain information.

emblue. noun. **1.** An extremely emotival reaction to an event. **2.** A remembrance that generates strong emotion. **3.** Emostriassion.

emboce. verb. **1.** To attack someone's feelings directly, particularly in their most vulnerable areas. **2.** Encompragn.

embreck. noun. *Psychology.* **1.** A person scoring low on an emotional coefficient test, generally a person who does not express emotions openly. **2.** An emotional cretin, commonly used to refer to a married man of medium to high intelligence who uses introversion to avoid interacting with reality. **3.** Emostagnous.*

embryosis. noun. *Medicine.* **1.** Prelude of a miscarriage. *Medicine.* **2.** Inflammation or degeneration of an embryo. *Embryology.* **3.** Ontosis.*

emetize. verb. **1.** To eject from the mouth, over someone, vast quantities of malodorous material proceeding from the stomach. **2.** To purposefully spread mucous and acrid material over someone. noun. *Informal.* **3.** Intentional barf. *Psychology.* **4.** Vomit nervosa.

emezzle. verb. **1.** To pretend or believe a person is illustrious and treat him or her accordingly. **2.** To wrongly believe a person is a celebrity of a figure of authority and be overly impressed. **3.** Eminentroll.

emiff. noun. **1.** The evaporation of time. *Physics.* **2.** Efluchronoxion.

emofluence. noun. **1.** Something or someone possessing an innate quality to soften the harshness of a man. **2.** Emoliandric.

emoniation. noun. *Psychology.* The power of a single thought to spontaneously generate an emotion.

emoppy. noun. *Informal.* **1.** Condition of decreasing height in older people due to feeble bones following degenerative conditions such as osteoporosis and osteoarthritis, among others. *Medicine.* **2.** Enchaporosis. *Informal.* **3.** Enmidget.

emostagny. noun. **1.** A complaint expressed by a woman frustrated by her husband not expressing his emotions. **2.** A persistent grumble from a woman married to an embreck* man.

empathectomize. verb. *Psychology.* **1.** To diminish or to systematically eliminate empathy in others. *Sociology.* **2.** To reduce the compassion and sensitivity of young people toward others by passive conditioning through excessive and repetitive violence in multimedia.

empathectomy. noun. **1.** A process to remove empathy from a person. **2.** A procedure to dehumanize a group of people or a population.

empathometer. noun. An intracranial device used for measuring and scoring sympathy and empathy toward living beings. The combined results are expressed in a numerical logarithmic scale with distinctive separation of groups in a pathic-ascending order: microscopic organisms, vegetable life, invertebrates, vertebrates, birds, mammals, marine mammals, primates, unknown humans, personal acquaintances, distant relatives, household pets, family members, personal pets, close friends and deepest loved ones.

empell. noun. **1.** A small, thin dart shot by electronic means. **2.** Electrazon. **3.** Darthflo.*

emperspectived. adjective. **1.** Becoming the center of attention of spectators at an event, especially for those spectators from further away. **2.** Becoming aware of being the focal point within a panorama.

emplethorize. verb. **1.** To introduce an excessive number of people, animals or things into a confined space that, at a certain point, becomes too small to contain them all. adjective. **2.** Cramming too many flowery words into a circumlocution.

emplot. noun. *Military.* **1.** A dysfunctional peculiarity of armies in general to concoct an order that could be misinterpreted and invariably is misinterpreted. **2.** Misconstruction of an order, which causes confusion in recipients. **3.** A mignius* receiving a command. **4.** Ejercindipy.

empomilled. noun. An object that presents the impression of voluntarily resting in or on a comfortable place.

emposh. noun. *Medicine.* **1.** A set of molecular and hormonal treatments combined with surgical procedures applied to mature adults or elderly people to provide them with the appearance of youth. **2.** Transformation of an adult or elderly man in an ephebe. *Philosophy.* **3.** Ephebination.

empratic. noun. *Politics.* **1.** A form of government in which each of its citizens is unknowingly a corporation, has virtual or symbolic rights and annually donates a portion of his estate and income to said government. *Economics.* **2.** Corporate fiefdom. *Philosophy.* **3.** Empheaucracy.

emprime. verb. To establish family relationships between people who have no blood ties.

emprion. noun. A sense of community with all human beings.

emprunetion. noun. An implosion of love between two persons that terminates the relationship without any apparent cause, but nonetheless engenders mutual blame.

emuphid. noun. **1.** An obstinate person incarcerated within his or her own thoughts in some deep intracranial cell network. **2.** Encepherred.

enacosed. noun. A person who is caught by complete surprise when accosted by someone who has fallen insanely in love with him or her.

enady. noun. **1.** The restaurant routine of settling diners, offering menus and taking drink orders from the worker-bees wearing ties and business suits crowded around tables to discuss topics that are considered important to their corresponding companies. **2.** Encorpoxy.

encareted. noun. **1.** A person who is wearing a mask. **2.** Someone who maintains an expression of disapproval or anger for a long time.

enchirl. verb. **1.** To grind one's teeth while sleeping uncomfortably or during a period of anguish, producing an irritating, deep scraping sound. **2.** To dontox.* noun. **3.** Stress-related bruxism.

endalgia. noun. Intense physical pain originating in the marrow of the bones and irradiating throughout the body.

endemocracy. noun. *Politics.* Authentic democracy born into the minds of the governed, which only seems to work in theory.

endolia. noun. **1.** Extreme feeling of betrayal and loneliness after experiencing treason or deception from someone previously trusted. **2.** Feeling of a rodaply.* **3.** A prelude to postfidence.*

endoperity. noun. Uncomfortable sensation following indoor climatic changes.

endosis. noun. *Medicine.* **1.** Contraction and collapse of a hollow organ. *Economics.* **2.** Collapse of a global financial Ponzi scheme.

endotheric. noun. *Telecommunications.* **1.** General, vague information manufactured and disseminated in a way that will be easily understood by the majority of the people. adjective. **2.** Providing information with little substance. **3.** Related to the making of small Dutch pancakes.

endratility. noun. Analogous qualities of two independent events that occur simultaneously.

enemmet. verb. **1.** To forcibly perform a punitive enema on someone. **2.** To carry out an enema viciously against a person's will. *Politics.* **3.** To make mandatory citizen participation in national election charades.

eneurosial. adjective. Drooling on a pillow in excess.

eneuvacuesis. noun. **1.** Involuntary defecation in bed. **2.** Puffery of fudder.* *Psychology.* **3.** Regression Syndrome.

enfer. verb. **1.** To confront something unknown with a positive and open attitude. **2.** Encumate.

enfeud. noun. **1.** Theatrical marital dispute that begins in bed. **2.** Eneurodrama.

enfocusy. verb. To focus upon and isolate a soliloquy within a crowd to hear and perceive the meaning of the words that a person speaks amongst all the additional noises heard.

engelity. noun. A peculiarity of an animal to cool the environment around itself by exhaling.

engglomation. noun. Amalgamation of pieces of information or ideas which become fused to the extent that they can no longer be recognized individually.

engoge. verb. **1.** To repeat the same word at the beginning, middle and end of a clause. adjective. **2.** Enleighing* people by repetition. noun. **3.** A method of mind control. **4.** Epanatriplosis.

enleddy. noun. Extreme attempts to project self-worth to become accepted within a community or a group by following subtle acceptance rules determined by peers of such social groups.

enledray. noun. **1.** Disconcerting mixture of simultaneous emotions. **2.** Guanilly.

enleigh. verb. **1.** To create cracks in the minds of people. **2.** Epeirogenate. noun. **3.** Development of severe cognitive dissonance.

enlergature. noun. *Informal.* Each one of the connections between the entrails and the body.

enlettuce. verb. To lift the dress of a woman while she is wearing it, and hold it tightly above her head to block her vision, to immobilize her and/or reduce her possibility of resistance.

enlill. noun. **1.** The addition of nonexistent words to clarify a meaning. **2.** Epeneoxegesis.

enllerg. verb. To open the creative mind.

enmidget. verb. *Informal.* **1.** The effect of time on musculoskeletal degeneration and height. **2.** Emoppy.*

enosphile. noun. **1.** A heavy drinker. **2.** Someone who is incapable of distinguishing the flavors or qualities among different types of wine.

enotic. noun. A clamorous thunder or boom that can cause disorientation, dizziness, auditory hallucinations and even loss of consciousness.

enoticate. verb. To purposefully provoke disorientation, dizziness, auditory hallucinations, or loss of consciousness with a shockingly loud noise.

enotrine. noun. **1.** Each one of the bodily points that seems to discharge electricity during excitement. **2.** Thrill pinpoint titillation.

ensausage. verb. To inlay people, animals or things so they become embedded or aplethorated* in a confined space.

enslipper. noun. **1.** A person wearing slippers who drags each step across the floor to prevent the slippers from falling off. **2.** Loogger.* **3.** Dysbeeper.* verb. **4.** To annoy someone by using a persistently slow tone of voice.

entenimism. noun. *Philosophy.* Philosophical theory which emphasizes that to reach a truth it must be assumed that everything is false.

enteroptosis. noun. *Medicine.* **1.** Intestinal disturbance following a distressing event. *Informal.* **2.** Cranky tummy. *Informal.* **3.** Punched or sour gut. **4.** Similar to puppy-love blues feeling in the tummy.

entetrime. verb. *Literary.* To profoundly move the essence of a sentient being in one of several directions, such as complete bliss, deepest angst or darkest night.

entilexy. noun. *Linguistics.* **1.** The true meaning of a word. **2.** Etymological and non-etymological meaning of a word.

entinaptosis. noun. Complete state of decline in body and soul.

entrefeet. noun. Space located between the feet.

entrella. noun. A hose or pantyhose for men.

entremediate. adjective. **1.** Occurring or done between the immediate and the mediate. **2.** Relatively near in time, relationship or rank.

entremortis. noun. Period between a past death and a future death.

entremundy. noun. *History.* A period of contestable peace between the Second and the Third World Wars.

entropilexism. noun. **1.** Incertitude and frustration when reading a text with abundant acronyms. **2.** Frustration caused by not being able to interpret the meaning of a text with technical terms or numerous abbreviations. *Literature.* **3.** Uncertainty when reading a text with abundant neologisms and exasperation in not being able to interpret the meaning.

enverit. verb. To make a person or persons see the truth.

epagh. verb. To rescue the economy of a group, organization or state at the proportionate expense of minions, subordinates, or citizens.

epementize. verb. **1.** To insert an idea or a memory in the mind of a person by artificial means. noun. **2.** Related to the wide technological applications, uses and consequences of the uses of epementism.

epeneothesis. noun. *Linguistics.* The insertion of letters in a word to create an obscure neologism with no apparent etymology.

epicosmogeny. noun. *Astronomy.* A theory advocating that all features of the cosmos are configured randomly during the cosmogony and not previously programmed at the beginning of time.

epicosmos. noun. *Astronomy.* Accessory phenomenon that accompanies the cosmos throughout its development without having any influence over it.

epilexic. noun. A person who looks up a word in a dictionary before meeting someone and then questions him or her on the meaning of that word.

Generally, after a negative response, said person defines the word to demonstrate erudition.

epinator. noun. A person who volubly voices his or her opinions to the most opinionated person in a gathering.

epistropher. noun. **1.** A person who suddenly and unintentionally changes someone else's life in a favorable manner. **2.** Eclampt.

epogomor. noun. **1.** The man who places himself on top of everyone else during an orgy. **2.** A domineering man in a gomorry.* **3.** Epigomorrider.

eponox. noun. The darkest of nights in each one of the poles.

equinemia. noun. A shared memory that was faithfully recorded and recalled between two or more people.

equinollent. adjective. Having no tide while day and night have exactly the same duration. Generally referring to a sea or a large body of water.

equirrogate. verb. To maintain the balance of arrogance in a group.

eral. verb. **1.** To produce or reproduce time particles and irradiate them. **2.** Efluchronotch.

ergonemia. noun. **1.** Differential in the energetic demands between a stored memory and an evoked memory. **2.** The energetic needs required for stockpiling various memories such as the associative memory, the dissociative memory, the traumatic memory, the photographic memory, the virtual memory, etc.

ericoteic. noun. A person who often becomes red-faced during foreplay and throughout copulation.

erocordia. noun. A sexual relationship between two people who have intense feelings of deep affection for one another.

erocubbio. noun. **1.** Enduring sexual liveliness in a couple. **2.** Erocordiated.* *Archaic.* **3.** Bicorpia carnalis.

eroghostic. adjective. *Psychology.* Being the target of constant sexual advances by a non-corporeal entity.

eroghostum. noun. **1.** Seduction, sexual advances or sexual intercourse believed to be carried out by a ghost or a spirit. **2.** Syncorpenty.*

erojection. noun. The feeling of being sexually rebuffed by a lover with no specific cause.

erollitude. noun. Possessing the quality of being sexually attractive.

erolucid. noun. A person with the ability to detect subtle or almost imperceptible signs of sexual arousal in others.

erommation. noun. **1.** Strong awakening of sexual emotion and desire. **2.** Irrepressible sexual arousal.

eromnesia. noun. **1.** Pleasurable remembrance of an infidelity without any sense of guilt. **2.** Iscariotic* memory of an extramarital affair.

eronescence. noun. Discreet and gradual increase of sexual desire in the absence of erotic stimuli.

erorgotist. noun. A person who makes exhausting efforts during copulation and frustrates the sexual partner.

eroscorsion. noun. Intense sexual desire in circumstances unfavorable for sexual interaction with anyone.

erosed. noun. **1.** Need and desire to experience sexual pleasure. **2.** Ardent appetite for venereal pleasure. **3.** Arousing sexual excitement. **4.** Uncontrollable sexual urge. *Informal.* **5.** Horniness.

erospection. noun. *Psychology.* **1.** Sexual relations of recognition between two or more young people of the same sex without feelings of physical attraction between them. **2.**

Mutual carnal exploration among non-homosexual young people of the same gender. **3.** Andrognery. **4.** Venerilence.*

erosphyxia. noun. **1.** Coitus without passion. **2.** Mild sexual arousal without increase of pulse rate. *Medicine.* **3.** Antaphrodisy.* *Medicine.* **4.** Leptolibido.

erospyrogy. noun. **1.** Matinal sexual desire. **2.** Frequent sexual arousal in the mornings. **3.** Matiprurigony. **4.** Matinflammitude. **5.** Matincalenda. **6.** Pyreosia.

erostally. noun. Sudden and unexpected sexual pleasure that triggers an intense and uncontrollable desire to continue and to increase the magnitude of said sexual pleasure.

erosthete. noun. A person who has or pretends to have a special appreciation for the seductiveness or sexuality of other people.

erotion. noun. **1.** Complete cessation of libido. **2.** Consequence of repeated crossimption,* antaphrodisy,* erosphyxia,* or sexidity.*

erostrepid. adjective. Having being infected by sexual desire.

erostropic. adjective. Having a strong attraction or tendency toward anything sexual.

erosynphally. noun. *Psychology.* Chronic sexual desire accompanied by nonspecific vivid illusions and penis erection or clitoris hardening.

erotersion. noun. Mental purification of abominable sexual urges.

erothrix. noun. *Commerce.* An instrument for producing varying levels of sexual pleasure, typically by applying electrodes to the neck.

erotrist. noun. A person who is sexually aroused by looking at or touching the hair of someone.

erovalence. noun. **1.** Qualitative value assigned to a person based on the number of simultaneous sexual relationships maintained. **2.** The combined eclectic coital power of a person.

erovoracy. adjective. **1.** Pursuing frequent and ephemeral sexual relations. **2.** Seeking sexual pleasure for diversion, entertainment or triumphal complacency. **3.** Having an insatiable appetite for coitus without erocordia.* noun. **4.** Gonajagger.

erovotion. noun. **1.** Persistent sexual enthusiasm and loyalty to someone. **2.** Persevering sexual compromise with a person.

errorization. noun. State in which a person believes he or she has solved a problem or resolved an error, but the error persists without the person's knowledge.

escalchism. noun. A machinery of state repression that has perfected, among others, conquest, imperialism, inquisition-like fear, tribute collection, false propaganda, subjects' surveillance and secret police in a brutal, yet subtle fusion of effective strategies for population control.

escatoph. noun. **1.** A person who has performed premeditated abominable acts against someone. **2.** Lecoby. **3.** Escolettuo.

eschemp. verb. **1.** To make a horizontal line with the lips simulating or hiding a smile. **2.** To smile without moving one's lips, like a Mona Lisa.

esclunate. verb. To curve the body in a fetal position, generally during sleep, when depressed or when being terrorized.

escolombra. noun. *Optics.* A shadow twisted by heat or light diffraction.

escrutine. noun. Opening and closing eyelids repeatedly and squeezing them tightly when closed.

esculation. noun. **1.** A group of words that come out of the mouth inaudibly. **2.**

Movement of mouth and lips that resembles the articulation of words. *Informal.* **3.** When the mouth emits a silent word salad of unheard ideas.

esculfation. noun. **1.** Expression of surprise and doubt a woman makes before the mirror prior to applying makeup. **2.** A pre-macastidity* period. **3.** The first of the three facial expressions a woman makes during a makeup routine, such as a grimace, a pout, or a moue followed by apprastide* or macastide* faces.

escurry. noun. Sardonic smile with an undertone of contentment a man tries to hide when a woman finishes moaning with pleasure during coitus.

escutack. noun. Protective metallic shield a precautionary vampire wears around the chest.

esfaciadum. noun. **1.** Expression of pain and anguish a man makes while ejaculating. **2.** A facial expression of mortification and discombobulation when experiencing pleasure.

esgarrio. noun. The loud weep a man emits when reaching an age of comprehending the reality in which he actually lives.

esmathism. noun. **1.** Sensation of incapacity, impairment and shock an intelligent person feels when reading for the first time a mathematical definition, such as "…is a polynomial equation where the highest degree is two," or "…is a relationship between a function sufficiently derivable, its variables and one or more successive derivatives of its functions." **2.** Hermechonny.

esnout. 1. A person who sniffs twice at any smell perceived. **2.** Echomisher. **3.** Echosniffer. **4.** Nasoriator.*

especret. verb. To await expectantly and with utmost curiosity the telling of a secret about someone known.

esquex. verb. To make efforts to protect one's honor on multiple social life fronts.

estercia. noun. The dexterity to operate a mechanical, magnetic or electric apparatus.

estimorce. verb. To remind someone of sad or upsetting events with the intention of pestering said person.

estinize. verb. **1.** To deceive oneself. **2.** To pretend to do what one is supposed to do when in solitude.

estomachic. noun. A quiet, calm and dependable person.

estomagtic. noun. A person with protruding jaw and mouth that resembles a snout.

estomhart. verb. To get distracted while someone is explaining something with interest, care and passion.

estongille. noun. **1.** Noise produced when blowing through protruding lips, making them flutter. **2.** Trompetille. *Informal.* **3.** Blowing raspberries.

estordinant. noun. A strong, rumbling, bass sound that produces internal vibrations in the body.

estornugen. noun. *Genetics.* The co-dominant gene that provokes exaggerated responses to estornugenous* stimuli in affected diploid offspring.

estracha. noun. A beautiful, congenial, intelligent and, in all senses, attractive woman who has a loud, revolting and deplorable laugh.

ESVIP. noun. **1.** Acronym for extra-super-very-important-person. **2.** A very, very important personality or celebrity. **3.** Abbreviation stamped on discount cards for supermarkets, convenience stores, stadiums and collective transportation.

etiodesy. noun. Set of particularities that differentiate human beings into fortunate and unfortunate, nobles and plebs, rich and poor, oppressors and subjugates, leaders and followers, employers and employees, etc.

etrimy. noun. Sense of complacency in not having something someone else has.

etry. noun. Change of location or residence prompted by success or studies.

etydler. noun. A person who contributes to the transformation of an etymy* into the final phase of truthful truth.

etygle. verb. To discreetly exaggerate a truth in order to lie with the appearance of being truthful. Example: "Yeah, right. I drove the car to the city, and really fast," was the response of a 12-year-old child to his father.

etymy. noun. **1.** The un-riddle of a deciduous truth that, following periods of absolutism and decadence, is transformed by full disclosure and knowledge into a truthful truth. **2.** The life cycle of a truth.

etythy. noun. Ultimate cause, set of causes, or manner of causation of a truth that cannot be rationally negated.

eubia. noun. **1.** Prerogative of human beings to live life with neither pressure nor demands. *Philosophy.* **2.** Cubiony.* **3.** A collection of citizens in a eucracy.*

eucracy. noun. *Politics.* A form just government without a profit agenda that practices peace and gets out of people's faces.

eujealy. noun. **1.** Benign envy. **2.** A certain degree of envy combined with admiration that prompts someone to emulate the person who is the source of such envy.

eumen. noun. **1.** A white lie not easily believed. **2.** A harmless or trivial lie told with good intentions or to prevent an unfavorable outcome.

eumenity. noun. **1.** A precautionary negative answer a man gives to a question from his spouse, when he anticipates potentially adverse consequences to a positive response. Examples: Did you see that gorgeous woman? Do I look bad in this dress? Do you think I am fat?

euminize. verb. To improve the performance of an artifact by making it smaller.

eumyth. verb. **1.** To believe that a fantasy, a myth, or a lie is true, forged by the hammer blows of repetition. noun. *Politics.* **2.** Facticity.*

eunecy. noun. **1.** Capability and strength of will to transform what appears to be inevitable or unchangeable. adjective. **2.**

Exhibiting the talent to alter destiny.

eunomid. noun. **1.** An ideal mode of governing. **2.** Exemplary leadership.

eupert. noun. Someone who considers potential future possibilities of everything perceived as a necessity.

eupht. noun. Unsolicited and unwelcome sound advice from an expert.

euthany. noun. **1.** A euthanasia programmed for the benefit of people other than the person being euthanized. *Law.* **2.** A law to deprive healthcare to selected groups of people. **3.** Thanatherapy.*

evacunym. noun. **1.** A person or a group of people who have become dehumanized via a doctrine in vogue with the intention to dispose of them as the doctrine representatives wish. **2.** A target of hecatonism.*

evacuous. adjective. **1.** Having no rights whatsoever. **2.** Being readily available for exploitation.

evaggio. noun. Someone so despicable and abhorrent that he seems to be an invagination of a four-legged vermin.

eventrate. verb. *History.* To cause the protrusion of organs through the abdominal wall or the rectum, generally during torture or execution.

exabrupt. noun. Sudden release of a strong emotion, generally a guttural outcry accompanied by an exaggerated gesture.

exabsciate. verb. To squeeze zits, pustules, blackheads, cysts, whiteheads, carbuncles, abscesses or furuncles in front of a mirror.

exacibia. noun. **1.** Expression of discomfort, nuisance, doubt, and revulsion some people make before the mirror while squeezing a pimple. **2.** Facial expression of an exabsciater.*

exagem. noun. *Geometry.* A polyhedron in which the internal faces are external and the external faces are internal.

exalienate. verb. **1.** To feel and believe one belongs to another country or motherland. **2.** To avoid communication totally or to circumvent direct contact completely with someone.

exaphrenic. adjective. *Psychology.* **1.** Acting furiously and out of control. **2.** Spreading indiscriminate violence. **3.** Turning into a delirious rabid beast.

exapusiasm. noun. An exclamation that expresses a mixture of surprise, enthusiasm, agitation and desperation.

excentism. noun. **1.** The appearance of complying with rules, standards, laws or socially accepted conventions while maintaining certain limitations and protecting one's rights. **2.** Euconformism.

excidiate. verb. **1.** To ruin someone slowly, persistently and totally. noun. **2.** Long-lasting depoilment.*

excognize. verb. To extract knowledge from someone by coercion or violence.

excuseyer. noun. **1.** Someone who asks to be excused when not hearing what was said. **2.** A person who says "excuse me" but does not mean to be excused. **3.** A person who says "excuse me" but means to request someone to pronounce something again. **4.** A person who asks to be excused but in reality is asking a rhetorical question after observing something or being the target of an imprudence. *Informal.* **5.** Mandestesser. **6.** Saygainer.

excusortion. noun. **1.** Mental processes through which excuses are formulated. **2.** Establishment specialized in the selection, assembly and sale of pretexts.

excussion. noun. Pre-programmed phrases that are verbalized as an excuse.

exdimen. noun. An interdimensional point, area, or place.

exdimensy. noun. The ability to depart from known dimensions.

execruant. noun. A corporate worker who acts as an executive and tries to manage employees in areas he or she does not understand.

exeginy. noun. *Psychology.* **1.** The personality disguise one uses through life that eventually becomes one's personality. *Literary.* **2.** The self-lie we project that becomes our truth.

exego. noun. **1.** The appearance of character and behavior a person projects to the outside world. *Philosophy.* **2.** Awareness that the only one who truly knows oneself is oneself.

exeturgh. noun. Someone who has survived a torture that would have ended the life of someone else.

exhilariant. noun. A person who perceives himself or herself as a witty comic, but is actually detestable to others.

exigan. noun. A woman who continuously complains of not having enough.

exinious. adjective. Maintaining composure and serenity during emergencies, adverse circumstances, tragedies and disasters.

existenosis. noun. **1.** The depressing perception of life by someone without options and with one unique, apparently predetermined, destiny. *Philosophy.* **2.** Awareness of unbecoming of what is or what exists into the non-semient.*

existrism. noun. *Psychology.* **1.** An altered perception of life. **2.** A sense of living between existential holes. *Literature.* **3.** A pilgrimage through the minefield of life. *Philosophy.* **4.** The absence of transition from existence to non-existence if the existence did not exist prior to its existence. **5.** The un-ontosis* paradox from non-semient to semient* to non-semient.

exmanition. noun. Vague instruction given to male adolescents who pernoctate in boarding schools or military barracks.

exoceptive. noun. A person who perceives what is not perceived by the five senses.

exochron. noun. A person who is out of place or out of time from where or when he or she originally was.

exochronicity. noun. **1.** Property of being outside a temporal constant. **2.** Ability to be outside time for an undefined period. **3.** Ectochronition.

exod. verb. **1.** To emigrate from a town, city or country. **2.** To furtively escape from an embarrassing situation. **3.** To slip away surreptitiously from a group of people.

exoglossia. noun. An adult with the infantile habit of sticking the tongue out.

exonema. noun. Memory stored and readily accessible outside the person who created it.

exonency. noun. Possibility that a thing or a living creature can remain without alteration, degeneration or damage outside its natural environment.

exopherome. noun. *Zoology.* A chemical substance or an intangible force produced and released into the environment by an animal, affecting the behavior or physiology of animals of other species, but not members of its own species.

exophile. adjective. **1.** Having affinity or favoring anything nonlocal. noun. **2.** A person who likes the looks and attributes of everyone else but himself or herself.

exoposs. noun. Being in the worst place and at the worst time.

exospectibility. noun. Capacity to see beyond the limits of the observable environment.

exospert. noun. **1.** A person with the talent to acquire experience through other people's experience. **2.** Someone who is capable of circumventing mistakes and succeeding thanks to the experience of others.

exosplosion. noun. *Astronomy.* Abrupt, swift, and inexplicable destruction of a celestial body.

experiate. verb. To perceive, to know or to feel something for the first time.

experifericity. noun. Rarity or extravagance in a person's character that surpasses his or her eccentricity.

experillition. noun. **1.** Continuous failure of an experiment despite multiple modifications of the variables. **2.** Frustrating feeling of incompetence when an experiment fails repeatedly. **3.** Incapacity to realize that a series of failed experiments failed by design and not through the purposeful wish of a higher being to deceive the experimenter.

exponder. noun. A person experienced and skilled in explaining complicated subjects with ease, eloquence and in detail.

extentic. adjective. Perceiving and feeling something happening away from a surrounding area.

extinnitus. noun. Thunderous, explosive noise that is so painful to the ear that, when repeated, it leads to madness or suicide.

extraoneiric. adjective. Happening outside dreams.

extravertient. adjective. **1.** Divulging something openly that may be socially unacceptable. noun. **2.** A person with the courage to acknowledge something that is not entirely accepted by the majority.

exureniac. noun. A person who, due to distraction, carelessness, inability, or compulsion, splashes urine outside the urinal or the toilet during micturition.

exwoven. noun. Finely threaded, transparent fabric used for female clothing that provides elegance and a certain warmth.

F

faceburse. noun. **1.** Expression of incredulity in a woman when pulling all items from her purse and not finding what she was looking for. **2.** Transduchial.

facident. adjective. Having a face with protuberances in the shape of teeth.

faciolipy. noun. **1.** Obsession with applying vast quantities of greasy substances to the face. *Informal.* **2.** Caramirah. noun. **3.** Multilayered, oily coating some older women smear on their faces and call makeup.

facsimilitile. noun. **1.** A man who is identical to his great-great-grandfather. **2.** A man who is the spitting image of his quatrigramps.*

factality. noun. Probability that a circumstance or an event will not happen.

facticity. noun. *Politics.* **1.** An effect of government propaganda, which after some time is erroneously considered truth by virtue of repetition. *Theology.* **2.** Effect of a doctrine on the faith or belief of its followers, accomplished by sheer repetition. **3.** Eumyth.*

fadition. noun. Gradual disappearance of something that is ignored.

faithycide. noun. Destruction of one's faith by logical, rational thinking that eventually leads to a feeling of well-being produced by accepting reality and assuming responsibility for oneself.

fallicity. noun. Trait of a person who fails in every project or venture undertaken.

falsechy. noun. **1.** Improbable goal a scientist sets provisionally and subsequently pretends to reject. **2.** Null hypothesis.

falsesteny. noun. *Psychology.* Depressing emotion of inadequacy when comparing oneself with other people who excel in a given field.

falsious. adjective. Believing that pursuing a path to being published is a path to discovery.

famalsity. noun. Sensation of emptiness many experience

after a life in search of fame and fortune as their only objectives.

faneggy. noun. Imprecision in measurement that varies according to the location where the measurement took place, who performed it, the tools used to measure and the precise points selected to define the measurement, among other variables.

fardel. noun. Non-anthological random collection of literary works published in one volume.

fardoh. noun. Obstinate, presumptuous divulgence of misconstrued information.

fatinamia. noun. Weariness of a soul in a decrepit body.

fatullation. noun. Illogical conclusion reached by a professional who guessed wrongly after jumping reasoning steps, making false, overconfident assumptions that marked the decline of his reputation.

faunaracy. noun. Clandestine abuse and violent treatment of animals.

fausitate. verb. To forcibly extract the truth from a person or persons by any means disregarding the consequences.

fautech. noun. **1.** Adverse effect of technological advances that, while simultaneously augmenting rate and speed

of telecommunications, also increase inactivity, asthenia and solitude in the youth. **2.** Fenacotechny.

fauxia. noun. **1.** Painted image in a place perceived as discordant to the intrinsic nature of the place. **2.** Incongruous *trompe l'oeil.*

fecatta. verb. To suffocate and even cause fainting in someone by defecating or emitting gases from the anus.

fecoffin. noun. Large safe deposit box, resembling a coffin, that banks reserve for special clients such as dictators, drug cartel leaders and bank executives.

feenisturny. adjective. Emitting no sound whatsoever when sneezing.

felizza. noun. A moment in life when one desists from the pursuit of happiness and appreciates life itself or the surrounding beauty.

femil. noun. **1.** Brilliant femininity in a person. **2.** Feminthioness.

fenacruelty. noun. *Sociology.* Pervasive use of extreme violence and cruelty in movies and multimedia. It generally involves digitally dramatized hyperviolence in humans and animals displaying hyperbolic bleeding, anatomical impossibilities and lavish torture.

fenession. noun. **1.** Putting an end to a passion voluntarily and without cause. **2.** Passiotolend.

fenester. noun. An aperture in a wall or roof to admit light or air that is placed inconveniently to see out of or for light or air to pass through it.

fenoneuron. noun. A type of neuron, a brain cell, with cocoa bean-like corpuscles where certain kinds of memories are stored.

feremobile. noun. Motorized coffin.

ferengill. noun. (from *firangi*, foreigner in Urdu and this from Persian) **1.** A disconcerting feeling when returning home after a long absence and perceiving everything as alien, exotic, distant and unfamiliar. noun. **2.** Sensation that everything surrounding oneself is foreign.

ferolite. noun. *Geology.* Each one of the pebbles and sand granules that comprise a minute landslide.

festeration. noun. *Medicine.* A wound or a sore that has become inflamed, suppurated and with fistula.

festition. noun. *Sociology.* **1.** A recreational activity that becomes routine by virtue of

frequency or prolongation. **2.** Phenomenon in which partying and recreational or pleasurable activities and diversions become boring when done in excess.

fiascologist. noun. **1.** A person specialized in failures. **2.** An underachiever for whom each fiasco is a success.

fibiony. noun. **1.** Degree of reliability on an electromechanical device determined by the number of specialized technicians required to maintain its operability. **2.** Quantifiable confidence in machinery, which is inversely proportional to the number and importance of people capable of repairing it.

fibioscent. adjective. Feeling frustrated and cheated by dependence on an electromechanical device that fails often and the specialized technicians who can fix it are unavailable.

fibriculation. noun. *Biology.* Spontaneous and rapid contractions of tissues or complete organisms.

fibulate. verb. To mentally link one's ideas with ideas of others, summarize them in writing and disseminate them with or without consent to demonstrate a prevailing ideological discrimination in a society.

fickery. noun. Assortment of health damages caused to a person by homeopathy or naturist therapies.

filachery. noun. A place where non-lascivious caresses and affectionate touches are purchased for variable periods.

filantness. noun. *Physics.* **1.** Property of viscous, mucilaginous, or mucous fluids that when poured or separated exhibit variable degrees of fluidity and form a thread which becomes thinner at perceptible stages before breaking. **2.** Stoichiofluidity.

filariant. noun. An exasperatingly boring speech.

filastine. noun. Extremely thin intestine of some invertebrate species.

finansepsis. noun. *Law.* Collection of sophisticated strategies used by financial organizations to defraud the majority of their clients.

finistretta. noun. **1.** A very small window. *Informal.* **2.** A dirty window with a worn wooden frame that cannot be opened.

fiscognatism. noun. Persistent and almost fanatical preoccupation with fiscal interests.

fisimity. noun. **1.** Principles or bases of friendship. **2.** Collection of intangible features which form an inexplicable link that joins two strangers in friendship.

fistugnasis. noun. *Medicine.* Cleft lip in the inferior portion of the mouth and jaw.

fistulation. noun. *Medicine.* Formation of an abnormal and narrow duct that opens to the skin or cavities and drains pus.

fixillity. noun. Intense focus on something, that leads to the perception and registration of minute details.

flabbus. adjective. Having large love handles and fleshy and fatty excess tissue in several parts of the body with wobbly consistency. Generally refers to a man.

flaggon. adjective. Exhibiting abusive treatment toward others in both verbal and physical senses.

flamalcolly. noun. **1.** Empathy not accompanied by internal pain or by sensation of pressure in the chest. **2.** Slight sympenassion* of tallophry.*

flamorous. noun. An affected, extravagant and ostentatiously dressed man who projects the opposite image of what he intends to project.

flanitic. adjective. Resembling, whether in movement or motionless, the texture and consistency of a partly congealed flan. Generally applied to a person.

flapellated. adjective. *Informal.* Having ears too big for head and body, with the shape, texture and movement that remind others of an African pachyderm.

flatta. noun. A woman with no breasts or with very small breasts.

flauttous. adjective. **1.** Possessing a tall, thin body and having a voice like the sound of a flute or an oboe. **2.** Fluttous.* **3.** Related to a person with a voice that resembles the sound of a wind instrument.

fleetzcaca. noun. (from German *Flitz*, arrow). **1.** Pointless attempt to reach a toilet when suffering from explosive diarrhea. *Informal.* **2.** Carrecarre.* **3.** Pyroclastic eruptive diarrhea.

flocuness. noun. Passive indifference toward existence, consisting mainly in living without perceiving or memorizing the relevant passages of life.

flophie. adjective. Having soft and spongy flesh that tends to hang, generally in overweight and obese men.

flovic. noun. A surface that has lost its tension when it should be tense and stretched.

fluctuneurosis. noun. *Medicine.* **1.** Relatively mild mental disorder without organic basis. The main symptom is loss of contact with reality alternated with depression, anxiety, obsession and hypochondria. *Psychology.* **2.** Drastic and exaggerated change in a disturbed personality that nevertheless does not reach psychosis. **3.** Teenagehood.

fluidipard. noun. *Informal.* **1.** A fluid chatterbox. **2.** A person who talks at length, without respite, with apparent fluency by repeating multiple synonyms. *Literary.* **3.** Inevident tautology.

fluminescence. noun. *Physics.* **1.** The emission of light by fire. **2.** An emission of light that varies consistently in color and intensity.

fluttous. adjective. Possessing an elongated, thin body that widens at the abdominal level, resembling a type of flute.

focant. adjective. Walking and barking like a walrus or a large pinniped.

folude. noun. Pungent and disagreeable smell coming from the genital area of a filthy person.

fondimeter. noun. **1.** Quantitative scale of fondness based on the empathymeter.* **2.** Tenderometer. **3.** Cariniometer.

forageniturous. adjective. Of alien parents, born in a foreign land, educated overseas, and living elsewhere.

foralsket. noun. (from *forelsket* in Norwegian). **1.** The euphoric feeling at the beginning of falling in love. **2.** An overpowering emotion of euphoria, possession and not wanting to be apart from a person with whom one just fell in love.

forandigeneity. noun. Quality of being native from overseas and raised with local children considered aliens as they were offspring of foreign parents.

foreignity. noun. **1.** Abrupt realization of being oneself when looking at one's own reflection and seeing someone else. **2.** Development of a sudden self-consciousness when realizing one is in a foreign land, in a different time and in another body.

forensist. noun. **1.** A technician specialized in performing autopsies. **2.** Autopsier. **3.** Necropsist.

forgeducate. verb. To beat or hammer ideas, repeated *ad nauseam,* accompanied by threats of temporal or eternal punishment, with the objective of molding a youth's belief and blind faith in a doctrine.

forgephene. noun. Flame of love that sparkles in oblivion.

forher. pronoun. Third person singular preceded by the preposition *for.*

forme. pronoun. First person singular preceded by the preposition *for.*

fornicatude. noun. Physical and mental fortitude to fornicate fortuitously.

fornicoling. adjective. *Informal.* Maintaining an immobile posture during coitus.

forumbulon. noun. *Medicine.* **1.** Coccygeal abscess that generally drains through the lumbar region. **2.** Abscess in the coccyx. *Informal.* **3.** A person who looks like a boil, a swelling, or a pussy bubo. **4.** A despicable prodon.

foryou. pronoun. Second person singular preceded by the preposition *for.*

fracosmia. noun. Particularity of an aroma or fragrance in maintaining the same intensity of smell despite dissipation or time elapsed from its initial release.

fractality. noun. Quality of something, made of finite or infinite elements, with an unchangeable aspect and distribution in any scale observed.

fractidea. noun. **1.** A big or small idea that is similar in concept to another small or big idea. **2.** A fractal thought.

frappel. noun. A person with an idiosyncratic, fastidious communicating manner.

frasall. verb. *Informal.* To rub words in someone's face for something said or done.

frassol. noun. A conflict caused by the combination of temperaments, desires, or opinions between two people.

fredonesis. noun. *Psychology.* **1.** Sexual arousal of a Peeping Tom in solitude. **2.** The fantasy of a *voyeur* when sexually engaged with someone else.

frembollance. adjective. Becoming part of the scenery or getting lost in movement, especially when walking in a crowd of people.

frepinnation. noun. Perception of freshness in an old memory of a landscape.

fresta. noun. *Meteorology.* Fog, or a distinguishable wave of humidity proceeding from the sea.

frettate. verb. **1.** To bother someone insistently. **2.** To stab repeatedly or rub someone with a blunt object.

frigio. noun. *Physics.* The SI unit of cryogenic energy. One frigio is the frigorific energy necessary to decrease by one degree Celsius the temperature of a gram of a cube of aluminum from 4.5°C to 3.5°C, at sea level.

frigistasis. noun. **1.** Momentary mental and physical incapacity during an emergency **2.** Loss of volition during a crisis. **3.** Frigistission. *Vulgar.* **4.** Shitless shock.

fritteration. noun. Erroneous impression of productivity or effectiveness when a task is performed under stress.

frondinella. noun. *Anatomy.* Space between upper lip and the nose with imprecise lateral limits.

froserb. verb. To worsen the conditions of the underprivileged.

frugerous. adjective. Displaying temperance during sporadic sexual relations, generally when influenced or under duress.

fudder. noun. Something of little or no value.

fugacent. adjective. Being able to disappear rapidly at the slightest provocation or stimulus.

fugastrous. noun. **1.** A person who involuntarily lives the three-dimensional present in fleeting astral trips. noun.

Informal. **2.** Extra-rapid trip by an astralite.*

fulmidrome. noun. Stadium where atrocious spectacles are shown for a public craving bloodshed and anatomical shattering.

fulmidrotic. noun. **1.** Transitory heterosexual lesbian. *Informal.* **2.** A homosexual woman who occasionally likes to pedal a man. **3.** Epactagonees. **4.** Ephemandrosic.

fumalation. noun. *Physics.* **1.** Etherectic resistance that interferes with the passage of photons, generally with undefined limits and exhibiting antiaerogenous differentials. *Physics.* **2.** Olopid conagration resulting from the onusthic and visible mix of corporeus gases. **3.** Abiotic vapor, granulated smoke, or particulated smog. These terms remain under onomasiological dispute.

funderk. noun. A person who is easily convinced and, without thinking, acquires faith in something highly improbable.

fundirrhea. noun. Illogical verbal entanglement of a preacher.

fundotist. noun. A person who attempts to reach the bottom of a subject in every conversation and annoys everyone else.

funegrate. verb. To make someone feel a deep sense of ill-fated finality.

furait. noun. A pleasure of a ticklish nature.

furelong. noun. Permission given to oneself to do something different from the daily obligations.

furphula. noun. *Informal.* A woman who heats her husband and molds him with the aid of hammer blows.

furtipediate. verb. *Psychology.* To strip away creativity or independent thought from a child by demanding blind obedience or faith.

fuscoll. verb. To blacken the mood of a person.

futilism. noun. *Philosophy.* **1.** Theory that invalidates any doctrine based on faith or eternal life, maintaining that death is death and hence, the end of life. **2.** Philosophical theory derived from nadism.*

futiloscope. noun. An instrument for detecting the inutility of a doctrine.

futulith. noun. *Psychology.* Depressive state after imagining oneself as a fossil in the distant future.

futupenia. noun. Event or circumstance that diminishes the probability of a future.

futupossession. noun. Quality of being controlled by an entity from the future.

futupresent. verb. To extrapolate the past into a predictable future based on present facts.

futupretill. verb. To envision the present as a past from the perspective of the future.

futupretize. verb. To imagine different conditional presents, each one with several future alternatives.

futurophobia. noun. *Psychology.* **1.** Aversion to the future. **2.** Sensation a person endures following a futupenia* or a futurpetry.*

futurephile. noun. **1.** A person attracted to the future and by the future. **2.** Condition of the phagiardized* or the healthy well-off.

fuwrain. noun. A person who converts to a religious doctrine that professes to believe in someone or something nonexistent.

G

gackness. noun. **1.** A feeling of guilt a person experiences when buying an object to replace a similar object broken or damaged by said person. **2.** Galsodynemia.

gaialism. noun. Theory proposing to globally unify all non-political and non-economic systems.

gallot. noun. **1.** A person who engulfs, ruins, destroys, eats, and swallows someone else's marriage for personal satisfaction. **2.** Gamophague.

gamarra. noun. **1.** A woman devastated physically and mentally after unremitting rape by several men. **2.** Gafould. **3.** Gahack.

gamiseptic. noun. A spouse who seriously affects a marriage after performing infidelity, treachery against her spouse, or other contemptible behavior.

gamiviacity. noun. Quality of long hair that bounces up and down rhythmically at the pace of a person walking energetically.

gamodrue. noun. The perceived instigator of a dissolved marriage.

gamofrag. noun. **1.** An irreconcilable marital difference. *Law.* **2.** Irrefutable argument that justifies a divorce.

gamophoric. adjective. Feeling the burden of carrying a marriage on one's shoulders.

gamotomy. noun. The sudden destruction of a marriage.

gamture. verb. **1.** To drastically put an end to a marriage. **2.** To ganembollate.

ganser. noun. A person who always has goosebumps.

garda. noun. First signs of a fashion before it is in vogue.

gardacle. noun. A person who fervently maintains his or her anal virginity.

garfism. noun. Any theory based on a weak, unproven concept.

gargepectation. noun. An expectoration in nonsmokers, in the absence of a respiratory ailment, that is caused by the habit of tickling one's own throat.

garhatrass. noun. Foodstuff of which the flavor is ruined when cooked by grilling.

gasolidify. verb. To convert a gas into a solid.

gastacanon. noun. *Psychology.* An avaricious person who squanders money on his or her own obsessions.

gasuleum. noun. *Chemistry.* A mausoleum of noble gases.

gauderism. noun. *Philosophy.* A philosophical theory derived from Epicureanism that advocates unrestrained pleasure and limitless enjoyment of the human existence.

gawloity. noun. *Psychology.* **1.** A feeling of repulsion, disgust, fascination, aversion, curiosity, when observing someone with abundant body hair. *Informal.* **2.** A feeling of revulsion or laughter triggered when seeing the upper body of a hairy man. **3.** Kwendy.

gazzle. noun. **1.** The admiration a husband has for his wife. **2.** Gamgynosophy.

gebranne. verb. To wait exasperatedly for a person who always arrives late to an appointment.

gelalgia. noun. Burning sensation, almost painful,

when the skin is very cold and touched gently by a warm hand.

geldghast. noun. **1.** Incorrectly executed castration. **2.** Neutedire. **3.** Desexion. *Medicine.* **4.** Irregular keloid scar in the castrated.

gelidious. adjective. Having an intense and paralyzing sensation of solitude in extreme cold weather.

gelidistasis. noun. A deep feeling of loneliness and cold bewilderment when surrounded by frozen particles suspended in a solidified air at an extremely low temperature while hearing, in the constrictive silence, the creaking sound of stiff nose hairs going up and down awkwardly with each breath.

gelidon. noun. **1.** Sudden and momentary pain around the forehead region when ingesting something cold. *Medicine.* **2.** Transitory postgelidic cephalea. *Informal.* **3.** Ice cream headache.

gelinaut. noun. **1.** A person who travels from one area of bitter cold to another when the season changes. **2.** Wintrinaut.

gelisather. noun. *Meteorology.* Unheard-of freezing cold that rarely occurs in a torrid area.

gelitrix. noun. adjective. A woman who practices or masters the art of diminishing the libido of a man.

gelosoid. adjective. Having skin with the gelatinous texture and undulating quality of a jelly.

gemeridy. noun. A collection of wailings, sobs, cries, moans and whimpers emitted by someone.

gemipater. noun. A man considered the progenitor or the father of an embryo created by genetic manipulation.

gemispiry. noun. Inhaling or sighing moan an aroused woman emits at the moment of the first vaginal penetration.

gendricism. noun. *Philosophy.* Philosophical theory derived from anthrovolution* that justifies and promotes the artificial conception of individuals and creation of new species since they are integral consequences of human evolution and, therefore, part of the natural evolution of the planet.

genimation. noun. *Medicine.* Extrauterine development of an embryo into a fetus.

genoid. noun. *Biology.* A gene that is the focus of the first mutation in an individual, which, in turn, is the first step in the changes in an evolutionary attribute of a species.

genubrid. noun. A cloned and hybridized being from whom the identity of its progenitors is undisclosed.

genucoxil. noun. **1.** A coital leg-hug someone being sexually penetrated does around the hip of the penetrator by anchoring his or her legs by the ankles on the back of the penetrator. **2.** Docogenucy. **3.** Desmogenuchia. **4.** Docotraction.* **5.** Pullasion.*

genuflexion. noun. Lowering of one's body by bending one knee to the ground for reasons other than respect or worship.

genula. noun. *Biology.* **1.** A human being at the pre-embryonic stage of development. *Theology.* **2.** Conglomerate of human cells that cannot be regarded, constitutively, as a human being. *Embryology.* **3.** The embryological period that occurs after the blastula and gastrula stages but prior to the neurula and organogenesis stages. *Philosophy.* **4.** A potential human being not yet human.

genustroll. adjective. **1.** Walking while the knees are bent. noun. **2.** A walk of someone handicapped. **3.** A silly walk. **4.** An exaggerated ambulatory manner of a person mocking someone else.

geocide. noun. *Ecology.* **1.** Disequilibrium and damage to the biosphere caused by one species. **2.** Chronic and irreparable georrhagia.*

geophobia. noun. Uncomfortable sensation of someone who feels he does not belong to planet Earth.

georrhagia. noun. *Ecology.* Erosion and destruction of various regions of Earth, by only one species, that seriously affect the integrity of the biosphere.

gerialgia. noun. A combination of multiple aches and pains that occur in old age.

germophobia. noun. **1.** A strong aversion to microscopic organisms. **2.** Extreme and irrational fear of germs.

gerundel. adjective. **1.** Using gerunds repeatedly and unnecessarily in written or verbal communication. noun. **2.** A region where people use gerunds commonly when speaking.

gigateer. noun. *Law.* A swindler specialized in fraudulent activities exceeding nine digits in any currency.

glamossa. noun. adjective. A woman who exhibits an exotic sexual enchantment that is a delight to some and repugnant to others.

glaswen. noun. (from *glas wen* in Welsh meaning blue smile). **1.** An insincere smile. **2.** Reflective, mocking or sarcastic smile expressing disapproval or disregard.

gleamine. noun. An extraordinarily beautiful woman who seems to shine with magical intensity.

gleamsity. noun. A quality of the skin of some young women that shines brightly, especially when reflecting light.

gliastrous. noun. A person who persists in accompanying another person somewhere when he or she has not been invited and his or her presence is not desired.

glitticity. noun. **1.** Property of something or someone who reflects light brightly and with varying degrees of twinkling. **2.** Scintimany.

gloema. noun. *Medicine.* Sticky growth of skin in the shape of a bladder.

gloriollum. noun. *Literary.* Psychological pedestal climbed by a vain man to receive praise.

glossad. noun. Any communication between people of different cultures via a common language, dialect, slang, patois, native tongue, lingua franca, *coiné* or foreign tongue.

glossader. noun. A person who exaggerates the pronunciation of words with long over-enunciated syllables.

glossochronology. noun. *Linguistics*. Study of various languages over time to statistically calculate the divergence among them and estimate a common root or origin.

glucophagous. adjective. Consuming great quantities of sugar daily.

glucryma. noun. **1.** A tear that is low in sodium and sweet in flavor shed by a woman spontaneously when she is the target of attention, receives an unexpected romantic gift, or is the object of an act of kindness. **2.** Sugweep. **3.** Sweetcry.

glutaminate. verb. To use a flavor enhancing substance in foods.

gluthark. noun. A compound that is used to enhance perception through sight, smell, taste, hearing and touch and does not interfere with mental processes.

gnowphobia. noun. **1.** Reluctance to admit something that is known with certainty to be true. *Psychology*. **2.** Defensive mechanism to inhibit recognition of what the ego or the id knows, feels or desires at the superego level.

gnoxtract. verb. **1.** To squeeze and extract knowledge or information from someone using monetary or sentimental coercion. **2.** To mindmilk. noun. **3.** Mind milking.

godsonship. noun. **1.** A sudden feeling of kinship for a person of certain authority or a celebrity with an intense, instantaneous impression of bond and mutual loyalty as if one was his or her godchild. **2.** Stepsonship.

gogation. noun. Tendency of transportation vehicles to agglomerate in certain points of a city.

gomorrisade. noun. *History*. An act of gomorry* that included acrobatic postures referred to as: The portal of Ur, the Phoenician Sail, the Sumerian Arch, the Mycenaean Square, the Ephesian's Hexagon, the Pharaoh's Pyramid or the Heptagon of Aristophanes, among others.

gomorrite. noun. **1.** A native or inhabitant of Gomorrah. adjective. **2.** Pertaining or relating to Gomorrah, its inhabitant or its ancient customs. noun. **3.** A man who engages in gomorry.*

gomorry. noun. *History*. **1.** Ancient sexual practice in Gomorrah considered abominable and eliminated from the Septuagint by divine order. Later on the term was erased from all books and dictionaries. **2.** Sexual orgy consisting of simultaneous penetrations through various orifices between several men.

gonadescence. noun. The condition of being regarded as having constitutively intrinsic and central maleness or femaleness based on the aspect of the gonads.

gonadometer. noun. Instrument of high precision used to measure the length of the male sex organ. It is generally used by a woman to prove and expose the false vanity of a man.

gonality. noun. **1.** A condition that defines being male or female based on direct observation of the external anatomy of the gonads. **2.** Quality that biologically and grammatically distinguishes maleness from femaleness and avoids the overlapping and multiple cultural and social connotations of the terms "sex" and "gender."

gonalized. adjective. Having one gonality.*

gonamb. noun. A sporadic healthy and hygienic act of infidelity a couple mutually agrees upon to boost happiness in a marriage.

gonocola. noun. A semen-flavored soft drink that is swallowed for instructional or rehearsal purposes.

gorfule. noun. **1.** A solid substance mixed with another solid substance below their corresponding melting points with the effect that the product resembles a gross smear of both. **2.** Matrimony.

gorhouos. noun. A lazy, demanding man who shouts orders indiscriminately as a strategy to get food and shelter from others.

gothiciality. noun. Quality of a decorative object or piece of art that grotesquely imitates gothic style.

gothility. noun. *Psychology.* **1.** Quality of several borderline personality disorders mixed with homosexuality and depression expressed in gothic style. **2.** Mode of dress that displays a person's incapacity to deal with his or her gayness, blotta,* and ignorance. **3.** Showy dressing style of a personality disorder.

gourmon. noun. **1.** Someone who is addicted to gourmet food and ingests it without savoring. **2.** A person who eats delicious dishes but cannot discriminate or value the flavors. **3.** Pseudogastronomist.

grammalexiology. noun. *Grammar.* The structure and system of the logical or arbitrary norms of a language that strives to unify what is temporally considered as the correct use of words, spelling, and grammar.

gramouck. noun. *Literature.* **1.** A heterodox writer who purposefully bends and contravenes grammatical rules with artistic, logical or scientific aims. **2.** Grammawouck.

graphocy. verb. *Psychology.* To write in a vacillating and difficult manner without any cohesion of ideas and with translocation of letters, and syllables.

grapholysis. noun. Detailed study of letters in a manuscript with such minutiae that dilutes comprehension in all its particulars, including patterns, context, perspective, and original information.

graphovore. noun. A person who visually devours texts, manuscripts and books and recalls typesets, spaces between words, paragraph distributions and all aspects of style and appearance of the printed matter but does not remember any of the information written in them.

gravipunity. noun. **1.** An intrinsic perversion of fate or of nature in general. **2.** Frustration of a person facing a seemingly selective gravity when something valuable falls from his or her hands and breaks another object of higher value.

gravitambule. noun. A person's perception of what happens due to a unification of time and space in which three-dimensional beings dwell.

greenosism. noun. *Economics.* Theory that invalidated the theory of the "Greenhouse Effect" and proved it to be a fabrication of purported man-made geothermal impact with the objective of imposing global taxes according to an estimate or an *a priori* quantification of a country's carbon monoxide emissions.

greyhole. noun. *Astronomy.* A hypothetical celestial object that does not contract or expand in a time-space singularity (different from the three-dimensional understanding of space-time) and recycles its time and energy.

greysity. noun. **1.** Quality of being dull, dirty, dusty or contaminated. **2.** Exhibiting several tones of colors between white and black. **3.** Degree of being dull and nondescript.

guacapia. noun. **1.** Fresh regurgitation of a bee immediately following ingestion of flower nectar that is highly valued by some people who believe it to contain curative attributes. **2.** Premiel. **3.** Prohonie.

guepidity. noun. Productive or creative potential someone wastes due to the voluntary recycling of throwaway ideas.

guiguila. noun. **1.** A series of constant, silly and light laughs emitted affectedly and uncontrollably in a nervous manner. **2.** Annoying, unstoppable giggles. **3.** Risignat.* **4.** Risiggle.* **5.** Risarit.*

guipsoid. noun. **1.** A person who, before saying something, declares that it will be brief, extends the recitation and when finished recites it again. **2.** Halcanous.

gumusev. (from *gumusservi* in Turkish). **1.** The reflection of the moon on water. **2.** The reflection of a celestial body on water. **3.** Lunar aranid.*

gyke. noun. **1.** A woman who exhibits aversion and disgust against anything feminine. **2.** Gynomisogyan.

gymelia. noun. **1.** A habit of eating while naked. **2.** Edisnude. **3.** Gymnophagia.

gymnisy. noun. **1.** To mentally undress one's own memories. **2.** To privately engage with oneself

about past events with blunt honesty. **3.** Gymnasimnesia.

gynadox. noun. A woman who changes her mind at a critical point in a marriage.

gynaphoric. noun. A male soul living in a female body.

gynelalia. noun. **1.** A peculiarity of a woman who says something to her lover, but wishes to convey something completely different. *Phonetics.* **2.** Dysmenparlia.* **3.** Dysgregally.

gynelid. noun. *Mythology.* **1.** Mythological woman with a semi-cylindrical body wearing spiraled rings in her limbs who feeds on the blood of men. **2.** Androhemaphag. *Vulgar.* **3.** Bloodsucker bitch.

gynephilia. noun. Honest admiration of female qualities. Usually applied to men.

gynesthenia. noun. The underestimated and unexplored strength of a female at the brink of womanhood.

gynesthy. noun. **1.** Female bravery. **2.** Gynezza. **3.** Ovulsy.*

gynesy. noun. A peculiar trait or *je ne sais quoi* of an intelligent woman who is not beautiful but carries herself gracefully and is considered attractive.

gyneticnia. noun. Reverberation or trace of femininity in someone who is not a female.

gynling. noun. **1.** An entity who feels natural or at ease in a female body. **2.** Ontogynic.

gynocky. noun. **1.** Genetically determined thickening of the body, particularly ankles, gluteus, hips and neck that occurs after reproductive age in women of certain Mediterranean nations. **2.** Gynchuk. **3.** Gynembarce.

gynolark. noun. A woman who gets upset with her lover for interpreting verbatim what she has said instead of what she actually meant to convey.

gynophimosis. noun. *Medicine.* Congenital condition characterized by a complete occlusion of the vulva, which is accompanied by recurrent vaginal inflammation and infection.

gynoscrott. noun. Unrestricted growth of the vulva that resembles a scrotum.

gynosophy. noun. Wisdom a woman develops after a long marriage.

gynovalence. noun. The number of women with whom a man is capable of sharing his love simultaneously.

gyntranct. noun. A woman who has severed the links to her femininity.

H

hadaism. noun. Doctrine based on the belief and popularity of said belief that after death believers will interact eternally with mythological beings.

hadouph. adjective. **1.** Exiting the age of innocence. noun. **2.** The commencement of a life phase in which someone ceases to believe in fantastic, mythical, fable, or fictitious characters. **3.** Civispavick.

hadryon. noun. *Physics.* Sub-subatomic particle sometimes formed after a collision between baryons and mesons.

hagiogeny. noun. *Religion.* Collection of acts or mannerisms allegedly performed that justify nomination or candidature for sainthood.

hagionism. noun. *Psychology.* Believing in the divinity of a person considered to be a saint by someone else.

hagionomy. noun. Habitually naming or invoking saints in routine conversations.

hagra. noun. A loud noise emitted by a mammal about to be annihilated.

haliation. noun. Unbearable sensation of feeling tied up by a coarse and heavy maritime rope around the neck.

halismegma. noun. **1.** Breath resembling the smell of a sebaceous substance secreted by preputial glands. **2.** Smeghalitus.*

halistercus. noun. Someone with breath resembling the smell of excrement.

halopren. noun. An object that stands out in a dark room because it is the focus of a halogen light source directed towards it.

haloreole. noun. A pale circle of tenuously bright light that floats over the head of a living person believed to be holy.

halotron. noun. An instrument that projects an aureole surrounding the head of a person pretending to be holy.

hamthral. noun. A just financial contribution made by a citizen to a non-corrupt government for the optimal functioning of a society.

harmodynia. noun. The mastery and graceful performance of a movement in any art, sport, or activity.

haucivoyant. noun. **1.** A person who perceives and realizes that someone is both desperate and confident simultaneously. adjective. **2.** Recognizing ambisahutianity.*

haxilegomic. noun. A person who speaks accurately, but only once and briefly, about a subject.

hebomest. adjective. Being condemned to seven years of bad luck after breaking a mirror.

hecatonism. noun. **1.** Collection of strategies employed to carry out the systematic extermination of a group of people. **2.** The making of evacumyms.

hecklept. verb. A public speaker whose oratory is interrupted in an aggressive and abusive manner.

hecrolate. verb. To go from one place to another in search of something.

hedonisaur. noun. *Paleontology.* A large omnivorous and bipedal dinosaur of the late Cretaceous period with massive head and three large horns like triceratops (*Triceratops spp.*), a formidable snout and a strong jaw resembling a platypus (*Ornithorhynchus anatinus*), claw-like front limbs like tyrannosaurs (*Tyrannosaurus spp.*), a double row of large bony plates along the back as stegosaurs (*Stegosaurus spp.*), a disproportionally long tail for its body, and the brain capacity of humans (*Homo sapiens*). It is assumed that it chased some prey to enjoy the hunt, had sex with them before killing them, and avoided eating their meat.

hedorrhemic. adjective. Containing various decomposing substances and emanating a repulsive smell more revolting than the sum of the individual decomposing smells.

hegedon. noun. *Paleontology.* A giant plantigrade extinct in the Pleistocene epoch, similar to present-day bears, with long fingers joined by membranes that allowed gliding when speeding after a prey.

helicomnem. A mnemonic technique to assist with recalling dates by imagining time as a spiral staircase in which each step is a year.

helicopoiesis. noun. *Biochemistry.* Phenomenon in which amino acids and nucleotides merge to form spiral-shaped molecules.

helicosed. adjective. Object acquiring a spiral shape which normally or naturally is not spiral.

helicosity. noun. A feature of the dispersal of the intangible, resembling a spiral.

heligonia. noun. *Medicine.* Latent hereditary condition precipitated by a viral infection characterized by longitudinal twisting of the penis resembling a spiral cylinder.

heliophile. noun. **1.** A person who sunbathes to excess. **2.** A person with purple skin covered with cancerous lesions who continues to frequently expose himself to sunlight.

heliothanasia. noun. **1.** Death by direct exposure to sunlight. *Informal.* **2.** Vamp-xpire. **3.** Suncroak.

heliphoton. noun. **1.** Visual perception of spiral luminous apparitions. *Medicine.* **2.** A group of spiral stellar lights that are perceived immediately after a traumatic event. *Medicine.* **3.** Sudden hypoglycemia, abrupt low blood pressure, or body weakness that triggers scintillating scotoma. *Medicine.* **4.** Teichopsia. *Physics.* **5.** In astrophysical bodies: The path

light takes following magnetic helicity.

helipodic. adjective. Walking fast and meandering.

helispade. noun. Electronic weapon made of two sabers of hard and light material that when fired causes severe damage to the targeted body.

hemacate. verb. **1.** To mumble repetitive unintelligible invocations with ritualized mannerisms and gestures to extirpate evils circulating in someone's blood. noun. *Informal.* **2.** Blood cleansing. adjective. **3.** Cleaning the blood from casted spells.

hemafervescence. noun. **1.** The boiling of someone's blood when in a highly irate state. **2.** A state of utmost emotional intensity.

hemalgia. noun. *Medicine.* Generalized pain that seems to circulate with the blood.

hemaricia. noun. Unrestrained desire to possess and store blood to cherish.

hemastic. noun. A person who paints with blood.

hemelgony. noun. Selective solidarity.

hemisperation. noun. Envy and resentment felt by the inhabitants of the southern hemisphere toward the inhabitants of the northern hemisphere.

hemispirosis. noun. Dizziness that occurs when climbing spiral stairs or standing on a motorized spiral.

hemoconglem. noun. A troubling sensation of rapid blood clotting throughout the body that slows down body movements and thought speed.

hemopyria. noun. *Medicine.* Sudden heating up of the blood in absence of fever.

hendistasis. noun. *Physics.* Cutting a fluid and solidifying the cut surfaces to create dry channels between the severed fluid sections.

hepatophobic. adjective. **1.** (of a person) Fearing or loathing ingesting liver. noun. **2.** A child who howls and wails when refusing to eat liver or other animal entrails at the dinner table.

hergure. noun. Stubborn bravery in females of some species.

heriugh. verb. To annoy an animal or a person with bright lights or loud sounds.

hermafront. noun. *Architecture.* **1.** Female appearance on the façade of a male building. **2.** Something or someone who appears to be feminine on the surface.

heroclivia. noun. A tedious recitation of a bold act someone did years before.

herpetise. verb. **1.** To crawl on the floor with undulating movements. **2.** To imitate the movements and mannerisms of a reptile. **3.** To coach a young politician.

hertiopy. noun. Something in nature with perfect curvatures and straight lines that fools the eye.

heterepic. noun. A collection of independent heroic acts, adventures, and tales of a group of people over a long period that converge into an impressive ending.

heterodict. noun. **1.** An individual whose every finger and toe is of different size and shape. **2.** A person who admires and is devoted to any new dictator who comes into power. **3.** A dictator who often changes the policies of his or her regime. **4.** Someone who constantly changes the tone or topic of a discussion, none of which can be recollected or described.

heterolesic. noun. A woman who is sexually attracted to effeminate men and overtly feminine or delicate women.

heterolysis. noun. **1.** Destruction of heterodoxy by orthodoxy. **2.** Phenomenon that turns heterogeneity into something or someone orthogeneous.*

heterom. noun. **1.** A rare or strange first name. **2.** A person who has two or more bosses or is employed to serve under several supervisors.

heterometer. noun. Instrument used to measure heterogeneity.

heteropoeia. noun. *Linguistics.* The study of the different pronunciations of etymologically correct words that are not accepted by the phonetic rules of a language.

heteroptulant. noun. (of a person) The display of varying levels of petulance according to the occasion.

heuroetimy. noun. A manner or a technique used in the discovery of the truth.

hexaliopodous. adjective. *Zoology.* A vertebrate biped who walks like an insect.

hialonicus. adjective. **1.** Dreaming of oneself as a crystal. noun. **2.** Related to or pertaining to a dream made of crystals.

hialorrhea. noun. *Medicine.* Massive excretion of crystals through an orifice.

hiatusgamy. noun. A temporary pause or break in a marriage mutually agreed by the couple.

hicentrip. noun. **1.** A trivial compliment or a phrase stated as an obvious excuse to change the topic of a conversation. *Rhetoric.* **2.** A short prosaic recitation. **3.** A brief psittacism.*

himatish. noun. *Geology.* Flat and extensive sand desert with no dunes, vegetation, or wind.

hippobradic. adjective. **1.** Having a slow horse. **2.** Having a horse that is unable to trot, gallop, or run.

hipsant. verb. To lift someone to the height of a third person.

hirsutophagy. noun. *Anthropology.* **1.** A practice of ancient cannibals consisting of ingesting the hair of the prey as a symbolic *hors d'oeuvre* prior to eating the flesh. **2.** Trichoantropophagy. *Medicine.* **3.** Trichophagia.

hisdolation. noun. **1.** Brief period of anguish during a consolation. **2.** A feeling of distress that accompanies a deslivy.*

hollandinous. adjective. Having the traits of falseness, pretension, apparent openness, and greed that prevailed in the Dutch culture.

holocier. noun. A person who talks too much about what he or she did, does or will do when actually he or she did not, does not and probably will not do anything.

holopathist. noun. **1.** A person who claims to be a specialist in several medical specialties and, without recognized study or accreditation, adopts the title of doctor. **2.** Chiropractor. **3.** Homeopath.

holorost. noun. A hugely intense sexual pleasure that sometimes can lead to unconsciousness.

hominophyte. noun. An insult uttered to an exceptionally passive person. Literally, it means human vegetable.

homocimen. noun. Collection of the ideal attributes of several men that a woman groups mentally to form an image of the perfect husband. This strategy, as the basis for selecting a potential husband, generally fails.

homonist. noun. **1.** A homosexual man who loves all men equally. **2.** Omniandrous.

homoprasism. noun. **1.** An alleged perception of the biosphere on the presence of humans on Earth. *Philosophy.* **2.** Theory proposing the biosphere as an entity that senses and endures changes, damages and consequences following the overexploitation and abuse of the planet by humanity, and thus recognizes it as a threatening and virulent parasite destined to be expelled or destroyed. **3.** Theory that conceives humanity as a poorly matched transplant on Earth and bound to be rejected. *Ecology.* **4.** A study on the factual effects of humanity on planet Earth.

horrocephalic. noun. A person with frightening looks and with an alarming way of thinking.

hortidermatic. noun. A woman with appetizing, maneuverable and lickable skin.

hortiphony. noun. To talk to oneself in a quiet and monotonous voice, as if not to be overheard.

hoslema. noun. An acronym of the three main targets where Spaniards swear to defecate: *hostia, leche y madre*, or the Host, breast milk and a mother.

hostiate. verb. To perform an occult art, daily or weekly, characterized by ceremonious incantations with the intervention of imaginary beings, pretending to successfully carry out the incorporation of a historical personage into bread or a wafer.

hostilalia. noun. An often unprovoked use of strong language accompanied by obscene gestures. Sometimes these are signs and symptoms of mental or organic brain disease.

humicodour. adjective. Smelling like a decomposing mix of animal carcass and vegetable refuse.

hydatibursa. noun. A bag made of water surrounded by water. It generally occurs by density differentials of two types of water.

hydatiburse. noun. A portable aquarium for transporting sacred aquatic goods to and from an altar or a temple.

hydopumble. verb. To knead water while preventing it from going between the fingers.

hydralute. verb. **1.** To make a person wet for no apparent reason. **2.** To throw water on people for diversion.

hydroseism. noun. *Earth Sciences.* Seaquake of high magnitude with oscillatory and trepidatory movements along with powerful alternating centrifugal and centripetal forces.

hydrostalgia. noun. *Medicine.* A severe pain precipitated by contact with water.

hydrozon. noun. *Physics.* **1.** Concentrated water. *Informal.* **2.** Water juice.

hyerathiny. noun. **1.** Intense emotion a person from an enclosed population experiences when establishing contact with people from a different population. **2.** Hirtacumbe.

hygoar. noun. **1.** A sensation of movement or change of position of one or more internal organ. **2.** Hypertosplenk.

hymenalagh. noun. Transposition of the hymen for another membranous element to guarantee the virginity of a woman.

hypercognicy. adjective. **1.** Suddenly becoming conscious of something and reacting in a dramatic manner. **2.** Realizing something or having an idea abruptly with no apparent stimulus.

hypercollius. noun. Strong and irregular yawn or exhalation that is perceived to have a colloidal, spiral, or herpetic shape.

hypergraviont. adjective. **1.** Responding excessively to the force of gravity. **2.** Disobeying the law of gravity.

hyperisfaction. noun. *Psychology.* **1.** Profound sensation of closeness to a person of authority or to a celebrity. **2.** A feeling of having family ties with a revered but unfamiliar person. **3.** A deep sense of stepsonship* or godsonship* towards an admired person.

hypermordence. noun. **1.** Mental repetition of an

act or acts that someone wishes not to have done. **2.** Frequent mental playback of repentance that decreases concentration, interferes with memory processes and produces an indefinable pain in indefinable parts of the body. **3.** Rammode.* **4.** A bite of the conscience. **5.** *Literature.* Agenbite of inwit.

hyperofanity. noun. Extreme profanation of something considered sacred by others.

hyperrority. noun. A talent to recognize other people's mistakes while not recognizing one's own.

hypertropism. noun. *Psychology.* An exaggerated admiration or attraction to someone that can attain a level of mania or psychosis.

hypnolity. noun. A hypnotizing fascination when looking at something very familiar that has not been seen for a long time.

hypnoloplegic. adjective. Feeling physical paralysis due to an extreme exaltation when seeing, hearing, or smelling someone of exceptional beauty.

hypnolussonity. noun. A condition in which a person stares in the eye of someone talking but does not listen at all.

hypnoluteness. noun. A somnolent state within a dream during deep sleep.

hypnopulsickness. noun. A soporific state of stupefaction when pondering how to solve a problem and encountering more and more unanswered questions and no way to come up with potential answers or even to begin devising a feasible system to interpret said questions.

hypnositic. noun. A relaxed expression in the eyes as if in a trance when half asleep.

hypnositis. noun. *Medicine.* **1.** Non-infectious acute sleeping sickness. **2.** Nistungulosis. **3.** A strong urge to sleep that makes a person either irritable or unconscious.

hypnotichny. noun. A passive, impassive, and vegetative state of watching television as entertainment, unable to think about the triviality of the information perceived.

hypnoticnia. noun. **1.** The trace of a dream. **2.** A footprint of a dream. **3.** An ephemeral memory of something perceived in a dream that appears suddenly and triggers the remembrance of said dream.

hypnoticnore. noun. Someone who is unwilling or unable to pursue a dream.

hypobolius. noun. A hypocrite who donates money to a cause because he or she feels guilty.

hypocolag. noun. **1.** A person of mature or old age with hanging skin appendages in several parts of the body. **2.** A delicacy made with a few fresh ingredients.

hypoflexible. adjective. **1.** Quality of a biological tissue or an organ that has lost elasticity. **2.** Unadaptable, strict person. noun. **3.** A stubborn person with a certain authority. *Informal.* **4.** An old phallus.

hypohexagio. noun. The art or technique of extracting honey from a beehive while maintaining the architecture of the hive intact.

hyponemia. noun. A memory buried under the heavy burden of traumatic memories.

hyporemorse. noun. **1.** A light pang of conscience. **2.** A pitiful act of repentance.

hypostrop. noun. A person who deliberately and tenaciously sabotages and eventually ruins someone's life.

hypoxerogony. noun. *Medicine.* A decrease in natural genital lubrication that causes dryness and alters sexual function.

hyprameutic. noun. A person who speaks in a singularly quiet tone of voice and is difficult to hear.

hystecalibria. noun. Measurement of the internal diameter of the uterus.

hysterionate. verb. **1.** To apply a gentle touch and lightly manipulate an erogenous region of the body as a therapy for someone with nervous and functional ailments. noun. **2.** Circumclitorization.*

hysteritomy. noun. A remedy consisting in slapping someone hard in the face until the hysterical fit ceases.

hytapreth. noun. Brief vibration of soft tissues without external physical stimuli.

hytric. noun. A silly facial expression of a man who thinks a baby kicked inside his belly.

I

iatrognitude. noun. **1.** A paradox patients encounter when their diseases cannot be diagnosed or treated due to lack of a physician with the appropriate training within a hospital filled with ultra-specialized physicians. **2.** The arrogance peculiar to physicians, particularly when wearing a white robe. **3.** The petulance of a surgeon in an operating theater. *Informal.* **4.** The impact of a white robe on a rube.

iatromanic. adjective. Having the urge to prescribe medicines without having studied medicine.

ichthyocephalic. adjective. Having a head that has the texture and shape of a fish.

ichthyosomnulism. noun. *Zoology.* The partial state of sleep of a fish or a marine mammal.

icompuous. adjective. **1.** A pontificating or pious posture someone adopts when adoring a religious image in public. **2.** Iconomprudish.

idemball. noun. Uselessly spreading ideas or doctrines to a non-receptive public.

ideogenism. noun. *Philosophy.* **1.** Philosophical theory that aims to explain the origin of ideas. *Medicine.* **2.** Theory that proposes the neurotransmissible origin of ideas within defined neural networks as connections of concepts. *Archaic.* **3.** A theory that contested the female nature of ideas, claiming that all ideas were masculine and thus proposed the name change to "ideo."

ideolytic. adjective. A thought or collection of thoughts that, due to their severity, acquire consistency and weight similar to those of a stone.

ider. verb. To see or perceive with the mind without making use of the senses.

idioneptitude. noun. Collection of characteristics or unique traits of ineptitude in an individual.

idiotomy. noun. Extirpation of stupidity from someone with punches and harsh shaking.

idolocracy. noun. **1.** A government system based on promoting idolatry of a selected puppet acting as Head of State, selected for his idiocy by small groups with vested interests. **2.** Yankeeism.*

idyllitude. noun. Permanent state of singleness of a person incapable of maintaining a relationship due to habitually fantasizing, without success, the perfect love affair.

igneosoid. noun. *Psychology.* A personality of any type, seemingly normal, who turns explosive and violent under stimuli not considered aggressive or provocative.

ignivore. noun. *Biology.* An organism that feeds or consumes fire as a nutrient.

ignode. verb. To desire with fervor something unknown.

ignolicia. noun. Intentional indifference toward someone or something.

ignomisia. noun. **1.** Action of ignoring the surroundings, the panorama or the people around by being totally engrossed with a telecommunications device. **2.** Effect that a cell phone, Smartphone, iPad, tablet or other small telecommunications device has on a person that consists of bringing closer those who are far away and pushing away those who are close. **3.** Ignophony. **4.** Telignosia. **5.** Inevitable consequence of the cabiphoned.*

ignostasis. noun. Capability to acquire trivial knowledge without thinking and while immobile.

ileoticnia. noun. **1.** The opposite to a *déjà vu*. **2.** A vice versa *déjà vu*. **3.** An experience that leaves a person trucufacted* or ascheplated.*

iliumic. noun. An anatomical organ or a structure that appears to be twisted.

immemocable. adjective. One or more lived events that were not recorded in the memory.

immeniation. noun. Question or doubt conveyed without oral or written communication.

immiration. noun. A superficial and infantile introspection.

immoleric. adjective. Pertaining or relative to someone or something having huge bulk, volume, mass or corpulence that buries said something or someone with no possibility of escape.

immoleter. verb. **1.** To bury someone alive. **2.** To purposely inter a living human. **3.** To kill someone by confinement in a dark and constricted space.

immortigenic. noun. **1.** An event or circumstance that awakens the desire for immortality. **2.** Anathanagenic. **3.** A commonplace occurrence that acts as a trigger to wish for immortality. Example: the first time one sees wrinkles or grey hair in one's reflection or the first time one discovers lack of recall of familiar past events.

immortity. noun. *Psychology.* **1.** A strong feeling of being dead while alive. **2.** The belief that life is not life, but a lifeless simulation.

imparlate. noun. **1.** Something communicated without spoken words. verb. **2.** To remain silent and convey more information with such silence than any other form of communication.

impecuniate. verb. *Economics.* To impoverish someone by legal, yet dishonest, immoral or unethical means.

impelation. noun. **1.** A feeling of being flayed from the inside out. *Archaic.* **2.** An incunabulum made of materials other than skin. *Psychology.* **3.** Someone immune to being impelled. *Medicine.* **4.** Phallacrosis artificiae. **5.** Generalized alopecia caused by non-therapeutic artificial means.

impercune. noun. **1.** Someone for whom money and wealth are the utmost and only values of life. *Psychology.* **2.** Someone with an inferiority complex. *Literary.* **3.** (of a person) Insecurity and ambition without intelligence are the paths to failure, poverty, and anonymity.

imperrorist. noun. **1.** A person who cannot be easily scared. **2.** A person incapable of feeling horror in extreme circumstances.

imphlegm. noun. A person who drowns in his or her own phlegm.

impiel. adjective. **1.** Having no skin. **2.** Unperturbed during extreme, life-changing or terrifying circumstances. noun. **3.** Imperrorist.*

implalgia. noun. **1.** A forceful sensation of centripetal emptiness when saying goodbye to a loved one forever. **2.** A sensation that precedes emotional vacuumness.*

impulsion. noun. **1.** The slow and unstoppable consequences that follow an implosion. **2.** A pullasion* with momentum. **3.** An act performed repeatedly by an energetic docotracter.*

impreludible. adjective. **1.** Beyond all doubt, having been thought and rethought after careful analyses of data from varying constants and variables and confirmed independent third party corroborations. **2.** Unquestionable although not readily apparent.

improstenible. adjective. **1.** Impossible to identify. **2.** Impossible to identify or to define when perceived for the first time.

improsticable. adjective. Impossible to explain even when suspending disbelief during improbable speculations.

inaliloquy. noun. **1.** Speaking aloud to an inanimate object or to a group of inanimate objects. **2.** Antibiony.* **3.** A purported conversation with an unresponsive inanimate interlocutor.

inalmat. noun. *Theology*. **1.** An intelligent being who lacks a soul. **2.** Unsoul. *History*. **3.** A non-European human being.

inaniment. noun. **1.** An impression that a mechanical or electrical apparatus or machine fails to work by its own volition at the least opportune moment. **2.** A mechanical or electrical apparatus or machine prone to vehivolition.*

inclipse. noun. *Astronomy*. **1.** Illumination of a dark celestial body by the passing of another that emits light. **2.** A temporary gain in significance, power

or prominence in relation to another person. *Commerce*. **3.** An influx of capital into a continually underfunded enterprise.

incognimancy. noun. Ignorance about what will be found prior to an exploration of unknown territories or disciplines.

incognitude. noun. A discreditable quality in an incognizant.

incomilation. noun. A feeling of self-satisfaction when completing a project, particularly a creative one.

incompetancy. noun. Analytical method to evaluate the incompetence of an employee.

incompetitude. noun. **1.** Quality of inability to do something successfully. **2.** Dispute or contest between two or more incompetents over something prestigious, generally a position at an organization. **3.** Tendency of an incompetent employee to ascend hierarchically to an appropriate level of incompetence at an institution.

incremal. verb. To pretend to be in a hurry when there is no reason to be in a hurry.

incustible. adjective. **1.** Related to the inevitable and insatiable avarice when ignorance is

mixed with power. noun. **2.**
An opiviet* politician with an
inextucible* attitude who klepts*
with mestoclasia* the goods and
money of poor and middle-class
families.

indead. adjective. **1.** Being
dead in life. **2.** Being dead and
alive simultaneously. noun. **2.** A
dead person continuing to have
corporeal life.

inesipiance. noun. A sensation
of incredulity at a time or at a
moment of success vehemently
wished for and realizing that the
likelihood of its happening was
almost impossible.

inesneeze. noun. **1.** A sudden
and involuntary propulsion of
air to expel it from the lungs
that is retained in mouth and
nose. It generally sounds like a
whimper. **2.** Sneezimplosion.

inextucible. adjective. **1.**
Inexplicable behavior or
phenomenon that occurs
extremely frequently. noun.
2. The everyday behavior of
a person that cannot be easily
described.

infatubility. noun. Ineffable
incapacity to control body and
mind when deeply in love.

infaud. verb. To remove the
eternity of the human soul.

infidery. noun. An
establishment where infidelities
are generated or carried out.

infusc. verb. **1.** To obscure
something by controlling the
intensity or covering the source
of light. **2.** To ruin someone's
reputation.

inlim. verb. To invite a stranger
inside one's home.

inopertion. noun. Affected
indifference toward someone
else's anguish.

inoport. noun. Someone who
arrives at the wrong place and at
the wrong time.

inopportine. noun. A person
who makes a comment at an
inappropriate time or place.

inopticable. adjective.
Impossible to see or visualize.

inosity. noun. **1.** Self-assured
ineptitude. **2.** Sesquintepcia.
3. Anasesude. **4.** Assertiveness
without a clue.

inquemity. noun. A custom
or habit performed routinely
when getting into bed in the
anonymity of darkness.

insasffective. noun. A person
who turns his or her back on
love.

inscrotum. noun. *Medicine.* **1.**
Anatomical area of the upper
and interior portions of scrotum
with indefinable limits behind
the pubic bone and abdomen.
This area is easily identified by
men who experience a traumatic
or chronic pain in the testicles.

Informal. **2.** A person who is a major pain in the balls.

insercivity. noun. The temporal dominance an inanimate object has over the person who possesses it.

insespathy. noun. **1.** A combination of voice, hygienic customs, dress and other physical attributes that makes a person detestable and hideous to others. **2.** Repugnopatility.

insopurnable. adjective. Something or someone without cause or raison d'être.

insospeling. noun. **1.** A person who does not belong to the country he or she is from. **2.** A person who does not belong in the family he or she were born into. **3.** An inhabitant of the Land of Insosperibility.*

insospennable. adjective. Unbearable feeling of non-afflicting anguish someone experiences when perceiving the trite and inevitable.

insosperibility. noun. **1.** A difficulty undergone by someone with no options when persuaded to live a new life with limited options and convoluted hopes. **2.** Related to or pertaining to the multidimensional time-space of that name. **3.** Quality of nonlinear time in the Land of Insosperibility.*

insosperible. adjective. **1.** Related to the reaction when experiencing or being in insosperibility.* **2.** Impossible to sosper.

inspipasticity. noun. A state of mental hyper-tonicity that generates a rapid sequence of ideas a person is incapable of processing, remembering, recording, or writing.

instand. noun. Each one of the semi-instants that, when put together, form a long period.

insticulate. verb. To proceed, speak, or act without thinking.

instinneb. noun. **1.** Routine imitation of gestures, speech mode, and opinions of the head of an organization or corporation by their subordinates. **2.** Corporate primulation.* **3.** Compamimesis.

intebrupt. verb. To interfere with an exabrupt* without interrupting.

intelmetism. noun. *Philosophy.* **1.** Theory advocating that the human intelligence does not increase in line with the rise in speed of communication nor with the logarithmic population growth, but that it remains constant in short-term evolutionary basis. **2.** Intelimetriation.

intemper. verb. **1.** To depart from indoors. **2.** To leave a building, a house, an establishment, or a roofed area.

intempestuous. adjective. **1.** Doing or saying something aggressively at an inappropriate time or place. **2.** Intempering* belligerently.

intempetive. adjective. **1.** Occurring at an inappropriate time or place. noun. **2.** Someone who is untimely and inopportune in both time and place. *Informal.* **3.** Mother-in-law. *Theology.* **4.** The god of a religion one does not belong to.

interfall. verb. **1.** To interrupt someone in mid-sentence to declare a ruling. **2.** To intercept the thoughts of someone to impose a verdict.

intestion. noun. *History.* **1.** A slow execution applied to deserters in a Mongol sect, consisting of the eventration of the intestines to let all the ordure fester the body until death. *Law.* **2.** The claim of an alleged inheritor in an intestate case.

intogobility. noun. Attribute of an idea generated simultaneously by two or more people when at least one person is unfamiliar with the subject matter.

intrafuge. noun. **1.** A person who intends to escape from himself or herself. **2.** Egofunest. **3.** Autofutilist.

intrality. noun. **1.** The collection of entrails, as a whole, of an inanimate object. *History.* **2.** The inside of the body of an inalmated* person.

intrament. noun. Distance between two thoughts in the same person.

intramentality. noun. *Philosophy.* **1.** Quality of all mental processes at the moment in which each one of them develops. **2.** The sum of a person's known and unknown intellectual capabilities. **3.** The unknown way of thinking of an introvert. *Psychology.* **4.** The transparent and characteristic mode of thinking of an extrovert with inferiority complex striving for superiority.

intranesch. verb. **1.** To mentally reiterate one's ideas to oneself. **2.** To stubbornly debate with oneself a concept just developed without sharing the mental discussion with anyone. **3.** To reintemize. **4.** To autodispute. noun. **5.** Endorment. **6.** Autoterch.

intrasom. verb. To enter a new dream from a dream one is dreaming currently.

intronsigence. noun. **1.** Action and effect of mentally penetrating oneself in high state of concentration to examine, without judging, deeds performed or emotions felt with the aim of achieving interior peace. **2.** Careful and persistent mental replaying of an inappropriate action committed without attributing one or more reasonable origins.

introscanable. adjective. The impassible feeling someone experiences when entering an intangible area.

introscoss. noun. Each of the nooks in the body or the mind.

introscusion. noun. Doubtful circumspection.

introsperibility. noun. Capability to enter into the Land of Insosperibility.

inupiate. verb. **1.** To manipulate the mental pivots of a person by subliminal innuendo. **2.** To steer the volitive* sexual arousal of a person with sensual insinuations.

inurquiciator. noun. **1.** An insinuator who loses control over his or her own insinuations. **2.** An inupiator* who is unexpectedly out of his mind for no apparent reason.

invarditure. noun. *Law.* **1.** A worldwide automatic process in which a law eliminates itself by virtue of being unjust. **2.** Collection of procedures geared to invalidate any law that violates any natural human right or is unilaterally oppressive.

ipsopensia. noun. **1.** Gushing sensation of incertitude when realizing that a thought is not a self-generated thought. **2.** An idea that appears suddenly with no mental link of any sort.

ipsothermic. noun. *Physics.* **1.** A natural condition, in certain circumstances, in which a body immediately acquires the temperature of its surrounding environment. *Informal.* **2.** The cause of an instantaneous sexual arousal.

ipsotice. noun. A vestige from the past that is detected immediately.

iraclampsia. noun. Sudden fit of rage with no apparent motive or provocation.

irariscient. noun. A person with eyes resembling those of a sheep.

irnatic. noun. **1.** A brilliant idea that comes from nowhere. **2.** A revolutionary idea that suddenly emerges with no links to any other previous knowledge. **3.** Isopensia.*

irnus. noun. Subaquatic snare that squeezes a terrestrial prey and asphyxiates it in a claustrophobically slow fashion.

irreturnable. adjective. **1.** Having no return. noun. *Literature.* **2.** What happened happened.

iscariotism. noun. **1.** Absence of guilt after committing treason. *Psychology*. **2.** Branch of psychology that studies the behavioral patterns and personality disorders of traitors. **3.** A method of eliminating the psychological hangover of potential traitors. *Informal*. **4.** Belief among traitors that guilt is irrelevant.

~ism. noun. The suffix of an ideology that when predicated for profit turns immediately into fraud.

istagh. noun. **1.** A phenomenal idea that seems to come spontaneously from a higher being. **2.** Inspiration with no apparent point of reference.

istrigacy. noun. Feeling of terrifying intrepidity when doing something with both determination and fear.

itsapeak. verb. (from *iktsuarpok* in Inuit). **1.** To go outside to check if anyone is coming. **2.** To glance through the window or door to verify whether someone is arriving. **3.** To check persistently if an expected person is about to arrive.

J

jable. verb. **1.** To persuade someone with consummate ease. **2.** To change, without breaking, the shape of something not easily malleable. **3.** Malleat.*

jablee. noun. Someone who is easily persuaded.

jalditic. adjective. Being pale as well as icteric or jaundiced simultaneously.

jaleb. noun. **1.** A person with an excessive psychological reliance on a partner who develops emotional dependence on said partner. **2.** Subsichedaneous. *Psychology.* **3.** A codependent person without a drug addiction.

jalot. noun. **1.** Someone who is constantly looking forward to receiving a gift. *Psychology.* **2.** A person with the obsessive need to be surprised with gifts.

jaloty. adjective. **1.** Showing with subtle gestures an evident yet obscure sign that one is ready to receive something. **2.** Sabafeign.

jamiz. noun. **1.** A man who hates urinating while sitting down. **2.** A calout* who reluctantly obeys a command.

jardier. verb. **1.** To be able to escape when cornered in a confined space. **2.** To sobrestine. noun. **3.** A resourceful person who commonly emerges intact from difficult circumstances.

jaust. adjective. **1.** Being suddenly enamoured with someone after a long friendship. noun. **2.** The unanticipated falling in love between two people after a long time of being acquaintances or friends. **3.** Melincandelament.

javelian. noun. **1.** A person who is spirited, proud, fierce and quiet. **2.** Sorviomuto. **3.** Tamofarro. **4.** Caobuco. **5.** Tacitrush. *Informal.* **6.** A tall, thin person with a pointy head.

jayick. noun. A forced laughter emitted when a joke is told by someone of importance.

jayus. (from *jayus* in Indonesian). noun. **1.** Involuntary or uncontrollable laughter after listening to a spectacularly unfunny joke. **2.** A person who giggles or laughs frequently.

jeek. noun. **1.** A facial expression on a stupid man that seems to compel everyone to punch him in the face. **2.** Dechonur. **3.** Mammudio. **4.** The facial expression of a desphiront.*

jejine. noun. **1.** The gesture of one person that resembles that of another person. **2.** An idiosyncratic mannerism of exaggerated mimicry. **3.** Maneriyic.

jelloid. noun. **1.** Visible vibration of fatty tissue on the skin of a fat person. **2.** Anecstatic* quivering of adipose tissue, frequently observed in the lower back of obese people and on the hips of overweight women. **3.** Fibrimation.

jenk. noun. **1.** Diarrhea in an adult with the consistency, color, and smell of meconium. **2.** Adult meconirrhea.

jesfascell. verb. To re-strategize the priorities and goals of one or more projects of a corporation that starts with laying off the executives involved in setting up the original priority strategies.

jick. noun. **1.** A self-nominated inheritor of a divine sovereign, thirsty for human blood and money, who patrols among illiterate people in search of gullible prey. **2.** Anthropohematophagous being of the working people, the socioeconomically disadvantaged, and the underprivileged of the third world. **3.** Siletropus. **4.** An evangelist.

jideate. verb. **1.** To pull something out and put it elsewhere in an intangible manner. **2.** To relocate intangibly.

joconalge. verb. To ease the distress of others by doing something silly.

joconalgia. noun. **1.** The act and effect of prompting a smile or a laugh in a person during a moment of anguish or pain. **2.** Commalive.

joffant. verb. To demand when demanding is not pertinent, appropriate, required or suggested.

joffer. noun. **1.** A beggar who, instead of asking, demands food or money in an arrogant and aggressive manner. **2.** Magnadier.

johartism. noun. *Philosophy*. **1.** Moral theory that critiques Manichaeism as doctrinal daltonism and proposes an infinite combinatorial diversity of moralities and behaviors. **2.** Malispectrism. **3.** Protanopsism. **4.** Deuteronomism.

jole. noun. **1.** Each of the valves that controls a sentimental compression. **2.** Mardagon.

jolp. noun. **1.** Lack of pain or confusion, and overwhelming self-empathy during an intense trauma. **2.** Absence of the ephemeral and forceful sensations of vacuumness* and confusion that are usually felt during an intense trauma. **3.** Materraneture.

jokantery. noun. Series of silly jokes among adolescents.

jokerious. noun. **1.** A silly person. **2.** Someone who is always fooling around. adjective. **3.** Pretending to be a clown.

jokestour. noun. **1.** A person who can make someone smile or laugh during a moment of anguish or pain. **2.** A person who is able to ease the distress of others by saying or doing something silly. **3.** Someone capable of joconalgia.*

jope. adjective. **1.** Having talent in several areas but conforming to remain a part of the mediocre majority. noun. **2.** Subdigiphrenic. **3.** Voluntary imbecility.

joumer. noun. **1.** A person who, at will, can move the eyelids in varied ways and not only up and down. **2.** Maleablefaric.

jubjub. noun. A bird in a poem.

jumenitor. noun. **1.** An item of furniture in the shape of an ass to sit on with legs astride. **2.** A portable ironing board.

junglize. verb. **1.** To enter into unknown or unexplored territory or field. **2.** To enter into a discussion of an unknown field when completely ignorant of the topic. **3.** To enter into a jungle. Generally applied to a city-dweller with no jungle experience.

juvenmally. noun. *Literary.* **1.** The wednesdarization of life in the fridaystage of life. *Psychology.* **2.** A yearning for youth in old age. adjective. **3.** Pretending to be young in attitude and style.

juvenoix. noun. *Informal.* An aging homosexual dressing and acting as a young homosexual.

juxtalgia. noun. A new and persisting pain that appears on the opposite side of other existing pain or pains.

juxtaphilia. noun. *Psychology.* **1.** Malady of always wishing to be on the other side from where one is. **2.** A personality disorder in which a person constantly desires to be in different circumstances.

juxtinamia. noun. *Psychology.* Recurring belief that an inanimate object wants to be located close by.

K

kaddaka. noun. *Informal.* **1.** A possessive woman who periodically forces her husband to stay at home instead of letting him go out with his friends. **2.** A controlling wife who operates as an active hangover preventative. **3.** Salvacruddian.

kaelling. noun. (from *kaelling* in Danish). **1.** A parent who persistently insults their children. adjective. **2.** Insulting obscenities aimed at children.

kahoon. noun. **1.** A person who projects his or her sexuality indiscriminately and affectedly. **2.** Erognathous.

kairocachia. noun. Negative circumstance or situation faced at the least opportune moment.

kairocrastity. noun. The most opportune moment to carry out the most onerous task.

kaleidogonous. adjective. Having multiple and ever-changing sexual partners.

kanckle. verb. **1.** To dispossess people of their possessions from highest to lowest value until they are left with nothing. **2.** To epicalk.

kanf. noun. **1.** A transsexual projecting his or her new sexuality indiscriminately and affectedly. **2.** A person announcing or promoting his or her new gonality.*

kanga. noun. A one-piece bathing garment made of narrow strings to cover certain portions of the body with the exception of breasts, buttocks and genitals.

kank. noun. **1.** Appearing quicker than anything conceivable. **2.** Episuddious.

kanny. noun. **1.** A mother who constantly carries an offspring in her arms. **2.** Kangaroottee.

kardois. noun. Some who enjoys squeezing pimples from other people's faces.

karmacky. adjective. Feeling the skin dry, wrinkle and tighten.

karmadumb. noun. Spiritual force or energy that condemns those few people who actually reincarnate to life in a religious or a political family.

karyosepsis. noun. *Law.* **1.** A drastic and full cleansing of all financial corruption from the core. **2.** A stepwise elimination of the finansepsis.* *Economics.* **3.** Corruptectomy.

kaskruttish. adjective. **1.** Pretending to have more capabilities than all other human beings. **2.** Epianthroid.

kasspat. noun. **1.** Someone who grunts incessantly with a half-smile on his or her face. **2.** Marmotong.

kataka. noun. **1.** Sudden lack of attraction toward a lover. **2.** Instantaneous frigidity during coitus. **3.** Erinsipidia.

katicky. noun. **1.** A feeling a person experiences hiding in a room while his or her lover's spouse suspiciously searches the room. *Psychology.* **2.** A stressful feeling of being persecuted or hunted. adjective. **3.** Experiencing a wape.*

kauticus. noun. **1.** Sexual arousal by someone or something foreign. **2.** Eroxenophilia. *Informal.* **3.** Turned on by someone or something exotic.

kayka. noun. **1.** A woman who hates men who hate women. adjective. **2.** Misandromisogynous.

keek. noun. **1.** A person totally inept at operating or utilizing any type of electronic or mechanical equipment. **2.** Oligomechanous.

kelk. noun. **1.** A person in a corporation who works in solitude to solve a problem and is absent from the meeting organized to define the necessary steps to solve said problem. **2.** Solitrespon.

kerackic. adjective. **1.** Impervious to promises. **2.** Acquiring thick skin after listening to false promises expressed with reiterity.*

kerackious. adjective. **1.** Attaining imperviousness to continuous slander. **2.** Acquiring the structure and texture of a horn in the process of attaining insusceptibility to burning. **3.** Keratocausted. *Archaic.* **4.** Becoming a tolerant cuckold.

kerst. noun. **1.** Variation in the weight of a memory that differs from memory to memory and from person to person, expressed in mol-grams or in a thousand or a million femtograms or 10^{-15} grams. **2.** Nemopesity.

kib. noun. **1.** Copious morning dew that makes everything thoroughly wet. **2.** Kilodross. *Informal.* **3.** A wet vagina.

kidnery. noun. *Informal.* **1.** Each side of the lower back above the hip. **2.** Rinoneira.

kie. noun. **1.** The outermost portion of a cuticle. **2.** Epicuticle.

kif. noun. **1.** A person who eats only mushy food. **2.** Magdaliphagous. adjective. **3.** Feeding exclusively on food transformed into a *purée*.

kifky. noun. **1.** Absolute certainty of being sober. **2.** Confident belief in one's own sobriety.

kigg. adjective. *Informal.* **1.** Exuding the worst breath smell. noun. **2.** A person with chronic borrifremic halitosis. **3.** Saprovafous.

kilotomy. noun. **1.** Strict low calorie, low carbohydrate, low fat dietary regimen combined with strenuous physical activity to lose weight in a short time. **2.** Sudden loss of weight by surgery.

kimmize. verb. **1.** To purposely raise someone's blood pressure. **2.** To suprasphingonate.

kimoko. adjective. **1.** Having skin like a reptile. **2.** Saurodermic.

kimole. noun. **1.** Quality and intensity of a friendship. *Psychology.* **2.** The quality and intensity of a friendship characterized by being inversely proportional to age in which the amistation* occurred. **3.** Pausamistation.

kimuck. noun. **1.** A person who deciphers or interprets prophesies. **2.** Presagist. **3.** Sagioclariator. **4.** Portender.

klatten. noun. **1.** Pain following repetitive pubic collisions during a passionate coitus. *Medicine.* **2.** Pubic inflammation after rough, bouncy and bumpy impacts. **3.** Vibrant episiopactalgia. **4.** Episialgia.

kleidoid. noun. **1.** Term for classifying organisms with additional glands that other members of their own species do not have. **2.** Extradenoidal.

klept. verb. To plan a theft in which avarice is the one and only motive.

kleptochrony. noun. Habit of stealing time from someone else, with total absence of empathy. It generally applies to sending an innocent person to jail or wasting someone's time with copious paperwork or being forced to listen to an endless, pointless monologue.

kleptolegal. noun. *Law.* **1.** Legalized state or corporate fraud. **2.** State's lottery. *Politics.* **3.** Banks' bailout.

kleptopathic. noun. *Psychology.* **1.** A person of medium to high intelligence with a mental disease characterized by the insatiable need to accumulate wealth by any means, which generally involves sophisticated, elaborate theft with a dubious veneer of legality. *Politics.* **2.** An incustible* person. *Finance.* **3.** A deceiviator.*

kleptophilia. adjective. **1.** Feeling pleasure when stealing, even when done for necessity. **2.** Bancking.

kleptophony. noun. **1.** Feeling that the sound of one's own voice does not actually come from one's own mouth. **2.** Disturbing sensation on remembering what one said seemingly being voiced by someone else.

kleptosadist. noun. **1.** A person who robs others with refined cruelty for pure pleasure. **2.** One who steals sexual dignity, respect, or freedom from others while experiencing a sexual arousal in the process. **3.** A bank executive.

klobb. noun. **1.** The perennial, infantile, and monotonous façade that disguises the caprice of a man.

klobsten. noun. **1.** A force with an apparent magnetic field that forms around two fleeting lovers.

klooph. noun. **1.** Finding that a corrected error was not truly an error prior to having been corrected. **2.** Equivomation.

klugg. noun. **1.** An orgy involving persons of the same gender. **2.** Unigonalidia. **3.** Gomorrism.* **4.** Erofectia.

kneepanty. noun. Belief, in some men, that a woman who farts while wearing pantyhose will reveal a sudden swell of the hose at knee level.

kockling. noun. **1.** Realization that one's destiny was tweaked by someone with specific motives. **2.** Megatorsing.

kodic. noun. **1.** An organism that inhabits the top portion of a cave. **2.** Epistrogler.

koggy. noun. **1.** A person who professes to know more about wines than everyone else. **2.** Epinologist.

koll. verb. *Informal.* **1.** To lie down on a bed with the hands outside the blankets. **2.** To exmanition* command.

komsie. adjective. **1.** A person who cannot help but divulge a confided secret. **2.** Secretaperio. **3.** Psittacrit. **4.** Psoricret. **5.** Secreterton.

koprett. noun. **1.** A black ghost inhabiting and scaring a Caucasian household.

koradorah. noun. *Education.* **1.** Teaching method that promotes individual pressure to deepen personal understanding and knowledge. **2.** Manognabatism.

kortick. noun. **1.** An error a man makes when doing something that a woman told him to do and not what she wished or meant for him to do. **2.** Malcertitude. **3.** Parasimiladia. **4.** Malandrosis.

koth. noun. *Architecture.* **1.** An architectural building that imitates ancient dwellings. **2.** A visually unpleasant and functionally defective architectural structure. **3.** Novarchiosis. **4.** New ruins.

kotox. noun. *Commerce.* Trade name of absorbent pads worn by men with urinary or fecal incontinence.

kumatuma. noun. The most intense silence, resembling a strong, empty and pulsating noise.

kummerspeck. noun. (from *kummerspeck* in German). **1.** Gaining weight from eating as a relief from stress or grief. **2.** Weight gain arising from compulsive eating habits. **3.** A fat person who eats without being hungry.

kustid. adjective. **1.** Having an irrational fear to evil deities of one's religion or to good deities of other religions. **2.** Mefistophobic.

kyntdom. noun. **1.** A sensation of deep victimization felt when, having endured damaging or adverse circumstances, new unrelated counterproductive events worsen the harm and generate new afflictions. **2.** Maligresity. *Informal.* **3.** Doubly screwed up.

kyverckon. noun. **1.** Someone pretending to comprehend the ideas of a deep thinker. **2.** Exontellinicist.

L

labenciate. verb. 1. To lower the edge of the lips frequently, deliberately or as a reflexive response to deception or sadness, but not petulant annoyance. 2. To pout habitually.

labencious. adjective. 1. (of a woman) Pouting frequently without expressing petulant annoyance. 2. Pucherian. 3. Puchorous. 4. Pertaining to a woman who labenciates* indiscriminately.

labialing. noun. Kissing and caressing the external and internal lips of the vulva with the tongue.

labila. noun. 1. A cosmetic, generally red, that a woman spreads over her lips to announce she is prepared to engage in coitus. *Medicine.* 2. Property of the vulva lips that turn turgid and red during an eromiation* and a erostally.*

labilation. noun. *Psychology.* 1. A custom of painting the lips red to imitate the color of the vulva during sexual arousal. *Psychology.* 2. Exteriorized neurosis characterized by the application of facial dyes with the objective of signaling that the sexual organs are prepared for copulation. *Psychology.* 3. Projection of libido.

laboritism. noun. *Religion.* 1. A belief that prolonged and excessive work is part of human nature and prevents boredom or abominable thoughts. 2. A workaholic doctrine that postulates that work must be a requirement to avoid asthenia and festition.* *Philosophy.* 3. Puritanidism.

lacayer. noun. Long, desperate, mute cry a common person frequently wails in the second half of life.

laciacor. noun. The last sigh of a person who never learned to breathe properly.

lacopend. noun. A person who routinely pays low wages to workers.

lagoonned. noun. 1. A person with olive skin that resembles stagnant, slimy and scabby green water. 2. A tint of olive skin.

Informal. **3.** A derogatory term applied to Mexican migrants in the United States of America.

lagrana. noun. **1.** The dried eye mucus generated after yawning with boredom for a long time. **2.** Lagranagra.

lagraner. noun. **1.** A viscous mucus on the conjunctiva that blurs the vision. *Informal.* **2.** The giant, granulose and sticky eye booger that blocks the vision. It generally refers to alcoholics with chronic conjunctivitis after a drinking spree. **3.** f. Lacustrane. **4.** Lagagnord.

laguthra. noun. *Psychology.* **1.** Occasional traits or behaviors that do not match one's personality. *Informal.* **2.** An elderly woman who openly displays the holes in her personality. **3.** Lagutrona.

lampade. verb. **1.** To open and close the eyes repeatedly. noun. **2.** Eyelidding.

lancefring. noun. *Literary.* The action of throwing a metaphorical arrow directed at the impossible.

lardathic. adjective. *Informal.* **1.** A fat, dirty and despicable person. **2.** Lardosious. **3.** Lardosebic.

larinity. noun. **1.** The quality or condition of long-lasting spouses who progressively resemble one another physically, particularly in advanced age. **2.** The quality or condition of long-lasting spouses whose habits and personalities become progressively similar. *Informal.* **3.** The state of husband and wife who look like brother and sister.

larion. noun. A mate, spouse, or partner selected due to the similarities to the person making the selection.

larpet. noun. **1.** A loud sound originating in the troposphere or stratosphere with the onomatopoeia of a grunt. *Informal.* **2.** A celestial sound that resembles a deity puffing or grunting. *Vulgar.* **3.** God's fart.

laruocholia. noun. **1.** Deep sadness after the presence of a ghost is no longer perceived. **2.** A feeling of gloom after a familiar ghost has departed a home.

laruoloquy. noun. A dialog with a ghost.

latrappa. noun. An annoying passive-aggressive pestering person.

laudophile. adjective. *Archaic.* Having a predisposition to abuse intoxicating substances.

laughincle. noun. Laughter from an unknown person that is irritating, but becomes contagious when said person becomes an acquaintance or a friend.

laxamanic. noun. **1.** A person who uses laxatives periodically as prevention or treatment of intestinal conditions. *Psychology.* **2.** An obsessive person who uses laxatives periodically to cure diseases outside the digestive tract.

leetost. noun. (from *litost* in Czech). **1.** Feeling of humiliation and despair at the sight of one's own miseries. **2.** Feeling of humiliation or ineptitude when someone mentions his or her accomplishments.

legalophobia. noun. *Psychology.* **1.** Extreme aversion to lawyers. **2.** Irrational fear of dealing or having to do with anything of a legal nature. *Ethics.* **3.** Justified hatred and disgust when dealing with lawyers or legalities of any nature. **4.** Abhorrence of dealing with bureaucracy. *Medicine.* **5.** Acute or chronic hypersensitivity to anything of legal nature.

legridy. noun. **1.** Ambition without knowledge. **2.** Luftmench.*

leilihood. noun. **1.** A stage of life between babyhood and childhood. **2.** An undefined period of life that occurs between lactation and the development of verbal skills. **3.** A stage of life in which a pre-lingual child, barely ambulatory, screams bloody murder to get out of the stroller for no reason apparent to anyone watching. **4.** Babylescence.

lentixore. noun. *History.* Cruel torture that consists of flaying consecutively defined and discrete areas of the body over long periods of time.

leptolargia. noun. Superficial lethargy.

leptolecticy. noun. A false hope of a medium- or long-term future success. For example the cryopreservation of someone's head and body.

leuscurity. noun. Quality of the momentary luminous blindness that happens after looking at a potent light source.

levibrach. verb. To make a sign by moving the left arm.

levinatitude. noun. *Philosophy.* **1.** The condition of being nonexistent before and after a life. **2.** The unbearable unbecoming of what is or what exists.

levobardic. adjective. **1.** Utilizing poetic rhetoric or a comic narrative to get out of a predicament. noun. **2.** A weefrond* rhymer.

lexestipia. noun. Frequent use of strong, metallic, hurtful words in spoken or written communication.

leximortization. noun. *Law.* **1.** Legal and lexical redefinition of the term 'amortization' to the more appropriate term mortization* that returned the definition of 'amortization' to its original etymological origin from Middle English: in the senses 'deaden' and transfer (land) to a corporation in mortmain. Related to *mortgage*, meaning literally, *dead pledge. Law.* **2.** Law that evolved from the crimortization* movement. *Linguistics.* **3.** A study that led to the replacement of the term 'amortization' with 'mortization',* meaning disguised fraudulent usury by a corporation. *Economics.* **4.** Revealing a madage.* **5.** Full disclosure of a swindilism.*

lexinary. noun. *Literature.* **1.** A book that lists and defines in alphabetical order the innominate words of a language. **2.** *Lexicography.* A dictionary of the ineffable. *Linguistics.* **3.** A reference book or electronic resource that lists nonexistent words of a language (in alphabetical order) and gives their meaning. **4.** A reference source in print or electronic form containing alphabetically arranged nonexistent words of particular subjects or disciplines in a language along with their meaning or alternative words.

lexitosious. noun. **1.** A person without talent that does not recuperate from a success and broadcasts said success. **2.** Someone who relives and embellishes with exaggeration some past achievement or feat for a long time after the event. **3.** Famaniac. **4.** Mythoximic.

libelbitch. noun. *Vulgar.* **1.** A person who slanders someone with affectation. **2.** A woman committing dramaviraggy.*

libetation. noun. **1.** The act of inflicting pain or suffering to a loved one. **2.** The ease with which someone can inflict suffering on a loved one. **3.** The act of hurting a loved person with iscariotism.*

libidiphage. noun. A libidinous person whose sexual prowess dwindles immediately before an orgasm.

lifule. noun. A sensation of movement in the bone marrow.

lignophagous. adjective. *Biology.* Pertaining to animal species that feed on wood but have no taxonomical relationship to xylophagous insects.

limagdation. noun. *Psychology.* **1.** A feeling of guilt without repentance. **2.** A feeling of having done something wrong, illegal or immoral or having failed to carry out an obligation without any sincere feeling of regret or remorse. **3.** Phantom iscariotism.*

lingeric. adjective. **1.** Spending more time than necessary in an activity. **2.** Staying in a place longer than necessary. **3.** Remaining in the same static position or persistently passive. **4.** Spending more time than necessary doing nothing. **5.** Wearing lingerie of the opposite sex.

lingualism. noun. *Philosophy.* **1.** Philosophical theory that promotes the deceleration of the rate of evolution of a language. *Linguistics.* **2.** A theory that proposes to preserve a language without any alterations over time. **3.** The purpose behind the theory to circumvent communication discrepancies among people from different geographical regions. **4.** The purpose behind the theory to facilitate posterity's comprehension of contemporaneous cultural, artistic, scientific, and historical records.

lipeiatrist. noun. *Medicine.* **1.** A physician specializing in sadness. *Psychology.* **2.** A professional therapist specializing in depressive personality disorders.

lipetic. adjective. **1.** Suddenly feeling fat and ugly. adverb. **2.** Antically. noun. **3.** Mesenty.

lipocian. noun. Quality of an inferior ice cream from a fast food restaurant franchise.

lipocrinkle. noun. **1.** The irregular and crenate aspect of skin with cellulitis. **2.** The wavering and gelatinous aspect of the skin in an obese person. **3.** The after-effects of liposuction. **4.** Lipocrough.

lipodomial. noun. The bloated abdominal fatness that gives a certain distinction to older people.

lipomio. noun. Dense smoke, irritating to the eyes and with a bitter smell, that emanates from burning human fat.

lipophagous. adjective. **1.** Feeding on fat. noun. **2.** A person who eats fat or greasy food exclusively. **3.** A customer at a fast food restaurant franchise.

liquitang. verb. **1.** To imagine that something intangible is converted into a liquid. noun. *Literary.* **2.** The love of an unfaithful partner for his or her lover.

litholiatry. noun. The study of fossilized physicians by an archeologist in the distant future.

livic. noun. **1.** A woman's expression of doubt and frustration when selecting which clothes to wear. **2.** Duplatic* and redubilant* expression of a woman during a livision.*

livision. noun. Anguishing daily feminine incertitude provoked by the selection of clothes to wear.

locusprious. adjective. **1.** Having an extremely boring manner of speaking. **2.** Having the ability of inducing somnolence in those listening.

logislegium. noun. *Law.* Simplification of all laws through logic and common sense in every legal aspect that liberates people from the time and costs entailed in maintaining, needing, and serving legislators and lawyers.

loog. noun. **1.** A person walking with slippers who emits a loud sound with each step. **2.** Exaggerated noise slippers produce during ambulation despite the soft materials used in their manufacturing. **3.** Ambulant dysbeeper.* **4.** A dysbeep* emitted by an enslipper.*

lucifarim. noun. **1.** A memory that functions as a trigger for all remembrances to arise. **2.** A sad memory that prompts an explosion of other associated memories, creating psychological trauma in the person attempting to re-remember the remaining recollections.

ludescivia. noun. Morbid pleasure someone experiences when toying effectively with the lust of others.

luffonian. adjective. Suffocating an illusion with sophistication.

luftmench. noun. (from *luftmensch* in Yiddish). **1.** Ambition without a clue. **2.** A dreamer devoid of practicality. **3.** An entrepreneur without a reasonable business plan and with no sense of reality. **4.** An impractical, contemplative person with no business or income.

luprenate. verb. To lubricate mucosae with non-oleaginous materials, generally during sexual relations.

luprenation. noun. **1.** Lubrication using non-oily substances. **2.** Action and effect of luprenate.*

luvertisch. adjective. **1.** Experiencing sustained dizziness after a fleeting episode of vertigo. noun. **2.** The feeling of disorientation and dizziness when recovering from fainting. **3.** Perlipothymy.

lymphphagous. adjective. **1.** Feeding on lymph. **2.** Consuming and drying out the

lymphatic system and paralyzing
the immune system of the host.
noun. **3.** A group of infectious
microorganisms that consume
or have affinity for vertebrate
lymph.

M

mabalon. noun. *Literature.* A mangrove where human shoots emerge, and briefly gasp fresh air and respite from their disincentivized, task-inundated briny life. **2.** Man-aspide.*

macahuate. noun. *Botany.* A gynodioecious tree from eastern México, family Laureacae, of 12 to 15 meters in height that bears a globular fruit named *ahuacate,* which is sweeter than the *aguacate* or avocado.

macastidity. noun. **1.** A fixed expression of mixed surprise and concentration, with eyes wide open and mouth half open, made by a woman when applying makeup before a mirror. **2.** Frozen apprastide.*

macilate. verb. **1.** To pulverize a solid metal. **2.** To mill something considered unbreakable.

macrima. noun. A tear shed by a man who sees a woman decades younger than him seductively undress during a striptease show.

madage. noun. *Law.* **1.** Disguised fraudulent usury by a corporation. **2.** Mortization.* **3.** Swindilism.*

madrage. noun. *Zoology.* **1.** A lamellibrach mollusk that inhabits the semitropical American coasts, has an ellipsoidal shell and is of delicate flavor. **2.** Madredage.

madroog. noun. **1.** Time interval post-midnight and before dawn. **2.** Matinade. verb. **3.** To wake up at dawn or very early.

magdalia. noun. **1.** The combined facial features following crying. **2.** A tired and sad woman with swollen eyelids and red nose after crying for a long time.

magnatron. noun. *Physics.* **1.** The largest of all cyclotron apparatuses in which both waves and subatomic particles are transformed into one another. *Informal.* **2.** Self-perception of an egocentric person.

magnefic. adjective. **1.** Causing harm or destruction with magnets. **2.** Performing magnetic bewitchment.

malfigure. verb. **1.** To assume something bad or negative about something. **2.** To form negative impressions about someone before knowing them.

malforbion. noun. An expression of arrogance, resembling smelling something fetid, on seeing someone or something perceived as inferior or of little value.

malihda. noun. **1.** A beautiful woman who flirts with an unappealing man for fun. **2.** An attractive woman who premeditatedly and with arrebocy* flirts with an unattractive man. **3.** Sarcastic hermeflirter. **4.** Sadistic crypterotan.

malleate. verb. *Physics.* **1.** To mold or manipulate something without changing form or behavior. *Psychology.* **2.** To mold or manipulate someone without changing his or her form or behavior.

mallugate. verb. **1.** To inflict a constant and long-term contusion on someone. **2.** To bruise someone consistently, uninterruptedly and excessively.

malude. noun. **1.** The state of an organic being with illness or injury. **2.** The state of a being with various of its functions working abnormally. **3.** Null

health. **4.** Multiaffection. **5.** Hadosanity. **6.** Rugradia.

malvion. noun. A creation against the regular order of nature.

mampinat. noun. (from *mamihlapinatapei* in Yagan). The look shared by two people who both desire to initiate something but are both reluctant to start.

manifeast. noun. A text written by a man with a fair amount of free time that, because of its superficial nature, seems to have been composed in between parties.

manocup. noun. Mannerism of respect or reverential thanks among Mexicans that consists of placing a semi-bent hand in a concave shape with the fingers together at the height of one's head, palm facing the head; the whole hand is shaken once without moving fingers or wrist.

manoptic. adjective. **1.** Capable of detecting pressure with sight. noun. **2.** A person with the ability to detect pressure differentials with sight. *Psychology.* **3.** A person who can immediately detect the pressure between two or more people.

maragonya. noun. A messy verbal imbroglio among several people.

marasa. noun. A depressive feeling when knowing

intuitively one is at the brink of discovering something important but the process is slowed down and critiqued by others.

marmoss. noun. **1.** A muffled grunt, sigh, or complaint of a person with a respiratory ailment. *Informal.* **2.** A grumpy old man suffering from allergies or asthma whose grunts and complaints seem as sounds coming from underwater.

marrowmeter. noun. An instrument to measure the distance between the bone marrow and a point in the skin.

marrut. noun. A man or a woman who when speaking sounds like a low-pitched purr.

marsupiation. noun. Formation of an abdominal pouch in some people.

marthera. noun. A woman who has sexual relationships with her sister's husband, boyfriend, fiancée, or lover.

martyrologist. noun. A writer of fictitious or non-fictitious biographies of martyrs.

martyrology. noun. *Psychology.* A branch of psychology that studies the motivations and psychological aberrations of those who suffer and die for a cause, conviction, or belief.

marvelation. noun. **1.** Astonishment when finding a hitherto unknown talent or attribute one possesses. **2.** Amazement after performing a feat one was unaware of being capable of. **3.** Maravillation.

masiosenous. adjective. **1.** Having big breasts. noun. **2.** A masort* man. *Informal.* **3.** A friendly insult between male friends.

masobarite. noun. **1.** An ascetic sybarite. *Psychology.* **2.** Personality disorder characterized by the doubly morbid voluptuary anchorite.

masochine. verb. To masochistically endure someone's actions for the benefit of others.

masogomorrism. noun. *Psychology.* Morbid sexual tendency of someone deriving pleasure from being humiliated or receiving pain during a homosexual orgy.

masogomorrist. noun. A promiscuous homosexual masochist man who frequents gomorrisades.*

masort. noun. **1.** An overweight yet muscular man with female breasts. **2.** An obese, senuous* and solid man. **3.** A man with jelloid* breasts.

massetetion. noun. **1.** Set of affected facial movements that, when listening to someone, occur occasionally as a nervous reaction or imitation of the person who is speaking. **2.** Affected imitation of the facial movements of a speaker of certain authority or celebrity.

mastuous. noun. **1.** A person with large teeth. adjective. *Informal.* **2.** Appearing to have dominos instead of teeth.

matrack. verb. To immobilize someone with a punch or a strike.

matterer. noun. **1.** A person who feels or expresses doubt, raises objections or questions a matter. **2.** A poshenmush* of doubt.

maxoficulty. noun. A feeling of impotency a person experiences on realizing that carrying out a task is very difficult or impossible, but in reality said person is capable of doing it with dexterity and without any difficulty or effort.

mecorrhea. noun. Explosive diarrhea in a baby or an infant that gushes outside a diaper resembling a leak of radioactive plutonium.

medagra. noun. Foul smell from the proximal portion of the ear's lobule.

medicass. noun. **1.** A physician specializing in terminal gastrointestinal diseases. **2.** Mediculist. **3.** Proctologist.

mediocrit. verb. To do something incorrectly or partially due to indifference or revenge.

mediocritate. verb. *Politics.* **1.** To reduce the quality and quantity of pre-university studies to diminish the educational level of a population and facilitate its control. **2.** To citizenate.* **3.** To decrease the salaries of pre-university teachers to promote their departure and encourage the hiring of dozetachers* in a region.

medullic. noun. **1.** A person with the capability of rapidly reaching the core of a matter, interrogative or problematic. adjective. **2.** Utilizing intelligence to the utmost and swiftly.

mefroluct. adjective. **1.** Interpreting body language in the absence of any apparent movement or clue. **2.** Deciphering imparlated* or sign-less communications.

megafausic. adjective. Having an excessively large snout.

megafrolic. noun. *Informal.* **1.** A crowded party or a gathering in a small establishment or room filled with tobacco and marihuana smoke, strident music, shouted conversations, and there is great consumption of alcohol and other intoxicating substances. **2.** Megalecera. **3.** Conrave. **4.** Soiréecide.

megamordence. noun. **1.** A long-term mental repetition of acts that someone wishes not to have committed. **2.** Chronic hypermordence.* *Psychology.* **3.** Intense mental playback and repentance for long periods of time that decreases concentration and interferes with memory. **4.** Continuous remembrances of a remorseful act that produces an indefinable pain in indefinable parts of the body.

melanary. adjective. Feigning a profound sadness or a deep sorrow.

melandoze. noun. **1.** A sadness that awakens when sleeping. **2.** Sadness that is exacerbated when lying down. **3.** Melancoliquenia.

melanimous. noun. *Zoology.* **1.** A Caucasian person with high concentrations of melanin in the skin. *Informal.* **2.** A black white. **3.** *Derogatory.* A white negro.

melasnot. noun. **1.** Black phlegm. *Medicine.* **2.** Melanophlegm. *Informal.* **3.** Dark buggers.

melation. noun. Cloying speech a husband utters to his angry wife who is upset for reasons he is unaware of.

melature. noun. *Literary.* One of the jowls of time.

melineous. noun. *Music.* A combination of sounds and melodious tones in the mind of a composer that do not have any analogue to the human ear and thus cannot be played or emulated by any instrument or cybernetic program invented yet.

melitoric. adjective. Speaking slowly in a monotonous tone of voice with long pauses about something not interesting.

mellibred. adjective. Having the flavor of rotten honey.

mellihesion. noun. Action and effect of slowly gathering together or adhering things together.

melotello. noun. *Music.* A person who composes songs about himself or herself.

memomedoric. noun. **1.** Someone who moves memories from one place to another. adjective. **2.** Remembering moments of one's life with no chronological coherence.

memortella. noun. A disagreeable memory one wants to forget but recycles endlessly, very loudly and clearly, causing mortification.

mencoleck. noun. (from *mencolek* in Indonesian meaning to tap someone lightly on the shoulder from behind and leaning on the opposite shoulder to fool them). A purposeless deception.

mengark. verb. **1.** To make efforts to tear a mental phlegm from one's mind. **2.** To cough inwardly in an attempt to clear a phantom phlegm after a tedious religious or political meeting.

menimung. noun. *Informal.* **1.** A person blamed for infecting the stump of an amputee who has to extend the length of the amputation as a result. **2.** A person blamed for causing an extension of an amputation.

menocrople. adjective. Maintaining false hopes for humanity with assurance.

mensalogy. noun. A study of the extraordinary mental abilities that sometimes are concomitant to mental illnesses or follow a cerebral trauma (such as exceptional photographic memory or rapid complex calculations), geared toward understanding their mechanisms and safe application in people not similarly afflicted.

menstrubation. 1. noun. Unexpectedly abundant menstruation. **2.** Surprising and massive menstruation that emotionally catarumbs* the mood of a woman and sometimes leads to mentalgia.*

mentalgia. noun. **1.** A generalized, persistent pain that is difficult to pinpoint and that alters the function of body and mental processes. **2.** (in men) A persistent inscrotum* that spreads throughout the body.

mentamble. adjective. *Literary.* **1.** Ambling slowly through mental labyrinths while dragging neurons with harsh ideas. *Informal.* **2.** Mental rambling.

mentapress. verb. *Literary.* **1.** To conceive an idea and to tighten it with virtual hands as to not let it go. **2.** To be stubborn. **3.** To be obstinate.

mentazoic. adjective. Having the ability to frighten the mind.

mentinous. noun. **1.** A compulsive liar with poor memory. **2.** A person with faulty memory who tends to lie and whose lies are frequently discovered because he or she cannot remember what the lie was about.

mercagloomness. noun. A slight feeling of helplessness when accidentally seeing an object in a store for sale at a lower price than one purchased earlier at a higher price after spending considerable time searching for the object's most competitive price.

meresion. noun. **1.** Action and effect of being in the center of the now, being simple, pure, and uncontaminated. **2.** A state of what is obvious and hence, considered unimportant or insignificant.

meretricle. noun. **1.** A man who lures women into prostitution and keeps a proportion of their earnings for protection purposes. *Informal.* **2.** A luring pimp. **3.** Proxeneit.

mergebrid. verb. **1.** To combine two different biological entities into one. **2.** To biomalgam. **3.** To biointegrate. **4.** Chimerabridization.

merition. noun. **1.** A collection of potential ideas that as a whole could be meritorious of fame and fortune. **2.** A patent application revoked for being submitted slightly later than a similar, yet inferior, patent application.

mesenult. noun. **1.** A person who suddenly realizes he or she has gained weight. **2.** A person who suddenly feels that he or she is indeed fat.

mesognosis. adjective. **1.** Refuting anything artistic or intellectual. **2.** Valuing indistinctly the excellent from the mediocre. noun. **3.** Incapability to distinguish a fine piece of art from a knickknack.

mestec. verb. *Theology.* **1.** To wander godlessly through the labyrinths of thought. *Philosophy.* **2.** To prowl through alleys of thoughts miditatively.*

mestoclasia. noun. Unethical arrogance.

metabrasion. noun. *Physics.* **1.** The process of scraping or wearing away at a distance or by immaterial heating. *Psychology.* **2.** A consuming passion felt for a person not known personally.

metaceive. verb. **1.** To perceive without the use of the senses. **2.** To ider.*

metaceptive. adjective. **1.** Possessing the capability to perceive without the senses. **2.** Having the virtue of perceiving external sensations or metadimensional* information without the use of the five senses. noun. **3.** Someone with the capability to ider* or metaceive.*

metachrony. noun. Beyond the perceived frontiers of time.

metacrastination. noun. Unilateral decision to postpone something indefinitely.

metactate. verb. To establish direct contact with something or someone in an intangible manner.

metatactile. adjective. **1.** Caressing one's own skin lasciviously to become sexually aroused. **2.** Self-siriciri.*

metadauphism. noun. **1.** Related to brothers or sisters with no biological or adoptive ties. **2.** Bloodless kinship.

metadimensional. noun. **1.** Beyond the perceived dimensions. **2.** Beyond the known and unknown dimensions.

metaduce. verb. **1.** To obtain matter and antimatter from quantum energy. **2.** To deduce after perceiving or absorbing metadimensional* or metachronial* information.

metaetaneous. adjective. **1.** Having the same age after a time. **2.** Having the same age while being from different times. **3.** Another term for metaeval.

metafetist. noun. A person who attempts to provoke a strong emotional impact on others from a long distance.

metalligence. noun. **1.** Beyond the capacity for simply acquiring, understanding, and applying knowledge and skills. **2.** Above and beyond the ability to 'read between the lines.' **3.** A capability to intellige far above all known intelligence levels.

metalogue. noun. A section in a book that is written outside the text as a commentary.

metalucidate. verb. **1.** To elucidate effectively what is beyond the third dimension. **2.** To explain efficiently and logically adimensional, paradimensional,* transdimensional,* achronical,* multidimensional and metadimensional* topics to three-dimensional beings.

metametate. noun. A Mexican flat stone for grinding grains that exceeds the size of ordinary *metates.*

metametry. noun. **1.** The joint branch of physics, mathematics, and philosophy concerned with the properties and relations of everything in higher dimensional analogues. **2.** Extradimensional polymetry.

metanution. noun. Presentiment of an exaggerated presumption in another person.

metaordinary. adjective. Pertaining to or relative to what is beyond extraordinary.

metapathy. noun. A group of physical attributes, tones of voice, gestures, and character that make a person very attractive to others.

metapraxia. noun. **1.** Incapability of voluntary movement when outside oneself. **2.** The failure of a traveling astral body to command movements in the physical body it has left behind.

metapursic. adjective. Having a body posture in the shape of a purse, generally due to unknown causes.

metariger. adjective. **1.** Someone who manages and counsels from another time or dimension. **2.** Someone who guides others through paradimensions* or achrony.* **3.** A person who leads others in dyschrony.

metastrophe. noun. A sudden event of immense proportion and magnitude that causes global damage and leaves long-lasting geological scars.

metasubmission. noun. **1.** An exaggerated submission from an insecure person. **2.** A surrender to a metariger.* **3.** The acquiescence of someone who is outside of his or her own time. **4.** The inevitable capitulation to oneself when in achrony* or transdimensionality.* *Psychology.* **5.** A drastic surrender when out of tune with reality. *Communications.* **6.** A submission carried out remotely.

metasummation. noun. Action and effect of carrying out all tasks that are linked to one another.

metaxist. verb. *Physics.* **1.** To augment the extension of a place through time. adjective. **2.** Existing beyond one's own physical life. noun. **3.** A life lengthened adventitiously.

Philosophy. **4.** The condition of what is or exists beyond the barriers of time or dimension. *Psychology.* **5.** The feeling of existing in a body, a place, or a time not considered our own. *Informal.* **6.** A taxi driver in a family-operated taxi company attempting to join a union despite the pleas from family members not to do so.

metenmemory. noun. **1.** A collection of human remembrances buried in or behind time. **2.** A transmigration of a memory from the distant past to the present. **3.** A transmigration of a memory from the present to the future.

metentrem. noun. **1.** A moment, event, or circumstance that is suddenly remembered without any apparent stimulus. *Medicine.* **2.** A sudden and desperate anal pruritus.

meteorize. verb. **1.** To spread a secret, or secrets, in a vertiginous manner. *Medicine.* **2.** To inflate areas of the gastrointestinal tract with a gas or air.

microtone. noun. *Music.* The shortest and highest-pitch note of all musical tones. **2.** The smallest note in sheet music.

mictum. noun. **1.** A stench emanating from a men's bathroom. **2.** A pungent olfactory hall of a urinal hell. **3.** A far-reaching mingodor.*

micuspic. adjective. **1.** Rejecting or inhibiting any sexual desire or arousal. noun. **2.** Erotersion.*

midhalved. adjective. *Archaic.* **1.** Being or occurring in the middle of a half and a quarter. **2.** Medimitamedium. **3.** Midmedium.*

midiconscience. *Sociology.* noun. **1.** A common thought or social norm. **2.** Human herd thought.

miditative. adjective. **1.** Being half involved or half absorbed in meditation. noun. **2.** A person who meditates partially.

midmedium. adjective. *Archaic.* **1.** Happening or being exactly halfway between one half and one quarter. **2.** Midhalved.*

mignitude. noun. **1.** The insignificant smallness of something. **2.** The minuscule importance of something. *Mathematics.* **3.** A numerical quantity of minimal value. *Astronomy.* **4.** A measurement expressed as a negative logarithm of size standardized to a neocosmic* constant.

mignius. noun. *Military.* **1.** Contemptuous treatment of a low-grade army recruit. **2.** Mineo.

millenite. verb. **1.** To play with numbers that have four or more digits. noun. *Mathematics.* **2.** A playful arithmetic teaching method.

mimetise. verb. **1.** To describe the character, qualities and attributes of another person using mimicry. **2.** To perform as a mime.

mimicentric. adjective. **1.** Attempt at centric imitation by anything peripheral. **2.** Centric imitation by anything peripheral that acquires a central structure, development, or a uniform panorama.

mingodor. noun. **1.** Pungent stench of fresh, old, or dried urine in public men's bathrooms. **2.** Mictum.*

minoctery. noun. *Medicine.* **1.** A hereditary condition characterized by a decline in fertility and sexual activity in young adulthood. **2.** Premature climacteric and menopausal appearance in young adults.

minuscabism. noun. *Commerce.* **1.** Literary tendency consisting of unrefined, simplistic narrative with no innovations that began in the twentieth century, promoted by large publishing houses with the objective of mass sales and short-term profits. **2.** Platitudism.* **3.** Delicuescence.

minuslation. noun. *Psychology.* Mental acrobatics by a mentally challenged person.

minutics. noun. **1.** The make-believe fight of children using the tips of the fingers. **2.** A gentle striking with the fingers a child receives from other children for losing a game.

miragio. noun. *Optics.* **1.** An optical illusion, which cause is other than the reflection of light when passing layers of air of different densities. *Philosophy.* **2.** An unreality of the real. *Literary.* **3.** A real unreality. **4.** The scary believability of a fictional work. *Politics.* **5.** The electoral process.

miramuerial. adjective. **1.** Precipitating death when being looked at. **2.** Ocumortis. **3.** Lookndie.

miristasia. noun. *Music.* **1.** Music of exceptional fidelity that is heard after long periods of sleeplessness. *Psychology.* **2.** Musical illusion transformed into virtual hallucinations during long bouts of insomnia or lengthy periods of anxiety-driven sleeplessness. **3.** Cancatic.

misaccomplice. adjective. Supporting a party, doctrine, or opinion of someone solely because of hatred of the opponent.

misandrope. noun. A homosexual man who hates men.

misantellist. adjective. Displaying hostility against intellectuals.

misasentic. adjective. **1.** Displaying hate toward anything promoting common sense. **2.** Showing intense dislike towards a person with common sense. **3.** Exhibiting discontent towards a person who is requesting use of logic or demanding common sense.

misastronomer. noun. **1.** A person who invalidates the belief in the influence that one or various stars, situated randomly millions and billions of kilometers between them and between them and the Earth, may have on the psychology or the destiny of one or more human beings. **2.** A person loathed by astrologers and horoscope followers.

misgalt. noun. **1.** The last defensive recourse that some prostrated mammals adopt. **2.** The ultimate opposing posture of a mammal, consisting of using the four limbs and the snout as both shield and weapons when about to be killed.

misogynecosis. noun. *Psychology.* **1.** A condition of a womanizing man who expresses his hate toward women by engaging in numerous fleeting and casual sexual relations. **2.** A neurosis in an effeminate man who expresses his hate of being thought effeminate by engaging in numerous fleeting and casual sexual relations with women. **3.** Filaninfatitis.

mistrovert. adjective. Being neither an extrovert or an introvert.

mistructor. noun. A person who opposes any new construction.

misvelia. verb. **1.** To pernoctate with neither purpose nor insomnia. **2.** To spend a sleepless night for no reason.

misvivole. noun. **1.** A person who opposes anything artificial. **2.** A person who opposes anything related to a civilization. **3.** Pronatural survivalist.

miyerdation. noun. *Commerce.* **1.** A phenomenon derived from prostimusism* by which, to achieve success, a female singer must dress seductively, move enticingly, and dance imitating coital movements. **2.** Prostimusism.* **3.** Prostitutional entertainment marketing.

mnemogoga. noun. **1.** A gathering or a meeting of memories. **2.** A virtual place

where a mnemogogation* occurs.

mnemogogation. noun. Conglomeration of memories.

mnephagon. noun. **1.** A person who bites and swallows his or her own ideas and believes them. **2.** A person at the moment of conceiving a schanpsid.*

mokitt. noun. (from *mokita* in Kivila). **1.** The truth everyone knows but no one talks about. **2.** Etymlick.

molluskad. noun. **1.** A solid substance resembling a mollusk. **2.** The body of a vertebrate that resembles a mollusk.

monohomonism. noun. *Anthropology.* **1.** A theory that rejects the existence of diverse species of the genus *Homo* on the planet in the last 100,000 years. **2.** A theory that confirms, based on archeological findings and their corresponding DNA sequences, the existence of at least twelve *Homo sapiens* subspecies or populations in the last 200,000 years, and thus rejects the notion that *Homo neanderthalensis, Homo floresiensis, Homo erectus, Homo heidelbergensis* and *Homo sapiens,* among others, were independent species of the genus *Homo* in this period, but rather a single species that, when interbreeding, produced fertile offspring.

monoloquy. noun. **1.** A tedious monologue that the speaker assumes is a conversation, disregarding any of the hearers. **2.** Soliloquy of one person during a conversation between two or more people.

moralty. noun. **1.** Exaggeration of a moral code to a point deserving of ridicule. **2.** Overt exaggeration of morality that is perceived as normal in a well indoctrinated society.

morbifest. noun. **1.** Inexplicable increase, worsening, or exacerbation of diseases during weekends and holidays. **2.** Unfathomable increase in the number of patients in need of a physician when most physicians are off duty. **3.** Baffling worsening of a disease in a patient during weekends or holidays when the treating physician has days off.

morbostupor. noun. **1.** Postcoital lethargy. **2.** A sluggishness and sleepiness experienced after copulation.

morla. noun. The tenacity and courage to carry out disagreeable tasks without complaint.

morniation. noun. **1.** Action and effect to be in mourning for someone not loved who has died. **2.** Dranduelo.*

morpery. noun. *Psychology.* **1.** An extreme feeling of despair where death is seen as the only possible option. *Literary.* **2.** A depressing state where reality is hopeless and death is the only hope.

morphosic. verb. *Phonetics.* **1.** To emit a sound pretending it to be a properly articulated word. **2.** To imitate sober mannerisms and tones of voice when heavily inebriated.

morponian. noun. A person who is anxious after making strenuous yet futile efforts to get rid of dirty thoughts.

mortization. noun. *Economics.* **1.** New term that replaces amortization and is defined as a manner to mortify someone chronically by perpetuating a debt, demanding and implementing minimum payment towards the capital and maximum payment to the interest. *Law.* **2.** Action and effect of a legal fraud. **3.** Crimortization.* **4.** Madage.* *Linguistics.* **5.** Leximortization.*

movistatic. adjective. Unmoving traffic that is supposed to circulate.

mucoserosion. noun. *Medicine.* A long and painful disease characterized by slow erosion of mucosae, which eventually ends as a dry membrane prior to the patient's death.

muepardious. adjective. Showing sudden good manners when habitually displaying despicable manners and foul language.

mujagra. noun. *Informal.* **1.** A woman over fifty years of age who delivers a baby for the first time. *Medicine.* **2.** Aging primigest. **3.** Analita.

multigress. noun. **1.** Persistent habit of changing subjects, unrelated to one another, in speech or writing. **2.** Incapacity to maintain one subject in a conversation or text. **3.** Habitual digresser.

multihomonism. noun. *Anthropology.* **1.** A theory that confirms the recent existence of diverse species of the genus *Homo* on the planet. **2.** A theory that supports the multispeciation of the genus *Homo* and confirms, based on archeological findings and their corresponding DNA sequences, the existence of at least twelve *Homo* species in the last 100,000 years and thus rejecting the notion that *Homo neanderthalensis, Homo floresiensis, Homo heidelbergensis* and *Homo sapiens* were the only representative

species of the genus *Homo* in this period.

multimonochromatic. noun. *Optics.* **1.** A property of something that contains multiple colors that suddenly is seen as having only one color. **2.** Greysity.*

multinent. noun. *Geography.* An arbitrary taxonomic union of two or more continents into one.

multipute. verb. *Psychology.* **1.** To give oneself multiple options or possibilities to consider. *Commerce.* **2.** To give people multiple options or choices to consider when purchasing something. **3.** To confuse consumers with multiple options of products that differ little in nature or price. **4.** To dischite.

multiseptic. adjective. Harboring numerous and different species of germs.

multisiration. noun. Consideration, urbanity and respect to all things, animals and people.

multiturny. noun. **1.** A period of non-parametric adversities that, without apparent cause, are followed by new tragedies. **2.** Occurrence of serial or simultaneous disasters and catastrophes.

mumblous. adjective. *Phonetics.* **1.** Speaking indistinguishable words. *Psychology.* **2.** Articulating unintelligible words. **3.** Morphosic.*

murdic. adjective. Speaking morbidly in such a manner to incite others to morbidity.

murgoya. noun. *Informal.* **1.** A woman denigrated for her aggressiveness, intelligence, and insolence. **2.** A woman rejected from some social circles for being unprudrish,* smart, and assertive.

murgrah. noun. Greasy biological refuse in decomposition used for cooking purposes.

museurish. adjective. Resembling a museum in size, furniture, illumination, level of noise and overall ambiance.

musicoven. noun. **1.** Tune or portion of a melody that is repeated insistently in the mind. **2.** A segment of a hated melody that is faithfully reproduced in one's brain and is impossible to stop.

musiscent. adjective. *Acoustics.* **1.** A natural or artificial sound or sounds that resemble music. *Music.* **2.** A collection of words that when heard or read in the intended order give the impression of a musical melody.

musistial. noun. *Music.* **1.** Beautiful musical piece that is played in the mind and is suddenly lost without being able to evoke it again. **2.** Admirable and complex musical composition, of apparent divine origin, that plays swiftly in the mind and is impossible to reproduce.

mutaphony. noun. A monologue from a parent that a child does not listen to.

mutuasturtion. noun. **1.** Mutual, simultaneous masturbation between two people. **2.** Amphidactination.

mydrias. noun. A condition in which someone's pupils are in constant motion of dilation and contraction, and appear to vibrate in the process.

mydriation. noun. Dilation of the pupils without esthetic or erotic stimuli or without decreased luminosity.

myotauric. adjective. **1.** Having strong overdeveloped muscles. noun. *Informal.* **2.** A burly man, built like a bull. *Informal.* **3.** A burly homosexual man, built like a cow.

mythification. noun. **1.** The accreditation of a myth. **2.** A piece of fiction or a myth that, with sufficient levels of belief or credulity can be transformed into truth or fact. **3.** Religion.

mythocide. adjective. **1.** Obliterating a myth. noun. **2.** A doctoral candidate in a science. **3.** Mythiric.

mythopenia. noun. Action and effect of tearing out the faith from someone whose faith is based on a myth.

mythophorer. noun. **1.** A theorizer who links events or data with deductive jumps. **2.** A conspiracy theorist.

mythoporia. noun. **1.** Strategy to get the truth using logic as bait and serial questions as a rhetorical hook. **2.** Questioning methodology used by doctoral examiners and some lawyers. **3.** Inquiring technique that differs from Eimerichism* in not extracting lies with lies nor with torture.

mythoria. noun. **1.** The seemingly erudite speculation of an ignorant person. **2.** Theorization without knowledge or data with the illusory appearance of being rational or educated.

N

nacastid. adjective. **1.** Remembering something bigger than it actually was. noun. **2.** A place that is remembered as being bigger than its actual size. *Psychology.* **3.** A pathology characterized by the dramatization or exaggeration of recent memories, recalling them as if they happened during childhood.

nachryma. noun. **1.** A small tear that flows with difficulty, between complaints and negative answers, in small children when sent to bed at bedtime. **2.** Pseudotear.

nadism. noun. *Philosophy.* **1.** A philosophical theory or belief that all living beings come from nothingness and after death they return to being nothing. **2.** A philosophical theory that served as the basis of futilism.*

naphukmy. noun. *Botany.* A small plant originating from Babylon, *Ugliuos caca*, of the family Umbelipherositae, with a thick resin used by ancient physicians as a purgative.

nagall. noun. *Informal. Vulgar.* A rude insult with imprecise meaning.

nairk. noun. The annoying sound of a nail scratching a blackboard.

nanite. verb. **1.** To snap one's wrist repeatedly while keeping the thumb and middle finger together and letting the index finger slap into the linked thumb and middle finger so that a sound is produced. This maneuver is generally performed by a self-styled edgy person and accompanied by reiterating an expletive. noun. *Medicine.* **2.** Microscopic robot that carries out programmed tasks.

nanoparla. noun. A habit, peculiarity, or talent for speaking in short phrases or sentences.

naphritis. noun. *Medicine.* An infected, extremely painful open sore caused by constant rubbing.

narcogenic. noun. A talkative person with a monotonous voice and nothing new to say.

narigen. noun. *Genetics.* A human gene that codes for long and pointy noses.

narinish. noun. **1.** Imprecise area that includes the wings in the lower end of the nose and the narines. **2.** The shape of a hole.

nariosis. noun. *Medicine.* **1.** The overgrown, inflamed, edematous, granulomatous, red, bulbous, and varicose nose in certain men of advanced age. **2.** Rhinophyma. **3.** Rosacea.

naritruous. adjective. **1.** (of a person) Showing the nostrils clearly and grossly when seen from the front. **2.** Nososuid. **3.** Rhinoporcine. **4.** *Informal.* Pignose.

narraesthesia. noun. **1.** A narration in which the speaker uselessly attempts to engage listeners with affected displays of emotion. **2.** An extremely tedious and somnolent monologue with ripples of faked enthusiasm. **3.** An affected monologue.

nasoriate. verb. **1.** To inhale several times in short, hesitant breaths while moving the head in a reptilian manner to detect the type and source of an odor. **2.** To nostrilt. **3.** To esnout.*

natard. adjective. Legitimate, biological offspring unwanted before birth.

nateism. noun. *Philosophy.* A philosophical idea that judges the current concept of *nation* (i.e. a large aggregate of people united by common descent, history, culture or language inhabiting a particular territory) as retrograde and invalidates it for not being close to the contemporary reality of many countries in the world. The nateism defines each one of those commonalities more strictly and uses them as the bases to propose the establishment of small territories to be named *microterras*, inhabited by people with true commonalities, granted autonomy and self-governance, and monitored by a global counsel lacking judiciary and executive powers.

nateist. noun. A person who negates his or her link between place of birth, nationality, and allegiance to a nation.

natrichryme. noun. Tears that contain a high concentration of sodium and cannot stop flowing despite strong efforts to suppress their flow, in response to a feeling of guilt.

natriophyte. noun. *Botany.* **1.** A plant, a fungus, an alga, or a lichen that grows in environments with a high concentration of salt. **2.** A plant, an alga, or a fungus that grows in unfavorable conditions or in environments.

nauthian. noun. **1.** A married man who organizes gatherings with gadabout acquaintances in an establishment for the sole purpose of not being at home. **2.** A man who visits other people elsewhere, without amistation* or fisimity* for the sake of not staying at home.

nayscowler. noun. **1.** A person who says the word 'no' prior to any statement, phrase or response. **2.** Naysayer. **3.** Neparlained. **4.** A person who shakes his or her head negatively prior to voicing any statement, phrase, or response.

nebulouscence. noun. **1.** Disconcerting emotion when feeling a decrease or absence of the power of physical sensation. **2.** The state of being uncomfortably numb.

nemanima. noun. **1.** One of the seven steroids for the soul. **2.** An ethereal chemical that effervesces, suppresses, or influences mood and behavior.

nemastule. noun. A compartment in certain neurons where memories or parts of memories are stored.

nemoptosis. noun. The sudden collapse of memories into a nanoscopic black hole of the mind.

nemorrhoid. noun. **1.** A memory that triggers itching or painful discomfort when being recalled. verb. **2.** To realize that one's memories are bloody and wrinkled.

nemoscence. noun. **1.** The act of comprehending that one memory triggers other memories. **2.** A feeling of satisfaction when comprehending that one memory causes the remembrance of other memories. *Education.* **3.** An effective method of recollection by combination of techniques. *Informal.* **4.** Dismissal of memorization-by-repetition techniques and promoting a synthesis of information, mnemonics, and planning an explanation in order to comprehend the material just learned.

nemostringent. noun. **1.** A self-memory, or a memory transmitted telepathically or by other means, that triggers a sour and dry feeling in the mind. *Psychology.* **2.** A memory, self or otherwise, that provokes depression concomitant to emptying the mind of other ideas or memories.

nemovority. noun. Forcibly robbing someone's memory by artificial means.

nenegate. verb. To negate repeatedly by shaking the head from side to side without saying a word.

neobardism. noun. *Literature.* **1.** Literature movement originating in the early 21st century characterized by numerous, unorthodox innovations and use of unlimited lexical resources such as an abundance of neologisms, delirious metaphors, descriptions of the innominate, magical hyperrealism, paradoxical prose, thematic complexity and multiple linguistic strata. *Informal.* **2.** Heterodox poetry or prose read by few, understood by fewer and appreciated by even fewer people.

neobranchia. noun. *Genetics.* Formation of aqua-respiratory tissues and gills in humans subjected to genetic manipulation.

neochondria. noun. *Medicine.* **1.** Sudden, unexpected development of natural or artificial cartilages in an elderly person. *Politics.* **2.** Conservative, but flexible form of twenty-seventh century government that actively favored concentration of wealth and power to a few while maintaining full liberties for the people.

neocosmism. noun. *Astrophysics.* A novel vision of the non-observable cosmos that is represented as an assembly of multiple universes scattered within and between overlapping dimensions.

neodermia. noun. *Genetics.* Rejuvenated appearance of a person following regeneration of skin following genetic manipulation.

neoembryosis. noun. *Economics.* **1.** A business where a person can purchase the development and growth of one or more self-cloned embryos to harvest cells and organs for future organ transplantation or cellular reconstitution. *Medicine.* **2.** A condition of unknown etiology that causes recurrent miscarriages.

neoforalgia. noun. A pain that occurs unexpectedly and appears to come from the outside.

neoglosia. noun. *Linguistics.* **1.** Every contemporary language. **2.** A theory, proposed by studying the roots of tongues from earlier millennia, that all contemporary languages are derived from more than one common language. **3.** A simulated projection of an isolated colloquialism fast-forward into the future.

neographist. noun. **1.** A person who recently acquired a taste for writing. **2.** A new, older author.

neoinfectology. noun. *Medicine.* A group of medical disciplines which are in conformity with *the second germ theory of disease* and apply corresponding prevention and treatment regimens to chronic inflammatory diseases, autoimmune diseases and some degenerative conditions believed to be caused, ultimately, by infectious agents.

neolibidic. noun. *Medicine.* **1.** A collection of a new generation of drugs that selectively inhibit phosphodiesterase 3, phosphodiesterase 4, phosphodiesterase 5, phosphodiesterase 6, phosphodiesterase 9 and/ or phosphodiesterase 10A to augment male libido and sexual function while improving memory and cardiac function. *Informal.* **2.** The renewed horniness of an aging man with a new, young lover.

neomaniac. noun. *Psychology.* A person exhibiting new manias that are added to, in alternation with or replacements for manias already established.

neonespot. noun. A bureaucrat that favors in-law relatives for contracts, concessions, or public employment.

neophaguism. noun. *Nutrition.* A group of techniques for food production based on inorganic molecules.

neophile. noun. **1.** A person who has an affinity for or favors anything new. **2.** A person with a tendency to value or appreciate anything new without having any knowledge or appreciation of the past.

neumescadine. noun. *Chemistry.* **1.** Aliphatic amine produced after the degradation of some products. **2.** An acyclic amine generated from human refuse, which is the cause of the whef* malodor. *Informal.* **3.** The ultimate cause of the smell in stagnant air of tires, stale fish, post-coital penis, and thrown away sanitary towels.

neumoscent. adjective. **1.** Having an atmosphere constituted by an ethereal substance resembling air outside planet Earth. **2.** Breathable, air-like gases on the surface of a celestial body outside planet Earth.

neurolization. noun. **1.** Intra-neuronal and inter-neuronal processes considered to be the origin of memory, thought, and generation of ideas. *Cybernetics.*

2. A process of interconnecting chips to produce thought generation in computers.

neuropunitive. adjective. **1.** Pertaining to the negligent or insensitive actions of a rough neurosurgeon during surgery. noun. **2.** The feeling of being palpated or medicated by a rough neurologist.

nictolopathy. noun. **1.** An uncomfortable feeling of confusion and pain a patient experiences when awakening from a long sleep without feeling the disease any longer. **2.** Unease and confusion when awakening from a period of unconsciousness.

nictopathy. noun. *Informal.* **1.** Feeling of embarrassment after awakening from a drunken stupor **2.** Sleep chronorrhage.*

nictonymph. noun. A single woman addicted to nocturnal sexual relations.

nifee. noun. Each of the dimples that some young slender women have on each side of the lower back.

nifeelic. noun. **1.** A woman who experiences deep and long orgasms. **2.** A woman with nifees.*

nintaction. A feeling of frustration a worker experiences when realizing that the task not done is of higher priority than the tasks accomplished.

nipazz. noun. **1.** The silence that follows awakening. **2.** Disconcerting silence when the dream is over.

niplost. noun. **1.** Artificial or seemingly tranquil ambiance that precedes a catastrophe. **2.** Ephemeral silence that heralds an explosion. *Music.* **3.** The drop. *Cinematography.* **4.** Cinematographic technique consisting of affected inactivity, slow motion, or silence that anticipates a dramatic action sequence to provoke suspense and shock in the audience.

nistagmite. verb. To oscillate the eyeball spasmodically around their horizontal or vertical axis.

nistagolia. noun. Natural and pleasurable sensation of sleepiness provoked by being physically exhausted.

nistangle. noun. A person capable of sleeping standing up.

noncoholic. noun. An abstemious person who has never been or is not an alcoholic.

noseblast. noun. Burning one's nostril hairs and enduring the scorching smell afterwards, generally accidentally when lighting a match or a lighter close to one's face.

nostalbick. adjective. **1.** Following the doctrine that planet Earth is the universe. *Philosophy.* **2.** Believing that there is nothing else beyond the observable.

nostaphilia. noun. **1.** An intense yearning for a normal home or a normal family. **2.** A vehement desire to live in a home without fights.

nostardition. noun. **1.** A deep nostalgic feeling that causes physical pain. **2.** Caustic nostardition: The most severe of the nostalgias. **3.** An excruciating pain that seems to take the form of a chemical burn caused by the absence of loved ones and the familiar. **4.** Hypernostalgia.

nubigous. adjective. **1.** Feeling or perceiving less, with a strange sensation of itching or prickling in the skin. **2.** Weepleness* accompanied by prickling sensation in the skin. *Informal.* **3.** Comfortably numb.

nunshee. noun. (from *nunchi* in Korean). **1.** A person capable of knowing the emotional state and the true mood of someone else. **2.** An insightful person who goes beyond the verbal and non-verbal clues of others.

nymphonocty. noun. **1.** A nocturnal gathering among adolescent or preadolescent girls where they talk and giggle about subjects important to girls of their age; they play, eat and, when they turn the lights off, pretend not to play erotic games between them. **2.** Female erospection.* **3.** Sleepover.

O

oblate. verb. **1.** To ritualize the movement of hands and arms while praying or during daily washing as an offering to a god. **2.** To manufacture wafers for Holy Communion. noun. **3.** An inhabitant of Oblat.

oblung. adjective. Having longer rather than deeper ideas.

obsolem. noun. *Psychology*. **1.** Progressively exacerbating depression relating to aging or nearing death. **2.** A joke that nature plays on intelligent beings. **3.** The realization that biocaducity* or DNA-programmed obsolescence is a cruel practical joke.

obsolinity. noun. Resources and space allocated for personnel dedicated to research in an esoteric area or an obsolete scientific field where data obtained, if any, are unlikely to be published in a scientific journal.

obstepodia. noun. **1.** The struggling, anserine walk of a woman in the last stages of pregnancy. **2.** Duckwaddle. **3.** Obswaddling gait.

obsuration. noun. A sensation of idleness standing on the triangular threshold of rite, routine, and obsession.

obviology. noun. A discipline where the subject specializes in observing and documenting the obvious, hoping to detect phenomena that have been previously undetected.

occulmenia. noun. An occult memory.

occultacle. noun. An ensemble of images outside the field of vision that are partially perceived when looking at something.

octoplegy. noun. *Medicine*. Lack of or a significant reduction in sensation and movement of four limbs along with the severe dysfunction of several organs as a result of shock, illness, or injury.

odredosis. noun. *Medicine*. **1.** A hereditary disease characterized by an uncontrollable facial skin growth. **2.** Facial hyperdermia.

odrelloid. noun. **1.** A person with an excess of skin and many wrinkles. *Informal.* **2.** An insult to someone with many wrinkles. *Derogatory.* **3.** Chow-chow face. **4.** Sharpeic.

ognoma. noun. **1.** The facial expression of a listener emulating that of a storyteller. *Literature.* **2.** A tumor of knowledge.

oleorell. noun. An oil painting executed in the style of an aquarelle.

oligodant. noun. **1.** A person who is easily dominated but who exhibits infrequent defensive outbursts and licentious behavior. **2.** Anadesic.

oligomophrenia. noun. *Psychology.* **1.** A disease characterized by emotional retardation and slight mental retardation. **2.** A condition that commonly affects aging or neurologically ill embrecks.*

oliguitrant. noun. **1.** An intrigant person with deficient memory whose intrigues usually fail due to lack of coherence. **2.** Oliguintrigant. **3.** An incompetent carrouha.* **4.** A deceiving mentinous.*

omnichronal. adjective. **1.** Absolutely encompassing all time. **2.** Understanding all time in an absolute manner. **3.** Related to all time within and beyond infinity. **4.** Chronoligic.* noun. **5.** Totitemporality.*

omnigen. noun. *Philosophy.* **1.** The cause of all causes. **2.** The ultimate causality. *Medicine.* **3.** The trade name of a useless antibiotic.

omnigonadic. adjective. **1.** A man who believes he possesses the largest penis. **2.** Possessing, involving, or relating to all gonalities.*

omnimity. noun. The capability to attract, repel, or exercise any action on things or people at a distance.

omnimnesary. noun. An archive of all past and future memories.

omphatist. noun. **1.** A person who subtly pulls the strings of a dialogue and suddenly leaves with dignity to the stupefaction of their listeners. *Literary.* **2.** A manipulative person who abruptly abandons a conversation while a perspicacious bell tolls an awakening call to smash the stubborn laxness of the abandoned audience. **3.** A person with a large, protruding belly button. **4.** An outty navel.

onanymph. noun. **1.** An attractive woman who flirts with a pubescent boy and triggers in him a series of uncontrollable masturbations in her honor.

Informal. **2.** Puberobonia. **3.** Flirtonanist.

onasomny. noun. **1.** A masturbation occurring during sleep. **2.** Somniturcy. **3.** Mastumbul. **4.** adjective. Masturbating while dreaming.

oneigarche. noun. **1.** Sudden exit from a dream. **2.** The overwhelming, inconceivable and frustrating emotion felt when changing realities when yanked out from a dream. **3.** A drastic wake-up call. **4.** A dream rudely ended by the sound of an alarm clock.

oneilytic. adjective. **1.** Related to or involving the rupture or destruction of a dream. **2.** Pertaining to an event or a person destroying someone's dream.

oneisca. noun. **1.** A bullion of dreams. **2.** Sequences with no logical flow or order in a dream. **3.** An eclectic dream. **4.** Amalgamation of remembrances or perceptions that are edited and reproduced randomly in a dream. **5.** A tornado of dreams within a dream.

oneitalloid. noun. **1.** A person who dreams of his or her own life instead of living it. **2.** Somnibious.

oneitude. noun. A vehement desire to return to a dream one was previously experiencing with such fervor that one is unable to perform any other activity.

onfaign. *Psychology.* **1.** verb. To psychologically corner a person with cognitive dissonance. **2.** To confront a person for deeds done against the confronter, especially when the confronted does not know that the confronter is the onfaigner.

onirophagic. adjective. **1.** Literally, swallowing one's own dreams. **2.** A systematic technique for remembering one's dreams and believing they were actually lived events. **3.** Using one's dreams as inspiration for writing fiction, composing music, or creating any form of art.

oniscape. verb. *Psychology.* To use or practice routine masturbation as a medium to escape life's tribulations.

onitactility. noun. The capability of feeling one's dreams with tactility. **2.** The ability to touch one's own dreams.

ontage. noun. **1.** The dysfunctional assemblage of a conscience into an entity. **2.** A crucial differential in the fine-tuning of an entity to an intelligent being. **3.** A radical dysfunctional fine-tuning of an onto* to become a being.

ontibelf. noun. A person who has a larger upper lip than lower lip.

ontilation. noun. *Biology.* **1.** A behavior inherited in certain individuals of one species that, in a generation, influences physical differences in future generations who together form a species different from the original species. **2.** Inherited behavior that is the cause of speciation.

onto. noun. *Biology.* **1.** A potential biological entity. *Philosophy.* **2.** A being prior to becoming a sentient being. *Theology.* **3.** A soul-bearing being before becoming an intelligent entity.

ontofanto. noun. **1.** A ghost who copulates with a corporate entity. **2.** A ghost involved in a syncorpenty.*

ontolilepsis. noun. *Biology.* **1.** Genetically programmed obsolescence. *Biochemistry.* **2.** DNA-controlled senescence. *Medicine.* **3.** The inevitable effect of time on biological beings and the prelude to ontosis* characterized by slower and increasingly erroneous cellular repairs and the conclusion of the average number of cellular reproductions. *Philosophy.* **4.** The

transit of what is or what exists toward what is not or does not exist.

ontosis. noun. *Biology.* **1.** The degeneration and prelude to death of a biological entity when numerous cells throughout the body have concluded the average number of cellular divisions. *Embryology.* **2.** The swelling of an embryo. *Theology.* **3.** The inflammation of an existence. *Psychology.* **4.** The indescribable physical consequences, such as overwhelming swelling, redness, heat, and pain, that every person experiences at some point in their life when beginning to feel the effects of senescence. *Politics.* **5.** A possible heterodox solution to the problem called life. *Literary.* **6.** The fatal surrender of a body to the claws of time. *Medicine.* **7.** The inevitable consequence of ontolilepsis.* *Philosophy.* **8.** Unbecoming of what is or what exists. **9.** The essence of the transition from existence to non-existence.

ontotheque. noun. *Philosophy.* The intangible space of an onto* prior to becoming a being.

onyo. noun. A legitimate child born from a clandestine adultery by the mother.

ophidiometer. noun. An instrument used to measure the idiocy of an intrigant or a gossipmonger.

ophthal. verb. To pay attention to something that is glanced at.

ophthalid. noun. *Anatomy.* The entirety of the internal and external parts of the eye including eyelid and eyelashes.

opinaut. noun. **1.** An insecure and indecisive person who navigates through friends and acquaintances asking their opinion regarding the decision said person must make, but who does not consider any of the opinions provided. adjective. **2.** Desimpinated.*

opivietistical. adjective. **1.** Believing in one's own superiority over others with a righteous feeling of being on the correct side of a doctrine. **2.** Mental astigmatism.

opstacle. noun. An ethereal balcony where one evaluates possibilities and selects an option.

opticate. verb. To look at something with more attention than optitting* and perceiving the surrounding panorama [total field of vision] in some detail.

optimick. noun. A man who maintains his focus on one precise point while urinating.

optite. verb. To look at something with attention without perceiving [what lies in] the total field of vision.

orastela. noun. The remaining puffing sound of a truncated word when a person is rudely interrupted.

orchibursitis. noun. Severe inflammation of the testicles in which they acquire the size and shape of a purse.

orchifratic. noun. adjective. *Psychology.* A wild obsession with frequently washing one's own or someone else's testicles, generally when falsely perceiving a bad odor emanating from them.

orchitrichosis. noun. *Medicine.* **1.** Abundant and persistent hair growth on the scrotum. **2.** Insidious scrotal hirsutism. *Informal.* **3.** Balls' mane.

ordate. verb. (in dance or sports): To rotate head first, before the rest of the body, to prevent dizziness when spinning or rotating rapidly.

ordeliness. noun. **1.** The state of mental equilibrium in a person who possesses no abilities or wealth. **2.** A feeling of acceptance, acquiescence, and satisfaction in a person with no abilities and no wealth. **3.** Total resignation on realizing one's own position or status in a society.

orgaplegia. noun. A series of uncontrollable and indescribable sensations following a strong orgasm that leaves a person with a delectable dizziness, trembling, and temporary paralysis.

orgarrobacy. noun. **1.** A strong feeling of being outside oneself during and after an orgasm. **2.** Placioustillia.

orgilation. noun. **1.** A feeling of pleasure beyond relief due to the absence of pain. **2.** The sudden sensation of comfortable ease and pleasure experienced by someone suffering an intense pain who unexpectedly discovers a posture where the pain completely disappears. **3.** A feeling of intense non-sensual pleasure that occurs when there is no perception of any internal or external stimuli.

ornithophagous. adjective. Feeding on birds of any type.

orofacic. adjective. Having an irregular face that resembles a mountain.

orofane. noun. An alpinist who considers a mountain his or her temple.

ortavel. noun. A sharp black shadow that travels at the speed of light at will.

orthemesize. verb. **1.** To verbally vomit out the teachings of a doctrine or a political system when their truth is realized. noun. **2.** The enemy within oneself.

orthogeneous. adjective. **1.** Uniform in character or content. **2.** Composed of a single nature. noun. **3.** A person who believes he or she is always correct. **4.** A man with a straight, flaccid penis.

orthopaternal. adjective. Pertaining or related to the filial art of correcting one's father.

orthovacy. noun. *Medicine.* **1.** A branch of gastroenterology and proctology studying the defects of bowel movements and the consequences of using toilets for defecation. **2.** A branch of proctology that promotes prophylaxis of various gastroenterological and proctological ailments by modifying the design of toilets so that a person can defecate naturally in a squatting position. **3.** A heterosexual priesthood.

orticate. verb. To become bothersome and irritating when touching another person.

osbeche. noun. **1.** A talented child whose talent is suppressed by an unbreakable moral rule that he or she must behave "well" at all times. adjective.

Informal. **2.** Smelling like the feces of an orphan.

oschille. noun. **1.** The shocking sensation of experiencing several disagreeable emotions simultaneously, such as fear, laughing, repugnance, crying, and shivering. *Informal.* **2.** Nianair. **3.** Something that induces the creeps.

oscillopath. noun. *Psychology.* **1.** A person who changes friendships frequently without a regular pattern and is incapable of maintaining long-lasting friendships. **2.** A person who is unable to have long-lasting friends.

oscufarse. noun. **1.** A fashionable trend among women to kiss the air during a photographic shot. **2.** The action of protruding one's lips to pretend to be sensual. *Zoology.* **3.** The protrusion of lips among primates in the absence of danger.

osculass. noun. A habit of women who are new to working out and are dressed in fashionable sporting clothes and elaborate makeup, who during an exercise routine protrude their lips in the motion of kissing and feign heavy breathing as if physically exhausted.

osculator. noun. An instrument used for learning how to kiss.

osculot. noun. **1.** An erotic kiss delivered to a person one does not love. **2.** A wabby* without affection. **3.** A glossioscle with no formal relationship.

oscuspum. noun. The saliva foam that develops in the corner of the lips of a person who is speaking.

oscutress. noun. A woman with an obsession to kiss a man's behind.

osfrand. verb. To capture an enjoyable moment of the past with the claws of a suppressed memory.

oslanic. adjective. **1.** Being annoying to others due to being uncomfortable, complaining about one's own uncomfortable position, or attempting to find a comfortable position. noun. **2.** A person who stands up, sits down, rearranges his or her position, in the attempt to find a comfortable posture.

osminist. noun. **1.** A person who studies or carries out memory transfers from one person to another. **2.** Transnoiter. **3.** Diamnener. **4.** Transomnemist. **5.** Mnemontist. **6.** Osmosimnemist. **7.** A person who is an expert in discerning smells.

osmiocrat. noun. A person with the ability to smell a bad government.

osmiodox. adjective. **1.** Changing one's opinion about the nature of a smell. noun. **2.** A person who pretends to have a good sense of smell.

osnid. noun. The occurrence of someone's opinions being dismissed by others on the grounds of contradictory or unlikely evidence, but, when reconsidered, the realization dawns that everybody's opinions about the nature of the discussion are also wrong or inconclusive.

osopabe. verb. To attribute qualities or defects to someone in an exaggerated manner.

ostenlate. verb. To display ostentatiously or to make apparent with affectation that something is great, brilliant, luxurious, or costly, that is actually common or has no value.

osteoflexia. noun. *Medicine.* A congenital disease characterized by soft, bendable bones and muscle atrophy.

osteospic. adjective. *Psychology.* A neurotic patient with extreme personality hardening or character ossification.

osteostenous. adjective. **1.** Having a light and thin bone structure. noun. **2.** A person with an extreme ectomorphic somatotype. *Informal.* **3.** Sylphily boned, whether gaunt or stout.

osteud. adjective. *Informal.* **1.** Having lots of bones. *Informal.* **2.** Having thick bones. **3.** Stocky. **4.** Osude. noun. **5.** A person with an extreme endomorphic somatotype. *Archaic.* **5.** Of bony trunk, but does not look scrawny even in famine.

ostriga. noun. **1.** An overwhelming feeling of frustration when, immediately after its purchase, a gadget stops functioning. **2.** The feeling of being mistreated when purchasing something that immediately stops working.

ostropy. noun. **1.** The uncomfortable and displeasing sensation of having a hair inside the mouth but being unable to find it and remove it, generally occurring in a public place. **2.** An annoying circumstance as unsettling as having a hair in the mouth.

osvelt. noun. An elegant and proportionally built person who is not slender.

othropsid. adjective. Lacking the spry, resplendent, and lustrous appearance of youth.

oticate. verb. To hear while partially listening.

oticuous. adjective. Having hairs sprouting out of the ears.

otiquett. noun. *Informal.* **1.** The area where the organ for hearing or the internal ear ends and the external cartilaginous ear begins. **2.** A bourgeois concept of being a good listener.

ovudious. adjective. *Informal.* **1.** A female displaying valiant behavior and not being intimidated by anyone or anything. **2.** Gynosadious. *Vulgar.* **3.** A woman with lots of female balls. **4.** Ovulsy*. *Medicine.* **5.** Denoting a woman with an excessive number of eggs in one or both ovules.

ovulsy. noun. *Informal.* **1.** A gutsy woman. **2.** A woman with strength and the ability to frighten others. *Vulgar.* **3.** A woman with balls and gynesthy.* **4.** The condition of being ovudious*. **5.** Gynezza.

oxyhalogen. noun. *Chemistry.* An ephemeral element created by the quantum fusion of oxygen and halogen. See the Periodic Table from 2836 AD.

oxythesia. noun. High fat, high sugar, and low protein meals prepared by franchises for mass consumption.

P

paleostenitisist. noun. *Anthropology.* An obstinate paleoanthropologist who adheres to only one theory of prehistoric human migration despite limited, incomplete, and inconclusive evidence.

palexost. verb. **1.** To complete someone else's sentence. **2.** To steal the words someone was about to pronounce. **3.** To kleptospeack. *Informal.* **4.** To paxalt. **5.** To pull out the words from someone's mouth. noun. **6.** The fastidious custom of completing someone's thoughts. **7.** The obsessive behavior of interrupting and concluding a statement another person was articulating.

palinate. verb. *Archaic.* To expose a person's past actions and the flimsy camouflage used to hide them.

palligule. noun. *Archaic.* Fictitious anatomical structure located between the thymus and the heart, associated with controlling romantic feelings.

palsnout. verb. **1.** To lift the tip of the nose by sliding it up with the palm of the hand. **2.** To scratch one's nose with the palm of the hand. **3.** To chironasate. noun. *Psychology.* **4.** A nervous tic consisting of scratching one's nose.

panalgia. noun. *Medicine.* Intense and hard-to-explain pain with mixed sensations of ardor, oppression, pinching, stabbing, whipping, dislocating, biting, striking, punching, and lacerating.

panapoh. verb. (From *pana po'o* in Hawaiian). **1.** To scratch one's head to encourage recall of the whereabouts of something misplaced. **2.** To scratch the scalp to enhance the memory of something forgotten.

panfleck. verb. To be incompatible and belligerent against everything.

pangnostic. adjective. **1.** Pertaining to each and all collective areas, disciplines, or sciences in which everyone thinks they are an expert. **2.**

(of a person) Being innately an expert in one or more fields, particularly politics, alternative medicine or therapeutics, meteorology, religion, and sports.

panlogism. noun. *Philosophy.* Theory that rationally affirms that everything unreal is in fact real, but not yet perceived.

panmisoiac. noun. **1.** A person who hates absolutely everything. **2.** A panflecker.*

pannet. noun. The alternative *worldwide web* that is free, threat-free, readily accessible, and immune to intervention by governments or big corporations.

panomnia. noun. **1.** The capability to perceive everything. **2.** Omnicivesence.

panoramate. verb. To observe all surroundings simultaneously.

panparlogy. noun. **1.** A conversation covering one or more disciplines, topics, areas, themes, or fields of work in which everyone can opine with confidence and perceived knowledge since everyone considers themselves experts. **2.** A talk in an area or areas in which any person can speak, discuss, or argue at length and assertively. **3.** Conversation, discussion, exchange, intercourse, dialogue, or

argument between pangnostic* people.

panpeek. verb. *Literary.* **1.** To glance beyond from a balcony called possibility. **2.** To panthopan.

pantoxis. noun. *Physiology.* **1.** A theory that recognizes that all substances are toxic when administered in excess or exceeding intrinsic pathogenic doses. **2.** Pantopoiss. **3.** Paracelsism.

pantrigue. verb. **1.** To consent fully to what one does not believe is just, reasonable, or true to end an argument, difference, or a dispute. *Informal.* **2.** To agree to anything just to make another person to shut up.

panusury. noun. **1.** Greedy practices, within the bounds of legality, globally spread by governments or corporations. **2.** Global ususepsis.*

pappoon. noun. **1.** A small skin cut made with a paper's edge that provokes a disproportionally strong pain. *Informal.* **2.** A pain on the skin that is inversely proportional to the size and depth of the wound. **3.** Papybrasion. *History.* **4.** A Chinese torture applied over long periods of time.

parablem. noun. **1.** A problem that in another place is not actually a problem. **2.** A problem that in a different place or time is not a problem because it has been clarified, solved, or simply is not a problem.

parabrupt. noun. **1.** A heightened moment of surprise or shock when in solitude. **2.** A dramatized exabrupt* when one is alone.

paraceed. verb. **1.** To proceed from another reality in time or space. adjective. **2.** Coming from a thing with no cognateness to such thing. **3.** Descending from a person without having blood relationship with said person. **4.** Having an origin from a parallel reality.

paraception. noun. **1.** Ability to perceive beyond current dimensions or time. **2.** Ability to perceive, ider* and metaceive* through dimensions or time.

parachronicity. noun. A peculiarity of being in a distinct time of the presently occurring time, precisely before the precise time happens.

paracog. noun. **1.** Alternative possibility of being or of being known. **2.** An illusion of having been paratherically* famous. **3.** Paracognostibility.

paracrastinate. verb. **1.** To partially delay or postpone something. **2.** To do the minimal amount of something while fooling oneself that one is not

putting it off. noun. *Literary.* **3.** A person who sees two tomorrows instead of one tomorrow in the tomorrow.

paradimensional. noun. Phenomenon by which it may be possible to go over interdimensional barriers heading to other bearings or a transdimensional* achrony.*

paradrigh. verb. **1.** To develop extra-corporeally a thing that is physically inside a body. **2.** To expand beyond the skin something that is intrinsically in a body.

paradrow. noun. A porous umbrella that stops the big drops of rain while allowing small drops to pass.

paragall. verb. **1.** To involuntarily assume a heroic act of someone else's as one's own. **2.** To daringdue. noun. **3.** A valourette. **4.** Couraginelia.

paragnoss. verb. **1.** To acquire knowledge of what occurs outside a perceived reality. **2.** To identify the nature of being by paraxing.*

paraguilt. noun. *Psychology.* **1.** A vivid feeling of guilt for what someone else did. **2.** Paramordiment.

parahabilitation. noun. **1.** Rehabilitation of offenders using unconventional methods. *Sociology.* **2.** Zurration.*

parahistory. noun. High proportion of information contained in history books.

parahue. verb. **1.** To give someone hope about his or her future when such future is truly uncertain. **2.** To parahuciate.

paralabic. adjective. **1.** (of a woman) Wearing extremely tight pants or shorts and revealing the contour of her genitalia. **2.** Paralabiated.

paralude. verb. To manipulate a manipulator, generally with a rehearsed passive-aggressive approach.

parament. verb. To think the same idea or concept several times pretending to be someone else each time with the intention of unraveling more.

paramerge. verb. **1.** To emerge sideways from a liquid. **2.** To come out laterally from the ether.

paramonition. noun. **1.** A strong feeling that something is happening simultaneously elsewhere. **2.** A signal or a warning from the paracoming. **3.** Parasage.* **4.** Concoviction. **5.** Parasentiment.

paramysticism. noun. **1.** Mysticism that does not involve deities or mythological characters. **2.** Extraordinary state of ecstasy in which a person feels in perfect union with an unknown, non-divine entity.

paranigma. noun. **1.** Incomprehensible thing or event that is outside or partially outside reality. **2.** A thing or event that is mysterious or difficult to understand and interpret because it is outside or partially outside reality.

paranostalgia. noun. *Psychology.* **1.** Melancholia triggered by remembering events in one's own life and realizing that they will never return. **2.** Deep sadness on being separated from close family or friends who, it becomes clear, were part of a past life. **3.** A strong and painful yearning for something that could have happened or been.

paraosmia. noun. *Medicine.* **1.** A degenerative neurological disease characterized by hypersensitivity to smells and, in advanced stages, olfactory hallucinations. *Psychology.* **2.** A psychological transposition of smells, in particular pleasant smells for foul smells, as a form of externalizing repressed childhood traumas. *Informal.* **3.** A condition of someone who claims to smell extraterrestrial smells.

paraperd. noun. The alternating joyous and embarrassing feelings when, seeing someone known from afar, one waves excitedly, runs up to the person and starts to hug or kiss him or her then suddenly realizes said person is a total stranger.

paraperson. noun. **1.** A stranger who looks like a close friend or a relative. **2.** Family doppelgänger. **3.** A loved one's doppelgänger.

parapheric. adjective. **1.** Pertaining to or related to saints whose lives were actually libertine. **2.** Being beside a periphery. **3.** Related to the silhouetted legs of a slender woman in tights. **4.** Having an attractive leg contour, generally a svelte woman wearing dark hose.

paraphody. noun. Capability to endure the adversities of others.

paraphoria. noun. A feeling or state of calm when perceiving someone else's wellbeing.

paraplethonoia. noun. **1.** A mental process in which memories are created from non-lived events. *Psychology*. **2.** Creation of fictitious life-long memories. *Literary*. **3.** A life constructed of invented memories. *Religion*. **4.** Intelligent design.

parapord. noun. A perplexing feeling when a stranger excitedly approaches and greets one as if one were a close friend.

pararcy. adjective. The collective look of people in an elevator, watching the numbers change, to avoid eye contact.

parasage. noun. **1.** A feeling that something is occurring elsewhere at the precise moment it is actually happening. **2.** A strong feeling that something may be happening in another present. **3.** Paramonition.*

parascend. noun. **1.** Relative position of a person through natural, artificial, or supernatural means. verb. **2.** To come from unnaturally, generally by futupossession* or by parateric* crononihilism.* **3.** To descend in an ascendancy.

parasignate. verb. To assign a task to a third person or an organization on behalf of a second person or organization assigned to it by an original person or organization tasked to do it.

paraspora. noun. **1.** Dispersal of people to either side of the frontier or border of their original place. **2.** Dispersal of something to one of the sides of its limits.

parastance. noun. *Physics*. Space or interval of place or time relative to the quantum state between two or more things or events.

parastrophe. noun. An abrupt event in someone's life that drastically changes his or her fate.

paratactia. noun. **1.** Disturbing sensation on perceiving a stranger caressing one's skin in a lusty manner. **2.** Contacting dystangibility.

paraterit. noun. **1.** Parallel past. **2.** Event that happened simultaneously to other events in an alternate time.

paratropistic. adjective. Having the tendency to attract something or someone.

paravrag. verb. To go from one part of a reality to another without a precise objective.

parawhile. noun. **1.** A temporal conjunction. **2.** A parallel period of time or a period of radialized* time. **3.** Conjunction of succession of instants during achrony.* **4.** A parallax happening.

parax. verb. To go from one reality to another maintaining certain order.

pardatheric. adjective. *Informal.* **1.** Having extremely large ears that undulate with any movement. **2.** Flapellated.*

paregoria. noun. *Archaic.* A potion used as medicine for children with coughs or diarrhea made of sweetened opium, camphor, benzoic acid and anise.

parexacticity noun. The quality of being at one side of the precise, immediately before the preciseness occurs.

parlament. verb. **1.** To speak or converse with one or more imaginary persons. **2.** To speak one's own thoughts aloud regardless of the audience in a dramatic play. **3.** To engage in conversation with members of a different party to settle a difference, surrender or force a peaceful agreement. **4.** Public soliloquy.

parlebb. verb. **1.** To drown out the voice of another person by increasing the volume of one's own voice or by shouting. **2.** To nullify someone's voice during a conversation. **3.** To purloin a word from someone forcefully.

paromimia. noun. **1.** A self-parody. **2.** An exaggerated imitation of one's own mannerisms. *Psychology.* **3.** The cartoon-like personality and character of oneself in elder years.

parpalile. verb. **1.** To pretend to babble without saying a word. **2.** To open and close one's mouth mockingly as if speaking rapidly without talking.

parrima. noun. *Psychology.* A deep emotion of resentment for what one did or did not do in a distant past that is as vivid as it would be if happening in the present.

parsipody. noun. **1.** Slow, claudicating walk of the elderly, generally when some parts of the body deviate at an awkward angle. **2.** Presbipodia.*

parsivation. noun. **1.** The act of declining a gift that is vehemently desired. **2.** The act of turning down a present with apparent indifference when knowing that such present would be extremely difficult or impossible to acquire. *Psychology.* **3.** A passive action to reject something that is desired but far away.

parturity. noun. The physical ability of a female to give birth.

parudomion. noun. A small dwelling or an apartment in a city slum.

pasuum. noun. A fleeting sensation that, for an instant, is erroneously perceived as a *déjà vu.*

paterfalter. verb. **1.** To lose the respect of a spouse and offspring. *Informal.* **2.** (of a head of household) To try and fail to govern a family. **3.** Patermasculate.

pathomnemonic. adjective. *Psychology.* Pertaining to or relative to a specific morbid memory in a patient with vegetative dystonia that helps to identify the trigger of the mental disease.

paulatide. adjective. Disappearing gradually at the rhythm of pulsations.

paywerck. noun. **1.** A person who is overtly insistent about paying for something. **2.** Someone who demands to pay for something when it is inappropriate or it is not his or her turn to pay.

peatonnic. adjective. **1.** Relating to an ignorant, unsophisticated common person. **2.** Pertaining to people who walk in an urban area as their only mode of transportation. **3.** Lacking insight or inspiration.

peavolic. adjective. Relating to a superficial, bulky, and unpleasant-smelling person.

pecton. noun. Any organism with a disproportionally large chest, generally with a small head, abdomen and limbs.

pecuniation. noun. *Economy.* **1.** Manipulation of currencies and commodities with state support. **2.** One of the strategies used in swindlism.* **3.** Pecunstraption.

pecuniseptic. noun. **1.** A place, region, or society in which avarice and greed are considered ethical and normal. **2.** A place or region where pecuseptic* people live.

pecunization. noun. **1.** Standardization of all currencies by implementing the same quality and quantity of gold in equivalent coins for each country in the world. **2.** Action that followed aurolition*.

pecusepsis. noun. A pervasive behavioral greediness in a society fostered by the glorification of wealth.

pederastism. noun. **1.** A systematic practice in an institution constituted mostly of men in which its members indulge in sexual relationships with boys. **2.** Organized sexual abuse of children in an organization whose main ostensible public purpose is to help mankind.

pedifont. verb. **1.** To tell the truth nonchalantly or without affectation. **2.** To speak sincerely and in a casual manner. **3.** To rest one's foot at the base of a fountain.

pedilardism. noun. **1.** Perversity of an adult who forcibly feeds and fattens a child with the sole purpose of making the child look well-fed and healthy. **2.** Child emporcment. **3.** Pedisament.

pedilation. noun. **1.** Official denial by the leaders of a religion of innumerable child sexual abuse crimes committed by ministers of said religion. **2.** Parishioner ignomicia* of perennial trastule* pederastism.*

pedilogist. noun. A person who narrates an event or an anecdote like a fairytale.

pedimania. 1. A habit of wiggling a foot while the legs are crossed. **2.** Podiomony.

pedimbule. noun. A game in which an adult suspends a child by the arms and swings it back and forth like a pendulum.

pedimism. noun. A school of thought that proposes not imposing rules and routine on children and treating them with courtesy and respect as if they are newly arrived ambassadors of the world.

pedipodia. noun. A quick and insecure walk of a child with alternating steps that, by turns, convey conviction and incertitude.

pelizant. adjective. Consistently and constantly horrifying.

peloster. noun. A wet clot that when drying and hardening emanates a putrid smell.

pelostrous. adjective. **1.** Having the tendency to become foul-smelling. **2.** Being prone to having pelosters.*

pentacapsicoid. noun. Something with five colors that

is irritating to the eyes when looked at.

pentalemma. noun. A situation in which a difficult choice has to be made, by selecting one of five alternatives, especially when the five are equally undesirable.

penulmition. noun. *Psychology.* A disturbing feeling that shakes the marrow when realizing that someone else observed or experienced what one convincingly believed had only been seen or experienced by oneself.

pepenable. adjective. *Informal.* Having flesh desirable for handling, manipulating, caressing, stroking gently, patting, fondling, licking, or fingering lecherously.

peraze. verb. To become conscious of something disagreeable, and then accepting it cheerfully and enthusiastically.

perbichery. noun. *Literary.* Lifelong habit of daily disgorging the same ideas disguised as new caprices.

pericapital. adjective. **1.** Moving around someone's head. **2.** An object moving around someone's head.

pericentric. noun. An eccentric and extravagant person who behaves normally when in the company of other people during habitual circumstances.

pericutive. noun. A highly specialized person hired as a corporate executive to supervise activities and strategize projects outside of his or her area of expertise.

periesthesia. verb. To feel something and to react to it much later due to other concomitantly distracting stimuli.

periffluist. noun. **1.** A person who, without agreeing or disagreeing with others, maintains an equidistant position during a discussion. **2.** Perimetrizing* around a potential conflict.

periloquy. noun. **1.** An act of reflecting and speaking aloud when by oneself, in total solitude, while walking in circles. **2.** Circumsoleparly. **3.** A vocalized stubbornness.

perimetrize. verb. **1.** To examine, analyze or study attentively the verges of a situation. **2.** To palpate carefully the edges of a place, thing or person.

perinvironment. adjective. *Ecology.* **1.** Surrounding the environment through its outer limits. noun. **2.** Periambiental.

peripluvious. adjective. *Psychology.* **1.** Inundated by problems and sorrows everywhere. noun. **2.** A person unable to perform any activity due to surrounding psychological torments.

peristellascope. noun. *Astronomy.* A telescopic instrument used to observe and study the purported peristellations.*

peristellation. noun. *Astronomy.* A cluster of stars that through imaginary lines can surround one or more constellations in the firmament.

peritative. adjective. Pertaining to or related to a person who maintains his or her distance to any relationship with words or actions.

peritravent. noun. A person who in conversation thinks the other person has a wrong opinion or belief and engages in verbal circumlocution to passive-aggressively circumnavigate around their difference.

perittave. noun. A heap of adornments or extra clothing on, between, or around attire already being worn.

perpodination. noun. The effect that money or power have on an otherwise honest person.

perspiler. noun. A perspicacious person whose perspiration increases as his or her perspicacity rises.

pervidia. noun. **1.** A dark fantasy that, due to its morbid nature, is eluded with loud mental noises or by vehemently thinking of something else. **2.** A fantasy a person denies, circumvents, or evades during introspection. **3.** A micromorbid idea.

petond. noun. A strong push or punch in the chest.

petrond. noun. The silly expression of doubt, ignorance, and negation that a man makes when his wife asks him a question.

petraposent. noun. *Anthropology.* A chamber in a speleological residence of humanoids before the creation of artificial dwellings.

petroid. noun. An irritating sensation generated when interacting with an odious person that feels like having a grain of salt in the eye or a volcanic pebble inside the shoe.

peyaflust. noun. A citizen with no social conscience.

phagiard. noun. *Psychology.* A person who nourishes bleakness and distress with false hopes.

phagology. noun. **1.** Study of habits before, during, and after eating, excluding nutrition and gastronomy. **2.** Prandiology.

phagoulous. adjective. Playing with food instead of eating it.

phalliapheresis. noun. *Medicine.* Removal of a penis by non-surgical means.

phallodont. noun. *Zoology.* A large, extinct mammal of the Miocene to Pleistocene epochs that resembled a giraffe with bulky and muscular body. Four to five meters in height, it walked erect with four legs and looked like an ambulant phallus.

phalloflaggia. noun. **1.** Sexual game that simulates flagellation with a penis. **2.** Opening ceremony of a gomorrisade* during a gomorry*.

phallosfy. noun. *Medicine.* Tremors and quivering of a penis caused by involuntary muscular fibrillation.

pharmapathy. noun. *Commerce.* **1.** Invention of diseases concomitant to the manufacturing of drugs with the goal of marketing the drugs to treat said diseases. **2.** Pharmpecuniary. **3.** Mercapathy.

pharmaphant. noun. A pharmaceutical corporation that seeks large profits and manufactures drugs to treat non-existent diseases or pharmapathies* which are fabricated during the development of such drugs.

phenacultry. noun. **1.** Pervasive 21st century trend of displaying gore and extreme cruelty in movies and multimedia. **2.** Digitally enhanced cinematographic violence in humans and animals characterized by hyperbolic bleeding, anatomic impossibilities, and stylized torture.

phenatechnia. noun. Increase of asthenia and solitude among young people as consequences of technological advancements and speed of telecommunications.

philarckish. adjective. **1.** Having affinity for or craving creamy foods. **2.** Philacreamious. **3.** Having attraction for cloying people.

philoclast. noun. *Psychology.* Depressive state that surges at the moment when two peoples' tastes and desires collide.

philoforous. adjective. Possessing an attribute or carrying something that makes a person believe he or she is appreciated or admired.

philogendry. noun. *Philosophy.* Philosophical theory from the 22nd century that endorses natural conception and reproduction while opposing artificial generation of organisms and species.

philogynist. noun. **1.** Someone who admires women. **2.** A man who enjoys being in the company of women, observing their anatomy, examining their behavior, analyzing possibilities on how they might respond to a certain stimulus, imagining how they would look naked, what shape and how firm their breasts might be and what type of noises and moaning they would emit when reaching an orgasm.

philomenia. A distasteful first name given to the ugliest girl in a Latin American family.

philonemia. noun. Multisensory didactic technique to facilitate and strengthen memory.

phimofistitis. noun. *Medicine.* **1.** Infection with the formation of pus-draining fistula due to an extreme preputial narrowing. **2.** Complete fistulated* phimosis. *Informal.* **3.** A brutal fistfight in a transvestite bar.

phleboctesy. noun. *Medicine.* **1.** Medical treatment in vogue that neither ameliorates signs or symptoms nor cures a disease. **2.** A fashionable therapy that can worsen the condition being treated, as did the bloodletting of yesteryear.

phlebotron. noun. An exaggeratedly muscular man, usually by artificial means, with many visible tortuous veins that appear to be inflamed.

phlegmaron. noun. Eruptive phlegm that is expelled involuntarily in an explosive manner.

phlegmogenous. adjective. Originating, promoting, or influencing the formation of phlegm.

phlegmoid. noun. A person whose presence alone suffices to spark in others the urge to spit in his face.

phlegmord. noun. *Medicine.* **1.** An overheated large phlegm that is either swallowed or spat out during a high fever. **2.** Pyrovomica. **3.** Phlegmacald. *Informal.* **4.** Hotspit. **5.** A person who has the impulse to spit frequently.

phlepsia. noun. An organism that appears to live normally despite environmental conditions swiftly deteriorating past levels in which life can be readily sustained.

phosperon. noun. Luminosity coming from the mouth of a moribund or recently deceased person. It is generally seen in darkness.

phosphorilic. adjective. Showing sudden and sporadic signs of intelligence and genius. Generally applied to a forumbulon.*

photorepulsive. noun. *Physics.* **1.** Phenomenon of certain substances or bodies consisting of repelling or destroying photons and, consequently, light. *Astronomy*. **2.** The intrinsic darkness surrounding a celestial body. *Literature*. **3.** The unique ability of Tragaluz, *Lightgulper*, the light-eater character of children's stories.

photoshopped. noun. **1.** Something real or unreal that seems more than real. adjective. **2.** Having embellished something by artificial means.

physconomist. noun. **1.** A bespectacled urban intellectual in the habit of reading at night. **2.** A metrophilic, noctambule, photophobic and stenophthalmic student.

phytanima. noun. The vegetable soul of each plant.

phytanimous. adjective. Having the animosity and the mobility of a plant.

phytocanibil. noun. *Botany*. **1.** Several species of herbivore or phytophagous plants that trap and ingest plants of their own species. **2.** A cannibal plant.

phytocide. noun. **1.** Destruction of vegetable life, chiefly for work. **2.** Annihilation of plants.

phytoctisy. noun. *Psychology*. Mania of collecting artificial flowers and plants.

phytohuman. noun. *Biology*. **1.** Recombinant cell derived from plant and human progenitor cells. **2.** Phytandrocyte.

phytosiphous. adjective. Having and passively showing the personality of a plant.

phytotomy. noun. Artistic or recreational activity consisting of amputating anatomical portions of living vegetable organisms to manipulate their growth for ornamental purposes.

piantazo. noun. **1.** A twist of an instant within a moment. **2.** A loop of time that happens in a specific instant.

picometaphor. noun. *Literature*. A metaphor composed of two words or fewer.

pielomutt. noun. A person who sheds his or her skin periodically.

pirounaut. 1. A person who does pirouettes in bed. **2.** Pirouettenaut. **3.** An acrobatic callisthencist. **4.** A performing gymnast during sexual intercourse.

planetator. noun. An massive apparatus used for provoking collisions between two or more satellites or planets.

plasmattrition. noun. **1.** An illusion of seeing someone else in one's own reflection. **2.** A mirage of something or someone in one's own reflected image. *Psychology*. **3.**

The phenomenon of seeing a live selfie doppelgänger in the mirror.

plasten. noun. **1.** A person who is frequently the target of practical jokes. **2.** An orgy worker or the liaison who accompanies clients to ensure their enjoyment or satisfaction.

plastiforic. adjective. Wearing hose, pantyhose, or tight transparent material.

plastrous. noun. **1.** A man who achieves a long marriage through adaptability, patience, and interpreting what his wife wanted or wished rather than what she said. **2.** Stabiloid.*

platitoic. adjective. **1.** Pertaining or related to the mediocrity of spoken or written communication. **2.** Flatness, shallowness, plainness, or unremarkable quality of an orator or a writer.

pleaphobia. noun. A sensation of unease in the middle of a strong pleasure.

pleater. noun. **1.** A terrestrial high tide. **2.** End or conclusion of the rising of a surface. **3.** The highest point of a solid surface that rises and falls like a tide. **4.** The tip of a ground wave during an earthquake stronger than 9.5 on the Richter scale.

plebony. noun. The twisted sympathy a plebeian feels for celebrities who have it all.

pleonasmity. noun. **1.** Quality of a pleonasm. *Linguistics*. **2.** An elaborate exegesis with numerous obscure terms that complicate interpretation and do not facilitate understanding.

pleoneiria. noun. A sensation of wellbeing when waking up from a pleasurable dream one does not quite remember.

plompous. adjective. **1.** Having generous, voluptuous flesh in hips, buttocks and thighs and a slim body, generally in women or androgynous men. **2.** Having well rounded, curvy, or full figure. **3.** Being awkward. **4.** Pertaining to or related to an ungraceful in style or movement.

pluribilation. noun. **1.** A deep misgiving shared by many. **2.** A widespread and common doubt shared by numerous people. **3.** A feeling of betrayal experienced by the majority of citizens of a nation after an election.

poikil. adjective. **1.** Having eyes of varied colors. *Medicine*. **2.** Poikilophthalmic. noun. **3.** A person with peculiar variation of colors in each iris. *Music*. **4.** A girl with kaleidoscope eyes.

poiky. adjective. **1.** Having an extraordinarily varied and plentiful diet. **2.** Poikilophagus. noun. **3.** Any omnivore with an extraordinarily wide-ranging diet.

politage. noun. **1.** Waste material contained in or removed from a parliament, senate or congress, including humans. *Sociology.* **2.** Human refuse.

poltoclian. noun. A stain on clothing or material that acquires fractal morphology.

polymegh. noun. An intense retch that provokes the simultaneous contraction of urethra, colon, uterus, and vagina in women and urethra, colon, urachus, and prostate in men.

ponurite. adjective. Believing oneself to have no agglomeration or confusion of concepts.

porcinette. adjective. *Informal.* Walking and snorting in a style characteristic of a pig.

porlicutor. noun. A person who dominates a conversation despite having less knowledge than the other people at a gathering.

pornodyte. adjective. **1.** Being drawn to prohibited pleasures. **2.** Being incapable of resisting prohibited pleasures. **3.** Pornomagnethropoid.

portitude. noun. **1.** Posture and gesture of a person who feels a healthy pride in his or her triumphs. **2.** Appearance of having solidity in mind, character, or finances.

poshenmush. noun. (from *pochemuchka* in Russian). A person who asks too many questions.

pospensivator. noun. A deep thinker ignored by his contemporaries who posthumously motivates others to ponder.

postabulation. noun. **1.** An action and effect of indirectly defining a word using two or more parables. **2.** Parabletion.

postchill. noun. **1.** Tiredness after going through a tickling session. **2.** Uncomfortable sensation of insecurity or disturbance following an oschille.* **3.** An uncomfortable sensation following prolonged laughter.

postcognition. noun. **1.** Capability of knowing the future of a person by knowing the past of another, separate person. **2.** Retrocognition of the future of a third person via the past of a second person. *Philosophy.* **3.** The knowledge of the future by extrapolating from the past. *History.* **4.** Future patterns, paths, and behaviors of cultures or nations, accurately predicted by analysis of historiographic records using a set of algorithms. **5.** Future history.

postcognitive. adjective. **1.** Assuming something reliably and predictably by extrapolation of verifiable past events. **2.** Pertaining to the predictability of history.

postfidence. noun. **1.** Lack of trust or greatly diminished confidence in someone. **2.** Decreased trust in a person who was previously fully trusted.

posthage. noun. Intuitive prediction, as a presage, of something unknown from the past that actually happened.

posthumorous. noun. **1.** A remembrance of a humorous event, watched or lived, that when spoken to others becomes more humorous than the original event. **2.** Cominemy.

postick. noun. **1.** A tickling nasal sensation following a sneeze that could be followed by another sneeze. **2.** Postornude.

postimity. noun. **1.** The probability that something will happen or not. **2.** A fifty percent likelihood that something may occur.

postmediate. noun. Posterior to the mediate, but not the immediate, in time, space, or degree.

postoneiry. noun. **1.** Unexpected appearance of sensations, images, smells, or moods of a dream one recently had. **2.** Unwanted repetition of a dream. **3.** Recollection of a forgotten dream.

postpretive. adjective. Being or happening after the past.

postride. noun. The resigning attitude and frustrating surrender to reading a manual or instructions after numerous failed attempts to install or start recently obtained equipment or apparatus.

preactivity. noun. **1.** Mental activity of a proactive person prior to being proactive. **2.** The mental process of how to create or control something rather than to respond to a future possibility.

precognicia. noun. Non-paranormal foreknowledge of present or future circumstances or events.

preconst. noun. Something that was demonstrated to be absolutely certain in the distant past.

prectasy. noun. An undefined period of pleasurable confusion that precedes a moment of ecstasy.

precutive. adjective. **1.** Preceding something else without interruption. **2.** Prefollowing* immediately before or in retrosequence. noun. **3.** An executive prior to his or her predictable dismissal from an organization.

predatorism. noun. **1.** Abuse and exploitation of associates, business partners, or loved ones. *Psychology.* **2.** Personality disorder characterized by the behavior of pleasing oneself at the expense of others.

predipuct. verb. **1.** To pose simple and logical questions to invalidate the arguments of a preacher. noun. **2.** A predipucting target. **3.** Predipuder.

predubilation. noun. **1.** Strange sensation of ephemeral doubt that precedes a sneeze or an orgasm. **2.** A fluctuating shiver that surprises someone before sneezing or reaching a sexual climax. *Informal.* **3.** Unsure if coming or going when coming.

prefollow. verb. **1.** To precede in a non-continuous fashion what is about to happen. **2.** To presseg. noun. **3.** Prenext.

pregeria. noun. Premature rejuvenation.

premadroog. verb. **1.** To wake up very early or well before dawn. **2.** To prematinate. noun. **3.** Time interval beginning after the madroog* and before dawn. **4.** Prematinade.

prembeile. noun. **1.** Varied feelings that people experience before dancing. **2.** A subconscious or instinctive mental rehearsal of the movements and steps to perform immediately before dancing.

prenostigy. noun. Intense and scourging emotion that a presemption* is a penitence imposed for an act committed in the past.

prepend. noun. **1.** A thought that has not been thought yet. **2.** Protopensement. **3.** Althought.

preperd. verb. **1.** To lose or to cease possessing something before owning it. **2.** To lose something erroneously assumed to belong to oneself. **3.** (of gambling) To lose the winnings prior to winning. *Commerce.* noun. **4.** An enterprise bound to fail, usually for obvious reasons. **5.** Preloss.

prephernalia. noun. **1.** A significant present given to a bride before marriage. **2.** Money or goods given to a female partner or a partner assuming the majority of a feminine role in a couple living together.

presbipodia. noun. *Medicine.* Assortment of types of gaits provoked by arthrosis, osteoarthritis, hypomyosís, arteriosclerosis, ankylosis, or any other degenerative disease common in senility.

presbitogeny. noun. A society that restrains children from playing and persuades or imposes on them the adoption of gestures and slow movements characteristic of the elderly.

presbitosis. noun. *Philosophy.* **1.** Final stage in old age when organs fail and hope is extinguished. *Medicine.* **2.** Terminal senility. **3.** Multiple failure of organs and systems where treatments help some conditions but worsen others. *Informal.* **4.** A condition in which a patient is a living textbook of internal medicine.

presemption. noun. *Philosophy.* **1.** The disturbing sense of the turbid weight of the perceived present. *Psychology.* **2.** Potent emotive reaction to a paramonition*. **3.** Manomescence.

presention. noun. **1.** Innate ignorance of the multiple convolutions of a present within the ephemeral present perceived.

2. A cluster of presents in a present that three-dimensional beings cannot sense due to lack of chronosensory organs. **3.** Perception of one of the presents not yanked out by the astromeleic speed of time passing.

presequent. adjective. **1.** Preceding something in hierarchical order. **2.** Ranked or graded precutiveness.*

presinate. verb. To alleviate or heal the sorrow someone will have.

presinolate. verb. To pretend to heal the sorrow someone will have or could have.

presnit. 1. Inhaling sound, or a sequence of inhaling sounds, a person emits prior to sneezing. **2.** Prefosturn.

presolar. noun. **1.** A defined area of land immediately before a lot of land. *Astrophysics.* **2.** Time preceding the formation of the solar system. *Astronomy.* **3.** The time elapsed between the departure of photons from the surface of a star and their arrival in the atmosphere of a celestial body.

pressinlation. noun. *Physics.* **1.** Acquisition of pressure and maintenance of the compulsion exerted after said pressure has ceased. *Psychology.* **2.** Acquisition of pressure and maintenance of the compulsion exerted after said pressure has ceased. **3.** Presincontulation.

presticide. noun. The loss of a friendship and money following a loan of money.

prestineuric. noun. *Medicine.* **1.** A neurologically normal person with high electroencephalographic activity. **2.** A person with no apparent ailment but with a high mental activity that can be only detected by medical diagnostic methods.

prestopht. noun. **1.** A comical squinting facial expression. **2.** The act of wrinkling the face to enhance vision. *Informal.* **3.** Making fun of a visually impaired person. **4.** A person over 50 years of age attempting to read small print without glasses.

pretangnose. verb. To comprehend the meaning of life an instant before dying.

pretargony. noun. **1.** Condition of a person with no profession or work who depends on others and repeatedly demands more from them without justification. **2.** Glifory. **3.** Catachidonity.

preterible. adjective. A conditional past that either happened or it did not happen, or it is doubtful that it occurred but it is sensed to have happened.

preternity. noun. **1.** Eternity minus one. **2.** Quasiperpetuity with beginning and end. **3.** Eternity minus a unit of time, which may vary between 1 and 10^{16} seconds [i.e. 316,880,000 years].

preteromnesia. noun. **1.** A remembrance that suddenly turns into a doubtful memory of an event lived. **2.** Opteromnesia. **3.** Disjuncated memory. **4.** Reconficsia.

pretinision. noun. *Psychology.* Instantaneous and uncomfortable emotion that precedes fear.

pretist. noun. A person who, when putting a belt on, routinely misses one belt loop on the back of the trousers, forming an awkward fold.

pretmory. noun. **1.** An innate and preconceived memory pre-lost prior to an existence. **2.** A memory recalled during levinatitude.* **3.** Remembering something in a metaxistance.*

pretrophy. noun. *Embryology.* A period preceding the absence of development of a vestigial tissue or organ in an embryo.

pretzeller. noun. **1.** A person who makes pretzels. **2.** A pretzel salesperson.

preversic. adjective. Taking a few steps back before approaching something hated.

primisnor. noun. **1.** The first person to fall asleep and snore loudly in shared bedrooms, dormitories, cells, tents, or bedrooms. **2.** Primironk.

primitage. noun. The first tragedy, sorrow, or misfortune that is inexplicably followed by other unrelated tragedies, sorrows, or misfortunes.

primulation. noun. Emulation, with varied levels of affectation, of the speech style and mannerisms of a person admired.

prionoid. noun. Artificial protein-rich organism created by assemblage of prions.

prionosis. noun. *Medicine.* **1.** Idiopathic group of infectious syndromes following a blend of prions from diverse origins in one or more tissues. **2.** Incurable and fatal infection in one of more organs following *in vivo* recombination of prions.

probletation. noun. Promotion of a person in an organization for merits related to the solution of a problem said person created deliberately and clandestinely.

procane. verb. To be reborn from a state of deterioration, decomposition, or collapse into a superior condition to the previous one.

proceept. verb. To demonstrate the existence of the unreal.

procolham. verb. **1.** To translate incorrectly a poem or the lyrics of a song into other languages and to make the translation more popular than the original work. **2.** To dye something a whiter shade of pale. **3.** A pale shade. **4.** Procolharumize.

procounsel. noun. **1.** Unspecific, paradoxical, or confusing advice. **2.** Vaguemonition.

prodelight. noun. **1.** A pleasurable memory that exceeds the lived experience in pleasure and delight. **2.** A memory of a pleasure that is more pleasurable than the real pleasure.

prodon. noun. *Medicine.* An abscess that oozes a necrotic fluid.

prodult. verb. **1.** To adopt an adult as a godson or goddaughter. **2.** Prosonament.

proforism. noun. A concise definition of a highly technical or complicated concept in layperson's terms.

profute. verb. To anticipate something joyful or pleasurable with exaggerated enthusiasm.

prognemia. noun. An unrelenting and cruel memory; the more one tries to forget the more it replays.

progusk. verb. **1.** To extinguish passion. **2.** To smother the will of a person to execute a planned action.

prontaneity. noun. **1.** Satiation immediately after beginning to eat. *Medicine.* **2.** Pre-prandial or intra-prandrial satiation. *Informal.* **3.** The loss of appetite when sitting down to eat.

propard. verb. **1.** To impede someone from achieving his or her goals or dreams. **2.** To obstruct the path of someone's success.

propasch. verb. **1.** To actively delay a bureaucratic or legal process, generally maliciously. **2.** To cease helping, attending, looking after, or servicing someone.

propensive. adjective. Pertaining to or related to a person who incites others to think, particularly after the death of said person.

prophiloquist. noun. A person who is unable to convince others in spite of providing incontrovertible evidence in an eloquent manner.

prosalaic. adjective. Having exceptional skill in explaining complicated subjects, excluding politics or religion, in everyday language.

prosaurion. noun. A juice made of reptile fossils that is prepared by melting the rocks where the fossils are entrapped and discarding the rocky eluant.

proscind. verb. To actively plan to deprive oneself of something.

prostance. noun. Nonexistent lapse or interval of time or space between two things or events that eventually become the same thing or event.

prostibilism. noun. **1.** Undisputedly and freely willing to pay excessive tributes. **2.** Fully accepting an avernocracy.* **3.** A population that is not civispabilated.* **4.** Full compliance with an empratic* government. **5.** Tribunation.* **6.** Un-hamtral.*

prostigyn. noun. A gynecologist who aims to attract clients by clinically examining patients in a shop window.

prostimism. noun. *Commerce.* **1.** Marketing strategy to promote musical products played by women. **2.** A cookie-cutter approach by music industry monopolies consisting of publicizing, in music video format among target audiences, songs interpreted by attractive young women dressed seductively, moving enticingly and dancing simulating heterosexual and

homosexual copulations. *Music.*
3. Merdation.*

prostinct. noun. **1.** A prolonged
state of alertness due to
precaution or fear that causes
chronic stress. **2.** An enhanced
and sustained instinct.

prostisible. noun. **1.** A whistle
or whistle-like sound a prostitute
emits to attract clients in
some countries. **2.** Sirenalio. **3.**
Nereidio.

prostruct. verb. **1.** To mentally
conceive a construction. noun.
2. A talented architect.

prosume. verb. **1.** To brag
about oneself over planned
future achievements. **2.** To have
a high opinion of oneself. **3.** To
boast about how attractive one
will be.

prosumption. noun. **1.** High
valuation of oneself for acts
not yet done. **2.** Action and
effect of prosume.* **3.** Perceived
arrogance in a person and their
shared plans or dreams.

protaphony. noun. Feigned
sorrowful tone of voice when
reading an obituary or sad news.

prothanasia. noun. **1.** The
killing of a person planned
long before his or her potential
suffering or when the potential
suffering is uncertain. **2.** The
killing of a person who may
suffer an untreatable disease

in the long-term future. **3.**
Thanaxis* of someone else.

protidiot. noun. *Informal.* **1.** The
worst insult directed at an idiot.
2. A person who is considered
or is catalogued as being worse
than a preidiot.

protoception. noun. **1.**
Perception of natural temporal
phenomena through the
senses, without identifying or
knowing its nature. **2.** Rare
and unexplained perception of
non-linear time. **3.** Awareness of
time metrodicity in non-linear
time units, without synarchic*
apparatus or instruments,
that compartmentalizes such
non-linear time units by
circumnavigating the presents
to detect a here-and-now that
co-exists with the parawhile,*
which generally escapes
perception by the senses
because three-dimensional
sentient beings perceive only
a paninclusive chronoprison*
where the amphafter, the
protofoward and the postbehind
are fissioned in beforeness and
afterness and perceived as an
ephemeral instant.

protemporaneous. adjective.
Pertaining or related to a person
or thing existing or present
in the same past as another
person or thing, including the

immediate, mediate, and distant past.

protonsel. noun. **1.** A partial counsel to help a person to solve a problem individually. *Education.* **2.** A coaching technique. verb. **3.** To prompt someone to come up with an answer with instructive hints.

protopreterition. noun. Speculation of what was but was not because if it occurred, it did not actually happen since the could-have-been did not take place and was not possible even if it could have been probable in the past, but was not, for reasons of temporal-spatial causality not clearly understood.

protujation. noun. *Psychology.* A feeling of claustrophobia or of being oppressed as if a tight space when one is outdoors and in solitude.

prounsel. adjective. **1.** Being prone to receiving unsolicited advice. noun. **2.** A person who is a repetitive target of advice, generally without apparent cause.

provanescence. noun. **1.** An image, color, sound, smell, or sensation that is perceived faintly and slowly by the senses or by memory, and suddenly is perceived in its entirety. adjective. **2.** Anasfumant.

proversity. noun. A non-innate, non-morbid debauchery a person pursues voluntarily.

proximeter. noun. **1.** A person's intuitive meter that (when operating well) senses the appropriate amount of personal spatial distance from other people to maintain. **2.** The intuitive sense that takes into account relevant cultural, psychosexual, amistatus* dynamics, and unique circumstances to maintain an appropriate personal spatial distance. **3.** Proximitude. **4.** Ejackler.*

pruniness. noun. *Psychology.* A strong sensation that one's body is not enough for one's ego.

prurit. verb. **1.** To cause an itch. **2.** To do something that provokes an urge to scratch.

pruritate. verb. **1.** To tickle someone. **2.** To cause in a person an emotion that triggers laughter. **3.** To bother someone slightly and insistently.

prut. verb. **1.** To cause or promote a puncture in the mood of a person. *Psychology.* **2.** To cause a depression in a person.

prux. noun. **1.** Sticky dew. **2.** Gluey humidity.

psalmonerist. noun. A person who openly pretends to like monotonous, graceless chants.

pseudologist. noun. A person who specializes in or studies falseness.

pseudopassion. noun. **1.** An intermittent, weak, or insecure passion, generally motivated by profit. Example: The feeling of an artist working as an artisan in a factory; the feeling of a person in a couple not completely in love. **2.** The feeling of acting in a profession or occupation.

psittacism. noun. **1.** Repetition of a word or a statement like a parrot. *Education.* **2.** A teaching method based on repetition to exercise the memory. **3.** Reiterity.*

psoricret. noun. **1.** A secret nobody can keep. **2.** Psittacrit. **3.** Secretapius. **4.** Secrepert. **5.** A secret that travels as fast as bad news.

psychalgia. noun. **1.** An oppressive and generalized pain in the body that cannot be pinpointed. **2.** Mild discomfort a person feels when sensing being a eumenity* target. **3.** A bittersweet reaction during a mythopenia* or a sacharigenous statement.

psychaspide. noun. *Psychology.* Maneuver or ruse someone uses as a psychological shield.

psychescribe. noun. A person who writes mental notes or texts without using any physical tools.

psychoclast. noun. **1.** A person who unintentionally exasperates another. **2.** A person who inadvertently and easily breaks the personality of another.

psychocumic. adjective. Having a sharp and pointy mind.

psychodiphic. adjective. Having the faculty to sense other people's intentions.

psychoelectric. adjective. **1.** Producing a hair-raising feeling of thrilling excitement. **2.** The feeling of a performing artist receiving a deserved standing ovation. **3.** A feeling of excitement, fear, and euphoria on being the center of attention of a large number of spectators.

psychoelectrography. noun. *Psychology.* A method to record the reactions of a person to various stimuli, compute the reactions to an algorithm of personality profiles, and display the 3D outcome on a screen.

psychoghostism. noun. A belief that attributes common psychology to ghosts and serves as the basis for exorcisms of people and haunted houses.

psychognator. noun. A person who projects his or her personality with affectation.

psychognomy. noun. *Psychology.* A study that analyzes and catalogs the personality of a person according to the person's name.

psychograph. noun. **1.** A person with the capability to discern the personality of someone at first sight. **2.** A person possessing innate psychodiphic* and psychographistic* abilities **3.** Psychodecipherer.* **4.** *Psychology.* An instrument that deciphers personality by detecting and recording physiological reactions to various stimuli.

psychographistic. adjective. Having the ability to perceive, from mannerisms and tone of voice, the thoughts and desires of others.

psycholm. noun. **1.** The action of extracting concentrated knowledge by squeezing someone's mind. **2.** Psychudderation. **3.** Psychomilk.

psychomencia. noun. *Psychology.* A condition in a personality characterized by anarchy that does not reach a level of psychosis.

psychosondist. noun. *Commerce.* **1.** A specialist who pretends to know the origin of a person's mental anguish after searching for subconscious impulses that may be repressed by conscious thought through long sessions in which the specialist inquires after said

person's particular lived events and emotions. *Psychology.* **2.** Psychoanalyst.

psychostat. verb. *Psychology.* To group individuals in an organization according to their personalities to maximize their productivity and to increase the likelihood of anticipating their reactions to possible events.

psychostregy. noun. *Psychology.* Strategy to select and assign a specific torture method according to the personality of the person being tortured to inflict the most severe mental and physical pain without killing the person.

psychoswindler. noun. **1.** Someone who is aware of a person's needs or desires and uses that information to abuse or swindle said person. **2.** Psychographilator.

psychotalisman. noun. A mental figure that is believed to have magical powers.

psychotize. verb. *Psychology.* **1.** To transform an organic ailment into a psychological disturbance. *Informal.* **2.** To drive someone nuts involuntarily.

psychoxenia. noun. *Psychology.* Sudden sensation of not knowing oneself.

pudentory. noun. **1.** A public lavatory exclusively for washing portions of the body that are covered by clothing. **2.** A genital bathroom. **3.** In some European countries: a menstruatory. **4.** A walk-in "vudeeh".

pugasyl. noun. **1.** A privileged refuge for runaway pugilists. *Archaic.* **2.** A place of refuge and solace for retired hit-men or mercenaries.

pulasion. noun. **1.** A pleasurable act by a person being penetrated during a copulation consisting of putting the legs on the back of the penetrator and pulling to increase the force and depth of the penetration. **2.** A docotracting* genucoxil.*

pulsandric. adjective. **1.** Pertaining to or relative to the innate impulses of human nature. noun. *Psychology.* **2.** Energetic vibrating monad without which mental processes cannot be executed.

pulsiocognition. noun. *Psychology.* Self-discovered psychic energy, generally during introspection, that orients one's behavior toward reaching a goal.

punescent. adjective. Having an excessively potent voice that seems to come out in solid particles which strike the hearers inside the ears.

punialgia. noun. **1.** A self-induced non-physical pain that is endured by some, but complained about by the weak. **2.** Consequence of the blotta.*

puniscald. verb. **1.** To publicly expose a slanderer or a liar. **2.** To polyscalt.

punitherapy. noun. *Medicine.* An ineffective and painful treatment that is administered on purpose.

pyrobrady. noun. *History.* **1.** Cruel and prolonged burning torture consisting of raising the temperature very slowly until the death of the victim. **2.** A torture consisting of slowly boiling or baking a living person.

pyrobramic. adjective. Related to or pertaining to sexual arousal during a menstruating period.

pyrobramy. noun. A sexual desire in a woman during her menstruation.

pyrocandela. noun. *Anthropology.* **1.** An ice lamp. **2.** A concave recipient made of bone where animal fat was lit for warmth and lighting among some genus *Homo* societies circa 500,000 B.C.

pyrofulmint. noun. **1.** A sudden gush of flames. **2.** An intense, rapid, and destructive fire. **3.** Raffage.

pyrogont. noun. **1.** A male labial cosmetic that is colorless, flavorless, and odorless containing concentrated yohimbine. **2.** An aphrodisiac a man uses clandestinely in a cosmetic or other substance to administer by kissing a person he would like to engage in copulation.

pyrokleptist. noun. **1.** A professional specialist in stealing fire. **2.** Someone who robs fires of diverse origins. **3.** Promethist.

pyroyoon. noun. Amusement and delight conferred by the controlled use of fire.

Q

quarky. noun. **1.** Quality of a non-cheese substance that has the smell, taste and texture of a soft cheese. *Physics.* **2.** A hypothetical meson-like subparticle unbound to its corresponding antiquark.

quatrigramps. noun. *Informal.* Great-great-great-grandfather.

quesity. noun. **1.** Quality of smell, shape or consistency of a cheese. **2.** Cheeseness.

queromize. verb. To rape brutally a man through the anus using only the hands.

quintingulated. adjective. *Zoology.* Having five fingers with nails at the distal part of each extremity.

quiornivore. noun. A person who regularly eats raw or bleeding meat.

quisnate. verb. **1.** To escape from a financial predicament immediately after discovering oneself to have been the target of a fraud. **2.** To exod* from an economic problem immediately after sensing a kynt* or a maligresity.

quister. noun. Membranous aura that develops progressively and surrounds a pernickety person.

R

rabosic. adjective. **1.** Pertaining to, related to or attributable to the two round fleshy parts that form the lower rear area of a human trunk. **2.** Buttocky. **3.** Having a disproportionally large caboose. **4.** Having an accented derrière.

racolia. noun. A firm conviction of certainty about something without having an idea of what it is about.

radialism. noun. *Physics.* Radial expansion dependent upon the radialant's departing dimension: zero degrees from one dimension, 180 degrees from two dimensions, 360 degrees from three dimensions and so on.

radiclism. noun. *Politics.* **1.** A political theory that advocates the truly full transparency of a state's finances. *Economics.* **2.** An economic theory that preceded the political theory of the same name that unveiled the manipulation of a state's income and expenses as the root of corruption and proposed controlling mechanisms to prevent said manipulation.

raffage. 1. An unexpected spurt of flames. **2.** A burst of fire directed to a specific location.

raggadic. noun. A person who develops jagged crags in their personality and new strange behaviors which do not match the previous mundane personality.

raggage. noun. *Literary.* The evanescent difference between the capriciousness of a man and a woman.

ragost. verb. To tie the fingers and hands of a person with rubber bands to prevent any defensive movement as done with live lobsters and crabs in a supermarket.

ralett. noun. One of the helicoidal extensions in a teletransporting chamber.

ramaph. noun. A stream of odoriferous waves that precede or are immediately below the smelling threshold capacity of a human.

ramb. noun. *Medicine.* A viral venereal disease discovered in certain clusters of prostitutes at the end of the 21st century.

rametina. noun. The youngest daughter of a prostitute.

ramixia. noun. Phenomenon of accelerated fracturing of one discipline into several sub-disciplines and of those into sub-subdisciplines.

rammocle. noun. *Psychology.* **1.** A mental activity within the collection of mental activities that constitute the feeling of guilt. **2.** Part of a supramaculation.*

rampittude. noun. *Statistics.* Amplitude of variation between weighted low and weighted high records collected in an investigation.

rapage. noun. **1.** The seduction of a consenting adolescent by an adult. *Law.* **2.** A love affair between an adult and an adolescent that is not considered statutory rape.

raptanime. noun. **1.** An abduction of a soul. verb. **2.** To kidnap someone's spirit.

rapuler. noun. *Informal.* A worker who, when in front of his or her supervisor, reacts and behaves as if caught copying during an examination.

rasdazz. noun. *Astronomy.* The corrosion of a celestial body without an atmosphere that seems to have rips on its surface.

raspous. adjective. Acquiring a loud, rasping voice as part of one's profession.

rastroid. noun. **1.** A penetrating, disagreeable and cloying perfume used by a person that facilitates following and finding said person sometime after change of location. **2.** Rastrogenous.

raveler. noun. *Informal.* **1.** A person whose voice and arguments are a constant repetition, seemingly part of one long bolero, with the same rhythm and the same melody interpreted by different manipulating instruments. **2.** A human bolero.

ravunal. noun. *Literary.* **1.** A group of large grey clouds that darken a day. *Meteorology.* **2.** A group of thick dark grey clouds that help in predicting a thunderstorm.

realimeter. noun. Instrument that measures reality with validated data.

reboist. noun. **1.** A phenomenon, triggered by one or more causes, that suddenly makes a person glow with beauty. **2.** A woman pregnant with a male fetus who radiates allurement.

rebostion. noun. **1.** The act of being ashamed of one's own beauty. **2.** The action of a woman who covers her face during an emotional moment or a reboist.*

recalliate. verb. **1.** To make something or someone more attractive again by adding decorations or features. **2.** To re-embellish, to re-beautify, to re-prettify.

recalp. verb. To powerfully affect someone's emotional state.

recalt. verb. To fully embrace a perception while sharpening one's senses.

recanaxia. noun. A reflex of alarm or a grimace when discovering one's first grey hair in a reflection.

rederm. verb. **1.** To apply or to acquire new skin. noun. *Commerce.* **2.** A business enterprise that exploits self-cloning technologies to harvest skin for autologous transplantation purposes. *Law.* **3.** Regulatory efforts from the early 24th century which applied specific restrictions to cosmetic rederm applications.

redoffalous. adjective. **1.** Lacking the capability to savor a delicacy. **2.** Samboter.

redotment. noun. **1.** The action of conferring a second dowry.

Linguistics. **2.** A habit of writing two dots instead of one. **3.** Camerriment. **4.** A woman who re-dowers* a husband. *History.* **5.** A telegram sent by a telegraphist with Parkinson's disease.

redrott. noun. **1.** A double treason in an act of treason. **2.** An unknowing self-betrayal while betraying another person. **3.** Repiffy.

redubilation. noun. *Psychology.* A feeling of apprehension when becoming aware of a personal doubt and a new doubt suddenly emerges.

reflaction. noun. **1.** A nervous and involuntary inflation of the cheeks when one is speaking with a person considered important. **2.** A nervous distension of the mouth when one is speaking of one's own actions and believing them to be of some significance. **3.** Callacotude. *Vulgar.* **4.** Smegation.

refranic. adjective. **1.** Having the ability to speak using multiple adages. **2.** Having the inability to speak without using proverbs. **3.** Having a capricious preoccupation with adding overfamiliar sayings during a conversation. **4.** Paremanous. **5.** Sabamic. **6.** Colemazinne. **7.** Maximic. **8.** Axiomistic.

refrinderm. noun. **1.** A quality of the skin that refracts light. **2.** The natural glitter of a young woman's legs or skin in general. **3.** Ridammy. **4.** Alosh. **5.** Respieldor.*

regaphio. noun. A flat, slender, and muscularly feminine abdomen.

regendrics. noun. *Genetics.* A branch of genetic engineering dedicated to studying regeneration of limbs and organs.

regettic. adjective. **1.** Related to a material that was elongated until losing its original shape and becoming unrecognizable. **2.** Pertaining or related to an amorphous enlargement. *Physics.* **3.** Molding or manipulating something until its behavior is changed. *Psychology.* **4.** Manipulating someone until his or her behavior is changed.

regisment. noun. **1.** Unwritten norms that govern the behavior of a menstruating woman in a public lavatory. **2.** Reglad. **3.** Rasfrent.

regree. adjective. **1.** Being ready, eager, enthusiastic or anxious to do something. **2.** Being of the most eager disposition to do something for someone else. **3.** Being impatient to experience something for the first time. **4.** Chineiric.*

reguedial. noun. **1.** A room in excessive disorder. **2.** A situation where several solid artifacts are scattered like a flood of liquid.

reinvisibility. noun. **1.** Quality of regaining invisibility. **2.** Quality of being able to become invisible for a second time or more. **3.** Camefy.

reironesia. noun. **1.** Theory that endorses laughter as one mechanism for prevention and treatment of diseases. *Philosophy.* **2.** A theoretical branch of rihistism* or rihistic philosophy.

reitebrate. verb. **1.** To reiterate something in a firm or punitive tone that shakes the hearer. noun. **2.** A belligerent reiterity.*

reiterity. noun. **1.** The state or condition of denoting a reiteration, of saying something again, of repeating statements, of stressing something obstinately, of mentioning and re-mentioning a masticated message, of accentuating an already voiced thought obdurately, of relapsing into articulating the same or similar words, of underlining the obvious in the wearisome story told and retold endlessly, of declaring recalcitrantly the same thing one more time, of stating a tiresome echo, replication, duplication, and recidivation of the same idea, of retelling

and re-retelling what has already been said, of going over and over the same thing, of pounding, battering, crushing or mashing something said earlier until hackneyed, of insisting obstinately a number of times, of remarking with brutal stubbornness a jejune point of view, of adding resolutely once more a minute, nauseating concept, of re-announcing a statement in a dull pedestrian fashion, of enacting a dreary recitation of a notion, recapitulating it redundantly and repeating it with different words, of decrepit tautology, of speaking with perseverance and with circular logic, of voicing tenaciously a chewed, tedious thought, a munched, insipid phrase, of pronouncing pertinaciously a monotonous postulate of minion quality, of vocalizing a mind-numbing opinion tediously, of uttering once more an uninteresting verbal regurgitation and to assume that the hearers are as equally incapable as the reiterant in retaining any detail of any information after hearing it innumerable times. **2.** Reaffirmation of something.
relecterium. noun. **1.** Instrument designed to facilitate reading in elderly people. **2.**

A lectern equipped with a potent light source and a large, adaptable magnifying glass. **3.** Sepitunk. **4.** Talesin. *Informal.* **5.** Readease.
relickerus. noun. A relic of an erotic nature.
relintive. adjective. Persisting without any sign of retraction.
remobiad. noun. A Friday soup, also called *rapipe* in some countries.
remomio. noun. **1.** An unpronounceable, untranslatable, and unrepeatable expletive a person pronounces during a state of agitation. **2.** A collection of unpronounceable, untranslatable, and unrepeatable words said when experiencing a barraphia.*
remute. verb. **1.** To re-deaden, re-muffle or re-soften a sound. **2.** To mute again. *Informal.* **3.** To hit twice the mute key on a television remote control or a phone following the insistent request of a girlfriend, wife, or partner. **4.** adjective. Refraining two or more times from speaking. noun. **5.** A person who has lost the power of speech for a second time.
renavatar. noun. **1.** An incarnation of an incarnation in a third incarnation happening immediately after an artificially

modified incarnation. **2.**
Rimpestar.

reoptonance. noun. **1.**
Prolongation of a visualized
image that is gradually fading.
2. A vision produced by the
revision of another vision.

reosmia. noun. **1.** The illusion
of smelling a smell again after
the original smell has dissipated.
2. Reffag.

repag. noun. **1.** A new clothing
item that, when worn for
the first time, is perceived by
everyone as a rag. **2.** Relimious.

repelation. noun. **1.** Action and
effect of removing the cortex
or the surface of something
and cataloging each one of
the internal components to
understand its nature. *Psychology.*
2. Action and effect of
removing the behavioral layers
of someone and cataloging each
one of the layers to understand
his or her personality. *Art.* **3.**
The process of dissecting, and
cataloging, each coating of a
painting to understand how it
was painted in order to avoid
another grumble like the one
that initiated the process.

rephlade. verb. **1.** To acquire
soft skin or to apply something
on the skin to make it smooth
and silky. **2.** To. affofate. **3.** To
reflatidate.

repomiation. noun. **1.** The
feeling an obese person endures
when observing an athlete. **2.** A
feeling a fat person experiences
when next to a slender, thin,
emaciated, splanchuose,* or
ríttic* person.

repotor. noun. **1.** A person
who affirms or responds to
something only after someone
else has affirmed or responded.
2. Repliverious.

repuntition. noun. **1.** A
sensation of guilt with
no motive whatsoever. **2.**
Rephebation. **3.** A sensation of
pressure throughout the body
felt by a Catholic man after
coming out of a confessional
booth, which intensifies after
arriving home to bicker with his
wife. **4.** Whepid.* **5.** Whammit.*
6. Telesm.*

rerretch. verb. To make the
sound and movement of
vomiting without vomiting.

respesn. noun. **1.** Feeling of
mute respect before someone
with impressive personality.
2. Silent respect. *Psychology.* **3.**
Feeling of humbleness or shame
that triggers inability to speak. **4.**
Inability to ask for forgiveness.

respieldor. noun. **1.** Natural
glow of a young person's skin,
principally in women. **2.** Skin
that appears to emit light. **3.**
Refrinderm.* **4.** Resplenderm.

restropy. noun. **1.** Indifference of a group of individuals or of all individuals within a species faced with annihilation. **2.** Inaction or indifference of some people or animals who act as if nothing is happening when witnessing other individuals within their group being hunted, predated, massacred, assassinated, or executed.

retabia. noun. Mucosal excretion coming out of the penis after coitus that has no purpose and makes no sense.

retette. noun. **1.** A dirty toilet with no seat, usually in public restrooms. **2.** Toilet, water closet or WC with no seatress.*

retharpia. noun. The remaining manhood left in a man after being in an impactful event.

retisensic. adjective. Saying nothing or almost nothing out of sympathy or empathy with the listener.

retrapern. verb. To withdraw a penis from a vagina for no reason before consummating coitus.

retrengyndamy. noun. A condition in which a woman gives and a man receives.

retreract. verb. **1.** To repudiate a sexual advance with words or gestures. *Politics.* **2.** To negate a negation adding a double negative, generally when

endorsing something. noun. **3.** Seggot.

retrochenation. noun. **1.** A group of amorphous and intangible scars that are accumulated in a relationship. **2.** Marital blotta.*

retrocognition. noun. **1.** Any knowledge learned retrospectively sometime after a lived experience. **2.** Retrospective knowledge.

retrodilection. noun. **1.** The distinct phases of predictable marital arguments that conclude in an irreconcilable dispute. **2.** Retrogamilection. *Politics.* **3.** The rhetoric of a successful politician that gives the false appearance of being logical. *Linguistics.* **4.** Deceiving utterance that contains tautology, circular reasoning, short-circuit tautologies, or dodecagonal rhetoric. **5.** Contrasts and similarities of rhetoric in politicians. *Literary.* **6.** Rhetorical circumlocution with no destination.

retrofluence. noun. **1.** A person or thing from the past with capacity to have an effect on the character, development or behavior of someone from the present or future. **2.** Influence of something to modify or control a process through time.

3. A person or thing with such a capacity or power.

retrognostic. adjective. **1.** Acquiring knowledge retrospectively. **2.** Learning by retrocognition.* noun. **3.** Specific retrocognition.*

retromaniac. adjective. Being obsessed with performing again, without modifying any variables or activities that previously failed.

retromord. noun. The feeling of having the need to possess an inanimate object after a similar one was discarded, donated, destroyed, or thrown away.

retropaff. noun. An intent to respond or react to an affront, insult or assault by voicing unintelligible sounds or incoherent words.

retrophet. noun. **1.** A person who claims to possess the supernatural ability to see past events not recorded in history. *Theology.* **2.** A person regarded as an inspired teacher or proclaimer of the will of past prophets.

retrophony. noun. **1.** A voice with a metallic quality that seems to have an immediate echo. **2.** A voice possessing an artificial or virtual quality of a paleocybernaut from the future in communication with the present.

retrosidia. noun. **1.** Audible hallucinations that appear spontaneously after three days without sleep. **2.** Miristasia.*

retrosentiment. noun. **1.** A remembrance that triggers a feeling or emotion that exceeds in intensity the original circumstance or event. **2.** The act of giving a person something intangible retrospectively for something said person may have done.

retrosequence. noun. **1.** A logical correspondence between the future conduct of a person and the future principles said person will adhere to later. **2.** Circumstance or event that prefollows* something that will probably happen.

retrosequent. adjective. Preceding or happening in relation to something that may happen in a conditional future.

retroserve. verb. **1.** To maintain or take care of something or someone that already happened or existed. **2.** To bring to life and to sustain without any concomitant harm to anyone who existed before. noun. **3.** A backward serve in tennis.

retrosteth. noun. An area of imprecise limits inside the chest where a feeling of emptiness and pain concentrates during a period of emotional anguish or grief.

retyrantion. noun. The conversion of a revolutionary leader into a tyrant after replacing a previous tyrant in a defeated governmental regime.

revehivolice. noun. **1.** Repetition of an act performed by an inanimate object. **2.** A repeated and seemingly voluntary act by an electromagnetic vehicle, machine, or apparatus that required fixing by a specialized mechanic or technician, but once in the presence of said mechanic or technician it begins to work or function properly. **3.** A repeated vehivolition.*

revemp. noun. One of the three inseparable units that constitute hatred.

reverbellation. noun. **1.** Delicate, undulating movement exhibited by proportioned breasts of a young woman while ambulating. **2.** Biological reverberation that can trigger an emotion when seen. **3.** Anecstatic* biological vibration. *Psychology.* **4.** Envy experienced by a woman when observing a younger woman with reverbellation. **5.** Esthetic or sexual pleasure felt by heterosexual men when observing same.

reyatt. noun. **1.** A scream a woman makes when sitting down without looking and falling down accidentally in a toilet without a seat. **2.** Retescreech. **3.** Toiyell. **4.** Holehowl. **5.** Barraphic* shriek. **6.** A woman's squeal when diving in a seatress.*

rhabdiate. verb. To refuse the use of a walking stick, cane, crutches, or other implement to assist walking.

rhapsomania. noun. Unconscious obsessive compulsion to imitate gestures, behaviors or expressions of other people.

rhetecord. verb. To remind someone of something of which they do not want to be reminded.

rhetophobic. adjective. *Psychology.* **1.** Being intimidated when listening to a person or persons versed in rhetoric. **2.** Having an aversion to physical or verbal challenges. **3.** Molesinic.

rheumster. noun. **1.** An extremely strict schoolteacher. **2.** Schallahan. *Archaic.* **3.** A person who chronically discharges mucous material from the eyes or nose. *Archaic.* **4.** A snotty boy.

rhinic. adjective. **1.** Pulling mucus from the nose with one or more fingers, whether in private or in public. *Informal.* **2.** Snottic. *Psychology.* **3.** Digirrhinic. noun. *Psychology.* **4.** Rhiner.

rhinning. adjective. **1.** Wrinkling one's nose as a sign of nervousness, uncertainty, or resignation. noun. **2.** Rhinofligation.

rhinodonous. adjective. Having a big head, proportionally small eyes, and teeth like a rhinoceros.

rhinogous. adjective. **1.** Pertaining to or relative to a person who pulls out mucus from the nostrils with one or more fingers and then ingests the extracted mucus. *Informal.* **2.** Boogeybear swallower. *Psychology.* **3.** Mucophagon. *Psychology.* **4.** Rhiniphagous. **5.** Pambuche. *Informal.* **6.** Snot eater.

rhinopodus. noun. An extraterrestrial animal that uses its nose for locomotion.

rhinoxic. adjective. Having a nose of disproportionate size and shape for head and face that gives a person a comical appearance.

rhizet. verb. *Philosophy.* To reach the root of a truth.

rhizeta. noun. Feeling of satisfaction and pleasant relief on having reached the root of a truth.

rhizolysis. noun. *Agriculture.* **1.** Destruction of roots. *Philosophy.* **2.** Destruction of truth's roots. *Law.* **3.** One of the mechanisms of a state's financial reconciliation with the radiclism* political and economic movements.

rhizoty. noun. *Philosophy.* **1.** Quality of having reached the root of a truth. **2.** Etymogy. **3.** Verilia. **4.** The last phase of etymy.*

ridace. noun. **1.** A brief mocking chuckle accompanied by tongue clicking and, sometimes, by a puffing sound. **2.** A sarcastic chuckle. **3.** Riflett. **4.** Risardia. **5.** Sarcachosquia. **6.** Sardiss. **7.** Risaculation. **8.** Churle.

ridipule. verb. **1.** To call loudly or to physically pull someone in public to make a scene or to ridicule said person. **2.** Public derision. **3.** Open and violent contumely.

riett. noun. *Medicine.* A schizophrenic patient with a certain ability to distinguish some hallucinations from reality.

riggler. noun. **1.** A woman given to habitual annoying giggles. **2.** A woman who guiguilates* loudly and irritatingly when speaking.

rigorific. adjective. **1.** Having body rigidity that resembles *rigor mortis. Medicine.* **2.** Being exposed to prolonged cold and having body stiffness.

rihistism. noun. *Philosophy.* A theory that promotes frequent laughter as a path to health and happiness.

ringling. adjective. Provoking fights outside a ring during a spectacle such as boxing or wrestling.

risaritt. noun. An affected, nervous laugh that is prolonged without impetus.

risigette. noun. A light giggling a girl perpetuates that is contagious to other girls.

risiggle. noun. **1.** Incessant and affected giggling without motive. **2.** Prolonged and affected giggling that is not provoked by a risinogenous* stimulus.

risinogenous. noun. **1.** A circumstance or action that provokes laughter. **2.** Something that makes a person laugh.

risperant. noun. **1.** The feeling of being in a time-still in the middle of a hardship. **2.** A woman who feels interminable instands* in each contraction during labor.

rittic. adjective. **1.** Having an extremely thin body despite eating great quantities of food. **2.** Ritopio.

rocime. noun. *Archaic.* **1.** A mix of resin with oil used in acts of gomorry. **2.** Sagari.

rockloid. noun. **1.** A person who is not a musician and imitates the gestures, mannerisms, speech patterns, and mode of dress of a musician in vogue. **2.** Inatimulater. **3.** Primulator*. **4.** Musical omnimimesis. **5.** Roculator.

rocolimous. noun. **1.** Dry and hard mucus adhered to the nasal mucosa that impedes the airflow. Said mucus does not come out when blowing one's nose, requiring a fingernail or a solid object to be extracted and, when coming out, drags a long, dense mucus that tickles a nostril. *Informal.* **2.** Hard and dry air-blocky snot. *Informal.* **3.** Megabugger.

rodaply. verb. **1.** To flay someone's spirit. **2.** To deeply disappoint a person who fully trusted in one. **3.** To endoliate.* adjective. **4.** Feeling postfidence.*

rodophant. noun. *Informal.* **1.** An obese person displaying awkward and clumsy movements. noun. **2.** An elephant lurching in the mud.

rodwaff. noun. *Informal.* An overweight woman with short legs, thick ankles, and widespread cellulite dressed in miniskirt or in tight shorts.

rotoric. adjective. Producing an annoying and repetitive noise, being a machine, an animal or an inconsiderate person.

routiler. noun. A bureaucrat who follows a routine strictly and unvaryingly.

rubrid. verb. *Literary.* To place an ethereal signature on the idea of another.

ruckacar. noun. *Informal.* An old decrepit person.

ruckloid. noun. *Informal. Vulgar.* A derogatory insulting expletive to an old or debilitated person with reduced mental abilities.

rumenine. verb. **1.** To repeat mentally an idea or a memory for long periods of time. **2.** To interrupt all activities to chew on an old idea or memory.

rumped. adjective. **1.** Having lost the rump curvature of youth. *Informal.* **2.** Old flat ass. **3.** Delabraic.* **4.** Rabadiperniated.

ruon. noun. *Physics.* **1.** Subatomic particle with no mass believed to be responsible for transmitting different forces into the charges of other particles to maintain symmetrical distances between each hadron. **2.** Cuon.

rupestrition. noun. *Psychology.* **1.** Fear felt by a young person considering the possibility of reaching old age. *Informal.* **2.** Loathing of becoming older.

rutiperation. noun. Irreparable damage on any part of the body caused by a routine performed for long periods of time.

ryphlet. noun. **1.** A laughter between teeth. **2.** A chuckle between teeth. **3.** A sardonic risaritt.* **4.** Inchision. **5.** Rinsispy.

S

sabime. noun. **1.** A person who nods insistently without saying a word when an expert explains a subject. **2.** An ignorant person who compulsively nods as a sign of understanding or agreement.

saboferon. noun. **1.** A person who develops rapid and intense physical response when chewing or ingesting tart or spicy foods. **2.** A person who develops immediate reactions of hyperthermia, sweating, and irritating pain inside the mouth when chewing or ingesting calitrigeneous* foods. **3.** Enchilous. **4.** Gastroward. *Informal.* **5.** A spice wimp.

sacackah. noun. *Vulgar.* Circumstance or event that induces panic.

sacapresage. noun. **1.** Something that seems to facilitate a conduit to happiness when one does not possess it. **2.** Something that forces us to plan our future, but to live in the present. **3.** Money.

sadispetrer. noun. A sadist who maintains an immutable posture when carrying out sadistic acts.

sadogomorrism. noun. **1.** Morbid sexual tendency of a person who enjoys causing pain or humiliation to others during acts of gomorry.* **2.** Gomosicalipsis.

safejester. noun. **1.** The delusion a safety belt provides when traveling in an airplane at a speed of 600 miles per hour and at an altitude of 37,000 feet. **2.** Safession. **3.** Safeass. **4.** Salphette.

sagatenn. noun. An oily substance.

saharrad. noun. *Archaic.* Purposeful self-cutting of the skin in multiple areas of the body.

saladery. noun. A phrase used to reimburse or thank a worker, assistant, donor, volunteer or care giver instead of giving money or barter in return. Examples: *God bless you. God will pay you. Bless your heart.*

salant. noun. The consummation of a marriage outside a nuptial chamber or a bedroom.

saltander. noun. A promiscuous person who jumps from man to man.

saltapatras. noun. *Informal.* **1.** An idiosyncratic effect of certain recreational drugs. **2.** A recreational mood-modifying drug. **3.** An involuntary backward somersault.

saltesher. adjective. *Psychology.* **1.** Having several personalities and alternating them at will according to the occasion. **2.** Inciting or manipulating loved ones or friends to do something for oneself.

salthon. noun. An unexpected and copious rush of salt from a saltshaker onto a favored dish.

samath. noun. **1.** Expression of horror by a woman who accidentally dives, bottom first, into a toilet with no seat. **2.** A facial expression that accompanies a reyatt.* **3.** Countenance of a barraphia.*

sambotic. noun. The waddling, propulsive gait of a horseman with tertiary syphilis.

samioty. verb. **1.** To over-stimulate someone in any educational aspect. **2.** To senambiate.

sapithemic. adjective. Changing a conversation suddenly to a subject matter one is familiar with.

saplate. verb. To raise and shake one's hand to silence someone, pretending not to be disrespectful.

saplatic. adjective. Having the urge to saplate.*

saposis. noun. A curd of dirt or grime on someone that resembles rotten soap.

sarcopathy. noun. *Medicine.* **1.** Any disease that consumes the flesh. **2.** A condition that seems to suck the skin dry. *Informal.* **3.** Mummylation.

sardogamist. noun. A married person who openly mocks his or her marriage.

sarf. noun. The ineffable and limiting pride in comprehending the universe held by a person who perceives only a minuscule portion of it through a tiny hole of his or her senses.

sarragre. noun. **1.** Verbal abuse by a husband to his wife. **2.** Cruel verbal treatment of a partner in a relationship. **3.** Verbal domestic violence.

sarrah. noun. *Informal.* **1.** A woman who pesters her husband daily. **2.** A woman who harasses her spouse continuously for no reason. *Vulgar.* **3.** A verbose bitch face.

sarwhess. noun. Embarrassing excitement a commoner feels in the company of distinguished persons or celebrities.

sarwick. adjective. **1.** Having a face that resembles the growth of fungi or algae on a marine rock. **2.** Sarguicheous. **3.** Sarguic.

sathkion. noun. A mediocre spouse who shines due to the triumphs of his or her spouse.

sauriol. noun. **1.** Fermented and distilled fossilized reptile concentrate credited with curative and life prolongation properties. **2.** Prosaurion* spirit.

sausade. (from *saudade* in Portuguese). noun. Ambivalent sensation of both happiness and sadness when yearning for something that is now gone.

schizophilia. noun. Having the disconcerting propensity of not knowing what to wish for.

sciencesology. noun. *Commerce.* **1.** Organization transformed into a religious system based on the seeking of self-knowledge and spiritual fulfilment through graded courses and training which everyone passes. **2.** Ideology of the semi-ignorant with recurring laziness of thinking. *Religion.* **3.** A pangnostic* association with contributing members who are unable to remember why they joined and what the association is about.

seatress. noun. **1.** Reclining seat without a lid on a toilet. **2.** Sentadeer.

sebate. noun. An instrument or apparatus that stops working moments before someone needs it for something important.

seducabb. noun. A coarse seducer with vulgar manners.

sedusten. noun. **1.** A stubborn seducer who persists with his or her seductive conduct following multiple rejections. *Psychology.* **2.** A man who utilizes seduction as a psychological mechanism as compensation for his real or perceived inferiority.

selepic. adjective. **1.** Relating to or characteristic of a fictitious epic story that resembles man landing on the moon in 1969. **2.** Saena. **3.** Mythepy.

semenarch. noun. The first ejaculation of an adolescent male.

semenemesis. noun. Vomit of semen.

semience. noun. *Philosophy.* A state in which someone is and exists.

semilexia. noun. **1.** A word that was pronounced incompletely due to an incident. **2.** A truncated word that is not a verbosury* and that usually occurs when conversing with a verbastigh.* **3.** Interruption in the enunciation of a word when it is perceived to be an inconceivable dysnomer* by a non-wonliner.*. **4.** Ceasing to converse suddenly when seeing oscuspum* in an interlocutor. **5.** Sudden sluggish speech when sensing oneself in insosperibility.*

semimbryo. noun. A vehemently desired embryo that will later on devastate a life.

seminophagous. adjective. Swishing, swallowing or savoring semen willingly.

semiinstant. noun. **1.** A portion of an instant. **2.** A fragment of an instant in the adopted chronal* systems.

semipregnation. noun. **1.** The condition or period of having a semimbryo* developing in the entrails. *Literature.* **2.** The condition of being half pregnant.

semisepsis. noun. *Economics.* **1.** An apparent state of financial convalescence during a massive economic crisis. *Medicine.* **2.** The apparent, yet unconfirmed, presence of harmful bacteria and their toxins in tissues.

senseguisis. noun. Lack of perception, subconscious tolerance, or complete unconcern about one's own body odor.

senuouse. noun. *Informal.* **1.** A man who, due to obesity or an endocrine ailment, seems to have female breasts. noun. **2.** *Medicine.* Gynecomastia primadonal gravis. **3.** Jelloid.

sepelon. noun. A well-attended funeral.

seperotile. adjective. **1.** Being uncomfortable in any posture or place. **2.** Being moviculatic. **3.** Being pleuridermic. **4.** Being an egonfort* in the company of others.

sepiation. noun. **1.** An impression about how colors were perceived in the past. **2.** Sensation or imagination that the mediate past was sepia-colored and the distant past was in multiple colors. *Psychology.* **3.** Depressive condition characterized by memories lacking color. *History.* **4.** The process of manufacturing ink or dye from cuttlefish.

septeration. noun. **1.** Rupture of a physical barrier that separated two enemy factions prior to a confrontation. **2.** A dispute between two neighbors through a fence. *Medicine.* **3.** Dissection of a septum.

septisocial. adjective. Causing a deterioration in a society.

serefi. noun. *Archaic.* Small container to carry liquids in a carriage drawn by four horses.

serenator. noun. *Mythology.* Ancient fat male deity who spread dew on outdoor surfaces at night.

serengraph. noun. **1.** A typographical error an author finds when receiving the first copy of his or her printed book and glancing at a randomly selected page. **2.** The depressing feeling of finding a typognicia.*

sesalivity. noun. **1.** An effect experienced when listening to someone saying a truth with a few, to the point, accurate and well-articulated words. **2.** The sensation of having one's mouth dried out or without saliva. **3.** Pinole.

sesquidozen. noun. Eighteen.

sesquintessential. noun. Representing more perfection than the most perfect or typical example of a quality or class.

sesquisane. adjective. **1.** Having more than a sound mind. **2.** Not having had any sign or symptom of sadness, anxiety, or any negative emotion.

sesquivirgin. noun. **1.** A woman who is more than a virgin. **2.** A person who has not touched or been touched lasciviously by anyone. *Psychology.* **3.** Female sextoh.*

sesquiwell. adjective. **1.** Being more than healthy. **2.** Being in more than full health. **3.** Being more than normal, natural, and desirable. **4.** Being more than satisfactory in size, amount or desirability.

sestry. noun. *Informal.* **1.** A man with experience in rapidly detecting subtle signs of heat in a woman. **2.** A fortunate erolucid* man. *Informal.* **3.** A persistent and lucky philanderer. **4.** Semacelogist.

setenabion. noun. *Archaic.* The seventh participant in a gomorrisade.*

setic. adjective. Having fun or experiencing pleasure while seated on fences, especially children.

sexation. noun. *Biology.* **1.** A separation of gender within members of an asexual species. *Evolutionary Biology.* **2.** The evolutionary split of gonality* within an asexual species. **3.** An outcome of a selective pressure to heterogenize the haploid nature of some members of a species. *Philosophy.* **4.** The origin of gender, gonality* or the sexes. *Literary.* **5.** The primordial spark that provoked the schism and allure of maleness and femaleness.

sexidity. noun. *Psychology.* **1.** Exaggerated frigidity accompanied by a violent opposition to any sexual activity. *Medicine.* **2.** Extreme antaphrodisiasis. **3.** A condition that follows the stage of marital erosphyxia.*

sextaessential. noun. More unblemished, finer, and purer than quintessential.

sextesimus. noun. *Archaic.* **1.** The most precise of the sextarius in ancient Rome. **2.** Something very small and valuable that requires an accurate and sensitive scale.

sextoh. adjective. *Psychology.* **1.** A pathologically celibate man. **2.** A man who, out of fear, has never had sexual intercourse. **3.** A psychopathic condition in a boy with Oedipus complex, castration complex and anchorite complex combined. **4.** A rare condition among Catholic priests.

sgrib. noun.(from *sgriob* in Gaelic, meaning itchiness in the upper lip before taking a sip of whiskey). Facial itch in anticipation of something enjoyable.

shnapsid. noun. (from *schnapsidee* in German, meaning alcoholic idea). **1.** Crazy idea. *Informal.* **2.** Crackpot idea. **3.** An idea that initially seems brilliant and later turns out to be stupid. **4.** A prodigious idea

conceived while drunk or under the influence of drugs that is actually foolish, dangerous or unrealistic.

shagshag. noun. (from *zhaghzhagh* in Farsi). The chattering of teeth from the cold or from rage.

shlimazzle. noun. (from *shlimazl* in Yiddish). **1.** A person who seems to be the persistent target of unfavorable circumstances. **2.** A persistently unlucky person.

sialixate. verb. **1.** To put an end to someone's repeated false promises.

siaxalk. verb. *Informal.* **1.** To dry the mouth of a liar. **2.** To vacuum the saliva of a compulsive hypocrite.

sibleton. noun. Nervous indecision that precedes the beginning of a crisis.

sigilian. noun. *Psychology.* **1.** An obsessively secretive person. *Commerce.* **2.** A trusted employee of a corporation or of a government spying agency.

signurd. noun. **1.** Someone who insists stubbornly on signing a document that does not concern him or her. **2.** Signecious.

sigojous. adjective. Pertaining to a person who protrudes and shakes the lips hesitantly and then presses them together to keep the secrets inside his or her mouth from being divulged.

sigon. noun. A siphon for malleable solids.

sigoquy. noun. **1.** Infantile exchange of words between two people after a copulation. **2.** Tafaly. **3.** Postcoital parvoparlia.

silesta. noun. An undefined collection of silences.

sillympretic. adjective. **1.** Bathing or showering immediately after having bathed or showered. *Psychology.* **2.** An anally retentive, hygienically compulsive person. **3.** Rispognic.

silomy. noun. **1.** Unexpressed anger or rage accompanied by insulting and threatening thoughts. **2.** Passive-aggressive pride.

siltanthroid. noun. **1.** An anthropomorphic or anthropoid silhouette in the shadow of an inanimate object. **2.** A dark human form produced by an object situated between rays of light and a surface.

simelation. noun. A mediocre imitation of the voice of a celebrity.

simolaicity. noun. **1.** The buying or selling of governmental privileges to modify laws or elections. **2.** Democracy.

sinistrism. noun. A belief that a dirty mind is a good source of creativity.

sinismercy. noun. *Psychology.* **1.** Insensibility, lack of empathy or lack of sympathy for the suffering of others in situations of generalized and extreme misery. **2.** Absence of mercy when it is perceived that it is useless. **3.** Sinampiety.

sinistine. noun. An unfavorable destiny that prevails in the underprivileged.

sinterity. noun. 1. Lack of skill in performing tasks. **2.** Talented in art privately, but unable to demonstrate it in public.

sinuolispic. adjective. *Informal.* **1.** Going through tangents lisping. noun. **2.** A verbose person who changes topics incessantly during a lisping monologue. **3.** Sinuoseser.

sireniage. noun. An old and ugly mermaid with cellulite on the tail.

siriciri. noun. **1.** Combination of caresses, kisses, and manipulation of erogenous areas that two people give each other for pleasure. **2.** Foreplay. **3.** Precopulio. **4.** Presex. **5.** Cotopy.

sisarro. noun. *Psychology.* Subconscious psychological compensation that counteracts a monadic burden.

sistron. noun. *Psychology.* **1.** A hindrance, or hindrances, to happiness. **2.** Psychological blotta* that accumulates throughout life and handicaps a person's ability to be happy.

slamadato. noun. (from *Slampadato* in Italian, meaning a person who frequently uses UV tanning beds). A person addicted to non-addictive substances, places or events.

smeghalitus. noun. **1.** Smell of a person's breath that resembles the odor of smegma. **2.** The smell of breath of someone who just licked a penis. **3.** Prepucedorious. **4.** Halismegma.*

sneeper. noun. A sniper who became a sniper because of cowardice.

sneezatory. noun. *Commerce.* **1.** An establishment where, for a price, a person can be made to sneeze repeatedly. **2.** A place specialized in inducing sneezes. **3.** Stornutory. **4.** An establishment selling estornugenous* materials.

snooch. noun. A person who hides somewhere in a room while his or her lover's spouse suspiciously searches said room.

snoochiness. noun. **1.** Anxiety about the probability of being discovered. **2.** A vehement desire to become invisible. **3.**

State of apprehension on being compelled to hide by necessity or danger.

sobamest. adjective. *Informal. Vulgar.* Foul expletive or gesture denoting incredulity at a premise, information, or a verbal statement.

sobardic. adjective. A liar who after being sobamested* admits to having said something untruthful.

sobart. noun. A person who lies and is not believed by others, but even when confronted or sobamested* maintains that the untruthful statements are true.

socimity. noun. *Sociology.* A degree of change by which a society modifies the personality of each one of its members.

sociosant. noun. A social cretin who is generally intelligent and uses introversion to stay away from reality.

sociometer. noun. *Psychology.* An instrument that measures a person's social capability of interacting with human beings.

sociostagnancy. noun. *Psychology.* **1.** A relatively mild mental illness characterized by a retardation of social interactions with others. **2.** A social debilitation as judged by low scores on a social quotient test and on the sociometer.* **3.** A difficulty in behaving with ease in the company of strangers.

socus. noun. **1.** The father-in-law of the brother-in-law of the mother's cousin of the sister-in-law of the second wife of someone. **2.** Socuniomprisuge.

solanimitude. noun. *Psychology.* **1.** A sensation of being without the physical presence of someone close to one. **2.** Feeling alone despite being in the company of loved ones.

solbid. verb. To touch a sleeping person gently, while avoiding tickling and awaking the person.

solible. noun. *Physics.* Property of certain solids that are able to be dissolved with other solids thanks to a solidophilic* action at the molecular level.

solidophilia. noun. *Physics.* **1.** A substance that absorbs or coalesces with certain solids. **2.** Chemical and magnetic force that is unique to solible* solids.

solilagy. noun. *Sociology.* **1.** A branch of sociology that studies the effect of punitive captivity of offenders on society in general. **2.** A branch of sociology that compares at a social level the ealm* with the effects of parahabilitation* and prophylactic delitherapy*

of incarcerated offenders upon their release.

solilocuous. adjective. **1.** Acting differently while in solitude than when in the company of others. **2.** Pertaining to or relative to a rhiner,* a rhinorhinogous,* or an ungoflexor* when by themselves. **3.** Solimochy.

solustalia. noun. **1.** Proximity of two or more souls. **2.** The degree of fisimity* between friends, lovers, or spouses.

somaphagous. adjective. *Zoology.* **1.** Feeding on and swallowing whole bodies. noun. **2.** Wholithron.

sometell. noun. **1.** Conspicuous body language that reveals more than words. **2.** A collection of involuntary gestures and nervous reflexes that tell more than one is willing to admit or reveal. **3.** Kinesics signs that do not involve haptics or proxemics.

somnatic. adjective. **1.** Sleeping solidly and deeply and being very difficult to wake by loud noises or shaking. **2.** Modorric. **3.** Somnamplumbic. noun. *Informal.* **4.** Brick-brain. **5.** Concrete skull. **6.** Tabicephalus. **7.** Somnadumb. *Medicine.* **8.** Eucachexia.

somniblass. noun. **1.** A profound sleep. **2.** The most intense of sleeps. **3.**

Semi-comatose sleep that squeezes all senses. **4.** Long and profound sleep that provokes a period of lethargy and confusion after waking up.

somnisage. noun. **1.** An event that already happened, is happening or will happen and is recognized as having been dreamed previously. **2.** Presomnisage. **3.** Oneirophesía. **4.** Dreamveration.

sonalgic. adjective. Of, relative to, or pertaining to a sound that causes pain.

sonosurro. noun. **1.** An audible whisper that a person wants someone else to hear. **2.** A person who utters a murmur with the purpose of being heard.

sonsonition. noun. A psychological torture consisting of playing a loud and endless recording of a portion of a disagreeable song.

sophextremism. noun. *Philosophy.* **1.** A philosophical school of thought that endorses the belief that all luxury has negative consequences. *Psychology.* **2.** A seemingly sophisticated, yet austere attitude held by a group of people in their devotion to things or customs typical of their place of birth or residence. **3.** An attitude aimed as a

preventive to being depaysed.* **4.** Extreme nateism.*

sophistimate. noun. **1.** A person who is sincere and refined, exhibits subtle elegance, and is adaptable to any situation while acting naturally. **2.** A person who uses affected words, archaisms, or cultivated words, and explains them without pomposity. **3.** Anasoflame.

sophroxenic. adjective. **1.** Exhibiting exaggerated caution while being abroad. *Psychology.* **2.** Feeling paranoid when away from home or country.

soplust. verb. **1.** To uselessly utilize a blunt, smooth object to pull something slippery from an inaccessible place. noun. *Informal.* **2.** A person who lacks common sense.

sosprack. verb. **1.** To find something a few moments after giving up the search for it. **2.** To find something in the ultifand* an instant following the telocease.* **3.** To ubitrack.

sotald. verb. **1.** To communicate something about someone to someone else without using verbal or written means. *Informal.* **2.** To point to a person stealthily to demonstrate to others that said person is to be blamed. *Vulgar.* **3.** To make a gesture in the direction of a person in an effort to ascribe the fart one just released.

sotamount. verb. *Informal.* **1.** To mount a female with a certain force while under her. *Informal.* **2.** To sexually ride a woman while she is the mount.

sothanat. noun. Anything that is or resides under or beyond death.

sottosublime. adjective. **1.** An artist who attains popular success without having talent, proficiency, or expertise in the corresponding art. *Informal.* **2.** A mediocre bestseller. **3.** An unimaginative, disagreeable, ungainly, ugly, or loathsome top-forty song.

sotule. adjective. **1.** Behaving foolishly. noun. **2.** A non-alcoholic drunk who drinks for the sake of it. **3.** A weekend drunk.

soverid. noun. Oblivious to a person's beliefs or convictions.

spacenate. noun. A person born in a space station or in a ship during space travel.

spacule. noun. **1.** A person who handles and speculates with money belonging to other people. *Law.* **2.** A 22nd century law that criminalized the act of speculating with money or goods from others. **3.** A person or an organization charged with the offence of handling or speculating with money or goods from other people without self-risk, and profiteering by charging fees and hidden costs.

spantility. noun. Ability to link developments of apparently independent events and maintaining composure when everyone else is consternated.

spectroscent. adjective. Resembling the aspect or intensity that reminds one of light.

speleospecter. noun. A ghost who roams caves.

speleostene. noun. A cave too small to be used as a shelter.

sperathron noun. *Literary.* An accelerator of hope in an amphitheater of despair.

spermhydrocide. noun. Mass annihilation of spermatozoids when ejaculated in an aquatic environment.

sphenositis. noun. *Medicine.* A short-lived and slightly painful sensation of pressure behind the eyes after a loud, forceful sneeze.

spherangle. noun. **1.** Geometrical spheroid figure outside the quantum that is formed by two or more angles made of curved, continuum lines. **2.** A union of two or more curvangles.*

sphinctorial. noun. A facial expression of surprise, satisfaction, and sarcasm, generally with a half-smile, made by a man when hearing the first orgasmic moans of a woman during copulation.

sphingolfacious. adjective. Being extremely disconcerted to a point of feeling inert and lifeless.

splanchuose. noun. **1.** An emaciated person whose abdominal organs can be distinguished through the skin. *Anatomy.* **2.** An anatomical organ that lacks lustrous surface.

splellate. verb. **1.** To flay the mucosae of a person with chemical substances. **2.** To destroy the gastrointestinal, genital or respiratory epithelia with caustic or acid materials.

spornality. noun. **1.** The state of satisfaction when having limited options or fewer choices to make. **2.** The feeling of happiness when possessing a scant number of goods.

sprigedick. noun. *Vulgar.* A person with a body that resembles a stock of wheat and who walks with no rhythm, as a vertical blob advancing mechanically.

spynemy. noun. The act of spying on a person's memories, without his or her consent, for morbid or profitable purposes.

stabiloid. noun. *Informal.* A loyal, faithful, and hard-working husband.

stalactic. adjective. Decreasing in intensity very slowly.

stalactize. verb. To fall or slide mellifluously like a stalactite.

stalagmation. noun. *Physics.* Slow slither of a thick fluid in any direction caused by any force with the exception of gravity.

stalogamy. noun. **1.** A phase preceding a couple's understanding that their separation is inevitable. *Informal.* **2.** An unstable marriage that is hanging by a thread.

stampoly. noun. **1.** A sudden rush of both predators and preys to escape together from a particular circumstance or stimulus. **2.** A city where a significant proportion of its inhabitants stammers.

staticism. noun. **1.** Action of remaining in the same position or unchanged. *Sociology.* **2.** A consequence of cerdilism.* *Psychology.* **3.** Pretension of remaining in the same position or unchanged. *Informal.* **4.** The principle and practice of a bureaucrat. **5.** An intense inclination to do nothing.

statix. noun. A variable and uncontrollable feeling of abandonment when a person stays at home alone and everyone else has left on a pleasure voyage.

stelalgia. noun. *Medicine.* **1.** A tightening pain. *Psychology.* **2.** A physical or mental discomfort that feels like compression and makes movement difficult.

stenobliny. noun. *Psychology.* **1.** The crushing feeling of being trapped. *Literature.* **2.** The oppressive sensation of being tied by the neck to a stranger with a slimy rope during a forced conversation.

stenocosmia. noun. *Astronomy.* Scientific theory that deals with the narrow nature of the universe, extrapolated from the morphology of galaxies.

stenofenest. noun. An extremely small window that does not admit sufficient light or ventilation.

stenopleasy. noun. **1.** Awareness of pleasure that vanishes the instant one realizes it is indeed a pleasure. **2.** Ephemeral evanescent pleasure.

stenorrhea. noun. *Medicine.* Explosive, high pressure discharge of a bodily solid or fluid caused by the tightened sphincter from where it comes out.

stenovaguer. noun. **1.** A person who wanders through narrow passages and cannot find their way. **2.** A mestecod.* *Education.* **3.** A senior undergraduate student with an undecided major. **4.** An imaginative chronopalent.*

stepsonship. noun. **1.** A feeling of reverence for an older figure, a person of authority, or a celebrity with a strong sense of familiarity as if one was suddenly his or her stepson. **2.** Godsonship.*

steralgia. noun. *Medicine.* Inflammatory pulmonary disease characterized by profuse pain during inhalation.

stercable. adjective. **1.** Having the potential of being converted into fecal matter. *Informal.* **2.** Manurable.

stercalia. noun. *Psychology.* **1.** Affective aversion to stepping into fecal matter. **2.** Neurotic fear of stepping into fecal matter.

stercamble. adjective. Having the tendency to frequently step into fecal matter.

stercogic. noun. **1.** Intransigent strategy, with the appearance of being logical, used to convince people to believe in a doctrine. *Psychology.* **2.** A person suffering from stercophrenia.* *Psychology.* **3.** Stercophrenic.

stercolaggy. noun. Change of one bad leadership for another bad leadership in an organization, a locality, or a country.

stercolapia. noun. Frustrating feeling of distress after numerous cleaning efforts to wipe the anus with toilet paper and every new toilet paper remains soiled.

stercopathy. noun. **1.** Profitable belief that administration of minimal doses of a poison, a toxin, or a noxious substance is healthy and applicable to the prevention and treatment of diseases. **2.** Homeopathy.

stercophrenia. noun. *Psychology.* **1.** A mental disorder characterized by an intransigent compulsion to convince others to believe in a particular doctrine. **2.** A sufferer of opiviety.* **3.** A disease affecting an stercogic.* **4.** A condition affecting the proponents of syncretinism.* **5.** The diagnosis often made of a deliragious* person.

sterexpression. noun. A hard facial expression someone adopts in a formal setting.

stermule. noun. **1.** A person who uses religion to control his or her debauchery. **2.** A person who utilizes religion as the only sedative for his or her own unruliness. verb. **3.** To use religion to dissipate dissipation.

sterohydralia. noun. *Psychology.* A sensation of perceiving water as a solid.

sterohydrosis. noun. *Psychology.* A condition in which a patient imagines their bodily fluids solidifying.

steromnesia. noun. **1.** Solidification of memories. **2.** A state in which, by own volition or following a persuasion, the memories stop changing.

steroscopic. adjective. Observing something solid meticulously.

sticot. noun. **1.** A person who claims to speak in verse, but his or her speech does not rhyme. **2.** Sticoid. **3.** A person who looks askance at anything out of the ordinary.

stilmatic. adjective. Pertaining to or related to an anchoret living as a sybarite.

stoicuse. noun. **1.** A person who stoically endures someone else's continuous abuses. **2.** Endurous.

strabinamic. adjective. **1.** Behaving in a strange manner and responding in an unpredictable manner to stimuli. **2.** Pertaining to or related to a pericentric* person who reacts differently to others in exceptional circumstances.

strafaiant. adjective. Inhaling air loudly or in an outlandish manner to demonstrate frustration or annoyance.

straggemnia. noun. *Medicine.* **1.** Irregular and anguished breathing in an acute and severe pulmonary disease. **2.** Breathing of despair in a person rescued from drowning. *Informal.* **3.** Exaggerated breathing of a person having just resurfaced after holding his or her breath for a long period of time.

stragorous. noun. **1.** A person with deplorable looks and dress that seems to have come from a disaster zone or a battle. **2.** Straguerrillous.

strandilar. noun. A society, a population, or a group of people who behave bizarrely and boisterously.

straspian. noun. An incompetent spy who acts and dresses as a fictional spy and is easily detected by other spies, neophyte spies, and common people.

stremizator. noun. A person with innate talent, looks, or fame who impacts others with a look or a smile.

stremis. noun. **1.** A stimulus that provokes shaking and trembling. **2.** Stremerogenous.

strenocyte. noun. *Biology.* A cultured cell that survives in extremely unfavorable conditions.

streptaricy. noun. Severe avarice that may corrode everything that surrounds a greedy person or persons.

stridia. noun. *Music.* Musical composition that must be interpreted very loudly or stridently and that, even when sung or performed quietly with an acoustic instrument, seems to be executed in a loud manner.

stroppegize. verb. **1.** (in a corporation) To change priorities or objectives suddenly. **2.** To pretend to have knowledge and experience and to have considered all options when announcing budget cuts and salary reductions to employees. **3.** To ruin the enthusiasm of company workers.

strotting. noun. **1.** Strategy of an artist to favor and purposefully seek adverse conditions in which to become inspired. **2.** Bellastropper.*

struondous. adjective. Pertaining to an extremely loud and deafening sound.

stummish. noun. *Informal.* A penetrating, hideous stench coming from a group of people.

stumpon. noun. **1.** An extremely ordinary person. **2.** A person who does not stand out and no one can remember.

subanthrosis. noun. *Anthropology.* **1.** A paleoanthropological postulation by Gastranen D'Luca in the 23rd century that states that absence of paleoanthropological evidence is not evidence of paleoanthropological absence. *Philosophy.* **2.** Scientific theological paradox. *Anthropology.* **3.** Underestimated number of species belonging to the genus *Homo* in prehistory with full knowledge that the limited paleoanthropological findings that survived erosion, degradation, and destruction have not been found or will never be found. **4.** Subestohomism.

subclam. verb. **1.** To quietly shout something of apparent importance away from a microphone during a speech to augment the curiosity of an audience in a passive manner. **2.** To say something that seems significant away from a microphone to attract the attention of a murmuring audience or silence them.

subconceptic. adjective. **1.** Frequently assimilating only part of a concept listened to or read. **2.** Frequently missing what someone said without having hearing impairment. **3.** Missing the meaning of something said.

subcrastination. noun. **1.** A gloomy vision of tomorrow by a non-pessimist suffering from depression. **2.** The desire to delay or postpone something being done under duress.

subdormit. verb. **1.** To be on the verge of sleep. **2.** To be between half-sleep and sleep.

subexistence. verb. To live without human dignity.

subfanic. adjective. Learning a revelation, stirring the abstraction in one's mind and then losing the meaning forever.

subflague. verb. To burn something slowly with modulated microwaves so that when it burns it glows in the center.

subfund. verb. To scatter something within itself.

subpice. noun. **1.** The lowest point or the lowest base of something. **2.** The smallest point. **3.** The easiest point or portion to solve of a complex problem or difficulty. **4.** Piconade.

subserge. noun. A subordinate to a sewage superintendent.

substirp. noun. A proud lineage of an ignoble family.

subterflugh. verb. *Literary.* **1.** To submerge oneself in a rhetorical labyrinth with a convoluted excuse. *Psychology.* **2.** To deceive others in order to achieve one's goal.

subtrication. noun. **1.** Inevitable failure of something when any of the variables that should be infallible are not carried out, stop functioning, fail or do not happen. **2.** Unavoidable fiasco experienced when any of the skills someone takes for granted are gone.

subundric. adjective. **1.** Being a native, inhabitant or proceeding from a place or country located below sea level. **2.** Subaharic. **3.** Sublowlander.

subungunal. adjective. Pertaining to, relative to, situated or applied under the fingernails.

suclur. verb. **1.** To intend to hide one's memories. **2.** To actively attempt to forget something and to be unable to do so.

sucoggio. noun. The action of disguising a deep sorrow with displays of half gloom.

sultria. noun. **1.** A woman who behaves in such a manner as to indicate she is in heat. **2.** A woman who announces with gestures that she is ready to copulate.

superternated. adjective. Being excessively disturbed and depressed.

supervalk. noun. A squall of time.

supervalt. noun. **1.** A lattice perception of time. **2.** A sudden rearrangement of time. **3.** Superlattism of a portion of linear time.

suprabaryc. adjective. **1.** Being subjected or assembled under great pressure. **2.** Living, working, or operating under tremendous pressure.

supracogot. noun. *Informal.* The lower portion of the rear of the cranium.

supraddictic. noun. *Psychology.* A behavioral pattern that is predictive of compulsive or exaggerated addictions.

suprafficient. adjective. Having the capability to achieve the maximum effect with minimal wasted energy, effort, or expense.

supramaculation. noun. **1.** A feeling of deep guilt that is commonly a consequence of a continuous regret for one or more deplorable actions committed. **2.** An overwhelming feeling of guilt where often the only conceivable repentance is suicide. **3.** Multiple circumvoluted rammocles.*

supraphasize. verb. **1.** To add stress on a word or phrase to give special significance to what is being said. **2.** To exaggerate gestures and expressions to add prominence to a spoken message. **3.** To highlight the importance or prominence of something with cartoon-like affectation.

suprine. verb. *Medicine.* To stoop the body in response or reflex to a pain.

suspiracle. noun. A large and deep sigh.

suspiricy. noun. A long and deep sigh while moaning, caused by a sudden burst of pleasure.

sustocle. noun. **1.** An improvised vantage point where, out of sight, a person can spy on the reaction of someone he or she has frightened clandestinely. **2.** A sneaky vybernaught.*

sutomendry. noun. A business establishment that repairs shoes that shoe repair shops cannot fix.

swindlism. noun. *Economics.* **1.** A fraud of immense proportions carried out by financial institutions or banks without any legal repercussions and with state support. *Law.* **2.** Strategic corporate fraud of enormous proportions with government endorsement. *Informal.* **3.** Megastaff. *Informal.* **5.** Megascamism.

swindlosaur. noun. **1.** A species of dinosaur that swindles

its prey and then eats it. **2.** Sandrasaur.

symbioliy. noun. Quality of reciprocity or camaraderie between two people.

symbionate. verb. To perform an artificial or projected assemblage between two entities of the same species.

symbionitis. noun. An uncomfortable sensation that occurs in an individual when symbionated* in another body.

symibiosis. noun. *Philosophy.* **1.** Philosophical theory that justifies research using live animals. *Ethics.* **2.** A movement that justifies research using live animals by arguing that during the evolutionary process there is always exploitation of one living being over others to secure its own survival and the survival of its species.

sympenassion. noun. Consolation two persons give one another when sharing individual distresses of discrete nature.

sympesiation. noun. Sensation of sad emptiness in response to the lack of empathy or sympathy experienced when listening to the tragedies of others through third parties.

sympodia. noun. A slow and nervous gait of a person

walking toward a podium in a public gathering.

symprionia. noun. *Medicine.* **1.** Combination of infective proteins in the tissues of an infected person. **2.** A cause for fulminant prionosis.*

sympyrosis. noun. A phenomenon that occurs when two or more fires of diverse origin join and form a bigger, devastating fire.

symuphon. noun. An intense *déjà vu* constituted by various simultaneous *déjà vus.*

synagy. noun. Peaceful state of mind and complacency about what one has and what one does.

synaligium. noun. Significant difference between the inventive productivity of one person and a group of people taking into account the decision-making speed and the discovery process.

synamnemia. noun. **1.** Lethal failure of experimental memory transfers and memory fusions. *Medicine.* **2.** Fatal transcranial mnemogogation* with obliteal dysmnemopulence. **3.** Fulminant iatrogenic transomnemia.* **4.** Antiontony. **5.** Nmemonic ontolilepsis.*

synaptism. noun. *Medicine.* Insertion of memories into certain types of neurones through synaptic hook-ups.

synarch. verb. **1.** To calculate or to estimate a rhythm. **2.** To perceive a rhythm. *Informal.* **3.** To feel as one with the rhythm of a musical piece.

syncept. noun. A mental process in which multiple disjointed ideas coalesce to form a concept.

synchroplause. noun. A spontaneous and long-lasting applause, in unison, from an audience.

syncognity. noun. A union of knowledge between cultures, peoples, or beliefs.

syncorpenty. noun. *Informal.* **1.** Copulation between a corporeal being and a ghost. **2.** Ontophantia. *Theology.* **3.** A sexual relationship between a person and a non-corporeal being. **4.** Anthiontonia. **5.** Barremacy. **6.** Immaculate conception.

syncretinism. noun. *Theology.* **1.** A movement that intends to unify and reconcile benign and malignant deities from different doctrines. **2.** A movement that pretends to unify all religions.

syndescend. verb. **1.** To condescend without being patronizing. **2.** To allow an action from a person for mercy or preference without a feeling of superiority.

syndemocretism. noun. A movement that tries to unite the countries of the world under a single global government.

syndemy. noun. *Anthropology.* **1.** A theory that maintains that the mixing of races among different human races augments with time. **2.** Synetnochia.

syndense. verb. *Physics.* **1.** To unify diverse densities. **2.** To amalgamate the densities of different components while maintaining their individual nature.

synerget. noun. verb. *Chemistry.* **1.** To adhere, unite, or cause two or more substances to interact to produce a combined effect greater than the sum of their separate effects. *Commerce.* **2.** To merge two or more organizations to increment the combined profits to a higher figure than the sum of their individual profits.

synespectral. adjective. **1.** Having or containing all colors. **2.** Toticolorous.

synfentrission. noun. A rhetorical resort an intelligent person uses to confuse an audience when said person is incapable of convincing the audience of a concept.

synfidence. noun. *Sociology.* **1.** Unified feeling of confidence within and between two or more groups of people. **2.** The open telling of private matters or secrets with mutual levels of trust between two groups of people.

synfisepsis. noun. *Commerce.* **1.** A business strategy forming financial conglomerates or monopolies that will eventually obtain exorbitant amounts of money from the state in the form of bailouts. *Law.* **2.** Swindilism.*

synflict. noun. An imminent conflict that was resolved prior to the beginning of a conflict thanks to an opportune mediation.

synglossia. noun. *Linguistics.* **1.** Creation of words with words or roots of words from several languages to define terms not previously defined. **2.** Synlexia.

syngression. noun. **1.** An accord between two stubborn people. *Politics.* **2.** A signed nonaggression pact between two or more nations with the knowledge that the pact will be broken in the near future. *History.* **3.** The temporal episodes of peace among ever-changing countries and empires in their quest for wealth and power.

synic. noun. A man who, knowing that a woman will use

the facilities soon, deliberately leaves a toilet seat up.

synlactyn. noun. A mixture of milks from distinct mammalian species for elaborating cheeses and gastronomical dishes.

synmule. verb. To represent a mule imitating its attributes and movements.

syntemporaneous. adjective. **1.** Happening, originating, or existing during the same period but in different dimensions. **2.** Occurring or existing in the same period of time but in a different place or location.

syntexity. noun. **1.** Skill and balance of both hands and feet in the fine or performing arts. **2.** Simultaneous adroitness in several parts of the body. **3.** Dexterity to perform several tasks simultaneously.

synvalescence. noun. **1.** Period in which someone partially recovers his or her health and strength after several debilitating, unpleasant, annoying or painful events. **2.** Gradual and partial return to being oneself after multiple blows. *Medicine.* **2.** Period needed for recovering from bimorbidity.* *Literary.* **3.** The mending of multiturnies.* **4.** Betterment from the tragictions* of life. **4.** Recovery from a zalahazar.*

syspondrial. adjective. **1.** Using sexual relationships as the sole physical activity to purposefully burn calories. noun. *Informal.* **2.** Sexercise.

systhesis. noun. **1.** A study of the function of one part of the whole. **2.** Backward synthesis. *Commerce.* **3.** Retroengineering. **4.** The process of programing the timing of failure during the manufacture of electronic devices.

T

tachychronicity. noun. Relative or real acceleration of time.

tachydesic. adjective. Having the attribute of being easily fixed.

tachyoptic. adjective. Searching rapidly and methodically with the eyes.

tacivity. noun. **1.** The pretension of not wanting or desiring something. **2.** Recomity. **3.** The action of rejecting a gift that is deeply desired. **4.** Parsivity.*

tafal. noun. **1.** A secondhand triumph. **2.** Feeling of contentment when someone close achieves a victory or a great success.

talasogeny. noun. Archaic origin of a contemporary being that eventually traces back to the sea.

talasophobia. noun. *Psychology.* **1.** Fear of the sea. **2.** Seafear.

taldo. noun. Intangible qualifier, whether positive or negative, that results from a count.

talempenia. noun. Decline or loss of a talent due to neglect.

talifa. noun. Cacique or chieftain of a small barrio in a metropolitan misery belt.

tallophry. noun. **1.** Sensation of emptiness without empathy after listening to a stranger, who will likely not be seen again, openly confess and cry over personal tragedies. **2.** Coldicout.

talot. noun. Each one of the half-siblings, none of whom know each other, each of them unaware that they share the same biological father.

talul. noun. **1.** The long and proportionate waist of a slender woman. *Archaic.* **2.** A brave Roman soldier who cheats at dice.

tamang. noun. Any soft material used to protect the skin from coarse garbs.

tamangur. noun. *History.* An undergarment of soft material some medieval hermits wore clandestinely under coarse clothing.

tamatude. noun. *Psychology.* **1.** An unprovoked anger toward inanimate objects, more commonly mechanical and electronic. *Physics*. **2.** Rignucity. *Cybernetics*. **3.** Abiodesy. *Psychology*. **4.** Aversion, fear or phobia toward electromagnetic devices. **5.** A traffic jam in a tiny town.

tangentiate. verb. **1.** To deviate from the main topic of a conversation by communicating something irrelevant that nevertheless appears significant. **2.** To use subterfuge to cunningly evade a predicament.

tangibilist. noun. A person capable of making tangible something intangible.

tangibilize. verb. To make tangible something intangible.

taprek. noun. **1.** Spontaneous anger with an inanimate contraption that stops working. **2.** Violent actions on an electromagnetic device that stops operating.

tarathel. noun. Any microscopic or macroscopic organism that lives in or frequently visits a urinal.

tarlatain. noun. **1.** A person who overacts in real life situations. adjective. **2.** Feigning professionalism and care in any everyday circumstance. **3.** Displaying affectation when performing any quotidian task. **4.** Serpity.

tarsemia. noun. **1.** A purposefully sadistic remedy. *Medicine*. **2.** An aseptic punitive treatment administered to a patient by an anempathic* physician.

tarsit. noun. Fictitious perception of reality following a prolonged insomnia.

tartemic. adjective. **1.** Having a blistered or blistering personality. noun. **2.** A Slovak sweetmeat dessert mixed with different types of sausages.

tartle. (from *tartle* in Scottish). noun. An uncomfortable feeling of embarrassment following the vacillation and doubt when greeting a person and not remembering his or her name.

tartroma. noun. *Medicine*. **1.** Exudative cutaneous affliction. **2.** A spontaneously occurring skin lesion without apparent cause characterized by exuding black vesicles that dry up in scales and fall off rapidly.

tartugge. noun. Disappearance of a historical fact from history books.

taxichronia. noun. **1.** The speed with which a taxi driver transports passengers from point A to point B. **2.** Tachytaxisia. **3.** Spicy food prepared from taxidermists' subjects.

teatist. noun. **1.** A man who claims to be a connoisseur of female breasts. adjective. **2.** Having an innate talent to manipulate female breasts.

technostutt. noun. Invented art or technology following incessant repetition of trials by an obstinate person with no training or experience.

tefanont. noun. A tall, hairy, and overweight man who speaks gutturally.

tegiction. noun. Strong and exquisite feeling of satisfaction with a long lasting, almost electric, pleasure when triumphing in something considered a lifelong destiny.

telanthropology. noun. *Anthropology.* **1.** The comparative study of prehistoric hominids of the genus *Homo* with anthropomorphized beings mentioned in oral history, fairy tales, folklore, legends, religions, and myths. *Literature.* **2.** Branch of literature that systematically correlates aspects of mythical anthropoids and prehistoric anthropoids in fictional narratives.

teleaudit. verb. To hear voices coming from far away.

telemat. noun. An automaton projected or transported through long distances.

telentrusion. noun. An action of a telepath who invades and infringes the thoughts and appropriates the memories of another person.

telepathe. verb. **1.** To communicate impressions, sensations, or ideas between two or more people without using physical signs or any physical means. *Informal.* **2.** To communicate mentally.

telesm. noun. *Psychology.* **1.** Frequent feeling of guilt arising from the mistaken belief that one is responsible for something that happened elsewhere. **2.** A partial whammit.* **3.** An incomplete whepid.* **4.** Repuntition.*

teletaxia. verb. To impose order from a long distance.

telocease. noun. To desist or to conclude the search for something lost.

telogonism. noun. A desire to equate or identify oneself with a secondary character of a literary piece, a theatrical play, a television show, or a cinematographic spectacle.

teloisle. noun. The last love of one's life.

telollusion. noun. **1.** An illusion acquired during the second half of one's life. *Literary.* **2.** The optimistic visualization of reality despite the evident, inevitable and irreturnable* devidalgia* during the autumn of life. *Informal.* **3.** Inexorable approach of a train to a final destination where a person will disappear but he or she feels happy and enjoys the trip.

tempeiric. noun. The attribute of building character based on welcoming the daily hardships of life.

templeter. noun. **1.** Interminable space of time. **2.** Infinchrony. **3.** Preternity* plus one.

temprot. verb. To pass from one time to another at a moderately fast speed without experiencing the passage of time and without traveling through time.

tenebrodon. noun. *Paleontology.* **1.** Extinct mammal of the family *Elephantidae,* genus *Mammuthus,* species *tremebundus,* represented massacring humans indiscriminately in cave paintings. **2.** Caviodon.

teratosoggical. adjective. Forgetting of a historical fact sometime after being invented by the rulers of a country or region.

tercolia. noun. *Literary.* A light-beam of stubbornness that sneaks through a cloud of certitude.

terechy. noun. **1.** Profound sensation of incompetence over having failed one's destiny. **2.** Common feeling shared by childless women over forty years of age. **3.** Sirgelle.

tergo. noun. Prolonged repercussion of similar intensity to the event that precipitated it.

ternopathia. noun. An independent third personality that emerges from two merged entities.

terolidon. noun. *Psychology.* A difficult fight endured against the monster of one's conscience prior to defeating it and becoming a true self.

terpache. noun. *Psychology.* **1.** A person who is simultaneously perspicacious, obstinate, irreducible, and refined. *Zoology.* **2.** A worm-like mollusk that drills into solid materials for food and shelter.

tertelic. adjective. **1.** Walking clumsily, pretending not to be falling down. *Informal.* **2.** Chocoletic. **3.** Campostric.

tesmaporation. noun. **1.** Profuse sweat that flows when feeling intense pain. **2.** Totisomalgic* sweat. *Medicine.* **3.** Endalgic* diaphoresis. *Psychology.* **4.** Implalgic* perspiration. **5.** Mentalgia* dampness. *Literary.* **6.** Wet nostardition.* **7.**

Paranostalgic* sudor. *Medicine.* **8.** Panalgic* exudation.

tesosmia. noun. **1.** The appreciation of an aroma with relish. **2.** The enjoyment of the odor of someone or something.

testamentemp. noun. Last declaration of a person's will stipulating aspects related to temporal after-death issues.

testinook. noun. *Archaic.* **1.** An undergarment to cover and protect the male genitals. *Informal.* **2.** An undefined area a man scratches as a habit, mania, or as a sign of nervousness. It generally involves scrotum and perineum.

thanatherapy. noun. **1.** A euthanasia arranged for a person in consideration of the people surrounding said person. **2.** A suicide planned for the benefit of others. **3.** Thanatotherapy. **4.** Euthany.*

thanaxis. noun. **1.** A suicide planned before an inevitable long suffering. **2.** Non-self-prothanasia.* **3.** Thanaprophylaxis.

theonigma. noun. **1.** The intrinsic enigmatic nature of the concept of a god. *Commerce.* **2.** The lucrative basis of a religion. **3.** The explanation of something nonexistent using patronizingly vague or enigmatic concepts.

theophagy. noun. **1.** Symbolic anthropophagy of a deity. **2.** Cannibalism of an incarnated god. **3.** Swallowing a muscle and blood macerate of a divinity in a wafer. **4.** Holy Communion.

theophobic. adjective. Having fear of a good god or a god who is in vogue in some specific place and time.

theopodic. adjective. Believed to be walking like a god.

theoviam. noun. *Philosophy.* Path toward accepting personal responsibility outside of a religion.

therapenent. noun. Attending or servicing someone who is lying on their own bed.

thermodence. noun. **1.** A substance or a belief that augments strength and courage. *History.* **2.** The effect that the waters of the river Thermodon had on the ancient Amazon warriors of Cappadocia.

thermonimia. noun. Simultaneous sensation of being hot and cold.

thirdcery. noun. A parent habitually referring to self in third person when speaking to their small child.

thirdiate. verb. To refer to oneself in third person when talking to an offspring or a pet.

thombosnant. adjective. Being continuously shocking and startling.

thoraxcle. noun. *Biology.* A small cavity in the thorax of some animals containing cells that secrete an antifreeze substance.

tictasy. noun. A convulsive movement of some part of the body in response to a physical or a mental stimulus, real or imagined.

tilomann. noun. *Psychology.* **1.** A sudden thought that appears when listening to someone, unrelated to the topic the interlocutor is verbalizing. **2.** Thoughts that frequently occur when listening to someone boring.

tingendipia. noun. The occurrence of a difficult circumstance that prompts a person to discover by chance something important or beneficial.

tintination. noun. **1.** Muscular twitching in some part of the body with ringing or buzzing in the ears. *Informal.* **2.** Feeling a wib* while hearing ringing in the ears. **3.** A wibbing* tinnitus.

tintinity. noun. Ability to vocally imitate with great accuracy the sound of a bell, a ring, or a trumpet.

tirigenosity. noun. Event, image, or memory that alters someone's emotional state to a point of shivering with goose bumps.

tirillent. verb. To shiver and to chatter teeth when perceiving the presence of a ghost.

tiritelia. noun. *Literary.* **1.** A tickle the butterfly wings of eternity cause when caressing a soul. **2.** Feeling one with the universe.

titeret. verb. **1.** To manipulate a person in such a manner that the person's movements display the awkwardness of a marionette. *Politics.* **2.** To handpick a ruler for a seemingly democratic nation.

tlack. verb. **1.** To walk making ticking or clacking noises that resembles the tapping of a keyboard. **2.** To produce or make sounds imitative of a person wearing flip-flops. **3.** An affectedly feminine lesbian.

tobilophant. noun. *Informal.* **1.** The thick ankles of a grandmother in a Mediterranean country. **2.** Anklephant.

tocoscad. noun. **1.** A smell, exciting to some and disgusting to others, that lacks singularity or life. **2.** A wheffy* smell without a bouillon-smelling quality.

tokkah. noun. (from *tokka* in Finnish). A large herd of reindeer.

tolasolapy. noun. **1.** An artificial ethereal field created jointly by the minds of several people. **2.** Soleggio.

tomand. verb. **1.** To reprimand someone in a nonspecific fashion. **2.** To educate or instruct someone about something using vague terms. **3.** To give a vague order and add "do it right" or "get it done." **4.** To yell an obfuscating command expecting no questions for clarification.

toniclonic. noun. *Medicine.* **1.** Intermittent and uncontrollable body rigidity with violent rhythmic contractions. **2.** A tropical cocktail prepared by mixing banana liquor, orange liquor, white wine, vodka, a cola drink, and evaporated milk.

torcugge. noun. A person who, not being a sadist, feels a sad pleasure in watching the suffering of others.

torshlosspanik. noun. (from *torschlusspanik* in German). **1.** A desperate feeling that something desired is fading, missing, or being taken away. **2.** A feeling of frustration when something one has is departing.

tortone. noun. **1.** A clumsy person who is incapable of catching something thrown and always makes an excuse to justify the incapacity. **2.** A polite fumbler. **3.** A nervous clumsiler.

tosnud. noun. **1.** Simultaneously occurring cough and sneeze. *Medicine.* **2.** Rare convulsive, spasmodic, noisy, and intempestive* movement, consequent to forcibly expelling air from the lungs through nose and mouth simultaneously following concurrent stimuli in nose and throat.

toticcent. noun. **1.** A person who pronounces with emphasis each syllable of each word. **2.** A person who stresses most syllables as if they had foreign language marks to indicate stress or pitch. **3.** An orator who uses speech affectations in each syllable to emphasize the message.

totiglion. noun. Recognition that each person is superior to another in a specific field, behavior, talent or quality.

totiplegia. adjective. *Medicine.* Paralysis of the whole body.

totisomalgia. noun. Intense, oppressive, and debilitating pain in the whole body.

totitemporality. noun. *Philosophy.* **1.** All time within and beyond infinity. *Physics.* **2.** A quondam conceptualization of time, from beginning to end, without considering radialism,* chronoradiality,* chronofusion,* preternity,* adimensionality,* transdimensionality,* achrony* or chronodimensialism.*

totiver. noun. A person or thing completely changed from their original form.

trachory. noun. **1.** An occurrence or group of occurrences that are perceived as treacherous. **2.** Chorizo and fried fish mixed with guacamole and wrapped inside a Mexican tortilla.

tracoluous. adjective. **1.** Being coarse in speech, manner, and intercourse. **2.** Tiraculous.

tragiction. noun. **1.** Serial accumulation of misfortunes, tragedies, sorrows in a defined period of time. *Psychology.* **2.** The psychological burden when misfortunes, tragedies, or sorrows happen in a short period of time.

tralga. noun. Action and effect of inverting or transposing the natural order of various things or beings simultaneously.

transdetiss. noun. *Literary.* A threshold through which a caprice enters and a disillusion exits.

transdimension. noun. A hypothetical relative state between one dimension and another.

transdimensional. adjective. Relative or pertaining to an undefined time-space (different from the three-dimensional understanding of space-time) during the transition from one dimension to another.

transdox. noun. *Informal.* A person who frequently changes opinions.

transfrady. noun. A union, guild, or syndicate whose people are separated in time or space.

transkinesia. noun. **1.** Idea or feeling of a past situation that seems to have been transported to the present in constant increments and hence, intensity and impact. *Physics.* **2.** Transfer of movement with nothing in between.

translegate. verb. **1.** To delegate an activity, a task, or a responsibility because of a complete inability to perform it oneself. **2.** To assign a task to someone with full knowledge that there are intrinsic circumstances that will impede its being carried out. noun. *Informal.* **3.** A transvestite judge in a courtroom.

transnostic. noun. **1.** An illiterate person with the ability to efficiently acquire knowledge by discriminate listening and observing. **2.** An old soul reincarnated in the body of a loser. **3.** A person in the highest percentile of cognometer* scores. adjective. **4.** Learning by proxy. **5.** Ecsyd.* **6.** Possessing metalligence.* **6.** Paragnossing.*

transomnemia. noun. Transmission of one or more memories from one person to another by artificial means.

transpacial. adjective. **1.** Occurring at the precise instant of dying. **2.** Occurring during a powerful impression that makes someone unconscious. **3.** The white tunnel with Jesus Christ at the end welcoming newcomers. **4.** Transaciagous. **5.** Transinfaust.

transparley. verb. To speak through a real, intangible, or imagined barrier.

transpecious. adjective. **1.** Transforming the exterior to appear as the opposite gender. *Informal.* **2.** Pertaining to an androgynous woman: a man among men. *Informal.* **3.** Pertaining to an androgynous man: a girl next door.

transpect. verb. **1.** To look without seeing. **2.** To stare with sentient yet inert eyes. noun. **3.** An empty look.

transpority. noun. **1.** Ability, under deep concentration, to make the sudoriferous glands excrete their contents through the pores. **2.** Capability of a person to perspire or sweat at will. **3.** An ardent wish of a perspiler.*

trarrask. noun. Abuse, excessive torture, or destruction of an inanimate object.

trascoque. verb. **1.** To grant someone rights of ownership and exploitation of something to be conquered, expecting nothing in return in the immediate future. noun. **2.** Land booty.

trastule. noun. A self-nominated terrestrial judge and executor who pretends to hold the monopoly on communications with celestial beings.

treccor. noun. **1.** Sudden and inexplicable reduction in affection between two friends. **2.** A contingency that may lead to dysrumpation.* **3.** A factor or factors that overshadow fisimity.*

trecide. noun. **1.** Elimination of the number thirteen from floors in buildings and rows in vehicles of mass transportation. **2.** A sarcastic response to a superstition in a supposedly advanced civilization. **3.** Unthirteenness.

treevisity. noun. The process of desire to possess a Christmas tree, going to a tree farm, admiring one tree from afar, then cutting it, transporting it to one's home, adorning it with useless decorations and lights that are later removed to throw away the tree in a dumpster.

trempello. noun. **1.** A predator that sees potential preys, selects one prey, chases it, knocks it down and harms it without the intention of eating it. **2.** A bold man who customarily wears wigs that imitate the hair of cartoon characters.

trepanator. noun. **1.** A metallic instrument with the shape of a corkscrew used to perform trepanations. **2.** A born-again vegetarian cannibal.

trepiambule. verb. To walk with vigorous steps while the body seems to go exaggeratedly up and down.

trepidatory. noun. Intense, jerky, vertical movement of the ground during a strong earthquake.

treverter. noun. (from *trepverter* in Yiddish). A witty response or comeback a person thinks of when too late to be used.

tribunation. noun. **1.** Annual donation to a government disguised as tax. **2.** Transfer of significant percentage of income, along with time-consuming demollent,* to a government. **3.** A coerced, unjustified, and periodic excessive excision of money.

tricynic. noun. **1.** Someone who acts cynically several times during the same day. **2.** A tricycle manufactured for adults who never learned to ride a bicycle.

trietomism. noun. *Philosophy.* Philosophical theory from the 23rd century that axiomatically establishes the triple truth: the truth perceived, the truth of others, and the cosmetic truth.

triligent. adjective. **1.** Being prudent and having a conscience about one's obligations and responsibilities. noun. **2.** The name of a Walt Disney cartoon character not yet conceived by the company.

triloquent. adjective. Having the ability to effectively manage simultaneously three spoken or written conversations.

triloquy. noun. **1.** A colloquium of three. **2.** A situation between three persons in which one believes they are conversing while the other two only hear a monologue.

triopt. noun. A person who has a third eye.

tripter. adjective. *Entomology.* **1.** Having three pairs of wings. noun. **2.** A clumsy and overweight stripper.

trisnid. noun. **1.** A sound produced when snapping one's wrist repeatedly and letting the index finger slap into the linked thumb and middle finger. **2.** The irksome sound of an edgy person doing a nanite.*

trisvernal. adjective. **1.** Being lost without a light source in an obscure jungle while hearing threatening noises. **2.** Entering a dense forest or a jungle and not having a clue on how to survive. **3.** Fearful junglization.*

tritheism. noun. *Religion.* A monotheistic religion that admits to having three gods.

tritsomn. verb. **1.** To grind one's teeth while sleeping. **2.** To enchirl.* **3.** To rumeninate* persistently during a dream causing stress. noun. **4.** Pervasomniate. noun. *Medicine.* **5.** Bruxism.

triumphasia. noun. Indifference or absence of enthusiasm after a great achievement.

trogloglossian. adjective. **1.** Speaking northern Dutch as a native speaker. **2.** Imphlegm.*

troglophant. noun. *Zoology.* **1.** A small, long-haired, muscular mammal with large tusks and small ears extinct during the Miocene epoch of the order Proboscidea, family *Elephantidae*, that inhabited caves. **2.** An Italian grandmother with a huge appetite.

trogodoster. noun. *Literature.* A fictional entity from the mid-23rd century that mutated from a prionoid,* preferentially inhabits caves and destroys everything in its path.

trompedille. noun. **1.** Repeated emission of gas from the anus in a semi-controlled fashion to avoid producing noise. **2.** Emission of intestinal gas in a manner similar to an estonguille,* to ameliorate an uncomfortable flatulence. It generally occurs in a public place. *Medicine.* **3.** Hemorrhoidal catarrhal typhlitis. adjective. *Informal.* **4.** Clearing the rear throat. *Informal.* **5.** Farting estonguille.* verb. *Informal.* **6.** To fart publicly.

trucufaction. noun. A state of profound confusion in an intelligent three-dimensional being subjected to a transdimensional* permutation.

truculency. noun. **1.** Collection of cinematographic strategies used to astonish and startle audiences. **2.** Violestesia* tactics. **3.** Creation of hyperviolent, ghastly and highly ghoulish spectacles. **3.** (in a film). Excessive number of scenes displaying hyperreal violence toward humans or animals. **4.** Cinematographic trarrasks.*

tucupulio. noun. *Archaic.* Manual decantation of the kidneys.

turbonation. noun. *Psychology.* **1.** Multitude of events that present themselves surprisingly in a fierce and stunning manner that impedes a person from continuing any activity. *Sports.* **2.** A competitive swimming style where swimmers propel themselves by blowing air or water through their mouths.

turbulate. verb. **1.** To imitate a turbulence with voice or action. noun. *Sports.* **2.** A swimmer who is expelled from a turbonation* race for moving any extremity.

tursitude. noun. An infrequent yet significant legacy a few people leave after their existence.

twelf. noun. **1.** A cardinal number between eleven and thirteen, equivalent to the sum of two and ten or to the product of three times four. *Linguistics.* **2.** A replaced spelling of the number twelve since it is a singular word ending in *f* and its plural counterpart ends in *ves*.

tympa. noun. *Informal.* **1.** Any internal part of the ear. **2.** An out-of-tune marimba that sounds like a person begging for mercy.

typognicia. noun. **1.** An undetected typographical error, despite multitudinous revisions by author, editors, grammatologists, and typographers, that is found after a book is printed. **2.** Serengraph.*

U

ubon. noun. **1.** A person incapable of performing a task appropriately. **2.** A person who is unable to produce something useful. **3.** A person unfit to practice a trade, a craft, or a profession. **4.** An inadequate in all senses.

uckloid. noun. **1.** A person who is frequently told to go fuck himself. **2.** Carahooslee. **3.** Fucksor. **4.** Fockloid.

udony. noun. **1.** Obsession with demanding respect, together with an inability to learn that respect cannot be obtained by raising the voice. **2.** Imperative imploration of respect by a tyrannical and paternalistic father to members of his family who support him financially and tolerate his eccentricity and abuses.

ulacoid. noun. A person who dresses unfashionably and is socially unfit.

ulatro. noun. *Literary.* **1.** The afterworld moan of a virgin being autopsied by a necrophilic forensic technician. **2.** A mute wailing of desperation.

ulciflitis. noun. *Archaic.* **1.** Deflowering a sore, an ulcer, or a wound from its lustrous appearance. **2.** Rough debridement of a wound. *Medicine.* **3.** Sudden hemorrhoidal ulceration that resembles the action of a vicious anal deflowering.

ulo. noun. **1.** The precise moment in life when a person surrenders to his demon or to his genius and follows a mysterious law that orders him either to ruin or to transcendence. **2.** Yourcernarism.

ulon. noun. **1.** A living being selected as an object of attack. **2.** A human target.

ultifand. noun. **1.** The last place where a missing object was found after an unrelenting search. **2.** Finirast. **3.** Telocluse.

ultrafission. noun. *Physics.* A series of nuclear physics techniques used for the discovery of the elementary sub-particles Ng y Wn. The sub-particles Ng y Wn, which when pronounced resemble a grunt, are considered the true atoms because they are indivisible despite their unknown nature.

ultratembile. noun. An involuntary, extremely rapid contraction of muscular fibers causing increase of heat in the area of the body where it occurs.

ultratomb. noun. **1.** Beyond the grave. **2.** On the other side of death. **3.** Afterlife. **4.** Afterworld.

ultratrophic. adjective. *Biology.* Acquiring characteristics beyond taxonomic genus, species or family due to a different nutrition.

ultrong. noun. *Politics.* **1.** Action and effect of controlling and exploiting a population to the maximum degree. **2.** Synergic effect when effectively combining technology and Machiavellianism.

umbiciled. adjective. Living at home with one's parents as an adult.

umbicilius. noun. A human parasite who receives nourishment and shelter but gives nothing in return.

umboh. noun. *Archaic.* The center of a shield.

umbration. noun. Taking a son turning fourteen years of age to a brothel to mark the beginning of his manhood.

umbril. noun. *Literary.* An area of imprecise limits at either side of a threshold.

uncinasious. adjective. Having a big and extraordinarily curved aquiline nose.

undecahedron. noun. *Geometry.* A three-dimensional shape having eleven plain faces.

unfond. noun. **1.** A person who is ignored or treated with indifference, neither loved nor hated, and easily forgotten. **2.** A weff.*

ungoflexor. noun. **1.** A person who after cutting a big toenail evaluates the resistance of the cut piece between his index finger and thumb. **2.** Onicosistor.

unguclet. noun. A person who stares flabbergasted at an ungoflexor* playing with a cut toenail piece.

unguiculan. noun. **1.** A person who due to habit, mania, bad manners, or pleasure, frequently scratches his or her own buttocks in public. *Informal.* **2.** Ass-scratcher.

ungulation. noun. Act or action of using toenails, fingernails, or hoofs for locomotion.

unibicity. noun. **1.** Quality of two in one. **2.** A peculiarity, proclaimed in certain doctrines, in which two people or two deities exist together in one entity.

unigendric. noun. **1.** A custom, a behavior, or a fashion that lacks gender assignation or distinction and is not subject to discrimination, abuse, joke or insult. **2.** Unigonal.

unigonal. adjective. **1.** Having one chosen gender. **2.** Having one gonality.*

unikini. noun. **1.** The lower part of a bikini. **2.** The portion of a female bathing suit worn in topless circumstances.

unimnema. noun. One specific type of neuron storing one memory.

unisensia. noun. *Psychology.* **1.** A feeling that life is worthless and unimportant. It generally occurs in people contemplating suicide and in certain persons facing death. **2.** Anegopathy* in individuals of certain species that could be part of restropy.*

unisthile. noun. Someone who thinks and acts slowly and is incapable of adapting to perform a task.

unprudish. adjective. **1.** Having had, but inexplicably losing any sense of modesty, especially with regards to matters of nudity or sexual nature. noun. **2.** A common trait when coming of age.

unwake. verb. To fall asleep.

unwakio. noun. The precise moment someone falls asleep.

urdic. verb. To palpate hesitantly and so softly that itching is provoked in the person being palpated.

urface. noun. **1.** A thing or an event that is important despite being under the surface or unnoticed. *Literary.* **2.** A person who does not know himself or herself and sees only the surface of his or her own face in a reflection. **3.** The emotion felt when looking oneself in a mirror and not recognizing the face.

urtick. verb. To hit someone with a cushion full of needles.

uscrine. verb. To strive to remember or to reflect on something said that was heard but not listened to.

usnagg. verb. To consider something indispensable that was previously a luxury item.

ustorish. adjective. Having the capacity to burn.

ususepsis. noun. *Law.* Pervasive usury that is legalized and concealed in numerous clauses full of legal jargon and ambivalent terms.

uxorinette. noun. A male wife.

uzun. noun. (from hüzün in Turkish). Feeling of despair on realizing that bad events taking place will get worse.

V

vaciosensia. noun. **1.** A feeling of burning emptiness from the stomach to the throat after going through an intense emotional experience. **2.** Improstenible* ayody* in the retrosteth.* **3.** Heartache.

vacitress. noun. Profound sensation of vacuumness* and other inexplicable discomforts in the retrosteth* caused by the loss of a loved one.

vacuumness. noun. **1.** An uncomfortable feeling of empty pain in the torso. **2.** Overwhelming feeling of emptiness as if having endured a bone marrow suction. **3.** Sustained implalgia.*

vagilostro. noun. **1.** Vaginal secretion of a virgin in heat. **2.** Exudative fluid of an erosedious* maiden.*

vagino. noun. A vagina in a man.

vanimerity. noun. **1.** A feeling of satisfaction when obtaining what was desired after a long period of unrelenting hard work. **2.** A deep feeling of pride after a success achieved by eunecy.*

vanimeter. noun. An instrument for measuring and indicating the degree of vanity in a person.

vanivainity. noun. Inexorable desire to be the focus of an apotheosis.

vapord. noun. **1.** Steam emanated from heated fat that irritates the pulmonary tract when inhaled. **2.** Volatilized scalding grease. **3.** Superheated oil vapor. **4.** Scalding fog made of burned animal fat. **5.** Calcined lard fumes. **6.** Vapardo. **7.** *Informal.* The smell of deep-fried butter. *Informal.* **8.** Vapolard. **9.** Mucocarbonizing steam.

varialization. noun. Repetitive modification of variables in an experiment until a desired result is obtained to support a theory.

vartrosil. noun. **1.** An artist whose art takes time to be appreciated. **2.** Innovative artistic style that appears to be asymmetric, chaotic, or ugly at first sight. **3.** A work of art that requires time to appreciate.

vartity. noun. Change in values and priorities when someone is suddenly in extreme poverty or diagnosed with a serious illness.

vastaguist. noun. *Psychology.* **1.** A person who discerns the personality of a father and a mother through the psychoanalysis of their offspring. **2.** A person who practices vastaguilogy.

vastugge. noun. A son or daughter who is not loved by their parents.

vegeton. noun. All projected passive reactions, irrespective of quality and intensity.

vehivolition. noun. **1.** A nonworking or malfunctioning vehicle, a machine, or an electromagnetic apparatus that in the presence of a mechanic or technician begins to work properly. **2.** A volitive* action of an inanimate object.

vejigation. noun. *Medicine.* **1.** Protrusion of the bladder through the urethra. **2.** Eventration of the bladder through the abdominal wall or the urethra.

vejigg. verb. To induce the urge to urinate on someone.

vejislescence. noun. An action or a desire that generates a feeling of uncertainty accompanied by an uncontrollable urge to urinate.

velaptor. noun. A narcoleptic night guard.

velug. verb. **1.** To hide actively, with some affectation, any indication or sign of femininity or acts considered feminine. **2.** To pretend not to be a woman. **3.** To conceal effeminacy with exaggerated zeal.

venerilence. noun. *Psychology.* **1.** The desire to engage in sexual relations between prepubescents, pubescents, or adolescents of the same gender who are not sexually attracted to one another. **2.** Desire for periodic erospections.* *Medicine.* **3.** Recurring non-homosexual gonagnotia.

ventilapse. noun. A breeze of time.

veramity. noun. A true friendship that is limited to a handful of people throughout a person's life.

veraspritude. noun. Tempo of a spoken truth that hurts more than a blaring slander.

verbastine. noun. **1.** A man with a high pitched, raspy, discordant, dissonant and annoying voice who talks loudly and excessively. **2.** A raspoun. **3.** A strident trapalon.

verbosurist. noun. **1.** A person who bastardizes and

degenerates a spoken language. **2.** Barramist.*

vergunt. verb. **1.** To scandalize those who are unconventional. noun. **2.** Epather.

veriperation. noun. An axiom of an undefined doubt.

vermigamous. adjective. Believing to be married to a worm.

versichy. noun. **1.** A peculiar property of a work of art made with coarse material that, when seen from afar, seems real. **2.** Versiquity.

verticon. noun. **1.** A light and fleeting dizziness felt after an intense orgasm or other potent pleasure. **2.** Kinetill. **3.** Plascoreo. *Vulgar.* **4.** Cum undertow.

vespert. noun. **1.** Period of the day from the time the sun is close to the horizon, approaching sunset, until the sunlight is not seen. **2.** Daily interval of time, around sunset, from when Venus is first seen until sunlight is not perceived.

vestiality. noun. **1.** Disregard for the vagaries of fashion and deliberate wearing of clothing attire that does not conform to the season. **2.** A habit or a mania of dressing in summer clothing in other seasons. **3.** Determined flouting of the social standards or the unwritten guidelines of an in-vogue dress code. **3.** Exestio.

vestiana. noun. **1.** A person dressed in see-through clothing. **2.** A person fond of wearing transparent materials.

victomarius. noun. A person who lifts the arm or arms of the winner in a competition, a sporting event, or a spectacle.

vidarrage. noun. The ghastly life story of a vidarrio.*

vidarrio. adjective. **1.** Not having been favored by life. noun. **2.** A person who finds numerous and frequent vicissitudes and unhappiness throughout life.

violestesia. noun. **1.** Unbothered reaction to violence or the suffering of others as a consequence of frequent exposure to them. **2.** Action and effect of recurrently perceiving with indifference extreme acts of cruelty and brutality in multimedia. **3.** Passive familiarity with torture.

virgeja. noun. *Informal.* A promiscuous woman who has not been penetrated vaginally.

virulenticity. noun. **1.** Quality of virulence. **2.** The potential of causing toxicity, serious infection, malignancy, or hostility.

visecritude. noun. Mania or perversity of a person that is perceived by others as a virtue.

vistreza. noun. The saddest of all sadnesses.

volit. verb. To exercise one's own volition.

volitivate. verb. To act, exercise, or to empower one's will.

volnirium. noun. **1.** Programmed dream. **2.** A dream that was planned or provoked by volition. **3.** A dream that is the product of a previous suggestion. **4.** A desired dream that happened.

voluptruous. adjective. Of, related to, or characterized by large curvaceous objects or furniture. Generally referring to eclectic pieces with renaissance patterns as a base.

vomilation. noun. **1.** Powerful nausea and strong impulse to vomit with uncontrollable spasms when there is no material left in the stomach. **2.** Vomit of gastric juice with no food in it. *Medicine.* **3.** Pre-prandial vomit. **4.** Self-induced vomit in anorexic bulimia.

vomilia. noun. **1.** Routinely vomiting after eating. *Medicine.* **2.** A disorder characterized by frequent self-induced postprandial vomiting, caused by various psychogenic conditions.

Psychology. **3.** Obsession with vomiting after a meal in bulimic patients.

voragine. noun. **1.** Impetuous whirlpool of utmost intensity and size from which escape is almost impossible. **2.** A very large maelstrom.

voraginosity. noun. **1.** A turbulent situation of confused movement. **2.** A violent turmoil with no visible ending. **3.** A tumultuous circumstance from which it is difficult to escape.

voraguous. adjective. **1.** Consuming conflicting emotions with no apparent solution. **2.** Attempting to confront conflicting emotions in others.

voragyn. noun. **1.** A domineering and violent woman with turbulent emotions and confused desires. **2.** A strong and violent woman with conflicting emotions. *Vulgar.* **3.** Crazy bitch.

vorrask. noun. *Meteorology.* **1.** An extremely rare and violent storm arising from the combination of a hurricane and a blizzard. *History.* **2.** A quick and massive revolution involving a high proportion of citizens in which most of the previous rulers are killed.

vortexian. adjective. **1.** Coming from a vortex. noun. **2.** A person's erratic behavior.

Psychology. **3.** A person who had a whirlpooled uterine life. **4.** Vortexish.

vupugarge. noun. A sticky mucous substance draining from an orifice of the body, which originates from an internal infection.

vybernaught. noun. (from *vybafnout* in Czech). **1.** A persistently annoying, silly person. **2.** An annoying sibling. **3.** A person who jumps out from a hidden area and says boo to scare someone.

W

wabbel. noun. **1.** Extraterrestrial food eaten by space travelers. **2.** Sideraxenophagial.

wabby. noun. *Informal.* **1.** Mutual contact, rubbing, or caressing with tongues between two persons. **2.** Lengthy kiss with mutual rubbing or caressing of tongues as a sign of sexual desire. **3.** Tongue touching following the beginning of an erommation.* **4.** Linguscle. 5. Glossioscle.

wabergy. noun. The quality or condition of a person who resembles his or her pet.

wabeic. adjective. Being intentionally baffling.

wable. noun. **1.** A perception of being followed by something intangible that suddenly acquires a nebulous tangibility when detected. **2.** Sentusculation.

waboh. noun. A microscopic intracranial microwormhole.

wabulious. adjective. **1.** Awaiting a fizzled orgasm not knowing that it already happened. **2.** Anticipating a vanished sexual climax. **3.** Sifustenity.

wacie. noun. **1.** An Eskimo who is always chilly and complaining of the cold. **2.** Glaciodaire.

wackle. verb. **1.** To be deprived of the power of sensation, feeling, or responsiveness. **2.** To feel uncomfortably numb.

wacklery. noun. The practice of making someone feel drunk by persuasion.

wadge. noun. *Informal.* **1.** Buggery between men clustered in confined quarters. *Medicine.* **2.** Sigmoidabrasion. *Religion.* **3.** Priesthood initiation. *Informal.* **4.** Sacerdotal novitiate. **5.** Siesordocio. **6.** Seminasodomy. *Nautical.* **7.** Kissing the gunner's father. **8.** Pegboyny.

wador. noun. **1.** Oppressive and burning sensation throughout the body when carrying a heavy emotional burden. **2.** Neuroabrasion.

waffin. noun. *Psychology.* **1.** A person with psychological retardation who is displaced, depersonalized, and disillusioned as a result of perceiving everything in slow motion. *Medicine.* **2.** A person suffering from restricted movement or incapacity of movement in one or several parts of the body following a neurological condition. **3.** Neurobradic.

wagger. noun. **1.** Someone who frequently gesticulates making ugly, twisted expressions of disgust, pain, or repugnance. **2.** Grimacillator. **3.** A Valley girl or a Valley girl-like person.

waildred. noun. **1.** Prolonged, high-pitched, hair-raising cries emitted with the sole objective that someone will please a caprice. **2.** Strident wailing a child, barely ambulatory, emits to get out of a stroller. **3.** A wail, resembling that of one coming from a torture chamber, from a spoiled infant during leilihood.*

wailinaut. noun. **1.** A spouse who shuts the door and flees without saying goodbye or concluding a marital dispute. **2.** Marifleer. **3.** Gamofugue.

waippier. noun. **1.** A person who writes an explanation or commentary of an abstruse word or an obscure text that is difficult to understand. **2.** Glossographist.

wamb. noun. **1.** A mode of transportation through death. **2.** Transthanatic.

wambleic. noun. *Zoology.* **1.** Any mammal with green fur. **2.** Glaucofont.

wamper. noun. **1.** A person who purposefully sheds a tear and has a hand ready to smear the tear on the face. **2.** Tacodrach.

wamprity. noun. **1.** Astuteness or dissimulation accompanied by subtle mockery that is effective for a short time. **2.** Supercarronery.

wanckitis. noun. *Informal.* **1.** A disease of unknown origin characterized by the anomalous presence of sweat glands in the glans and as a consequence, excrete copious quantities of sweat during any physical activity. *Medicine.* **2.** Glandispordia. *Vulgar.* **3.** Sweating dick. **4.** Sweaty weenie. **5.** Wet willy. **6.** Soggy knob.

wancle. noun. **1.** A first impression someone has of a language when heard for the first time spoken by a fast-talking native speaker. *Informal.* **2.** Tahbletic. **3.** Weeckie. **4.** Waboh. **5.** Enkondle. **6.** Kow-kow. **7.** Whabb. **8.** Grutugock. **9.** Chac-chack. **10.** Jeck. **11.** Whable.

wancoid. noun. *Informal.* **1.** A person who voluntarily accumulates air in the esophagus or stomach and rapidly expels the air through the mouth with an obnoxious noise. **2.** A person who frequently burps uninhibitedly. *Medicine.* **3.** A patient suffering from neumogastry. **4.** Neumopesic.

wape. noun. A vehement desire to be invisible.

wapilly. noun. **1.** A custom of smoking tobacco following copulation. **2.** Tobbacarn.

wapord. noun. **1.** A person who, for a fee, requests and processes permits, licenses, authorizations, or submits proposals before an extremely bureaucratic government office on behalf of another person. **2.** Gestionnaire.

wappitude. noun. **1.** Incapacity to process memories. **2.** Inability of a bigendric* being to remember the memories of its host. **3.** Neurogestity.

wappour. noun. **1.** Disconcerted emotion when remembering lived events that seem different from documented recordings of said events. **2.** Nemoconsternia.

warkish. adjective. **1.** Having a protracted and raspy mode of speaking. **2.** Glossagolt. noun. **3.** Verbastine.*

waubness. noun. **1.** The introduction and spreading of an external memory into one or more neurons. **2.** Nemneudity. **3.** Nemosubfundition.

waxout. noun. **1.** A thin U-shaped plastic or metallic object sometimes used to pull out earwax from the ear. **2.** Sacacerila. **3.** Bobby pin. **4.** Hairpin.

weab. noun. *Informal.* **1.** A method for growing of a fetus outside a womb. *Medicine.* **2.** Ectoembryogenesis. **3.** A set of techniques for the extrauterine development and growth of a fetus in a surrogate person. **4.** An artificial chamber for successfully growing a human fetus to birth.

weacle. noun. **1.** A sensation that is simultaneously pleasurable and disconcerting when tickling the palate with the tongue. **2.** Gingisquill. *Informal.* **3.** Creepy palate.

weacy. noun. **1.** A woman who treats people with affected sweetness, thinks she is a nice person, but is regarded as cloying and detestable. **2.** Glucogynous.

weady. noun. **1.** A person who, without realizing, causes inconvenience to others in obtaining something for self-convenience. **2.** Necevenient.

weaf. noun. **1.** Perception of a smell that is both known and unidentifiable. **2.** Unpleasant and confusing perception of a whef.*

weaggoon. noun. **1.** A person who communicates with other people without following any system or structure of language. **2.** Grammofog.

weamy. adjective. **1.** Inducing rapid and inevitable queasiness and nausea, but not vomit. **2.** Nauseagenic.

weaple. noun. *Informal.* **1.** The taste of inhaled tobacco smoked immediately after sex. **2.** Tobbacarnish. **3.** Fleshbit. **4.** An after-sex pleasure not only confined to wapillists.* *Informal.* **5.** A weappy.*

weappy. adjective. Feeling pleasure with the first puff of cigarette smoke immediately after coitus.

webron. adjective. *Informal.* **1.** Having limited mental capacity. *Psychology.* **2.** Paucophrenic.

weck. noun. **1.** The invariable obsolescence of a concept or a technology once it is finally comprehended. **2.** Retrognolysis. **3.** Detragnosy.

weeland. noun. **1.** A sequence of spontaneous actions that include filling the mouth with air, inflating the cheeks, expelling the air out quickly, chuckling, and covering the mouth with a hand to hide laughter. *Psychology.* **2.** One of

the reactions provoked by a welp.* **3.** Varied reactions and feelings, ranging from laughter to disgust, triggered by seeing the furry back and shoulders of a bare-chested man. *Informal.* **4.** Disparate bodily responses when looking at an obese person in tight clothing or an old person wearing a skimpy swimsuit. Examples of other visual goads that elicit it: a person with the head in the shape of a cone, a person with disproportionately large ears, a person with a body in the shape of an egg. **5.** A sequence or mixture of feelings that could lead to a wenollious* situation.

weem. verb. To humiliate a person persistently to the point of causing depression.

weemier. noun. **1.** An involuntarily high-pitched pronunciation of certain syllables that renders speech with a melodious and sometimes questioning quality, generally in little girls. **2.** The diction in a small girl that is sometimes a prelude to a chirittage.* **3.** Acution. **4.** Pediagudition.*

weeple. adjective. **1.** Being dazed and sleepy with twisted sensory perceptions and clumsy movements. noun. **2.** A sensation of feeling with less intensity. **3.** Deggude. **4.** Nubeciment.

weexy. adjective. **1.** Well known for oddness in facial features or ugliness. **2.** Being the center of attention for physical features or peculiarities. **3.** Weikuss.

wefeck. noun. **1.** A nickname a belligerent wife gives to her exasperatingly calm husband. **2.** A psychoclast,* melatious,* dysonaudic* or embreck* husband who is a nightmare to a conflictive wife. **3.** Tacitulerant.

weff. noun. **1.** A person without distinction who is easy to forget. **2.** Stumpic. **3.** An ordinary person who is difficult to remember. **4.** Unfond.*

weisson. noun. **1.** The ability to learn or the innate faculty to comprehend the displacement of non-linear time. **2.** Capability to conceptualize the alinearity of time or the entrance to a paradimension.* **3.** Transteropty. **4.** Protoception.*

welck. noun. **1.** Action of pulling a curtain cord in a hotel room whereupon the curtain glides into a position opposite to what is desired. **2.** Synencord. **3.** Adextrosyncordy. **4.** Sintrosyncordation.

welger. noun. **1.** A person who has an obsession with tinkering with contraptions or devices

that do not need repair. **2.** Traheener. **3.** Tinkmaniac.

welk. noun. **1.** A style in which a man holds his penis during urination. **2.** The number, types of fingers, and positioning of the fingers a man uses to direct his penis during micturition. Examples: thumb-index or pipe holder, index-thumb, index-middle or cigarette holder, middle-index or cigar holder, thumb-index-middle, index-middle-thumb, etc. **2.** Mingidactia.

wellott. noun. **1.** A person who uses an exclamation, affirms or agrees, looks, hesitates, and then states or explains the initial intended message. Example: "Well, all right, I see, I suppose, but what I mean is…" **2.** Pannagreish.

wellough. noun. **1.** One of the destinies that beneficially transforms a disadvantaged person who has persistently worked against the original, unfavorable predestined destiny. **2.** Dextrotine.

welp. noun. *Psychology.* **1.** A stimulus that triggers a wide spectrum of feelings. *Informal.* **2.** A visual goad that provokes varied spontaneous reactions, from laughter to disgust. **3.** A stimulus that induces a weeland.*

wemmie. noun. **1.** A person who is afraid of the sea. **2.** Talasophobic.*

weng. noun. **1.** A person with a habit or fixation of arranging, fixing, moving or repositioning objects in front of him. **2.** A person annoying to others during a conversation due to his or her constant compulsion to place in order or make shapes with objects only to change the order or the shape moments later.

wenk. noun. **1.** Someone unable to discern the brilliance of another person. **2.** Campther.*

wenolliosity. noun. **1.** A mixture of the utmost intense feelings. **2.** An extreme weeland.*

wepard. noun. **1.** A solid and opaque object that when illuminated on one side does not produce shade or a shadow. **2.** Panascio.

wepple. noun. *Informal.* **1.** The precise instant in which the hymen is broken in a virgin. *Archaic.* **2.** Transhimecrage.

wepucius. noun. **1.** A factor, circumstance, or person that mitigates the severity of a harsh condition. **2.** Anexhaustoid.

werfian. noun. **1.** An earlobe attached to the posterior part of the jaw in its entire length. **2.** A person exhibiting this trait. *Informal.* **3.** Something or someone not to be trusted.

werfidia. noun. **1.** A feeling endured by an intelligent child when an adult talks to him or her as if they were mentally challenged. *Psychology.* **2.** Tiricletsia.

werg. noun. **1.** A person who walks in a rush, chin up, chest out, with affectedly rapid gestures, pretending to display an image of authority or vigor. **2.** Tachyondic. *Informal.* **3.** A person feigning authority or celebrity status.

whaffor. noun. *Psychology.* **1.** A pathognomonic sign of senility. *Literary.* **2.** Transposition of a dream for a grunt. **3.** Permutation of illusions for remembrances. **4.** Transoneration.

whag. noun. **1.** Repetitive actions of an adult consisting of moving the head backwards with the eyes wide open, slightly opening the mouth to conceal a smile, and stubbornly reiterating a word or words in a high pitched and excited tone of voice when interacting with a baby. **2.** Ternapule. **3.** Weechie.

whalloid. noun. **1.** An impertinent person who becomes conscious of his or her impertinence. **2.** An intempestous* person who realizes his or her inopportune behavior.

whammit. noun. *Psychology.* **1.** A feeling of guilt when thinking that one is responsible for something that happened elsewhere, exacerbated by not being able to do anything about it. **2.** Projected supramaculation.* **3.** Telesm.* **4.** Whepid.* **5.** Multiple rammocles.* **6.** Exaggerated repuntition.*

whamour. noun. An extraordinary and impactful feeling of mutual love at first sight.

wharfel. noun. **1.** A wall or a solid division between rooms through which sounds travel easily. **2.** A place where one hears unwanted noises, conversations, or moans. *Informal.* **3.** An apartment in a building where the neighbors are easily heard. *Physics.* **4.** Transopuld. *Archaic.* **5.** A brothel close to a wharf for sailors who have limited time to explore a city.

wharteic. adjective. *Medicine.* **1.** Having extremely dirty external and internal parts of the ear. noun. **2.** Otoscopally soiled. *Archaic.* **3.** Miner's ears.

wheddiness. noun. **1.** Aversion to monsters who supposedly inhabit distant lands. **2.** Teratoxenosis.

wheelicle. noun. **1.** Momentary illusionary sensation in a vehicle that the vehicle is moving when it is actually static. **2.** Wrong perception of movement in one direction that, when on a train or an airplane, one feels when observing another train or airplane move in the opposite direction.

whef. noun. *Informal.* **1.** A smell that has in common the stagnant air of tires, stale fish, post-coital penis, and thrown away sanitary towels. **2.** Metruscade. **3.** Tocoscadd.

wheggard. **1.** A man urinating who cannot help but stare at other urinating men in a public bathroom. *Informal.* **2.** A heterosexual man peeing in a public restroom who looks around and watches other men peeing.

whemoud. noun. **1.** Learning that is only acquired with time. **2.** Tempalement.

whemp. noun. *Psychology.* **1.** Excessive sadness for the death of an unknown person. *Medicine.* **2.** Pathoxenothania.

whepid. adjective. **1.** Having a feeling of deep guilt, but not having done anything immoral, illegal, or unethical. *Informal.* **2.** Having a feeling of remorse after experiencing a highly vivid erotic dream with another person or persons while in bed with one's spouse. *Psychology.* **3.** Whammit.* **4.** A prelude to telesm.* **5.** Repuntition.*

whess. verb. **1.** To numb a person's mind by assigning to said person an overwhelming number of tasks. *Politics.* **2.** To overburden a person or a population by communicating a plethora of trivial information. **2.** To put a mind to sleep. **3.** To timesomniate.

whiss. verb. **1.** To squeeze something while in locomotion with the intention to extract its internal contents in motion. **2.** To transpress.

wholithron. noun. **1.** A being that feeds on other animals and swallows the entire body. **2.** Somaphagous.*

whotta. noun. A masturbation executed by passing the forearm behind the thigh.

whurl. noun. **1.** Passing from one dream to another with no interruptions. **2.** Transomnism. **3.** Transitionless dreams.

wib. noun. **1.** Muscular twitching accompanied by a tingling sensation in some part of the body. *Informal.* **2.** Acuchinlidy. **3.** Tingliny.

wiclaw. noun. **1.** A person who questions each inconsistency of

a conspiracy theorist, a gossiper, or an intrigant with logic and precision, and successfully invalidates and discredits each machination. **2.** Anhintrigant.

widgeic. adjective. **1.** Having a crenoid* skin resembling a geometric assembly of numerous monotone Rubik's Cubes. **2.** Cubcrenoid.

wieff. noun. **1.** A static state of the soul. **2.** Animastasis.

wiegon. verb. **1.** To turn the chest insistently from one side to another, wagging the abdomen and jerking the head, waving and flapping both arms and legs back and forth, up and down, and in circles, while wiggling hips with psychotic, ungraceful movements until a garment is satisfactorily put in place. **2.** To aschytunne.

wikle. verb. **1.** To observe with interest and in detail through something. **2.** To transoptiate. noun. **3.** A sophisticated peeping Tom.

wilp. verb. **1.** To pierce, prick, stab, or impale something with force. *Informal.* **2.** To penetrate someone without consent. **2.** To transhimet.

wippour. noun. **1.** An abnormal sensation, typically pricking, tingling, and itching while sensing a morbid tranquility when the feeling of power is fused with the feeling of remorse. **2.** Anesthetisia.

wirrell. noun. Confusing agglomeration of events, people, or things in movement.

withinme. 1. pronoun. First person, singular pronoun preceded by the preposition within. *Theology.* **2.** Pronoun used by a speaker to refer to himself or herself as a divine entity that is talking through him or her. *Archaic.* **3.** Ethereal entity that is part of or inside someone else.

withouther. pronoun. Third person singular preceded by the preposition *without.*

withouthim. pronoun. Third person singular preceded by the preposition *without.*

withoutme. pronoun. First person singular preceded by the preposition *without.*

withround. noun. Anything immediately peripheral to or encircling someone or something in a defined space.

wod. noun. **1.** An artificial state of being in which either the body or the memories cease being part of the entity. **2.** Transnoisism.

woft. adjective. **1.** Being emaciated, without color, with hanging, loose skin and in an extremely weak condition. **2.** Detrimacrated.

wogren. adjective. **1.** Having the capability to offend or irritate with innovative insults. **2.** Creative foulmouthedness. **3.** Majaderic.

wokay. noun. A dish that tastes like meat or fish but does not contain any meat or fish.

wole. noun. **1.** A person who often gets out of trouble in a clever way. **2.** Someone who uses an ingenious sense of humor to wiggle their way out of compromising situations or problems.

wolt. noun. **1.** Pain present in the majority of the body. **2.** Migrating pain in tissues and organs that occurs during the aging process. **3.** Any pain present in a medical condition ending in ~*itis* or ~*osis* while aging. **3.** Panalgia.* **4.** Devidalgia.

womanity. noun. The condition of having the sensibility, emotional responses, maternal instinct, and other characteristics considered to befit a human female.

womprock. noun. **1.** A fast succession of thoughts with or without congruity between them. **2.** Pensiperg.

wonckle. verb. **1.** To endure a circumstance or to put up with someone through an intermediary. **2.** To transmegunate.

wonliner. noun. **1.** A speech disorder characterized by naming one thing or person for another. **2.** Transnomia. **3.** Dysnomer.*

woogh. noun. An intemperate passion.

wrank. noun. **1.** The undefined moment when someone enamored discovers the truth about the person he or she is in love with. *Literary.* **2.** The threshold where the feeling of being enamored ends and reality begins.

wug. noun. *Informal.* **1.** Someone who naïvely tries to convince a person who is enamored about something. **2.** A person who stupidly tries to persuade a womploid.*

wust. adjective. **1.** Possessing the ability to overtake or pass through barriers. **2.** Transphragmatic. noun. *Physics.* **3.** A wave or a particle that can go through a solid.

X

xeneck. noun. **1.** A collection of forgotten remembrances. *Psychology.* **2.** An assortment of forgotten memories that have one theme, sentiment, or time period in common. *Medicine.* **3.** Event-related amnesia. **4.** Pancela.

xenogonady. noun. Imagining being of the opposite gender during masturbation or copulation.

xenogote. noun. An *in vitro* generated zygote from the ovule and sperm of two strangers, implanted in an anonymous woman with an unknown husband.

xenomnia. noun. **1.** A collection of memories projected from one being to another, regardless of the time separation between them. **2.** Mnemobigendria.

xenonuninema. noun. A rare neuron in some intelligent beings that stores a sole non-instinctive and non-genetically inherited memory.

xenopaternity. noun. A quality of a father who is not aware of being a father of someone in another country.

xenopornophilia. noun. An obsessive preference for exotic or foreign prostitutes.

xenotoxin. noun. A rare poisonous substance found in certain meteorites.

xerotoic. noun. A person with an extremely dry personality.

xipham. noun. A martial arts technique that aims to strike with hands and feet at the opponent's cartilaginous section at the lower end of the sternum.

xorus. noun. **1.** A person who has facial wrinkles of deceit. **2.** Facial expression of an older liar. *Medicine.* **3.** Small corrugations on the face generated during adulthood from frequent, almost imperceptible muscle contractions that occur when telling a lie. *Literary.* **4.** The face of falsehood. *Politics.* **5.** A seasoned politician.

xuonon. noun. **1.** An unsophisticated wooden image of a deity. **2.** A crude representation in wood of a god or a demi-god in vogue, depending on the mythology being turned into a religion.

xylocybernia. noun. A retro marketing strategy that promotes the use of wooden computers.

xyloldo. noun. **1.** An object, made of a hard material, shaped like an erect penis used for sadomasochistic sexual stimulation. **2.** Punitive dildo.

yagran. noun. **1.** The act of a parent consisting of reciting numbers in ascending order to nonspecifically threaten a child into obeying a command previously given. **2.** Numenaza. **3.** Yagrumation.

yankeeism. noun. A State strategy, disguised as democracy or freedom, to invade other countries and implant puppet regimes to boost its own economy.

yerrory. noun. **1.** A belief that a corrected error did not need to be corrected in the first place. **2.** Antenemertalia. **3.** Yerroricia.

yeyey. verb. *Phonetics.* **1.** To pronounce the phoneme *ye* in an affectedly relaxed or petulant tone as the letter *g* in Italian or Catalan or the letter *j* in English. noun. **2.** The despicable mania of a Dutch verbosurist.* **3.** A habit of a Flemish barramist.*

yokmesh. noun. (from *yoko meshi* in Japanese, meaning a meal that is eaten from both sides). An unsettling feeling when speaking a foreign language.

yuput. noun. (from *Yuputka* in Ulwa, meaning walking in the woods at night). The feeling of something crawling inside one's skin.

yuxture. noun. **1.** The precise moment in life when one finds oneself. *Literary.* **2.** A moment in life when a confluence between morality and need occurs.

Z

zalahazar. noun. **1.** A cluster of three causalities that occur simultaneously. **2.** Various independent events that fortuitously occur simultaneously. **3.** Triazar. **4.** Troidom.

zambotor. noun. *Informal.* **1.** A husband who is easily controlled by a manipulating wife. **2.** The husband of a kaddaka.*

zarcostic. noun. **1.** A fixed smile commonly perceived as a sardonic smile. *Medicine.* **2.** Spastic paralysis of the masseter muscles of the cheeks that gives the impression of a fixed smile. *History.* **3.** Punishment established by King Zardon of Sardinia (8th century BC) for those accused of slander, consisting of cutting both cheeks.

zarga. noun. *Literary.* **1.** The action of seeing both present and future through the keyhole of a metaphysical door. **2.** Perceptive chronunlimitation. *Medicine.* **3.** A pincushion for sterile surgical needles.

zelostenoity. noun. *Psychology.* **1.** Collective mental processes that trigger a feedback loop of suspicion and envy causing blurry thoughts, somatic pain, and alterations of the personality. **2.** Pathologic consequences of an overwhelming blotta.*

zeloxenity. noun. *Psychology.* **1.** Fear of sharing love. **2.** Pre-jealousy. **3.** Fear of sharing or losing the monopoly of romantic or sexual attachment of a partner in a couple.

zohorie. noun. *Archaic.* **1.** A person who penetrates into the most obscure or deepest part of something. **2.** A person who tends to deepen every topic or aspect of life.

zollornouth. noun. **1.** Sobbing combined with a sneeze. **2.** The weeping of a person suffering from a severe allergy who cannot contain simultaneous congestion, whimpering, and sneezing.

zoophonic. adjective. **1.** Reproducing or faithfully imitating animal sounds. noun. *Informal.* **2.** A person who sounds like an animal when speaking.

zurration. noun. *Sociology.* Frequent exertion of excessive terror meted out to juvenile offenders as a rehabilitation or therapeutic strategy.